GLASS TOWN

GLASS TOWN

STEVEN SAVILE

ST. MARTIN'S PRESS

NEW YORK

GLASS TOWN. Copyright © 2017 by Steven Savile. All rights reserved. Printed in the United States of America. For information, address St. Martin's Press, 175 Fifth Avenue, New York, N.Y. 10010.

www.stmartins.com

Designed by Devan Norman

Library of Congress Cataloging-in-Publication Data

Names: Savile, Steve, author.
Title: Glass town / Steve Savile.
Description: First edition. | New York : St. Martin's Press, 2017.
Identifiers: LCCN 2017032060 | ISBN 9781250077837 (hardcover) |
    ISBN 9781466890152 (ebook)
Subjects: | GSAFD: Mystery fiction.
Classification: LCC PR6119.A95 G58 2017 | DDC 823/.92—dc23
LC record available at https://lccn.loc.gov/2017032060

Our books may be purchased in bulk for promotional, educational, or business use. Please contact your local bookseller or the Macmillan Corporate and Premium Sales Department at 1-800-221-7945, extension 5442, or by email at MacmillanSpecialMarkets@macmillan.com.

First Edition: December 2017

10 9 8 7 6 5 4 3 2 1

To the greatest magician of them all,
David Fredrick Matthews,
who conjured a family out of the raw materials he inherited

GLASS

TOWN

I

THE UPRIGHT MAN

January 13, 1994

Obsession is difficult to explain to someone, especially if they don't share it. Let's be honest here, no lies between you and me, boy, what are the odds of someone else sharing your obsession? Slim. Incredibly slim. If by some quirk of fate it happens, that two of you are driven by the same strain of madness, well, that would be unfortunate to say the least.

Eleanor Raines.

That was her name.

My obsession.

The object of my desire. I was going to say affection, but there was nothing remotely affectionate about it. Desire is a much better word. Less wholesome. Desire speaks of dark places, of yearning, sweat. It reeks of sex. Affection is something best saved for your grandmother.

Eleanor. My Eleanor.

Sometimes you see a face and you just know. You look at it and something inside you comes alive. I'm not sure I can explain it any better than that. It's strange trying to remember it now, trying to put into words a feeling felt in 1924 about a face that until yesterday I hadn't seen for seventy years. But I'm going to try, because I need you to understand. *Otherwise everything's been for nothing. I couldn't bear that. She deserves to be remembered.*

She's particularly sharp in my mind this morning because it's the anniversary of her disappearance. It's funny when you think of it, time being this arbitrary thing we conjured up to delineate a day and assign it a number of hours. Of course hours are equally fictitious. There is day and there is night, the rest of it is all just the space in between where the living is done.

January 13, 1924.

A lifetime ago.

The day Eleanor really became a star.

Before then she'd been working for Gainsborough Pictures on a film, Number 13, *Hitchcock's ill-fated effort that ended up as so much silver nitrate on the Gainsborough books. Eleanor had been cast as one of the down-on-their-luck residents of The Peabody, a low-income building down in Rotherhithe. She never really talked about the experience, or about Hitch, just to say he was a sweet young man with his own demons. I never really thought of him that way—the sweet part—he was always just a man with demons as far as I was concerned. But to be fair it didn't help his cause that he was instrumental in introducing Seth Lockwood into our lives.*

It's not a name you hear all that much these days, but back then the Lockwoods were the original gangster family running the East End. Nothing happened without their say-so. There was talk, of course. Eleanor was a beautiful woman, Lockwood was a dangerous man, and they were in each other's orbits. Their courtship had been the talk of certain seedier parts of the town, but the police could never prove anything. But I've always thought Lockwood had something to do with her disappearance, even if that meant she'd ended her days propping up some foundation over on Friars Mount. New five- and six-storey buildings were ten a penny back then. They were always building something. Gentrifying the city. The council could try and pretend that the Old Nichol Street Rook-

ery wasn't a slum and pretty it up with a new name. They could even take the scum out of the slum, but what they couldn't do was stop it from being a slum, not when men like Seth Lockwood still ran it. It didn't matter if Cock Lane was called Boundary Street. Those places couldn't change. Not really. The world doesn't work like that.

The entire family were nasty pieces of work, but Seth was always the worst of a bad bunch.

I don't know how he wormed his way in with Hitchcock—money, no doubt. Lockwood had plenty of it, none of it clean, and Number 13 was bankrupt—but from the moment he laid eyes on Eleanor I knew there was another person who truly understood my obsession. And like I said, that was unfortunate.

I heard someone the other day say, "No stories ever truly begin; neither do they end. They just go on off the page, and continue living." I like that idea. I mean, when I think about it, I could say that this all started at that moment, when Seth Lockwood walked onto the set of Number 13 down in Rotherhithe and fell in love with Eleanor Raines, but that's not really where it all begins, is it? Because he had to fall in with Hitch first, and Hitch had to run out of money midshoot on Number 13 for that to happen, and none of it would have mattered if Eleanor hadn't decided she wanted to be a star of the silver screen like Isobel Elsom, who'd captivated her so completely during Onward Christian Soldiers and A Debt of Honour, and of course was a dear friend of Hitchcock's—you see the convoluted patterns life weaves? Even then, there are a dozen other inciting incidents the tragedy around my life owes its existence to.

They are all here, of course.

And if you've found my journal, then I imagine you've found everything else, Boone. The newspaper cuttings, the reams of notes from my investigation as well as the official police investigation, which was declassified twenty years ago. All of this stuff is in the public domain. There are no secrets here. There are hundreds of *interviews and testimonies from people who knew her or were work-ing in the area when she disappeared. Plenty of people who'd run afoul of the Lockwoods came forward with their personal grievances, but eventually the police stopped looking for her. I must have read this stuff ten thousand times over the last seventy years, all of it's here, and all of it points toward Glass Town and Seth Lockwood. Every-thing that could possibly help I've tried to gather together into one place. This is it, your family legacy, my boy. My gift to you now that I'm gone. There're old photographs, headshots and stills mainly, and what I believe might be the only extant footage of Number 13, just a few minutes worth of material with Eleanor outside the fictitious Peabody, but it's all I have left of her to give you. Our celluloid angel.*

I've tried so hard to forget her—God knows I have tried. I tried for your mother, who has had to live her entire life knowing her husband was in love with her sister and that she could never compete with a ghost, and for my own piece of mind. You cannot live day-to-day with this perfect imaginary woman taking up all the space inside your head and still try and devote yourself to a woman who just happens to be her sister. It won't work. You're cheating three people if you try. Not that this is meant to be a lesson in morals—I'm not sure they'll last after your generation grows up anyway. I can't remember the last time I saw someone give up their seat on the District Line. Holding the door open for someone is a lost art. Everyone is in so much of a hurry they're forgetting about the best part of being alive—the here and now. If there's one thing this old man would love to teach you, boy, it's that. Live and love in the now. Don't mourn the past or yearn for the future. I know, I know; do as I say, not do as I do. Not that I think you can. I couldn't. I never found a way to escape the past, but that was because I never truly wanted to. It's a dangerous country, the past. Seductive. Al-luring. Easy to lose yourself in. Maybe you're a better man than me. I hope you are, for your sake.

But here you have it, all the elements of my confession. It's for you to do with as you will. I'm not even sure if I want to hand my obsession on to you. It consumed my life—why should I feed it yours? So ignore it, take it out and make a huge bonfire out of the stuff in the backyard, and be free of this thing. Or don't.

I'm fighting the urge to tell you more about the personalities involved. I really want to paint you a fuller picture of the Lockwoods and the Raineses, of how they existed in each other's orbits, and to conjure up some of the other players, too, like the young Hitchcock who's at the center of it all, and Claire Greet, the actress; Ruben Glass, the King of Glass Town; Damiola, the stage magician; and Eleanor, of course. But I don't want to color your discovery with my own prejudices. Better that you come at this with new eyes. Perhaps they will see something else? Perhaps after all this time they will see the truth? Or maybe there is no truth? That frightens me. The fact that everything I've dedicated my life to could be lies and deception. That frightens me almost as much as Seth Lockwood.

Only one thing remains for me to tell you here, one final confession. I've hinted at it already, but here it is: I saw her yesterday. It was a crowded street around Spitalfields. She stepped out of a narrow grotty little alleyway; turned, saw me, but didn't recognize this grizzled old face of mine because time is such a feckless bastard and makes husks of us all. She disappeared into the crowd before I could catch up with her. I don't know what I would have said even if I had. I can't even be sure it was her. It might have been the weight of decades of grief on my soul, the burden of all that longing manifesting itself in her presence, because she hadn't changed. Not in the slightest. She was still the same heart-stopping beauty. For a few seconds I saw the face your mother might have had, but for a crime that ripped her out of my life and, for a couple of years, was the talk of the town.

I know. I know it's crazy. Impossible. But there you have it. Perhaps it was an episode. Isn't that what you like to call it when your old man starts losing his mind? "Oh, don't worry about Dad, *he's just having an episode." I'd love to tell you the marbles are all inside the bag and not rattling around on the floor, but I did just confess to seeing a ghost, didn't I? Or if not a ghost, what? A doppelgänger? Eleanor reincarnated? Or maybe I saw the impossible? Maybe I saw Eleanor Raines step out of 1924 and that's the reason why no one could ever find her?*

So now you have it all—my confession that I never loved your mother, not truly, because my heart belonged to her sister, that she reminded me every day of what I had lost, that in my dotage I'm losing my mind, and that for all of my adult life I have hoarded every piece of memorabilia around your aunt Eleanor's disappearance, and that's it, I am unburdened. I wasn't a good father to you. I know that. You know that. I hope that during the coming weeks and months as you walk a few miles in my shoes you come to understand what drove me, at least. I don't expect forgiveness. I'll be rotting long before you ever forgive me. Life isn't all hearts and flowers. Sometimes it is just holding onto pain too long before letting it go.

Your Father,
Isaiah Raines

Joshua Raines folded up the letter, not sure what to make of it. Twenty-four years had passed since his great-grandfather's deathbed confession to his son—Josh's grandfather, Boone. Isaiah Raines had died that year, 1994, just a few weeks after writing the letter, judging by the date. Not that Josh remembered it well, he'd only been eight at the time and the only things he recalled about his great-grandfather were the old-man smell and that he used to leave his false teeth in a glass on the kitchen sink. Isaiah had been nineteen when Eleanor Raines had disappeared, though he hadn't been a Raines at the time. Isaiah had taken his wife's name in the summer of 1926, after a long courtship. Reading his confession it was obvious that he had changed his name to be closer somehow to Eleanor, as if by sharing a name they were linked even more so than by the ties of marriage to her twin sister, Lilly. His given name was

Isaiah Lockwood. Seth had been his older brother. It was a messy family history, but weren't they all?

Josh had found the letter among his grandfather's things that morning. His name had been written on the envelope. One last gift from Boone. He had no idea if his grandfather had ever done anything about it, and as of six days ago the chance to ask him had disappeared forever. Boone Raines, son of Isaiah and Lilly Raines, loving husband of Katherine Raines, devoted father of Barclay Raines (deceased) and doting grandfather of one Josh Raines and his baby sister, Lexy, had shuffled rather ungraciously off this mortal coil at 4:06 a.m. after pitching head-first down the stairs on the way to the toilet.

His grandfather's broken neck left Josh and Lexy as the last of the Raineses. It all ended with them, the weight of generations, the continuation of the family name, the passing of the baton, it stopped with them, and given Josh's inability to nurture a relationship beyond the one-month mark, it was likely to stay that way.

He looked at the grandmother clock in the corner of the room. It ticked on. He had two hours until the funeral. What he didn't have were the promised notes and pictures Isaiah had left to Boone twenty-four years ago, and he didn't have the faintest idea where to go looking for them, either.

Josh slipped the letter into the back pocket of his jeans and went through to his grandfather's kitchen. Like everything else of his grandfather's, it was impeccably organized to the point of OCD obsessiveness. There were seven aromas of coffee bean in the cupboard and a Swiss-made hand grinder on the bench beside the percolator so he could decide exactly how fine the grounds for each should be depending upon his mood. The cupboard smelled like his grandfather. Everything in the house did. He wasn't ready to deal with the loss—he didn't have any coping mechanisms in place. After his father's death, which he'd been too young to really understand, Boone had stepped up and been the man in his life. But even then it was one thing when death was expected, but it was something else entirely when it came sweeping down from nowhere. Barclay Raines had gone out one morning to pick up his Sunday paper and packet of cigarettes from the corner shop—a habit his wife had always said would kill him one day—and never came home. Some kid trying to rob the store had stuck a six-inch blade in his kidneys and that was that. There was no big argument to hang guiltily over his head for the rest of his life, no last words to hold on to. One minute his father had been there, the next he wasn't.

Josh saw the pair of tickets for tomorrow's Leyton Orient game at the Matchroom Stadium still pinned to the fridge by magnets.

He ground the coffee, but stopped halfway through. His head was all over the place. He needed to get changed. He hated wearing a tie, but it was the least the old man deserved. He was supposed to say a few words, but so far had nothing beyond "As granddads went, Boone was pretty good, mainly because he was mine. I remember watching *Four Weddings and a Funeral* with him, and when John Hannah read out W. H. Auden's "Funeral Blues," he looked at me and in all seriousness said, 'I don't want any of that bollocks at my funeral, son. Promise me. I don't want people crying. Make sure they play Israel Kamakawiwo'ole's "Somewhere over the Rainbow" and if you can possibly swing it, have some dancing girls to put a smile on everyone's face.' So, smile you miserable bastards, he might be watching." He wasn't sure he could do it, though. It was one thing to imagine saying something, saying it over and over again in his mind, even sounding pithy, but it was quite another to let the words out of his mouth.

Suddenly the house felt claustrophobic. His whole life was in this place gathering dust. All of those firsts; first loves, first kisses, first broken bones, broken hearts, and everything else that had happened to him after he'd moved in here with his mum in the wake of the first death. He could hear her bustling about in the front room, puttering around to keep herself busy. This was the second time the man in her life had died on her. He felt an overwhelming surge of sadness and wanted to go and hold her for a moment. She was the last grown-up in his life. Lexy might argue with that, but not for long. She always said she had no intention of growing up if she could help it.

He went through to the lounge.

She looked so much smaller than she had a week ago.

"Mum," he said, from the doorway. "Strange question, did my great-grandfather know Alfred Hitchcock?"

She cocked her head slightly. It was what she did when she was trying to remember something. "Where on earth would you get an idea like that, love?"

"Just something I read. Did Boone ever mention anything?"

She shook her head.

"Did he ever talk about an actress who disappeared? Eleanor Raines? I guess she'd be my great-great aunt."

She shook her head again. "He didn't talk much about the past, you know that. Something happened with his father and the rest of the family before Boone was born. There was life before, and then there was life after, and in the afterlife they were all dead to him." Josh resisted the temptation to point out that people were usually dead in the afterlife. "You know what a stubborn old bastard Boone could be at the best of times. I don't think your dad ever met his grandfather. He never talked about it, but you know what families are like," she shrugged a little. It was an eloquent gesture that basically said: *They're all as nutty as a fruit-cake.* "And now, well, it's all ancient history."

"Don't you ever get curious? Don't you ever wonder what happened?"

"Not really, love. And you need to go and get changed, people will be here soon. I've laid your suit out on the bed. You can be curious all you want later. Come to think of it, I'm sure some of Boone's old friends will be at the wake, you can ask them about your great-great aunt." And with that, his mum turned her attention to the dusting, moving the picture frame on the mantel above the open fireplace she'd already moved half an inch to the right back half an inch to the left. She'd move it back again before we left.

The 1970s flowers in the middle of the stair carpet were worn threadbare from forty years of shuffling feet. Boone's heavy sheepskin winter coat still hung on the hatstand at the bottom of the stairs, as did his flat cap. Josh must have seen him in that hat and coat a thousand times. His tobacco tin and Rizla rolling papers would be stuffed deep into the right-hand pocket. There was something comfortably reassuring about knowing they'd be in there. Like everything was right with the world, even though it wasn't.

He couldn't look at the bottom of the stairs without imagining Boone lying there, broken.

Josh hurried up the stairs.

His suit was laid out on the bed. It was his interview suit. It was also his "posh" suit for whenever he had to dress up. Now it was his burying-his-grandfather suit. He wasn't sure he'd ever wear it again after today. In a small voice, Josh mimicked the Wicked Witch of the West, *"Help me, I'm melting . . ."* and that was exactly how he felt.

He stripped off, showered quickly, and dressed, transferring the letter from his back pocket to the inside pocket of his jacket. As he struggled with the Windsor knot on his black tie he saw the hearse pull up outside the front door. There were already a number of somberly dressed people in the street; neighbors come to see Boone Raines on his way. Within half an hour there were more than five hundred people out there lining the street. There were people wearing brightly colored scarves declaring their love of Orient, people from his bowling team in their kits, people from the social club where he hid from the rest of the world with a quiet pint standing beside people he'd worked with down at the machine shop, even though he hadn't worked there for the best part of forty years, and so many other people come to pay their respects.

"Have you looked outside?" Josh said, coming back downstairs in search of shoe polish.

His mum nodded. "A lot of people loved your grandfather." She had put on her mourning dress, a high-necked black lace gown that wouldn't have looked out of place at a Victorian funeral.

Josh towered a good six inches above her. He crushed her in a fierce embrace and said, "No one more than us." And kissed her on the top of the head. He really wasn't looking forward to the next few hours.

There was a soft knock at the front door.

The undertaker stood on the doorstep in his morning suit. He was a cadaverous soul, gaunt to the point of emaciation. Every bone of his skull protruded starkly from his pasty white skin and the pockmarks where his stubble grew through were deep with shadow. He held a top hat and bone-handled cane in his hands, and looked studiously down at his feet. "It's time," Father Death said.

Josh looked at his own shoes, and figured that Boone would let him off with a few scuffs. Without thinking about it, he grabbed his grandfather's sheepskin coat off the coatrack and put it on.

"It's a bit tight across the shoulders," his mum said, ruffling his hair.

"Doesn't matter," Josh said and stepped outside.

Not sure what to do in the situation, he shook hands with the undertaker and waited for his mum to emerge from the house. He locked the door and walked arm in arm with her to the lead car. She leaned on him every step of the way. Josh opened the door and helped her in, then closed the door and walked around to the other side. He was incredibly conscious of everyone watching him.

The undertaker walked to the head of the two-car procession, put his hat on, and tapped the cane three times on the asphalt. Taking their cue the drivers started their engines, and followed the undertaker at walking pace through the streets of the Rothery Estate. As the cars pulled out of Albion Close the people on the side of the road began to clap. It was the strangest thing. At first it was only one or two of them, but by the time the hearse bearing Boone's coffin had rounded the corner all five hundred were clapping. And they followed behind the cars forming a funeral procession that had over two thousand people in it by the time it reached the gates of the church with more people joining the cortege on every street.

The Rothery wasn't the poorest neighborhood in the city, but it was a long way from middle class, forget any pretensions of polite society it might have had. It was working class to the core. On either side were red-brick terraces, but the estate itself was functional 1970s boxes, no frills, the streets all lined up in neat rows that had long since gone to rack and ruin. Down beyond the communal garages it was more like Beirut than Belgravia, and if you made it as far as the shops—four units squashed in side by side, a bookies, a florist, a newsagent, and a convenience store that doubled as a liquor store—you were taking your life in your hands. Back during the riots last year the worst parts of the Rothery had been torn apart brick by brick. There were still a dozen corpse cars down by the garages, burned-out shells up on bricks like some sort of postapocalyptic nightmare frontier. Back when Boone had moved in, the place had been so full of promise. The parallels with Isaiah's memories of Friars Mount made Josh smile. He was right, the council men could try and pretty places up and pretend that they weren't slums, but they'd find a way to slip back into their natural state soon enough. The Rothery had no delusions of grandeur. It was what it was, home to a few thousand Londoners and graveyard for a few thousand dreams.

Layers of inventive graffiti had been sprayed across the shutters of the shops. There was a colorful gang tag on the corner claiming the street for one bunch of thugs or another. No doubt they'd kill for it, too; a lousy street corner in a lousy housing estate. Hardly worth dying over, but people died for less every day.

The cars eased to a stop just inside the wrought-iron angels of the churchyard, tires crunching gravel chips. "Are you ready for this?" his mum asked, leaning over to pat Josh on the knee. He felt like he was ten again. He wasn't okay, far from it, but he wasn't about to tell her that. This was the part where he was supposed to be strong. That was just how it worked. He could be weak later, when he was on his own. It didn't matter that it felt like an invisible vice was crushing his skull, grief applying another ounce of pressure every few heartbeats.

Four pallbearers waited by the church doors with the vicar. They were laughing and no doubt sharing larger-than-life Boone stories. There were plenty of them to share. That was just the kind of man he had been. One of them finished the cigarette in his hand and scuffed it out underfoot. Josh reached into his coat pocket. He had been right, his grandfather's tobacco tin and rolling papers were stuffed deep inside. He closed his hand around it. The men nodded to him. He nodded back. All very formal.

"Rosie," the vicar said to his mother, offering her his hand.

His mother sighed and inclined her head slightly. Sometimes there were no words.

"Well, gentlemen, shall we?" the vicar asked as Rosie Raines entered the church. The pallbearers gathered around the hearse as the undertaker opened the hatchback and together eased the coffin out and onto their shoulders. It was balanced unevenly, as one of them was a good five inches shorter than the others. Josh took a moment on the threshold to turn around and just take in the sheer amount of people who had come to pay their final respects, before he went inside.

The pallbearers carried Boone down the aisle behind him.

Josh walked down the aisle to the front row where Alexandra—Lexy—and his mum sat alone on the family bench. There was no more family to fill the row, but the rest of the pews were packed and people were standing at the back and along the sides. As Josh took his seat, the vicar climbed up to the pulpit, looked out at the congregation, breathed deeply, and said, "A lot of people I haven't seen in here since they were christened. I wouldn't have recognized some of you if you hadn't lost your hair." That earned a few chuckles. "The last time I talked to Boone he asked me if I thought there was a heaven. I told him I was sure of it. He looked me in the eye and asked, in all seriousness, how did it work? Would we be ghosts up there drifting about? Would he have to learn to play the harp? He seemed really worried about it, so I assured him his lack of musicality wouldn't be a problem and we are reunited with our bodies in the Hereafter. Never a man of many words he simply said, 'Bugger.'" That earned a proper laugh from some of the men at the back, who obviously shared the sentiment. "That summed Boone Raines up for me," the vicar said, looking toward Josh. "But I'd like to ask someone who knew him far better than I did to say a few words. Joshua?"

He eased his way out of the pew and walked up to the lectern.

Looking out at the sea of faces he wished he'd written something down. It was only when he was up there that he realized he hadn't taken Boone's coat off. He breathed deeply, inhaling his grandfather's scent, and it was as though the old man was up there with him. That was magic. "As granddads went, Boone was pretty good," he said, offering a slight smile. "Mainly, I must admit, because he was mine." He saw a few smiles on the faces of the congregation. "I remember watching a film with him once, *Four Weddings and a Funeral*, you've probably seen it. When John Hannah read out W. H. Auden's 'Funeral Blues,' he looked at me and said in all seriousness, 'I don't want any of that bollocks at my funeral, son. Promise me. I don't want people crying. Make sure they play Israel

Kama'—crap, I can't pronounce his name. I must have practiced it a hundred times. Sorry, Boone. He asked for some dancing girls to put a smile on everyone's face." He let that last line linger, offering a slight smile of his own. "So, smile you miserable bastards. Knowing Pops, he's watching right now wondering where the dancing girls are."

And after that he had nothing.

The silence lasted five seconds. Those five seconds felt like they lasted five minutes.

Josh looked at them all, hoping he'd see someone familiar and that would make him remember a Boone story.

There were a couple of polite coughs from people worried he was about to break down. He had to remind himself they were all friends out there. No one wanted him to screw up.

The church door opened.

Two men were framed in the sunlight: one standing, the other in a wheelchair. People moved aside to let the newcomers in. It took Josh a moment to recognize the pair—Gideon Lockwood, the patriarch of the Lockwood family, in the chair, and a younger man, in his midtwenties pushing it. All heads turned as they came in. The old man raised a hand, as though giving Josh permission to carry on reminiscing. He didn't. Not at first. His mind raced. *Lockwood, here, at Boone's funeral?* The pair weren't friends. In fact, until he'd found Isaiah's letter, he would never have known there was anything to link the pair of them, let alone that they were cousins. Josh looked around the nave and realized that more of Lockwood's people were in attendance. He had no idea what was going on apart from the fact that the silence was growing uncomfortable.

He saw the vicar begin to move toward him, like a comedian getting the hook to haul him offstage, though this was probably a crook, given the whole shepherd of men thing and the presence of the gangster in the congregation. He smiled at that.

"You can tell a lot about a man by the people who come to see him off. Some, probably just want to make sure he's gone," he was looking at Lockwood as he said this. "Take a look outside. The streets are lined with people. Some of them are from his bowling team—they gave us an honor guard as we drove here from the house. Then there's about two hundred football fans out there wrapped up in their scarves and battling the chill. I recognized most of them from the terraces. Boone was part of more than one band of brothers. That says something about the man, doesn't it? That he could fit in. That people wanted to be around him.

"I remember years ago some kid broke into his house and robbed him after Gran died. He never had much to begin with. They took everything he had apart from the radio. All of Gran's jewelry. Everything he had of her. I could have only been ten or eleven at the time. We stayed up all through the night listening to the test match ball by ball, talking about Grandma, holidays we'd had down in Brighton, and day trips to Canvey Island. I learned more about my family and who I was in that night than I did over the rest of my life. I understood him. He never had insurance, no private pension, no savings; he lived pretty much hand-to-mouth, but he was a proud man. I remember him telling me how he had to carry sacks of coal home ten miles on his back when he was my age because they couldn't afford to get it delivered. And how, when he was younger, he'd had trials with Orient, but had to go to work instead because no one paid footballers back then. He was always a giant to me. And that night and every night after he was frightened to be alone, but would never have admitted that to anyone. It was our secret.

"People say things like 'he'd have given you the shirt off his back' or 'he was the salt of the earth' or some other dreadful platitude that basically means they don't know how to describe someone, but want to say something nice. I mean, here I am in my grandfather's coat talking to a room full of people that loved him, and all I want to do is take his tobacco tin out of my pocket and roll a cigarette because that's exactly what he would have done, but knowing my luck I'll set off some sort of divine sprinkler system and get drenched in holy water," he chuckled at that, no more than a little shrug of the shoulders. "But that's the Boone I'll remember. That's my grandfather. The man who wanted dancing girls at his funeral and I think I should probably shut up now before I offend God or something and they end up keeping him out of heaven." Josh looked across at the vicar, "Then again, if that means he gets a shot at a better body maybe he'd thank me for that?"

He wasn't sure what he expected, applause, silence, a few muted mumbles and nods; what he didn't expect was for Gideon Lockwood to call from the back of the church, "If I may say a few words about my cousin?"

The young man pushed Lockwood to the front when there were no objections. The old man rested a hand on Boone's coffin on the way past. For Josh, looking at the younger man was like looking in the mirror at his darker, wicked twin. Or at least that was how he rationalized it. Where he was fair, the young man was dark, but they were clearly chiseled out of the same genetic building blocks. The young man, for his part, didn't give Josh a second glance. He angled the wheelchair toward the pulpit, then turned him to face the front and locked the wheel brake in place. He offered a hand and helped the old man rise unsteadily to his feet. This was the king of East London, this frail old shrunken soul. It was hard to imagine him terrifying anyone, and yet even now Josh fancied he could see the steel in the old bastard's spine and the flint in his eyes. In some people, age should never be mistaken for weakness. Gideon Lockwood was one of those people.

He leaned on the wooden pulpit, surveying his domain.

"The greatest regret of my life is that I never got to know Boone," he said. "That probably surprises some of you—especially those of you who knew him. And those of you who know *me*. From what I understand of him, my cousin was a decent, honest, hardworking man when the world allowed it, and then just a decent, honest man when it didn't.

"I doubt you even realized we were related, did you? I didn't, until my own grandmother's funeral, when the priest said 'Miriam, beloved mother of Seth and Isaiah,' and I thought, 'Who the fuck is Isaiah?' Not the best way to find out you've got an entire family you've never heard of, right? Burying your dear old gran. That was a long time ago, of course. Christ," he looked over at the vicar. "Sorry, Father. Bad habit. It was 1963. Boone was already thirty by the time I tracked him down and his old man was already too far gone for help, in and out of Cane Hill

Asylum, really not holding it together. We met two or three times that year, but it was hard for Boone. I tried to convince him his place was back with the family—you see, Raines wasn't his real name; he was a Lockwood, just like me, just like my grandson here. I know, shocking, isn't it? How can a good man like Boone be related to a sadistic old bugger like me? We could have ruled this place side by side. He could have been the brother I never had.

"Here's the thing, and this is why I am here, to pay my respects to a rare man. With all the bad blood between our families Boone found a way to stay out of it. He walked the line. He was an upright man. Ain't many of those about in this world of ours, believe me. So I wanted to come here and say, in front of everyone, as God is my witness, as far as I am concerned it ends here. Our families are straight; the past is a different country. For the good of everyone, from this day forth and so on and so forth, what happened back then is dead and buried with the last good man in London. It's for the best that it stays that way. Joshua, son," Lockwood looked at him. There were no smiles. The threat was there in that last line—*Don't go digging around in stuff that doesn't concern you.* The rest of it was just talk for talk's sake. "You have my word, the old debts are settled. They don't carry over one generation to another." He turned to face his own grandson then, the message he came here to deliver delivered. "If there's any way for you and Josh here to find each other, then maybe something good can come out of this after all. It'd make this old man very happy if you two could become, well, if not family . . . then friends, at least." Lockwood turned his attention back to the congregation. "And the rest of you, think on this when you walk out of here in a few minutes: the world is a lesser place today than it was yesterday. It is diminished by the loss of an upright man." There was a tear on his cheek, and sentimentality aside, Josh couldn't begin to believe it was genuine. Men like Gideon Lockwood didn't show emotion in public. Emotion was weakness. They couldn't afford to be seen as weak. Lockwood wanted the people here to mourn Boone to believe he was genuine. That was different. And that just made Josh all the more determined to find out what secrets the old man was so keen to bury. "Let's make death a time of healing. I think he would have approved of that." He nodded to himself. "Yes. I think he would have approved of that. Vale, Boone Raines."

Lockwood walked unsteadily down from the pulpit to his wheel-chair, allowing his grandson to help him into it. As the younger Lock-wood pushed him slowly back down the aisle, he reached out and rapped hard on the side of the coffin. Then smiling to himself, said, "Definitely dead then. Had to make sure," which earned a chuckle from a few parts of the congregation. The old man looked less than amused.

2

THE CROOKED KING

"Do you think it will be enough to keep him out?" Gideon Lockwood asked his young companion as they returned to The Hunter's Horns, the public house in the warrens of the Rothery. All the streets had names that harked back to a more mythological past with echoes of Albion and an England that never was. There was a Herne Drive and a Goodfellow Lane both leading away from the green and dozens more within a hundred yards. The pub, like the rest of the estate, had seen better days. It was surrounded by herringbone rows of terraced houses with red clay tiled rooftops and wheelie bins in the yards. From above there were little pockets of green, notably around a big old lightning-blasted oak tree in the very heart of the estate the kids called The Hunter because of its branching horns, and beyond that rose the shadows of Coldfall Wood, one of the last primeval forests in the country. How many kids had lost their virginity in the fairy circle in the heart of the old forest? Half of those brought up on the Rothery, at least. Most of the streets were more concrete jungle than untamed wilderness, though. Not that its own form of dangerous game wasn't out on the prowl, but the Lockwoods had nothing to fear from those particular feral youths. This was their place. Their patch. No one would come at them here. That would be a declaration of war, and no one was strong enough to fight a war with them on their home turf. Not now. Not ever.

"It had better be," the young man said, sinking into the seat in the back room. The jukebox was playing some long-forgotten '80s one-hit wonder in the other room. In here it was muffled beyond recognition. "But if not, well, then we have to deal with him."

"I don't know, it's not like it was, we can't just make people disappear anymore," Gideon Lockwood said.

"That's exactly what we *can* do."

Gideon reached into his pocket for a packet of filter-tipped cigarettes and fumbled one out with trembling hands. It was quite an operation for the old man, but he stubbornly refused any help. The younger man waited for him to light up.

Everything in life isn't as it seems to be. The surface is constructed from a patina of lies. That was the first thing the young man had learned from Damiola, the magician. But that was an obvious lesson for one of the world's greatest liars to teach. He lived his life through deceits, showing one truth while hiding another quite different one. There are layers of existence. Layers of consciousness and understanding. Just because your eyes work well on one level doesn't mean they won't be blind on another. That was what Damiola had given him; eyes to see.

"It's not like we haven't done it before. And, if the worst comes to worst, at least we know no one will accidentally stumble across his body. Not where we'll hide it." The younger man wasn't talking about hiding Joshua Raines's body in the foundation of some bridge, either. He was talking about burying it in Glass Town.

"Then we better hope it was enough."

"You worry too much, boy," the younger man said. "Sometimes you just have to trust your old man."

Gideon Lockwood didn't say anything for the longest time. He offered no contradictions, because it was true: of the two of them he was the boy.

Marcus, the bartender, brought over a pair of brandy glasses slick with Rastignac XO and put them on the table between the Lockwoods, and then left them alone in the back room. This wasn't the kind of bar where the drinkers wanted the bartender to solve the woes of the world. They wanted to be left alone and he knew when to disappear.

"Look at it from my perspective," Gideon said finally. "I thought you were dead for the best part of my life. I grew up without a father. I grew old without a father. When the nuns told me who you were, I mourned you. When I learned your story, how you had disappeared, I hated Isaiah. I was sure he had murdered you. I couldn't let it go. So I watched him. He had no idea who I was. I got close enough to watch him obsess over your relationship with that bloody woman, like a ratter down a hole. He just wouldn't give it up. And I hated him for it. More than I *hated* her for taking you away from me. More than I hated you. Everything I became, that was down to your not being there. I was just a baby."

"Don't blame me for the choices you made in life. That's weak and it's bullshit. I didn't force you to do any of it, and given the choice I would never have come back, remember that. But I didn't have a choice."

Gideon grunted. "And how does that help me? You don't even want to be here. I'm dying and you don't want to be here. It doesn't matter that you haven't aged a day and I'm this withered old husk of a man; you're still my father, and all you can think about is that place and getting back there."

"Life isn't fair, boy, less so now than it was in my day. Back then we had our ways of doing things, but you knew where you stood. The family was firm but fair. People didn't dare cross us. You made an example of one man and let it serve as a lesson for all of them. You don't get to run a place like this without getting your hands bloody. But if you did it right, you only ever had to do it once." Gideon didn't disagree. The physicalities of control hadn't changed much over the best part of a century. "So we didn't get to play happy families? So what? Looks like you did all right for yourself without me. Ain't like you were a girl who needed me to dust off your knees when you fell down. Some might even say being forced to stand on your own two feet made a man out of you and you should *thank* me for going away. As for the dying, self-pity doesn't become you. We're all dying, son, it's a fact of life. It's just some of us are going more slowly than others. Look at it this way, at least you lasted longer than that bastard Boone, that's something to be grateful for, and I could still go before you. There are no guarantees in this life."

"Was she worth it?" Meaning was she worth giving everything up for? Meaning was she worth walking out on your life, turning your back on your brother, on the empire your father and his father had built? Meaning was she worth missing out on my entire life for? Meaning how could anything be worth that, explain it to me.

"Always, boy. Every single sacrifice, and I know you don't want to hear that, but that's the way it is. But if that boy gets his hands on Isaiah's papers—if he even begins to suspect what we did . . . how we did it . . . My brother was so close to solving the riddle of Glass Town, to seeing past the smoke and mirrors . . . And its defenses are weaker now. The frames are already flickering. The walls are growing thin. It can't last forever . . . If the boy pieces it all together, even if it's just to see through the frames for long enough to glimpse what is on the other side," the young man, whose real name was Seth Lockwood, shook his head as though it was all too much to countenance. "Then it's in danger of all coming apart. That can't happen. I won't let it. I won't give her up. Not now. We have made a life together."

"What are you going to do?"

"I think someone should pay his dear cousin a visit, don't you? There are bridges to be built. After all, your eulogy was very touching. How could he not be moved by it?"

3

FAMILY REUNION

Josh moved around the gathering like a grim moth—butterfly wasn't an appropriate simile because there were no bright colors on display inside the Scala, the old-domed bingo hall and social club on the edge of the Rothery where the mourners had retreated to raise a glass and share Boone stories. Everyone wanted to shake his hand and tell him how sorry they were for his loss, what a great man Boone had been, what a loss he would be, and share a reminiscence.

Three victims of middle-aged spread and male-pattern baldness propped up the bar, half-drained pints of stout in their thick hands.

Despite the smoking ban, the air was thick with the stuff.

Seeing him, the baldest and fattest of the trio raised a hand to call him over.

Josh didn't have the will to resist because if it weren't them, it would be another group just like them with another story, so he walked over to the bar to join them. "Gentlemen," he said, forcing a smile.

"The apple really didn't fall too far from the tree with you, did it? Bloody hell, it's like looking at a picture of your old man as a boy."

"Uncanny, isn't it?" the middle man agreed, setting his pint aside.

The third man agreed with a slight nod.

Josh didn't have the slightest idea who they were.

"How you holding up?" the first asked, but before he could answer the middle man said, "Pretty tough day, eh?"

The third man nodded his agreement again.

They were like some overweight balding version of the Fates, with the third weird brother remaining silent while the others made their pronouncements.

"Yeah, it's been a tough day," Josh admitted. "A tough week, really, especially for Mum. I'll be glad when it's all over."

"You're a good lad," the first offered.

"Like your old man," the second agreed.

And still the third man said nothing.

"Anyway," the first continued, "we just wanted to offer our condolences, face-to-face."

"It's appreciated," Josh said, managing a half smile.

"Did Boone ever tell you about the first time we met him?" the middle man asked. Josh didn't have the heart to tell him he had no idea who they were, so he shook his head. "It was going back some, we were kids, no more than eleven or twelve, I reckon. Right in the middle of The Blitz."

He settled in to tell his tale, leaning back against the bar now that he had a captive audience.

"It was one of those dark nights when the Krauts were in the sky with their bombs, just waiting . . . the air was thick with them. If I close my eyes, I can still remember the whistle from the doodlebugs and then the silence, and that was so much worse because you'd just know, shit, here it comes and there was nothing you could do but hide and hope it missed you . . ." he shivered, and it was obvious he really could remember. "Anyway, this old warden, Norman, was on the searchlight duty for our street. The lights were dotted across the rooftops to help our boys spot the Luftwaffe, strafing the sky. When the air-raid siren goes up and the blackout's meant to start, only Norman's light doesn't go out.

"Everyone's running for the air-raid shelters, but not Boone. See, even then Boone's a bit of a handful. What we used to call a good old-fashioned guttersnipe back then. When the sirens go off and people run for cover he's off to work. He finds an empty house, breaks a window, and climbs in, looking to grab some food from their pantry. We were all hungry back then, see. Properly hungry. Living hand-to-mouth. There just wasn't enough food to go around. My old mum would queue up for hours just for a bit of dripping and a crust. Stuff likes eggs were a treat. Bet you don't even know what dripping is, do you, lad?" he didn't wait for an answer. "So anyway, Boone's in this butcher's parlor helping himself to a plate of fried sausage when he realizes the place is still lit up like the middle of the day and he can't hear anything. That's the worst of it. The place is *eerily* quiet.

"Then he realizes what he can't hear: the drone of the doodlebugs. And the place is lit up like Christmas. The warden's only gone and had a fucking heart attack and his light's still on, guiding the German bombs right to the end of our street!

"Boone didn't hesitate—and remember he's still in short trousers— he scarpers out of the place like his arse is on fire, still eating that sausage mind you, and runs toward the light, not thinking about his own safety. It'd been drilled into us, see. That light had to be out. He climbs up onto the roof and uses a stone to shatter the bulb, even as the bomb explodes three streets away and takes out four houses in the terrace leaving nothing but a crater behind. And if that ain't enough, he only carries the old guy back down to the street, making enough noise to raise the Devil and get help for him. A second bomb landed less than twenty feet from where Boone stood—"

"Jesus, but how—?"

"Didn't detonate. Someone was looking after him that day."

"Someone's been looking after Boone all his life," the middle man said. Josh hadn't heard this story before. He shook his head, trying to imagine what it must have been like. "That old warden was my dad," the middle man continued, ending the story. "I wouldn't be here if it wasn't for your granddad, lad."

Josh nodded. As Boone stories went, it wasn't a bad one.

The three raised a glass to toast Boone Raines before Josh left them to their stories. He needed to get some fresh air, so he snuck out the back, closing the fire door behind him, and just stood in the shadows, breathing in the fresh air.

"All getting a bit emotional for you, eh, Cuz?" said a voice from shadows.

"Jesus Christ," Josh said. "You scared the crap out of me." He fell back against the wall, laughing. It was a nervous laugh full of relief that the thing in the shadows didn't mean him harm.

"Ah, sorry, that wasn't my intention. After Gramps's speech in the church I thought maybe he was right, you know? It's not *our* war. We should get to know each other. I mean, until today I didn't even know I had a cousin." He still didn't step out of the shadows. Josh heard a curious clicking sound. It took him a moment to realize it was Lockwood's tongue on the roof of his mouth.

"I'm not sure we are cousins," Josh said. "Not in the strictest sense."

"Well, we're blood. I mean you just have to look at us," and so saying Lockwood eased away from the wall, the shadows relinquishing their hold on him. The likeness was disturbing. He was right, there was no denying the genetic blend behind their faces. "And apropos of blood, do you know anything about this bad blood between your great-grandfather and mine? That's right, isn't it? The great part? It all sounds very mysterious."

"Not much," Josh said. "It was about a girl."

"Isn't it always?"

"Eleanor Raines."

"Pretty name—and I'm guessing your great-grandmother, then?"

"Nope. I'd never heard of her until this morning. My great-grandmother's *sister*."

"Oh, now that sounds like a scandal."

Something stopped Josh from telling his new cousin everything he knew. Instead he blew out an exaggerated sigh and shrugged. "Eleanor was the love of his life. There was some big falling out between Isaiah and Seth and that was it, the family split. Isaiah turned his back on the family, became a Raines, and my family was born."

"Oh, what a tangled web. Families, eh?"

"Families," Josh agreed.

Lockwood stubbed out the cigarette he hadn't been smoking, and ground it out under his foot. "Amen," he said.

Josh shook his head. "But, like your grandfather said at the funeral, it's not on us, is it? There's no need for it to define the next ninety years of our family."

"Agreed," Lockwood said, inclining his head slightly as he looked at Josh, weighing up what to say next. Josh wasn't sure Lockwood believed him when he said he didn't know what the feud was about, but couldn't see why it should concern either of them. Like he said, it was ninety years ago, and that is a hell of a long time for old grudges to smolder on. "Anyway, look," Lockwood held out a hand for Josh to shake, "I just wanted to say I'm sorry for your loss. I really am."

"Thank you," Josh said, taking the proffered hand. "I don't even know your name."

"Seth," he said. "Yeah, Looks like we're not the most original family when it comes to naming our offspring. It's just a curse I have to bear. Thankfully, no one remembers the old bastard these days. Anyway, by all accounts your grandfather was a good sort. I can't begin to imagine how it'd feel to lose Gideon, so, you know . . ." he said.

He let go of Lockwood's hand. Those were the last kind words that the pair would ever say to each other, not that Josh realized that at the time. His cousin turned to walk away, but stopped on the edge of the shadows and turned to look back at him. "Hey, nah, it's nothing. Forget it."

"What?"

"It's stupid, don't worry about it. I was just wondering if the old guy left you anything, you know, a memento. Like I said, it's stupid. I just keep thinking about Gideon and wondering what I'd want of his to remember him by."

Josh's hand moved instinctively toward the letter in his inside pocket before he could stop it, but rather than pulling back and making it obvious he carried on and pulled out Boone's battered silver tobacco tin. "This," he said, holding it up in the brightness of the security light for him to see. "I think he was trying to get me killed." The joke fell flat.

Lockwood left him alone in the dark.

4

THE RUSHES

"He's lying," Seth Lockwood said. "And rather badly at that."

"So what do we do?" the old man in the passenger seat asked. The degenerating nerves in his right cheek twitched, making it look as though he was struggling not to smile.

"We bring in the Rushes," Seth said.

"The what?"

"You'll see soon enough. I don't want to spoil the surprise. We're getting into Boone's house, and we'll tear it apart if need be. We're going to find what he left behind. Anything that leads back to Glass Town, we destroy. It's as simple as that."

"Remember, he's just a kid. He's not part of this."

"Don't go getting sentimental on me, sunshine. We do what we have to do. Whatever it takes. That's how we survive. Sometimes we even go so far as to enjoy it. And don't bother trying to pretend you've never enjoyed causing pain. I recognize it in you. We're kin."

They were parked at the side of the road, three streets away from the back of the Scala, overlooking the ruin of the old Latimer Road cinema. It had been a long time since any celluloid gods had entertained on that particular silver screen. It had been almost thirty years, in fact, since the last Saturday morning picture show.

Given the value of prime real estate in the heart of London the land itself must have been worth a not-so-small fortune regardless of the fact the building was a death trap, but still the old cinema stood abandoned and slipping evermore into decay without any sign of redevelopment. That might have surprised the casual observer, but a little digging in the right places would have revealed the name on the freehold as one Gideon Lockwood, the sale having gone through at the price of a peppercorn the week the old cinema owners filed for bankruptcy. More digging would have unearthed articles about the incessant vandalism the old Latimer Road cinema had been subjected to, including two attempts at arson, which suddenly stopped after ownership changed hands. A suspicious mind might draw certain conclusions from that evidence. There were reasons the Lockwoods had wanted the old cinema, of course. There were *always* reasons.

Seth took two things from the glove compartment: a box of matches and what looked like a Victorian wind-up toy.

"What on earth are you doing?" Gideon Lockwood asked as his ageless father turned the carousel. He saw the flicker of movement within the inner circle of mirrors that lined the carousel. "It's a praxinoscope, an early projection device. It is called Damiola's Carousel, and was part of the illusionist's stage show and quite unlike any zoetrope that came before or after it. Just sit back and watch. There are different ways to put the frighteners on guys now. Like this." The old man's cheek twitched again. His fingers had the same flutter, a sure sign that the disease was spreading. It made him look even weaker than he was. Seth Lockwood had no stomach for weakness. "Now do not fight me, boy, or disease won't be what kills you."

He planted the carousel on the dashboard, fitting a paper with a woman's silhouette cut from it onto the drum, and turned the small handle through seven revolutions until it spun under its own momentum, then he teased a match from the box and struck it, holding it in the center of the carousel as it turned. He opened the carousel's hood, and a moment later the flickering match light was projected into the middle of the street in front of them. Slowly, with each rattling revolution of the carousel, a stuttering silhouette began to take shape within the light. Two more turns of the handle and the flickering frames settled on the shape of a woman, though her face was horribly blurred from the carousel's erratic motion. It didn't become any clearer even though the image became more and more substantial until an actual woman appeared to stand in the middle of the road—though as the clouds shifted to reveal the moon, the moonlight streamed through her, undoing the illusion.

The match burned out and the carousel came to a stuttering stop.

She didn't disappear.

The woman conjured up by the carousel turned to face them. Her face remained a featureless smudge, but every other detail was in sharp focus. She wore a white dress that billowed around her knees and accentuated her movie star bust. She had a blond bob cut short above her shoulders. There was no color anywhere on her. She was a stark black-and-white projection made real in shades of gray.

"Meet the Rushes," Seth said.

He opened the car door and clambered out. He walked up the middle of the road to stand face-to-face with his invocation.

In the car, Gideon couldn't hear what his father said to his creation. He didn't need to. He knew he was filling its head with orders and sending it out to hunt. He couldn't bear to look at the apparition; it did strange things to him. It stirred things inside the old man he'd been sure were long since dead.

After a moment the conjuration seemed to shift ever so slightly, causing the moonlight to diffract, and moved off, not running, not walking, but seeming to blink in and out of existence with each jarring step because her new body lacked all the frames it needed to move smoothly.

And then she was gone.

Seth Lockwood walked back toward the car.

"She's off hunting," he said, clambering back into the driver's seat. "She will tear Boone's house apart. If there is something to be found, she will find it and bring it to us."

"What is that thing?"

"I told you."

"Not its name. I mean what *is* it?"

"It's from that place, that's all you need to know. Think of it as a dream if that helps."

"It doesn't."

"An ancient spirit. A thing of the mist. A demon. A succubus. Eater of Souls. There are lots of names for what she is."

"Dear God," Gideon said,. "You've turned that thing loose to *feed*, haven't you?"

"I am just protecting what I love, son, like anyone would."

"Can you control it?" Gideon Lockwood shook his head at the sheer staggering stupidity of what his father had just done.

"Well enough. She has Joshua Raines's scent," he held up the dog-end of Rizla rolling paper and a few tufts of burned tobacco that Josh had stubbed out before entering the church that afternoon. "She won't fade out until she has finished her duty to me. I didn't lie; the feud ends now. Joshua Raines is the last of Isaiah's line. I will not lose Eleanor. Not now. Not after all this time. I will not stand by and watch the dweomers around Glass Town fail one by one until any idiot can stumble upon our haven and take her away from me. I have sacrificed *everything*. I will not let Isaiah win. The bastard is dead. If Joshua Raines has to die for Isaiah's hold over me to be laid to rest, then so be it. It is a price I am willing to pay. By the time I am through I will have scoured every last recollection of his damned bloodline from the world. There won't be a living soul that remembers so much as his name, never mind his obsession with Eleanor. He won't win. He *can't*."

And there, in that last confession, Gideon Lockwood heard the depths of his father's madness. He didn't understand half of what was happening. Words like dweomers meant nothing to him. What he did understand was the intensity of his father's hate. The same emotion had fueled most of his adult life. The rest of it came down to one thing: Damiola's magic, whatever it was, was failing and Glass Town was coming undone. Seth would do anything to stop that from happening— including murder.

5

WHITE NOISE

Josh didn't go back inside.

He couldn't face the noise and the heat and the smell of too many people crammed in too close together drinking, but more than anything he couldn't face any more sympathy. Instead, he decided to sneak off. He figured Boone would forgive him even if his mother wouldn't. Real life was going to kick in soon. A day or two at most and then it'd be back to the office in Soho and the endless phone calls to strangers trying to sell them ad space in a magazine going not so slowly out of business. There was nothing more soul-destroying than dialing number after number, reading the script, and trying to inject some sort of *life* into it all.

Meeting his cousin had thrown him. There was something about the guy he didn't like. It wasn't just that he was slick, smarmy, or any other unpleasantly greasy adjective that came to mind when he thought of secondhand car salesmen. It was more fundamental than that. There was just something inherently *off* about him. Of course, it was quite possible his judgment had been clouded by the fact that he was a Lockwood. Old hatreds ran deep, even when you'd just inherited them.

People said names had power, the Lockwood name certainly did, and that had nothing to do with the arcane or mystical and everything to do with cricket bats to the knees, coshes made from socks stuffed with pool balls and wrapped around the side of someone's skull, shivs in the base of the spine and other makeshift weapons of pain. They were particularly good with pain.

Josh rolled another cigarette.

There was an art to it that he hadn't quite mastered, but then he'd never been a smoker. Since Boone's death it had felt like a way of being connected to the old man, so he lit the straggly rollie and sucked on the end of it, allowing himself to remember his grandfather.

He coughed out smoke and fell back against the wall, half-laughing at the ridiculousness of it all and flicked the cigarette end over end toward the trash. He walked away, leaving the faint strains of conversation and laughter behind. The Rothery at night was a curious animal at the best of times. Tonight was not the best of times. He walked with his hands stuffed into his grandfather's pockets, head down, from one puddle of streetlight to the next puddle of streetlight. He could hear the forlorn cries of a siren somewhere in the distance and the roar of a car racing around the fringe of the estate. It didn't take any great imagination to link the two together: boy racers out for a joyride.

He used the narrow alleyways between the terraces to cut across the municipal park without having to so much as set foot on a blade of grass, and then cut through the garages and up the hill toward home. He saw kids coming out of the sports hall, sweaty from football practice. There'd been something about one of the lads in the magazine recently, a local interest piece, he was supposed to be the real deal. A genuine talent. The route avoided the shops and shaved about ten minutes off the walk.

Long before he made it to the door he saw the peculiar flickering light through the chink in the curtains of the downstairs window, like someone had left the television playing to itself. He tried to think back, but it wasn't like they'd watched anything for days. The house had been a silent shrine since Boone's death.

Josh stopped at the end of the drive. He could just make out a darker shadow around the doorjamb where it was slightly ajar. He knew he'd locked up. Someone was in there. Some little bastard was robbing them on the day of his grandfather's funeral.

Something inside Josh snapped.

Instead of calling for help he ran to the door and flung it open, making as much noise as possible as he entered, hoping that it would scare the intruders off. Perhaps it would have, had they been kids looking to get in and out to make a quick score. But this was no simple smash-and-grab. The downstairs rooms looked like a war zone: the contents of every drawer had been turned out; papers, bills, magazines, and everything else that had been accumulated over far too long was scattered across the carpet; the furniture had been overturned, the back of the couch peeled away to expose the wooden frame and springs beneath the thick corduroy; glasses and ornaments from the dresser added to the debris, a tiny porcelain dancer in pieces beside a Herefordshire bull and a Shire horse. The horse's matchstick cart was in splinters; broken frames were discarded on the floor beside the torn photographs that catalogued generations of their family that had been torn out of them and cutlery glittered like treasure amid the ruin of their lives.

Josh's heart hammered wildly as he reached down for a knife, not that it was sharp enough to do anything more than butter someone to death.

He realized that the television, the Blu-ray and satellite decoder and all of the other expensive electricals were untouched, and he saw Boone's watch amid the mess. It was an old gold fob watch and chain, probably worth three or four hundred pounds, easily portable, simple enough to sell on. This wasn't just wanton vandalism; they were looking for something.

But *what*?

He picked his way through the mess, calling out, "I know you're in here. I don't want to hurt you. Just go and I won't call the police. I won't chase you. I won't even look to see who you are. Just go and we can forget all about this."

No answer.

He walked through to the kitchen.

The ransacking was every bit as thorough in there, with every drawer turned out, crockery broken on the linoleum floor, the plant pots in the window overturned and spilling their dry dirt across the sill, but the room was empty.

He heard something upstairs: the groan of a floorboard above his head.

Josh gripped the handle of the knife as tightly as he could and walked back through to the hallway and the phone. He dialed 999 and interrupted the operator as she asked which service he required. *"There's someone here,"* he whispered urgently. *"Upstairs. I can hear them."*

"There's someone in the house with you?"

"A break-in."

"And they are still in the house?"

"I can hear them moving about."

She confirmed the address with him, then said, "Listen to me carefully; don't say another word. I am dispatching officers to your location. They will be there in less than five minutes. Do not draw attention to yourself. Go outside. Wait for them. Do not remain in the house. Do not take any unnecessary risks. Let us do our jobs. Property can be replaced. The most important thing is that you do not put yourself in harm's way. Do you understand?"

Josh could hear the intruder moving around upstairs.

"I understand," he said, laying the handset back down beside the phone. He could still hear the operator telling him to go outside now and wait, but instead of doing what he was told, he climbed the stairs one step at a time, listening at each one until he was at the top.

He could see the weird flickering light bleeding out from under the door of what had been Boone's bedroom.

He thought about going back downstairs, doing what he had been told and going outside to wait for the patrol car, but five minutes might as well have been an eternity. They were in the room *now*, rifling through Boone's stuff. He kept thinking about Lockwood and how he'd asked if Boone had left him anything. It was too much of a coincidence that within an hour of that he'd returned home to find the place being torn apart, wasn't it? Isaiah's letter had promised a wealth of material from his obsessive investigation into Eleanor Raines's disappearance. Did the Lockwoods know about that stuff?

Of course they did, he thought bitterly. They were wrapped up in this and had been from the very start.

All that talk about a clean slate, about new beginnings, it was all rubbish. Life wasn't random; it was a weave of complex events, causes and effects both on a personal and an impersonal level. Things didn't just happen. Lockwood hadn't just happened to be outside the Scala. His "cousin" had been lurking in the shadows, playing lookout. Gideon Lockwood had sent some of their thugs around to hunt for Isaiah's legacy while they knew he was at the wake. It was the one time they knew for sure Boone's house would be empty.

The thought scared him.

Really scared him.

He'd grown up hearing stories of what they were capable of, and always thought them exaggeratedly tall tales, but suddenly risking coming face-to-face with the reality was so much more frightening than any gossip, no matter how colorfully violent.

He knew he should have waited outside like the operator said, and on any other day he might have, but not today. He wasn't going to run scared today. Boone hadn't been in the ground more than a couple of hours. This was his home, and anything Boone had left here, he'd left for Josh to find, not some bastard in Lockwood's pocket.

Josh crept across the landing.

He stopped outside the door to his grandfather's room and listened.

He could hear them tearing the place apart.

Josh pushed the door open.

The room was a mess.

Sheets had been stripped from the bed, the mattress overturned, and clothes pulled from the wardrobe and strewn about. In the middle of it all, the source of the weird light: a woman in a dress so white he could barely stand to look at it. She had her back to him, and was tearing into a pillow, though what she hoped to find inside it, he had no idea.

"What the hell do you think you're doing?" Josh said. The adrenaline flooded out of his system at the sight of a woman where he'd dreaded seeing a bunch of hoodie-wearing thugs or old-school bald-headed, overweight, Doc Martens–wearing bovver boys.

The relief was short-lived.

She straightened up slowly, seeming to flicker with each jerky movement, hands still deep in the foam of the pillow, and turned to face him—but without a face that was next to impossible. Where there should have been eyes there were dark hollows, where there should have been cheekbones, brow, and nose, they were smudges of light and dark that blurred together as though her creator had tried to erase her from the face of the world. The tear of her mouth opened and a sound like the crackle of white noise emerged.

Josh dropped the knife.

He stepped back a half step, shaking his head. She didn't come into focus.

Every movement was jerky and incomplete, like a film reel skipping over vital frames. A dark smear opened in the middle of her face and she cocked her head to the left. He realized she was sniffing him out, drawing his scent down into her like some kind of ethereal bloodhound. And then when she had it, she came at him, bursts of static crackling out of the tear in her face.

Outside, he heard the distant wail of sirens.

The police were still streets away.

The woman in the white dress rounded the bed.

For just a second her face seemed to come into sharp focus and he *knew* her. How could he not? She had one of the most famous faces of the twentieth century, blond bob cut to her shoulder, high cheekbones, pencil-thin arched eyebrows, sharp nose, and rich-red adulteress's lips and smoky eyes: Myrna Shepherd, one of the first beauties of the silver screen who had smoldered beside the likes of Louise Brooks, Greta Garbo, Hedy Lamarr, Fay Wray, and Mary Pickford. The poster of *Wallflower Girl* was a student dorm room classic. That poster had hung on the wall above his first girlfriend's bed for all the months they had been together. The look the photographer had captured in her eyes was anything but platonic and had caused thousands of young men down the century to fall in love with an impossible-to-live-up-to girl. Vicky—an earnest, intellectual, tragically hip girl trying to work out the woman she was going to become—never had a chance. How could she have when every time he made love to her he was looking up into Myrna Shepherd's eyes?

The woman in white was a young Shepherd, but unmistakably and impossibly her. The Hollywood icon stood in Boone's cramped little bedroom in the middle of the Rothery—the same Hollywood icon that had been buried in a cemetery in Los Angeles for twenty years.

Josh remembered the line from Isaiah's letter when he confessed that he'd seen Eleanor Raines again, or thought that he had: *she hadn't changed. Not in the slightest. She was still the same heart-stopping beauty. . . .* And here he was, face-to-face with another woman who hadn't changed in the slightest from that same golden age of silent cinema, another actress who still wore the face she had during the '20s.

It had the quality of a dream, at once illusive, chilling, and impossible to wake from; alone in a bedroom with one of the world's first true sex symbols and there was nothing erotic about any of the thoughts tumbling blindly through his mind. Josh tried to back up a step, moving toward the doorway.

Myrna Shepherd moved another juddering step toward him, closing the gap to touching distance as she reached out for him.

Another burst of white noise crackled out of her mouth, but this time he could have sworn he heard his name hidden within the rush of static, full of sibilant *hiss.*

And then she was gone; those beautiful impossible features burning up like a strip of celluloid under the intense heat of the projector's lens, and the faceless woman stood before him again. A smell—a fragrance he couldn't name—filled the cramped bedroom.

She reached out a hand for his face, to make a connection. The tear in the featureless plain of her face opened, the crackle of static desperate, hungry.

The sirens were louder, but still too far away to help him.

Josh didn't hesitate.

He ran.

Out of the room, down the stairs, through the door, and out of the house: away from the woman whose face had hung from his girlfriend's wall and into the darkness.

6

MYRNA SHEPHERD'S EYES

Responding to a call in the Rothery was a case of taking your life in your hands at the best of times, and a late-night call promising a burglary in progress could never be described as the best of times. Police Constable Julius Gennaro—who had been saddled with the unfortunate moniker of Julie from his first day on the job eighteen months ago—and his partner Huw Carter—known forever as Taff—pulled into the cul-de-sac where the open door of Boone Raines's house was backlit like something from a Spielberg movie.

They rolled to a stop outside the house. The headlights lit the front up like a Christmas tree.

"Fifteen minutes," Taff grunted. That was how long until the shift change. Fifteen minutes and they would have been back in the station and the call to 11 Albion Close would have been someone else's problem. Fifteen minutes and their lives would have been oh-so-very different—and in Taff's case longer.

He reached up and killed the siren. He hated the damned noise. Every copper on the beat did.

"Come on then, Julie, let's go be heroic for a few minutes," the big Welshman said as he unclipped the seat belt and opened the door. Taff wasn't in good shape, and it wasn't just a few extra pounds, either. It was all about discipline or the lack of it, temptation, and excess. Taff Carter was just a boy who couldn't say no. And as he'd always known, it would be the death of him.

He eased his girth out of the car and straightened the baton on his belt, ready for trouble. There was *always* trouble. It was just part and parcel of their everyday lives. It was getting worse though and had been for the last few years. The streets were nastier than they had been in a long time. Brexit had given people an excuse to revel in their prejudices. Race crime was up, religious hate crime was up, violent crime was up, criminal damage was up. But it was okay because the vicious little bastards had got their country back. There was an edge of brutality to it that hadn't been there when he'd started out walking the beat thirty years ago, in that weird time between the '70s brutality and the '90s new police. It wasn't just that people were more desperate now; they'd always been desperate if you looked far enough down the social ladder. Put simply, if they wanted something now, they'd take it. It didn't matter if they were coveting mobile phones, laptops, fancy designer trainers, or cars, if it caught their eye, nothing and no one could stop them from taking it; especially not a fat old policeman like Taff.

Gennaro closed the passenger door. He was younger and fitter than his partner, and still idealistic enough to think that he could make a difference so his name was always the first up on the notice board for outreach programs and community policing days. Three nights a week he volunteered down at the youth club, playing table tennis and pool with kids who two hours later were out on the rob in Taff's bitter, cynical world. Julie's was different; where Taff saw shit, he saw the chance for things to get better, and Julie always saw the best in people when they were trying to make their lives better.

"What do you make of it?"

Taff pulled the baton from his belt and extended it, ready for the worst. "Keep your eye on the car."

The big Welshman walked down the drive to the open door. Gennaro walked to the curb and waited in that no-man's-land between the vehicle and the crime. This was always the worst part of any call: not knowing what they were walking into. It wasn't anticipation; that was the wrong word. It was apprehension. Until they crossed the threshold they had no way of knowing what waited on the other side of the door. Anything was possible—right up until the moment it wasn't.

There was something disquieting about the peculiar light spilling through the open door of number 11 Albion Close. But before unease could mutate into dread, Gennaro saw a woman emerge from the house. The light left her looking as though a thin gauze had been draped across her face like a veil, but even so her bob of blond hair and smoky eyes made stark by dramatic makeup was hauntingly familiar.

He felt like he'd seen her somewhere before, but that wasn't his first thought as she came through the door. His first thought was: *She's far too beautiful for the Rothery.* And she was. She was uncomfortably beautiful.

Taff retracted his baton and clicked it back onto his belt, an eager smile spreading across his chapped lips.

"Everything okay, love?" Taff asked as she walked toward him.

Julius Gennaro couldn't hear her response as she leaned in close, but she seemed to sniff at Taff Carter's neck. He was sure he heard the sharp *huff-huff-huff* of her breathing. Instead of dispelling the unease, the sight of the woman, dressed for the red carpets of Hollywood not the feral streets of the estate, only served to heighten it. There was a long moment when he felt sure she was more dangerous than any gang kid, but he couldn't have said why, and then the sharp staccato crackle of the radio clipped to his belt broke the tension and she was just a beautiful woman on her own and they were her White Knights.

Not that she needed rescuing.

The woman turned her face toward Gennaro, and walked away from Taff Carter without another word. She moved with a curious faltering grace; a weird flickering interrupted each step she made. Gennaro found it hard to focus on her, but at the same time couldn't take his eyes off her. He knew the woman, he was sure of it, but couldn't place where he had seen her before. With no thought for personal space she leaned in close, her nostrils flaring as she sniffed around the young policeman's throat, like she was sniffing out his pulse. He felt her lips against his skin; she had lips like clay. Julius Gennaro shivered—it was the kind of shiver that would have had his second-generation Italian mother saying someone had walked over her grave—and then she moved on, sniffing at the night air and he was left feeling like he'd just lost something precious to him.

Neither of them followed her as she walked down the middle of the road and out of the cul-de-sac, but both watched her every step of the way. She drifted between the pools of streetlights, flickering between the bright light and night as she went.

The night was colder than he remembered it being when he'd clambered out of the car.

"What did she say to you?" Gennaro asked Taff Carter as the big man shuffled back up the drive toward him.

Taff shrugged and shook his head. He looked lost. Utterly and completely lost. "I have no idea," he said, touching a fat finger to his neck where the thick vein pulsed. "I'm not sure she said anything, but did you *see* her? That's a woman to lose your mind for, my friend." There was something in the way he said it, something that was echoed in his eyes that said he already had. Gennaro couldn't argue with him. She was something else. What, though, he wasn't sure.

"We should check the house out," he said, realizing the eerie blue light had gone, leaving number 11 in darkness.

"No need, Julie, it's fine. False alarm," Taff assured him. "Let's call it in and head home."

7

SECRET PLACES

It was difficult to run anywhere when he had nowhere to run to.

Josh thought about heading back through the estate toward the Scala and Boone's memorial, knowing there were a few friendly faces there, at least, but the fact that there were friends gathered together in the bingo hall was enough to prevent him running that way—he didn't want to bring this *thing* to their door.

So he kept his head down and ran hard, driving himself on, arms and legs pumping furiously even as his lungs started to burn. Running and thinking was difficult. It was conditioning: he ran to empty his mind. But now he needed to think. That *thing*—it was a thing, his mind kept screaming, a thing, a thing, a thing, because it couldn't have been Myrna Shepherd, not really, the rational part of his mind knew that was impossible. But what was it then? It had come to Boone's place looking for something.

It had ransacked the house and was still in the process of tearing things apart as he'd interrupted it, so it couldn't have *found* whatever it was looking for. But that didn't mean it wasn't there. The only problem with that line of thinking was that Josh had lived in that house for most of his life; if there was something to be found, he would have found it before now, surely?

So where else could Boone have hidden something?

It wasn't as though the old man had a lot of secrets, but, even as Josh thought that, he remembered something Boone had said to him once: *I'll let you in on a secret truth, sunshine: a man has maybe a dozen secret places during his life. It may start with a camp in the woods and end with a shed at the bottom of the garden as an old man, but there are a good few in between. If you ever find all of them, you'll truly know the man, but not until then.* They'd been talking about women at the time, and how much of yourself you were supposed to give to a relationship because Josh had always found it hard after his dad's death to let anyone in, but could Boone have been talking about something else as well? A secret place where his true self lived?

There were a dozen cars out on the road. They were the pack animals of the city. They hunted in numbers. He heard the deep-throated rumble of a gas guzzler redlining it around the roundabout three streets over. Josh risked a backward glance. He couldn't see the woman in white, but he could see that lambent glow that emanated from within her lighting up the sky like a low moon.

It was hard to believe all of this was about a few clippings and assorted "treasures" of Isaiah's obsessive research into Eleanor Raines's disappearance. The woman had vanished over ninety years ago. Even if there was a crime there it was almost a century old and everyone involved was long gone. When Gideon Lockwood had said the past should stay buried, he was right; it really was time for a clean slate. There was no need for Josh and this new generation of Lockwoods and Raineses to get dragged into the feuds of their forefathers. But just because it hadn't been a thug in a hoodie upstairs didn't mean that his first instinct had been wrong—for all his talk about clean slates Lockwood was behind the break-in, and what else tied Gideon Lockwood to Boone apart from Isaiah's papers?

Josh gritted his teeth and ran on, the soles of his trainers slapping against the paving slabs as he cut across the road toward a narrow path that squeezed between the terraces, leading through to a back alley lined with plastic wheelie bins overflowing with rubbish and torn bin bags. He didn't slow down. He was in good shape without being a gym rat, preferring to run through the park or swim on a Sunday morning to the endless repetition of weights. He cycled into Soho half the time, when he felt like taking his life in his hands. Drivers in London were a special breed of impatient on the cramped and crowded roads. They treated cyclists like an inconvenience to be squashed. His breath came in ragged gasps as he reached the end of the alleyway. Up ahead he saw the cut that led to the allotments and realized he'd been running toward the sheds and the vegetable plots all the time. This was where his grandfather hid himself away from the world.

Low-hanging telephone wires were strung like garrotes over the entrance to the path. Despite the fact that it hadn't rained for two days the ground beneath his feet was still muddy. The sides of the path were lined with thick hedgerows; a quintessential little slice of Britain in the middle of all of the concrete with the plots themselves on the side of a steep bank that ran all the way down to the river more than three hundred feet below. Josh ducked under the telephone wires and slipped and slid down the bank until he reached the red gate of Boone's old allotment. The vegetables had run to seed and the hedges gone wild in the months it had been left untended. Rotten apples still hung on the trees in the middle of the tall grass. In the plot beside Boone's the door of an empty pigeon coop rattled in the wind.

Josh slipped through the gate.

Boone's shed was at the far side of the field. It was up on paving slabs so it didn't sink into the earth with the torrential spring rains undermining it every year. The door was locked with a heavy padlock. Josh didn't have the key. There were two small dusty windows, but neither was big enough for him to climb through even if he broke them. It was easier for him to worry the entire hasp out of the wooden doorframe than try to break the lock. Even so it took him the best part of ten minutes to pry the door open and get inside because he was a lousy boy scout and hadn't come prepared.

It wasn't exactly an Aladdin's cave of treasures; there was an old grass-smeared lawn mower hanging up on a series of nails and thick loops of orange power cables coiled beside it; shears and hoes and spades and all manner of plant pots, both plastic and red clay lined the workbench;

there was an old vice and a pair of wellington boots beneath it; there were saws and hacksaws with sharp teeth lying on oily rags and beside a tea chest that had been converted into a makeshift seat, a copy of a book his grandfather would never finish reading: *Green Men and the Mythical Secrets of a Lost England*. There were candles and a box of matches beside it. There was a bright red toolbox on the floor that was open, and inside it he could see an assortment of every screw and nail imaginable scattered around various screwdrivers and spanners. What there wasn't, as far as he could see, was anything that might have hidden Isaiah's legacy.

He closed the door and sank down onto the tea chest, cold and alone.

He was tired of running around in circles getting nowhere fast.

He didn't risk lighting one of the candles. He didn't want the attention an errant light might have drawn.

Josh had been looking at the set of keys hanging from a hook on the back of the door for a good five minutes before he realized what they were. He checked to be sure, but even before he measured the teeth side by side with his own, he was sure they weren't for the house on Albion Close.

Could they be the keys to Boone's secret place?

There was only one way to find out.

He pocketed them.

8

LONELY AVENUE

"Hey, Julie, I'll drop you here if that's okay," Taff Carter said, pulling up beside The Hunter's Horns. The pub traditionally marked the end of the Rothery and the beginning of civilization. He didn't indicate as he slowed. An old woman shuffled down the street struggling with a bulging plastic shopping bag. No doubt it was stuffed full of cigarettes, a bottle of something to make the pain go away, and comfort food; what else would she venture out for at this time of night? The police station was a five-minute walk from the public house and looked more like a prison than a haven.

"I've got a couple of errands to run. It might drag on a bit. Figure you'd want to get home as soon as possible, not tag along with me." It might have sounded reasonable, but for the fact that in the eighteen months they'd been partners it was the first time they hadn't clocked off together. "Do me a favor, punch me out would you?" He handed his partner the key card from his wallet. It was also the first time Taff Carter had asked his partner to break the rules and clock him out. One change of habits wasn't necessarily a red flag, two could, at a stretch, be a coincidence, but given Taff's odd behavior back at the crime scene he was already looking at the third and final warning sign. It was the rule of three. The devil was in the details. It took three changes in behavior before the old bullshit detector went into the red zone and alarm bells started to ring. That weird look in his eyes when he came face-to-face with the woman in white didn't count as a third thing by itself, but it all added up to something. What, exactly, Gennaro didn't know, but something rather than nothing.

"No problem," Gennaro said. "Catch you tomorrow, matey. Sleep well." He pocketed his partner's key card.

"You, too, Julie."

Gennaro clambered out of the car and slammed the door behind him. Without thinking about what he was looking for, Julius Gennaro cast a quick backward glance in the direction of the Rothery. And for just a moment the reflections made it seem like there were two moons in the sky back there, but the trick of the dark soon faded. Head down, he trudged along the lonely avenue toward the station.

———

Taff watched him go.

When Julie turned the corner and disappeared behind the creaking sign of the old pub, he eased out into the middle of the road, executing a careful three-point turn, and headed back toward The Hunter's Horns.

It was a few minutes after closing time when he pulled up outside the pub but that didn't matter. Lockwood was expecting him. He didn't go in through the main door. He went around to the side and knocked twice, sharply on a boarded-up door. The walls on either side of it was a patchwork of whitewashed bricks and clever graffiti. The door opened a moment later. It was a young man—Lockwood's grandson—who answered. "Ah, our bent bastard; nice of you to grace us with your presence."

He stepped aside to let Taff inside.

"Don't call me that."

"Why not? That's what you are, isn't it? A bent bastard."

"I don't like it."

"I don't care what you *like,* but if it makes you feel better I could just call you our cunt? How'd you like *that*? I mean, you open yourself wide for our money, so that's what you are, isn't it?"

"Go fuck yourself, kid."

Lockwood smiled. "Ah, so you've still got a bit of self-respect hidden in there somewhere have you? Good. It's no fun if you're completely broken. Come in, Granddad's expecting you."

Taff followed Lockwood Junior down a dank regency-wallpapered corridor to a heavy oak door that led through to the snug where Gideon Lockwood waited. The carpet was sticky under his feet.

Lockwood stopped just short of the threshold. "Just remember, one day not too far away now, all this will be mine. You will be mine. Pleasant thought, isn't it?"

Before Taff could answer, he opened the door.

The old crook maneuvered his wheelchair around to face Taff as he entered the smoke-filled room. There were three untouched drinks on the table. Gideon Lockwood nodded toward one of them. Taff took his seat. There were cigarette burns in the upholstery. Like everything else inside The Hunter's Horns, it had seen better days.

"You wanted to see me?"

Gideon Lockwood reached out with a trembling hand for the brandy glass on the table. He hooked his fingers around the stem and raised it to his lips, savoring the rich flavor of the drink before he deigned to answer his pet policeman. "I did. I do. And no doubt I will again."

"Can't live without me, eh?" Taff Carter said with a good deal more bluster than he felt. This place gave him the creeps. It was like something out of a '60s gangster movie. He half-expected to see the ghosts of Ronnie and Reggie Kray leaning against the bar, looking on approvingly as one of their kindred spirits put the frighteners on the copper.

"I believe you responded to a call to a burglary on the Rothery tonight?"

Taff nodded. "Nothing exciting."

"Au contraire," the old villain said. "It was quite exciting, actually. The thief was looking for something I would dearly love to lay my hands on, but she failed me. The object of her search is rather precious to my family. An heirloom, I suppose you'd say. It was taken from us many years ago, and we've just recently learned that the thief was none other than the much-loved and late of this parish, Boone Raines. That's where you come in, Mr. Carter. I want you to recover it for me."

"We've known each other a long time, Mr. Lockwood. You know you can trust me," the Welshman said, already rubbing his palms in anticipation of the silver that was about to cross them.

"I know I can, Huw. My grandson doubts your dedication to our cause, but I don't. I know exactly what your loyalty costs in pounds, shillings, and pence." His smile was wry. "And that's what counts after all, isn't it?"

Taff didn't contradict him. "So what is it I'm looking for?"

"As I said, an heirloom. A piece of Damiola's glass."

"Is that some kind of ornament? A necklace?"

"Not really. It's more like a custom-ground lens."

"A lens? You mean like a contact lens or for a camera?"

Lockwood shook his head. "In principle, yes, but again, neither are terms I would use to describe it."

"Okay so how *would* you describe Damnwhatsit's lens then? I need to know what I'm looking for."

"Damiola's glass," Lockwood repeated the name slowly, as though he were talking to a child. "It's about the size of a cricket ball." He demonstrated, fighting the shakes to put thumbs and forefingers together to make a rough circle. "But shaped like a disc rather than spherical, hence referring to it as a lens. You'll find it in a brass compact case."

"Compact? Like a makeup case?" Lockwood nodded. "Okay, and what's so special about it? It can't just be sentimental value. No offense, but in all the years I've known you, Mr. Lockwood, you've never once come across as the sentimental sort."

"People can change, Huw," Gideon Lockwood half-smiled. "But its relative value is none of your concern. All you need to know is that it is precious to me. Bring it back to me and you shall be rewarded handsomely."

"So, not to put too fine a point on it, but where am I going to find this precious compact?"

"On a dead man," Lockwood said. "Assuming he took it with him to the grave. Otherwise, it could be anywhere. That is why I am paying you." The old man reached into his jacket for his wallet, and began to count out five hundred pounds in crisp fifties. "This should cover any incidentals you might incur."

"What if I said I didn't want your money?" Taff said, earning a snort of derision from Lockwood's grandson as he reached down for his own glass. He hadn't taken a seat at the table. It was about intimidation. By standing over them he was exerting power, showing his dominance. Taff had to look up to him whether he wanted to or not.

"I'd say I didn't believe you, but for the sake of argument, what *do* you want, if not my money? Let's open negotiations, Officer Carter."

"The woman."

"What woman would that be?"

"The woman in white. The one you sent to find the looking glass."

"You want me to *give* you the woman? How's that supposed to work?"

"Just one night. That's all I want. One night with a woman like that." Taff was shaking; his tremors were more pronounced than Lockwood's even without the old man's affliction. He struggled to master them.

"Just say I could arrange it," Gideon Lockwood said, waiting for the hope to register in the policeman's eyes. The eyes could never lie, he'd found, not when the temptation dangled in front of them was fashioned from desire. "What makes you think I would?"

"I've been good to you, Mr. Lockwood. Never seen you wrong. Looked out for your interests. Kept my colleagues off your back."

"And you figure I owe you, is that it?"

He didn't want to say that. Not out loud, but yes, that was exactly what Taff figured.

"Ever heard the saying: Be careful what you wish for?"

"One night," Taff said, "that's all I want. Just one night with someone like that. Dear God, could you imagine?"

A slow smile spread across the young Lockwood's face. He knocked back the shot of whiskey in his own glass and slammed the tumbler back down onto the ring-stained table right in front of Taff Carter. "I could, but I don't think you can," he said.

"Why? Because I'm overweight? A fat fuck like me would never get to have a woman like that go down on me? Do me a fucking favor. All

I've got is my fucking imagination," Taff said bitterly. "Just once I'd like to have the real deal, so if it's all the same to you, fuck your money, I want the woman. And not just some whore you send around to my place. Her. I want her. I want her to fuck me like I'm Brad *fucking* Pitt and George Clooney rolled into one. And I want her to pretend she likes it. If you can get her to do that, I'll get the glass for you and I'll get you anything else you want."

"Well, then, I think we have ourselves a deal, Huw," the young Lockwood said, gripping his shoulder. His fingers were uncomfortable as they pressed deeper than they should, digging into the muscle. "I'll send her around to your place tonight. You're right. You deserve it. And it's the very least I can do for you."

"Thank you."

"Oh, don't thank me, you bent bastard. You're going to get exactly what you asked for because I am a man of my word. Words are important. But in terms of our little arrangement, it's purely business, remember that when you're lying back and trying to think of England. I hope she's worth it."

"She will be." Taff turned to go, then stopped and said, "One more thing."

"Don't push your luck, Taff."

"His name . . . this dead man, who am I looking for?"

"Cadmus Damiola."

"What kind of name is that?"

"An old one. It used to mean something around here."

WHISKEY DREAMS

When was a key not a key? It wasn't so much a metaphorical question as it was a metaphysical one, like the tree falling with no one to hear it. A key with nothing to open has no purpose. Josh felt it rattle against Boone's tobacco tin in his pocket. Through the narrow window he caught a glimpse of that eerie blue-white flickering light as it swelled. He hesitated, caught in indecision, frozen between throwing the door open and running, or shrinking back into the shadows of the shed and pulling the old blanket up over his head and hoping the wraith bride just passed him by.

That hesitation took the choice out of his hands.

Josh saw her through the cobwebbed glass, heart-stoppingly beautiful, and utterly terrifying as she ghosted across the foxtails, dandelion clocks, and seed potatoes toward the shed. He scuffed back a step away from the glass, his foot fetching up against a discarded flower box and making it scrape across the wooden floor with what—given as he was trying to be church-mouse silent—sounded to him like enough of a racket to raise the dead. Josh fervently prayed she hadn't heard it. Mind racing, he ducked away from the window. How had she followed him here? How had she known this was where he would run to when he hadn't known himself? Or, more pertinently, perhaps, more bitterly, certainly: How had he been stupid enough to allow himself to be cornered here with nowhere to run?

The air *felt* peculiar. It was as if it was heavy with energy. Charged.

He risked a careful step back toward Boone's makeshift chair, transferring his weight from one foot to another very, very carefully so the old boards beneath them didn't protest, and then another, putting him out of direct line of sight through the window. He could hear her out there, moving through the allotment. He could hear the rustle of her long white dress through the high foxtails and the whisper of the long grasses in her wake. And he could hear something else, too, even if he couldn't understand *what*: a burst of static, like a radio that had fallen off-station, a cackle of white noise as it tried to retune, and somewhere inside that, the ghosts of voices that couldn't quite come through.

The shed was filled with an array of makeshift weapons if worst came to worst, but he wasn't sure he could fight the woman. Could a rusty old sickle cut her? He didn't want to ever find out the answer. That didn't stop him from taking down the sickle. It didn't have a particularly good edge on it, but given that the last thing he wanted to do was swing it the lack of cutting edge really wasn't a deal breaker.

The diffuse blue light filled the window, casting shadows across the workbench and tools inside the shed as it created a stark new geography for the place that consisted of black shadows and sharp angles. He caught a glimpse of her blond bob through the glass as she crossed the window.

The static crackled again.

It was at the door.

The eerie light crept beneath it, seeming to edge closer and closer to his feet, reaching out for him.

Josh tried to shuffle back another step, but there was nowhere to go.

The handle rattled.

Josh could half-hear the voices trapped inside it as another burst of static filled the night.

His grip tightened on the sickle's wooden grip.

The handle turned.

The door groaned open an inch.

Two.

The wraith bride's weird luminescence spilled into the shed.

The light touched every corner of the interior.

There was nowhere to hide as she opened the door.

Myrna Shepherd stood in the doorway, the folds of her white dress coiling around her, her chest flushed, rising and falling shallowly, breath coming fast. Her eyes were smoky hollows. She opened her mouth and another burst of white noise and ghost voices crackled out of her. He heard words in there, they were faint, coming from a long way away—another time, another place—and they made no sense to him: *"Gimme a whiskey sour . . ."*

"What do you want from me?"

"Gimme a whiskey sour . . ."

Josh didn't know what to say to that. "I don't have any," Josh said, feeling stupid and terrified at the same time. It was beyond surreal, facing a movie icon in the doorway of his grandfather's allotment shed, listening to her ask for a drink, and knowing what she really wanted was to shred his soul. His free hand closed around the key in his pocket. All he could think was that he couldn't let her have it.

"C'mon baby, you don't want to disappoint a lady, do you?"

"I can't give you what I don't have," Josh took his hand out of his pocket and held up both the sickle and the empty hand to show Shepherd he wasn't holding out on her.

"You don't want to disappoint a lady . . ."

She crossed the threshold.

Just a single step.

And then she stopped, tilting her head as though listening to something—a sound so far away or pitched so high—he couldn't hear. Her face twitched. Her head straightened. Those smoky eyes of hers bore into him. Her nostrils flared. And then her entire face flickered and for the silence between his hammering heartbeats she wasn't there.

And then she was.

Another burst of static filled with words, an old movie line, he realized hearing the echo of that famous statement of hers: *"Loneliness is good for the soul."* And, good to her word, the thing that was Myrna Shepherd backed away from the door, leaving Josh Raines to stand there and stare at the open doorway and wonder what had just happened and how the hell he was still alive.

He didn't move for a full five minutes, but the light had long since faded. Whatever she was, she wasn't coming back. He didn't know what had stopped her, but whatever the reason it had saved his life, so he wasn't about to start arguing with it.

He dropped the sickle on the old workbench and sank down onto Boone's tea chest seat, exhausted as the flood of adrenaline left his body. He was shaking so hard the key in his pocket rattled against the tobacco tin as though to remind him it was still there.

When is a key not a key? He riddled himself again; only he did know what it opened, just not where it opened it. It opened the door to Boone's secret place. He even knew what was inside it—or at least thought he did. It couldn't be far away; he knew that, too. The old man hadn't traveled much in his last days. So in point of fact he knew a lot more than he had even a few hours ago. And he wasn't fumbling in the dark. Boone had left him Isaiah's confession for a reason, hadn't he? It had to be a clue, didn't it?

But there were no addresses in that old letter, were there?

10

WRAITH BRIDE

Taff Carter felt particularly pleased with himself as he arrived home that night. He'd got one over on those smug bastards. They'd been so sure he'd do anything for the money—and truth be told he probably would have, if he hadn't had to put up with Lockwood's brat calling him a bent bastard, like he was somehow *better*. How could a piece of scum like Lockwood think he ever had the moral high ground? The man was worse than the shit you dragged in on the bottom of your shoe. But that only made his little victory all the sweeter.

Taff slammed the car door and damn it if he wasn't *whistling* as he walked the short distance down the driveway to his front door. If any of the neighbors had heard him mangling that happy tune, they'd have assumed he was drunk or stoned. Taff might have been many things, but he was not a whistler. He glanced back over his shoulder as he put the key in the lock. The habit was ingrained. Trust no one. You never knew who was out there or who might have followed you home. Better safe than sorry and a dozen other little pat truisms. He'd given the speech a hundred times at Victim Support meetings. It was all about taking responsibility for your own safety.

He was alone.

He opened the door and went inside.

The house was quiet. It was always quiet. That's what came of living alone. It would have been nice to be one of those guys who came home from work to the smells of cooking in the kitchen and the bustle of kids running up and down the stairs, toys everywhere, the family dog jumping up and down excitedly, but that life wasn't for him. He'd accepted the truth of that years ago. He'd never been a ladies' man and even when he had managed to find someone who liked him enough to say yes he'd never learned the secret of making it last.

He turned the lights on and locked the door behind him.

Home sweet home.

He had his routines: through to the lounge to put some music on, Miles Davis tonight, *Kind of Blue* accompanying him through to the kitchen to brew a pot of coffee, before getting out of the uniform and kicking back for an hour just unwinding. Davis's melancholic sax was perfect for his mood. There was something inherently lonely about it. It was the music of solitude. It was also the soundtrack of his life.

The fragrance of freshly ground coffee beans filled the kitchen.

Taff kicked off his shoes and sank down into the couch.

He wasn't a bent bastard, whatever they said. He wasn't even a bad cop. He'd started out as an idealist, just like Julie Gennaro, full of spit and vinegar. He'd gone toe-to-toe with some of the biggest villains in the city and won—or at least hadn't lost, which was an important distinction in this day and age. And then that bastard Lockwood had found his Achilles' heel, and just like that he was in his pocket and no matter how much he wriggled and struggled and kicked back he just couldn't get out now. He was too far gone. So it stopped being about getting out and became about taking the money, keeping his head down, not getting caught. He wasn't proud of what he'd become, but Taff Carter was a survivor, he'd live with the shame.

And his "vice"?

Drink?

Drugs?

Sex?

No, no, and no.

Gambling?

No. No cards, no ponies, no big-game rollovers. He didn't even play the lottery.

He was a mother's boy.

She was in a nursing home, bills spiraling and threatening to get out of control because her treatment was so expensive—it had started out at 600 quid a week that became 770 within two months and that was better than the 900 it had been for the last eleven months. A letter had arrived that morning extorting another 150 quid out of him a week that he simply didn't have, putting her care at 1,050 quid a week—and that treatment only amounted to waiting for her to die. But that was the money-grabbing Tories running the country for you, with their health panels and care councils and everything else that made them money and cost guys like Taff everything they had. They'd started taxing bedrooms and god knows what else in their austerity program and sent good people to food banks to survive while giving themselves big fat pay raises. It was a new, ugly world they were living in where profit mattered more than life. He worked extra shifts, pounding the beat all hours God sent. It wasn't enough. He just wound up feeling guilty as the dementia claimed her deeper by the day. She didn't recognize him when he went to see her, so he stopped going to see her, but he kept paying for her like a good son even as it cleaned him out. Of course, he should have declared it to the suits higher up the food chain, that was his mistake.

When Gideon Lockwood had offered to see his old mum right, make sure she was taken care of, how could he say no?

He closed his eyes and listened to the music, waiting for the woman to come.

Lockwood had promised him she would, and one thing the Lockwoods were good for was their word.

The music swelled, filling his mind until there was nothing else in the world to think about, only the cascading notes. Over fourteen minutes worth of them. It regulated his breathing. If he'd been a smoker, he would have had a cigarette as the song ended like some postcoital ritual, with John Coltrane's haunting tenor sax not playing so much as sighing its way through "Blue in Green."

He didn't have long to wait.

She didn't knock at the door or ring the bell. The first he knew of her presence in his two-bedroomed terraced house was the cold chill that accompanied the eerie luminescence as the wraith bride's light touched his skin.

He opened his eyes.

She was beautiful.

More beautiful—if that were possible—than he remembered from their brief encounter. Her face belonged to that rare and precious breed capable of driving a man to the depths of despair and the heights of covetousness in the silence between breaths. He envied the Lockwoods their hold over the city, their ability to get anyone to dance to their tune, even a woman as stunning as this to come and fuck a fat man like him just because they said so.

"Tell me your name," Taff Carter said, looking up at her.

She didn't say a word.

She reached down for his knees and parted them, and knelt between his legs. He squirmed beneath her silent touch. Somehow she conveyed so much raw sexuality without uttering a single word: not for her the boorish entreaties to *"Fuck me now, I want you inside me,"* or any of those other fifty shades. She was too classy for that, just as he'd known she would be. And no matter what Lockwood has said, he couldn't believe this was just business; not the way she looked up at him with her smoldering eyes as she traced her fingers across his zipper and teased it down.

He trembled beneath her touch, chewing at his lower lip.

Taff reached out to tangle his fingers in her hair. He wanted to savor this moment, this victory. He wanted to enjoy it. Fuck that, he wanted to *revel* in it as she took him into her mouth. He wanted to own her, just like Lockwood owned him.

He wanted to win for once. Just once.

He gasped and grabbed a fistful of her hair as she went down on him, throwing his head back so hard it hit the wall behind him.

He couldn't think.

Every muscle in his body was taut.

Taff opened his eyes again as he clenched his fist. The suddenness of it tore at her hair. He couldn't help himself. He wanted to see everything, to burn it onto his mind forever, because he knew this was a once-in-a-lifetime thing, but the agony and the ecstasy of it combined was too much for him. His head went back again and he closed his eyes as he gasped a "My God," up toward the ceiling. But there was no God for a man like Taff Carter, not here.

She climbed up him, her hands on his arms, taking her weight, until they were eye to eye. He couldn't focus on her. She flickered uncontrollably, blurring before his eyes before coming back into sharp focus. There was nothing romantic about the look she gave him; it was pure appetite. She opened her mouth again, a burst of white noise shredding the silence of the room. There were words in it, he was sure, like before, promises that reached all the way down to the core of his being and promised him devotion, desire, and eventually the gentle release of death.

"Tell me your name," he begged her as she reached up to place both of her hands on either side of his head, fingers pressing a little too hard, a little too hungrily, into his temples.

She said nothing.

She traced her thumbnails across his eyes.

She traced her fingernails around his temples.

She moved against him, taking him deeper.

And this was all he'd ever wanted.

This was better than money.

This was worth losing his soul for.

How could Lockwood even question it?

And he held onto that thought as he looked at her—really looked at her—and she pushed her thumbs into his eyes, making Myrna Shepherd's ethereal face the last thing he saw even as he came inside her.

When she finally spoke to him it was through a crackle of static that masked her voice. *"Is there anything better than this?"*

"No," he said. And meant it. Now that he was blind he could truly see his goddess for what she was and she owned him body and soul because of that.

"Worship me."

He did, with blind devotion.

II

THE ANGEL

Josh Raines read Isaiah's letter again, for the second time that day, looking for answers.

He had been wrong; there were addresses in it. Boundary Street—or as it had been, Cock Lane—Spitalfields, Friars Mount, but there was one that seemed to stand out because it was more than just a street, it was a building, too; The Peabody in Rotherhithe from Hitchcock's unfinished *Number 13*.

All roads led to Rotherhithe.

It was late. Getting on for midnight. Cross-city traffic wasn't the best, the last Underground had already rolled through, and he wasn't about to walk all the way to Rotherhithe, but he couldn't go home, either. Not while that *thing* was still out there. A chill ran down the ladder of his spine as he thought about the white wraith with Shepherd's face and those haunting static-filled recitations that spewed from her mouth. Things were happening. Things he didn't like and didn't understand. Reading Isaiah's letter just left him with more questions.

But if there were answers to be found, then maybe just maybe he had the key. The only way to find out was to go to Rotherhithe and see for himself.

The candle had burned down to a stub while he'd been reading.

He snuffed it out, leaving the shed in darkness.

He didn't know anything about Hitchcock. He had no idea if The Peabody had been a real building or if they'd used the façade of some old warehouse down by the waterfront to double as the low-income housing project from the movie, and if they had, what were the chances that it would still be there now and not have been converted into some luxury apartments for city boys with more money than sense?

Even five or six years ago it would have been next to impossible to find anything before sunrise. That was just the way it was. A decade ago a mobile phone could barely even be called that, at worst it was a brick, it certainly wasn't smart, but now he had access to all the information in the world in his pocket, all he had to do was sift through it. Hitchcock was a public figure, and even a lost film of his had to be the stuff of film legend, surely? There were people out there who were experts on this stuff and he had access to them without having to leave the shed.

Josh used his phone to sift through the hits his search returned.

Within a minute he was looking at a grainy black-and-white behind-the-scenes still of Claire Greet and her leading man, Ernest Thesiger. They sat on the steps of what, he hoped, was The Peabody building from *Number 13*. It appeared to be an intersection in Rotherhithe, but it was hard to really see any details and there were no real landmarks to speak of to help him get his bearings. There was a set of high steps leading up to the door while the footpath curved around the portico of a shop. No, he realized, studying the tiny image. It wasn't a shop. The signage read: *The Ang*, the rest of the name invisible as it curved around the façade. He could only think of one kind of establishment that had a "The" like that in their name: a public house. The Angel? The Anglers? Assuming the place hadn't been torn down during the intervening years— or flattened during The Blitz—there couldn't be that many pubs in Rotherhithe with "*The Ang*" in their name, could there?

There was only one way to find out.

Josh eased the shed door closed behind him and used a broken stone to hold it shut. He checked his watch. His mum would be getting back to the house soon. He really should go home to make sure she was okay, and at the very least warn her what she was walking into. He couldn't imagine how it'd feel finding her entire life turned out all over the floor on the day she buried one of the two men left in her life. But he couldn't go home. And calling her to tell her what was waiting for her rather than doing it in person, standing side by side with her as she surveyed the damage, felt somehow cowardly, so he called his sister, Alexandra. Lexy. She picked up on the second ring. No hello, just a barked, "Where the *fuck* are you?" The emphasis heavily on the fuck.

Josh didn't even try and deflect the question; he ignored it completely and told her, "Sis, I need you to go home with mum. Don't let her go home alone. Promise me."

There was silence at the other end of the line. He could hear the cogs in her mind grinding.

"What's going on?"

What did he tell her? The answer was obvious: as little as possible. Nothing, if he could get away with it.

"Please, just promise me. Don't let her go back by herself."

"What's going on, Bro, you sound weird."

"I am weird," he said. He wanted to say that he was good, everything was fine, but he didn't. "There's been a break-in. The place is a state. The police are here. I don't want her going back there alone. She doesn't need it tonight."

"Christ. What kind of sick cocksniff robs someone when they're at a fucking funeral?"

"Welcome to the Rothery. You've been gone too long."

She breathed in sharply. "Okay, I'll keep her away from there." Another hesitation, then she asked, "You aren't trying to find them are you?" She knew him too well, but then that was brothers and sisters the world over, wasn't it? "Promise me you're not doing something stupid, Josh."

"Promise," he said, and they both knew he was lying.

"I don't believe you."

"I don't expect you to. I'll be home soon. Don't worry, it's going to be fine." He killed the call before she made him tell her any more lies.

He walked out of the vegetable gardens, back up the muddy hill, and eventually back out onto the main road. The streetlights weren't working in this part of the estate, and several cars were almost invisible in the darkness because of it, but unlike a lot of his neighbors Josh had never nurtured the necessary skills that would have allowed him to drive off in one of them without the key.

He kept his head down and walked back toward the edge of the Rothery, hoping to flag down a passing taxi. The night was bracing. He felt the sting of the wind on his face and wished he were better dressed. But at least it wasn't raining.

Kids far too young to be out at this time of night loitered on the street corner, hands stuffed in pockets, heads down, feet scuffing the pavement. There were half a dozen of them with lightning bolts and other decals shaved into their scalps like the urban equivalent of a peacock's feathers. A couple of them eyed Josh suspiciously, but none of them moved. On a normal night they would have been intimidating. Tonight, though was anything but normal. They looked exactly like what they were: kids. He passed near enough to overhear what they were saying, but it sounded like a foreign language to him.

It would take ages to walk to Bermondsey, but he had nowhere else to go.

The Rothery was a warren of streets that all fed back toward the green, The Hunter's Horns and the lightning-struck tree in its heart. Getting out of it felt like a rat trying to work its way back out of a maze after it had snaffled the cheese—something that wasn't meant to happen. A pair of trainers hung from the arms of one of the lampposts; it wasn't quite LA with the trainers strung up to mark fallen gang members, more like a bully who'd decided to make some kid's life hell for a morning. Josh passed a dozen boarded-up windows. Some of the houses had been left empty after a fire in the summer had gutted them. The bricks around the windows were still blackened with soot. There were cars up on bricks where their wheels had been spirited away. *England, my England, this green and pleasant land,* Josh thought as he crossed the road and made his way toward the real world outside the Rothery.

He saw the back of a red night bus cross the mouth of the housing estate in front of him, and the light indicating that it was pulling in.

He ran after it, barely reaching the doors before the driver could close them in his face and drive off.

Josh paid his fare and made the journey as far as Tower Hill with the drunks and the damned, that entire subculture of London that only came out at night. He sat upstairs at the back, and spent the best part of an hour gazing out of the window. At one point he found himself staring at two young Goths in the relative seclusion of an overgrown cemetery. It took him a moment to realize that they were fucking up against one of the gravestones while across the street a guy filled his car with petrol from the all-night garage. If he'd been a philosopher, Josh might have drawn some kind of conclusions from the juxtaposition, but he wasn't looking for the ties that bind. He just wanted to get to Rotherhithe.

He rested his forehead against the glass, feeling the vibrations of the old bus as it rumbled down the potholed road.

Drunks stumbled up the stairs, drunks stumbled down the stairs, and the only thing they left behind them was the stench of kebabs. A group of Chinese tourists looked less than impressed in their corporate windbreakers. They talked among themselves animatedly, their voices like birdsong. Josh liked listening to languages he couldn't understand; without the structure of words and knowing where one ended and another began, the sounds became musical. It didn't take him long to get caught up in the rise and fall, fall and rise of their strange tongue to the point that he almost missed his stop.

He thanked the driver out of habit and stepped off the bus into the shadow of the Tower. Rather than try and find a connection, he started to walk around the back of the tourist attraction toward perhaps the most famous bridge in the world and crossed the river. There were so many songs about the city, from "Waterloo Sunset"—which was still a few hours away—to "Baker Street" and "London Calling," and walking across the water it was easy to see what it was about the place that inspired so many artists. He caught himself trying to hum at least half a dozen of them without actually knowing the tunes well enough for anyone to distinguish one from the next, but it put a smile on his face for the first time in what felt like forever and helped pass the half an hour it took to walk to Bermondsey.

Now that he was there he didn't know where to start looking. It wasn't exactly a small borough, but given every reference to *Number 13* mentioned Rotherhithe not Bermondsey it was safe to assume he could head down to the end of the Jamaica Road and start looking from there.

Jamaica Road could have been any inner-city road in England; it had the same red-brick snakes of terraced houses with the downstairs converted to shops and restaurants, all of the shop fronts covered by roller shutters, the roller shutters in turn covered by fly-posters for upcoming concerts in and around the town. It was a concrete-and-steel version of the old woman who swallowed a fly and didn't know what to do. There was no one on the street, but unlike the Rothery, Josh didn't feel like he was taking his life in his hands venturing out alone.

Soon enough he had crossed through Southwark Park and King's Stairs Gardens and reached the roundabout at the end of Jamaica Road. He was confronted by choices, as he stood facing the water. It wasn't just a simple case of eeny-meeny, left, right, or straight down to the waterfront, either. Yes, there were three main streets in front of him, but within a hundred feet those three streets became seven, and a hundred feet after that those seven became nineteen as Neptune Street, Albion Street, and Brunel Road fed into the Norwegian mission and the Finnish church and a warren of courts and estates all the way to Surrey Water. A man could get lost trying to track them all street by street, he realized, confronted with the reality of trying to do a predawn grid search of the place. There were too many places to get turned around. He decided to start down by the water for no better reason than it meant there was a clean dead end he could keep returning to as he worked his way along the riverbank.

Josh followed the path down the side of the King's Stairs Gardens, which were a vast field of black out of the reach of the streetlights. He could make out a few outcroppings of stone that appeared to be some sort of ruin that had been half-excavated. A boat out on the Thames sounded its horn. It had to be one of the most melancholic sounds of the city, encapsulating the loneliness of so many of the people who lived in London in one forlorn note.

After a couple of minutes Josh found himself face-to-face with The Angel pub, which stood all alone against the backdrop of the Thames.

Even isolated from all of the workhouses and other buildings that had been in the grainy photograph with it, Josh knew he was standing in the exact same place Hitchcock had stood when the photographer had taken the photograph of Claire Greet and Ernest Thesiger on the steps. There was something wonderful about that, the way it connected one place and two times. Not, he realized, that it helped. None of those old buildings were still standing, so any hope of walking up to a door and finding The Peabody or some other clue left like a trail of bread crumbs by Boone came crashing down with them. He took a moment to really take in his surroundings; aside from the lonely public house there was a terrace of what appeared to be dockworkers' tenements on the far side of the green, there was a fairly modern block of apartments or offices, it was difficult to tell, and of course the railed-off section of the Bermondsey wall excavations.

All in all, not very much.

He walked across the street to check out the pub. The sign beside the door told the story of the old building, claiming it had stood in the same place for over five hundred years and hosted the likes of Samuel Pepys; Captain James Cook before his journey to Australia; and Christopher Jones, captain of the *Mayflower,* who hired his crew from inside The Angel. The place fairly reeked of history. There was mention of an old priory and how the monks themselves had brewed the ale for The Angel. Behind the pub was a stretch of land known as Cuckold's Point, where the corpses of river pirates had been strung up as a deterrent to the rest of their kind. It was also the starting point for the riotous Horn Fair, where the mores were discarded for the day and women especially could surrender themselves to indecency and immodesty while the men drank and fucked with merry abandon. The legend was that King John himself had given the land to a miller he cuckolded after a hunting trip. That certainly set the tone for the wild fair.

There was no mention of a place called Glass Town, no images of glassblowers or anything else to do with fashioning glass or optics or lenses, nothing that might have linked the place to Isaiah's letter, and nothing to suggest Hitchcock's career had begun, if falteringly, on this very spot.

Josh didn't need to close his eyes to imagine the press gangs working the waterfront and the old wharves or the women dancing with wild abandon, drunk on laughter and lust.

There had been so much life here, and The Blitz had left it a wasteland.

Yet The Angel survived.

The pub was locked up tight for the night.

Josh did a circuit around the building, walking the same steps those condemned pirates must have walked to the gallows, but despite the slightly unnerving thought, it offered no clues. There was nothing that screamed out Boone. He was beginning to doubt himself, or his late-night reasoning at least, but before he gave up entirely and went back home, Josh decided to check one last thing. He walked back around the edge of the priory land, following the rusted railings to the workers' cottages. He opted to start there because that row of houses offered the most possibilities, or at least he hoped they did. They were the only buildings that could reasonably have been around when Hitchcock filmed *Number 13*. He was clinging to that, that somehow it all came back to the film, otherwise why would Isaiah have made a point of mentioning it at all?

The first thing he looked for was a number 13, but he was never going to be that lucky.

There were twelve doors on the street, and all of their numbers were even. That was typically English, too, a conspiracy to confuse the hell out of the postal workers. In the absence of a 13 he looked for something else to hang his hopes on, another clue that might have led back to Hitchcock or his family.

Josh half-expected to hear sirens after a few minutes; he couldn't have looked more suspicious if he tried, moving from door-to-door, checking them and then moving on to the next, but it was late enough that even the nosiest neighbor was asleep.

Each of the doors had buzzers, each buzzer seemingly calling multiple occupancies. Most had names that meant nothing to him. Most. There was one, in the middle of the street, that was more than just a little familiar.

It said: "Lockwood."

More precisely, it said: *Isaiah Lockwood*.

It took him a second to realize what was wrong with that, and that second was all he needed to be sure he was in the right place. Isaiah must have secured the place before he changed his name, or used his real name to hide it from his brother, Seth. Or Boone had, and chosen to hide behind his father's real name. This was it, he realized; Boone's secret place. Once he opened the door there could be no going back. Everything that had obsessed his great-grandfather and consumed his life was on the other side of the door.

Josh had the key out of his pocket and in the lock before any second thoughts could stop him.

The key turned in the lock.

The door opened.

He went inside.

12

TIMELESS BEAUTY

Isaiah Lockwood, whoever he may be, owned an upstairs flat. The narrow hall had that distinctly damp smell of abandonment.

Josh turned on the light.

A bare bulb burned too brightly after the darkness, sizzling.

He closed the door behind him.

The stairs rose steeply, the outsides of the runners whitewashed, the inside bare floorboards. It had obviously been carpeted once. Now the only carpet was one of ignored fliers, special offers, takeaway menus, and discount coupons that covered the floor completely.

He picked a path to the stairs and climbed them.

Upstairs was no better. As his mum was fond of saying, it looked like a bomb had hit it; but where the aftermath of a bomb was chaos, there was a madman's order to the mess here.

Josh walked into what had obviously been intended by the architect to be the lounge. It was utterly devoid of anything that could remotely be called furniture. It wasn't empty, though. It was full of crazy as far as Josh could tell. Every inch of the place was covered in newspaper cuttings with color-coded threads strung from one to the next. Strings stretched from wall to wall crisscrossing the room like a loom. He saw headlines from familiar papers like *The Standard, Daily Mail,* and *The*

Times, to ones he'd never heard of where the presses had long since stopped turning, *The Westminster Gazette, The London Daily News,* and a mix of *Informer's* and *Ledger's* and *Advertiser's* that catalogued London life from the '20s all the way through to the turn of the century. The old papers were so much more crammed with words—as though they could barely contain all of the stories they were trying to tell—than the more modern ones.

They weren't all about the disappearance of Eleanor Raines, either, but plenty were, chronicling the investigation and the frustration at the lack of evidence it unearthed, suspicion gradually coming around to Isaiah, the jilted lover, with the lack of anyone else to blame. Josh couldn't absorb it all in one cursory glance; it would take some serious reading to digest everything gathered in this room. Suspects' names came and went, some like Jack Sykes appearing over and over, then suddenly never appearing again, while others were mentioned only once, instantly forgettable.

Some of the threads, he realized, seemed to be charting sightings of Eleanor after her disappearance.

And there were finds, too. Bodies of unfortunate women they thought were her but weren't. For a while there every corpse in London was Eleanor Raines. It was as though the press were willing her to be dead rather than just gone, like it would have been a better story for them. Which of course it would have been, a dead actress would sell more papers than a missing one. Stay gone long enough and the world forgot you were there in the first place. But turn up murdered and you would never be forgotten.

As difficult as it was, Josh turned his back on her story and moved across to one of the other walls. This one couldn't have been more different if it tried. It was filled with weird drawings of Celtic knots and green-leafed faces, images of stone circles and dolmen, some huge like Stonehenge, others tiny like the fairy ring in Coldfall Wood. There were maps of ley lines and all sorts of endless knots of what might have been occult paraphernalia, he really couldn't tell. He saw words scrawled in a language he couldn't read, and others, like old earth magic, that he could. They were repeated all over the wall. There was one word he'd never seen before, *Annwyn,* and beside it a question: *The land of the dead?* Among the paragraphs of crossed-out research he saw the words *primeval forest,* and another drawing of the fairy ring like the one in Coldfall Wood. There were other drawings of chalk giants. It all seemed so out of place against the rest of it, which was so mundane by comparison.

An entire section was given over to gangland feuds between the Lockwoods and various East End families. Much of it was just bloody knuckles dishing out back-alley beatings, a proper '20s turf war with the kind of trademark brutality that would have gone down well in the Chicago of the same era judging by the reports. Skimming the headlines and the story leads for the meat, Josh learned a lot about his great-grandfather's family and the brutal extremes they had gone to when they took over the streets. It wasn't pretty, but then very little had changed, had it?

Beside the papers was an array of fly-posters for Damiola, Lord of Illusions, with grand claims promising to confound the mind and delight the heart. His illusions included self-decapitation, levitation, talking with the spirits of fallen soldiers, and mystifying legerdemain in a theater of wonder. In the center one poster boldly proclaimed: *Witness the Wondrous Opticron! Watch As It Opens Windows into Fabulous New Worlds! Marvel at the Miraculous Sights It Has to Show You! You Cannot Believe Your Eyes!* And again beside that new-worlds promise he saw the handwritten question: *Annwyn?* Beside that one word was a photograph of the Lord of Illusions himself, a very smug-looking Damiola. It was quite the juxtaposition against the mythologies and crime reports on the other wall.

There were maps, too; old-fashioned street maps from the 1890s and 1920s with the same area ringed in red. And then there were other maps and it just wasn't there anymore, like the cartographers had erased it and joined the ragged seams it left behind to mask its disappearance.

His head was spinning with it all. There must have been a thousand articles cut out and pasted up on the walls covered with the same barely literate scrawl, which he took to be Isaiah's, but some no doubt were the result of Boone adding to his father's obsessive detailing of the crime.

He found a name in red marker: *Ruben Glass.*

It stood out because Isaiah had mentioned him in his letter. Josh worked his way around the walls quickly, scanning the articles as he went, but at first glance he couldn't find any other mention of Ruben Glass.

But of course there were other rooms, and Isaiah's confession had promised him all of the answers. What had he called him, "the King of Glass Town"? Perhaps the link was to the organized crime detailed on the other wall—the Lockwood purge? But there were no colored threads for him to follow back there, though, so maybe that wasn't it. Maybe he was linked to Hitchcock, or the actress, Claire Greet? Isaiah had mentioned her, too. If there were answers, it would take time to find them in here, that much was obvious.

The second bedroom was no better, either, though it did at least have a single piece of furniture: an old cinema projector resting on an East India Company tea chest. The East India Company had ceased trading over 150 years ago. The right someone would no doubt have considered the tea chest a treasure. There was a single canister on the floor beside the tea chest. The reel of film was already in the projector, which faced the only wall in the entire flat that wasn't covered in cuttings documenting Isaiah Lockwood's obsessive search for his beloved Eleanor.

And then of course there was the shrine to Eleanor, otherwise known as the master bedroom.

Her face was everywhere, over every inch of the wall; publicity stills, candid shots, newspaper cuttings, just thousands upon thousands of photographs of her. This was the room Isaiah slept in, surrounded by her face. There was a mattress on the floor in the corner and the sweat-stained sheet that hadn't been washed since it had been bought covering it.

Josh stood in the middle of the room trying to look at the pictures all at once. There was no doubting she was an incredibly beautiful woman, but there was something about them that didn't feel right. He couldn't put his finger on it. He stared and stared, turning and turning about, taking them all in, every angle of her beautiful face. Eleanor Raines had been blessed. The camera loved her. It didn't matter if the images were candid or posed—color, sepia, or black and white—her bone structure and perfect porcelain skin was the stuff of Max Factor dreams, but it was her eyes that transformed the photographs into art. There was so much pain in them. This was a woman who understood loss.

That was unexpected.

Whoever had assembled the shrine had gone to pains to cut out all of the accompanying texts, and considering her brief time in the sun this room quite possibly collected every single photograph ever taken of Eleanor Raines. The bedroom was decorated with one man's obsession.

And then he realized what it was that jarred in his mind: some of the photographs just didn't look old enough.

Josh walked up to the wall, peeling one of the newer-looking ones away.

The date and timestamp on it, added digitally, claimed that the shot had been taken nineteen years ago. *1994*. He'd seen that date before, on Isaiah's letter. That didn't make any sense. Eleanor Raines would have been pushing her midnineties by the time that photograph had been taken, but the woman looking back at him was *young*.

He would have thought it was some kind of mistake—that the photograph had actually been taken from an existing negative of something that was much older—but for the fact that people in the background were dressed very much in '90s fashion. One clutched a pre-CFC-free polystyrene burger box from McDonald's. Josh was pretty sure that the backdrop of heart-attack burgers and fries weren't pre-1924. He recognized Spitalfields market.

Josh took Isaiah's confession from his pocket and skimmed through it again, looking for one paragraph in particular:

I saw her yesterday. It was a crowded street around Spitalfields. She stepped out of a narrow grotty little alleyway; turned, saw me, but didn't recognize this grizzled old face of mine because time is such a feckless bastard and makes husks of us all. She disappeared into the crowd before I could catch up with her. I don't know what I would have said even if I had. I can't even be sure it was her. It might have been the weight of decades of grief on my soul, the burden of all that longing manifesting itself in her presence, because she hadn't changed. Not in the slightest.

And here it was in a photograph, the proof of that letter. She hadn't changed. He looked at Eleanor Raines's face captured in 1994 by some photographer's camera lens and knew it was true. She hadn't changed in the slightest. It was *exactly* the same face as the one in the photographs from seventy years earlier. Exactly. Like she wasn't a day older.

He had no idea how that was possible.

1994.

He checked the letter again. Isaiah had written his confession in January that year, and died soon after. This photograph was from January 1994. He'd written that she hadn't recognized him, but what if it wasn't a coincidence that he'd seen her right before the end? What if she'd somehow found a way to come back to see him one last time?

On any other night he would have castigated himself for letting his imagination run away with itself, but hadn't he just walked in on Myrna Shepherd in his grandfather's bedroom? Didn't that mean *anything* was possible?

Another photograph caught his eye. It took him a moment to realize what he was looking at—his first impression was of Eleanor standing in the rain—it took a little longer for the context of the image to settle in. It was a beautiful shot, of course, haunting in its simplicity, the woman silhouetted against the backdrop of broken angels and mausoleums, but that wasn't what drew his eye to it. She stood with her head bowed beside a grave. He couldn't read the writing on the headstone, but recognized it nonetheless. It was in the old Bunhill Fields cemetery, famous as the resting place of Bunyan; Defoe; the comedian, Al Clamp; and a smattering of Cromwells. He recognized the gravestone because he'd visited it before.

It was Isaiah's.

So there was a photograph of a woman who was a dead ringer for Eleanor Raines at the graveside of the man who after being accused of her murder had spent his entire adult life obsessed with discovering the truth about her disappearance?

It was hard to believe that it was just a coincidence.

It was hard to believe that *anything* was a coincidence now.

It was as though the world around him was actually a fractured mosaic, that there were cracks that broke the pattern and made it difficult to see how things connected, but cracked or not that didn't mean they didn't connect somewhere, somehow.

Josh left the shrine and went back through to the room of crazy with all of its cuttings and colored threads, and took up a place in the middle of it all.

It was only then, standing on top of it, that he noticed the damage to the floorboards. He hadn't noticed it before because of the thick layer of dust. They had been scored and scorched over and over again, but not like someone had tried to start a fire. The damage was much more precise than that. It gradually dawned on Josh that it wasn't damage at all, but rather a drawing. He dropped to his knees and began brushing the dust back to reveal the image it hid. Someone had scored a map of a part of London into the floor. The reason he hadn't recognized it for what it was initially was that it was wrong. Even the curve of the Thames was off.

There was an entire borough between the landmarks of Spitalfields, Aldgate, and Shadwell that just wasn't there in the real world.

Was this the mysterious Glass Town Isaiah had written about?

Closer inspection and more frantic brushing with his bare hands revealed thirteen curious indentations in the wood, as though a knife had been dragged back and forth across them repeatedly to make its mark, but only for an inch or so in either direction. The strokes were neat, and the same on each of the thirteen points, but their distribution across the map wasn't even, or seemingly logical. Beside them someone had carved three words—*one for one*—deep into the floorboards, scoring over the letters again and again to be sure they'd never fade. The first *O* was within Coldfall Wood, over what would have been the old fairy ring, he thought.

Josh tried to place the rest of the indentations in the real world, but he wasn't all that familiar with the area, certainly not well enough to pinpoint the corresponding places without a map—but of course he had a map, he had lots of them up on the wall, some with the red-ringed area that had to be Glass Town marked on them, others without. He started to check them against each other, trying to picture where, exactly these deep scored marks referred to in the cityscape he knew from almost thirty years of living inside it.

But it just didn't fit.

Not in any meaningful way.

He couldn't join the dots.

It was as though a part of London had been excised and the only proof that it had ever existed at all was plastered all over these walls.

Could people simply forget somewhere existed?

Could they be made to forget?

He looked up from the floorboards to see the smug face of Damiola, Lord of Illusions, looking down at him. That look seemed to say: *Yes, yes they could if you knew the trick . . .*

But even if they could, it wasn't as though an entire warren of streets could simply disappear without a trace, was it? It wasn't like a ship going missing inside the Bermuda Triangle. Streets were physically rooted to the earth. The ground couldn't creep over them and bury them away without a trace. Rip them out of the city and surely they would leave behind a physical wound where they had been. Cartographers could erase them from maps, sure, any line that could be drawn could be erased, but that didn't take those streets away from the city proper. There was no All-Seeing Architect who could rearrange the geography of London to hide an entire neighborhood.

The world didn't work like that.

One for one.

There was no magic powerful enough to make it happen that wasn't conjured by books or films or computer games. In other words there was no magic, no matter how hard men like Damiola tried to convince you otherwise, no matter how many endless knots or horned gods or green men he drew. That was the brutally mundane reality of it all. The world was going to work, coming home from work, sitting in offices staring out of windows, dreaming of something bigger, something wonderful, even magical, as you begged strangers to pay thousands of pounds to place glossy ads and clever copy in a dying medium, but that was all it ever was, a dream.

Nevertheless, there was no getting around the fact that Myrna Shepherd had broken into his house tonight.

That wasn't a dream.

But that didn't make it magic, either.

13

NUMBER 13

There was food in the fridge, but he wasn't sure he could trust any of it not to poison him. Everything in there had a jaundiced hue. There was a jar of instant coffee on the counter, though, surrounded by a scattering of granules that Boone hadn't cleared away. It wasn't exactly manna from heaven, but it would do for now. Josh boiled the kettle and made a too-hot brew before going back to the projection room cradling the cup in his hands.

How many hours had his grandfather spent in this place during his life? It was hard to imagine Boone's secret life, but there was no escaping the fact that the old man must have been living one. It was like discovering he'd been living with a spy all these years.

Josh closed the door behind him.

He liked closed doors; they gave the illusion of safety.

The film reel was already in the projector; all he needed to do was plug the machine in and flick the switch to turn it on. The motor hummed slightly alarmingly as he did, and a dust-filled light speared the wall. The reel clicked as the film was drawn between the lens and the light and the images began to flicker unsteadily across the wall. There was no title sequence or anything else that he would have associated with a movie, but of course he was looking at something that had never been finished, something the rest of the world thought was lost: raw footage from Hitchcock's *Number 13*.

That the projector started at all was testament to the fact that someone had been paying the bills for this secret place.

There was no sound, so Josh had to try and guess what the story was meant to be. Even without the sound, though, he found himself being caught up in the facial expressions and body language and realized there was a fundamental truth to the story he was interpreting, and that without words it was harder to lie. There was a life lesson in that, he realized, watching the rough cut.

Two minutes in, Josh recognized the pub across the street from where he was now, but everything else was new—or rather old, lost to the German bombs and the avaricious developers who had moved into the area. Every now and again he caught a glimpse of Eleanor Raines in the background, but she never seemed to be the center of any shots. She was instantly recognizable, though, because her face was plastered all over the walls around the makeshift screen.

He watched the way she moved.

He watched the way she inclined her head.

He watched the way her lips twitched as she smiled.

And in all of those things he could see exactly why she'd stolen Isaiah's heart so completely and utterly. She came alive in the moving pictures in a way that she just didn't in the stills. It was as though the film had caught part of her essence that stills just couldn't, no matter how wonderfully they were lit or how perfectly her makeup was applied. And even then she was never the center of attention. She didn't need to be. She smoldered, drawing the eye no matter where she was in the shot.

One thing caught his attention early on in the film: a poster for Damiola pasted to the wall of a crumbling tenement. He recognized it immediately because the same poster was on the wall in the other room. The fact it was there, here, and in Isaiah's letter had to mean something.

Claire Greet dominated pretty much every frame, and with good reason: She was a beauty in the realest sense of the word. It wasn't sultry or sexualized. There was an innocence to her. She possessed the kind of beauty that would be out of place today in today's world of manufactured precision. She lined up outside The Peabody with other hopefuls, suit-case stuffed to overflowing on the ground by her feet while Thesiger moved down the line, picking out people to go inside. Josh couldn't help but think that with it being a Hitchcock movie, no matter how desperate they were supposed to be, the lucky ones would be those who *didn't* find themselves with a room inside.

He sipped at his coffee, and then decided to make himself comfortable on the mattress despite the health hazard it posed.

The scene changed, moving along the street toward the wharf, the camera focusing on one of the big steamships on the Thames, presumably highlighting the influx of poor fresh off the boat and the increased pressure their arrival put on the city. The imagery was every bit as stark as anything Hitchcock had ever captured on film with subtleties woven into the fabric of the city itself. But there was no denying it was flawed. Erratic. And without the lies of words to drive it, there was no tension.

Josh found it difficult to concentrate on the film, realizing that there was nothing of any real worth to be found within it. He slumped up against the wall, his head dipping as the night gathered around to claim him.

And then he saw him, a face in the crowd, and all thoughts of sleep fled.

Josh pushed himself up from the mattress and scrambled to his feet. He knew that face.

Josh had almost missed him because the camera moved on quickly, but it was so jarring to see someone he knew in a film that was over ninety years old: Seth Lockwood.

Seth was just milling around in the background, not actively part of the film. Josh watched him. He did nothing. He didn't move. Didn't interact with any of the main cast. But in one unguarded moment Josh saw something: the camera caught him looking at Eleanor Raines when he thought no one was watching, and it stripped away all deceits. His expression was purely covetous; his need stark, urgent, like it hurt so much to look at her he wanted to claw his eyes out, and yet he still couldn't look away.

Hitchcock had seen it, too, and focused the lens on Seth.

The director, like the magician he was, used Seth as a classic piece of misdirection, creating the illusion of an external threat to the heroine, something from outside The Peabody. It created doubt in the viewer's mind, allowing the real threat to move throughout the film unnoticed for a while longer.

Josh watched the frames again, stopping the projector when he had seen enough. It *had* to be Seth, he thought, even though he'd never met the man, but the similarity between him and the newfound cousin who had waylaid him in the yard behind the Scala a few hours ago was unmistakable.

He had cracked a joke about the apple not falling far from the genetic tree in their family. In every good joke there was more than a grain of truth. The similarities were beyond unnerving.

There was nothing else of note in the twenty-seven minutes of footage. Eleanor Raines occupied the screen for perhaps two minutes of that time, Seth Lockwood barely thirty seconds, and never without Eleanor, but those were the only two minutes of *Number 13* that mattered.

14

BLOOD, SWEAT, AND TEARS

How far would you go for love?

What extreme becomes too extreme?

Would you kill to save someone you loved?

Of course, and without a second thought in Seth Lockwood's case. Two people? Five? What about someone you were obsessed with? Once you were committed, it was the same, wasn't it? If anything, obsession was purer. There was no art so dark as the human art, as far as he was concerned. It was all about committing to a course of action and sticking to it no matter the cost. That single-minded determination was the difference between winners and losers, and Seth didn't lose. Ever.

He closed the door.

He needed to be alone and couldn't stand all of Gideon's grousing and worrying. How could the old bastard be the fruit of his loins? It wasn't as though he'd been born without a spine. At one point, in the late fifties and into the early sixties he had been one of the most feared men in London. Seth knew. He'd watched from afar. But the years had sucked the backbone out of his boy leaving a jellylike invertebrate in the gangster's place. It was sickening, really, to see him so diminished.

Seth would have crushed the kid if he hadn't needed him.

But good things came to he who waited, and Seth was nothing if not patient. This was still his city no matter what year it was.

He looked at the clock on the wall.

It was time.

It didn't matter what the hands showed, he'd always known it was time. He'd known since he'd set foot in the church for Boone's funeral. Things were happening that couldn't *un*happen. He'd caught sight of Eleanor among the mourners along the side of the road, watching as the funeral procession went by, but he hadn't been able to catch her. That she was so easily able to slip in and out of Glass Town now was a worry. It meant that the dweomers holding the grand illusion in place were failing faster than the damned magician had anticipated, which was bad, but unavoidable. He didn't understand exactly what the magician had done, or how he had done it, but he knew enough to grasp the implications when one of the ancient lenses cracked. That *shouldn't* have happened. The integrity of the entire illusion depended upon the glass. A single flaw could shatter it completely once and forever. And then what for him? Was he simply supposed to allow time to catch up with him and die like a normal man? He needed to replace the lens and restore the dweomers, and he couldn't do that without Damiola's help— which wasn't going to be easily had, given that the illusionist had vanished from the face of the earth back in 1924.

Of course, the fact that the lens had cracked was also the only reason he was out here now. He wasn't blind to the irony. It was an unintended casualty of war, a German bomb had taken down the building it was anchored to and in the process opened the way back here. He'd paid laborers to repair the house a long time ago, but hadn't concerned himself with the crack because it allowed him to slip in and out of Hell as he pleased. That broken glass could end up being the single most important piece of luck they'd had since Damiola sealed up their little slice of London town and they'd disappeared supposedly to live happily ever after. Without it, he would never have known Isaiah's obsession had been handed off to a new generation. Seth had hoped that after all this time they'd have given up looking, and gradually forgotten all about Eleanor, him, and everything else and just gone on with living their way into the future while they left the past where it belonged.

He was in the manager's office of The Hunter's Horns.

A leather inlaid mahogany desk dominated the room along with a high-backed green leather chair that would have looked at home in the Bank of England circa 1880. The room smelled of that well-waxed leather. An old cinema projector was the only thing on the desk. Filing cabinets and shelves filled with ledgers going back to the '20s finished the furnishings. Behind the desk was a battered green capstan safe.

Seth knelt in front of it, and pressed his left hand to the cold iron as he spun the dial.

He knew the combination off by heart: 130124.

The numbers would have meant nothing to anyone else, but they were more than just dear to his heart; they were the foundation of his entire life. The thirteenth of January 1924 was the day Damiola had pulled off his greatest trick ever and hidden away Glass Town from the rest of the world. It was the day he had finally owned Eleanor Raines, body and soul. He didn't think about her heart—he'd never owned that. Seth had accepted that a long time ago. It had taken a while, but he had learned to be happy with what he had. Seth was a practical man.

He had acted impetuously releasing one of the Rushes. It had been a mistake. He knew that. He'd known it at the time, but when his boy had questioned him it had only made him all the more stubborn. That wasn't a good trait. So now he needed something more surgical to send after the boy. Ideally he would have summoned the Negative, but that particular monstrosity was already patrolling the boundaries of Glass Town, keeping what needed to be kept in, in. So that left the Dailies or the Reels. The Dailies were more creatures of defense than attack, though like all of Damiola's invocations, equally capable of wreaking havoc. They were insidious little things that came and went in the course of sunrise to sunset, only to rise again with the coming dawn. No good for a night fight. The Reels came in pairs, and unlike the Rushes, which were a quainter evil, what made the Reels more interesting from his perspective was that they were capable of something approaching thought. If the Rushes were bloodhounds, the Reels were sharks.

He opened the safe and removed two of the three brown envelopes in there. One contained cash; lots of it bundled up in tight wads of twenties. Another contained documents pertaining to his life both then and now. All the papers he needed to pass in either time. The one that he wanted contained two reels of film that fit onto the arms of the old cinema projector on his desk.

This was no ordinary projector; it was one of Damiola's finest creations, a prototype for what became his greatest illusion of all, the Opticron. The films it showed were no mere show reels, either.

He teased the two small reels of film from the envelope, handling them with gentle firmness, cautious urgency, barely contained excitement, all of those things and more that conferred ownership and right. He unspooled a little of the film and held it to the light, looking through the frames until he found the silhouette he wanted: the Comedians.

Seth cleared a space out in the center of the room before fitting the reels into the projector.

He winced as the brittle film cracked as he curved it around the armature, and hoped it wouldn't break completely before he was done with it. He needed what was on that reel. The film cracked twice more, alarmingly, before he'd finished easing it into place and wound it on over the fractures. It stayed in one piece.

The power cable snaked back across the rug to the plug in the wall. Unlike the carousel everything in this invocation was electrical, a much more modern magic. At the time of its invention it had been otherworldly, now it was dated, like the Mismade Girl, the Chinese Water Torture, and other staples of the stage magicians trade. But it worked. That was what mattered. It was as simple as flicking a switch and the reels turned. The projector was slightly unbalanced and rattled against the desktop as they did.

Seth waited for a moment as the frames fed through between the lens and the flickering bulb, then lifted away the cap, bringing the image of the Comedians forth. The movement caused a flickering image to be projected against the back wall, the projection stretching from the center of the floor all the way up to where it joined with the ceiling. A gray image of the city filled the wall. But that wasn't what he was interested in. The reels spooled on, until finally the Comedians stepped into the frame, and were suddenly larger than life, standing on the floorboards in the middle of the room even as the bottom right corner of the image on the wall began to blister: one obese, the other unusually thin to the point of being gaunt, both instantly recognizable to a child of a certain age.

Marty Crake and Al Clamp, one of the most irreverent comic pairings of the last century. They weren't exactly darlings of the silver screen in the way that Fatty Arbuckle and Harold Lloyd were, or the more famous pairing of Laurel and Hardy. Crake and Clamp were pioneers of black comedy. There was nothing gentle or slapstick about their physical routines.

The image threatened to break up completely, a gauze of flickering frames blurring the Comedians as the projection lost its focus, and the film began to blister. The acrid tang of burning filled the room as wisps of black smoke curled away from the projector.

The film burned under the heat of the bulb, damaging the invocation. Something was wrong with the Comedians, Seth realized. Where there should have been two men there was only one, conjoined at hand and hip where the film had blistered during their summoning.

Behind them, the image of the city began to melt as the film burned inside the projector.

The stench of sodium nitrate was overpowering now, completely drowning the subtler, richer smell of old leather. There was nothing Seth could do. He couldn't force the invocation to accelerate or rip them out of the film, they had to emerge naturally, in their own good time, but the flames did more damage to them by the second. He breathed deeply and waited. No amount of damage to the Comedians would prevent them from doing what he needed them to, though it would limit their efficiency and how they could be deployed. They couldn't walk unnoticed through the streets of London if they were badly misshapen, fire-damaged freaks.

The Comedians looked at him expectantly as their film world burned out around them. Gradually they became more substantial, taking on the physicality their comedy was famous for, until they were finally whole. Behind them the cityscape was consumed in a blackened blister of burned film. It was like watching the end of the world through the lens of a 1920s disaster movie. The only sound in the office was the quick *slap-slap-slap* of the broken end of the film strip coming up against the metal projector as the reel spun around and around with nothing to show for its effort.

It was done.

Before the projection of the Comedians could burn out along with the rest of the film, Seth took a letter opener from inside one of the desk drawers and sliced his finger with it, drawing blood.

He winced as he held the wound over the projector, squeezing it to force his blood drip onto the lens.

As the first drop hit, it sizzled away on the glass, the second and third likewise, coming together to form a thin crust over the glass. Fueled by his blood, the Comedians would be trapped here for as long as he needed them to serve him.

Seth Lockwood sat down behind his desk.

He needed to think through his next words carefully, because once the Comedians were released, there was no recalling them until their task was done. He couldn't afford to waste them. He needed to think this through and be absolutely sure he knew what he was going to demand of the conjuration; and that meant finding the precise words. Precision was vital. There was no room for misinterpretation. Once the Comedians were fed, they wouldn't forget. Those words would become their life-blood. They would draw sustenance from them. They would draw strength from them. And they would find purpose in them.

The Comedians waited patiently for his instructions.

"It is time," he said, finally, drawing a deep breath. "The dweomers around Glass Town are failing, and soon must fall. I believe Damiola left instructions for this eventuality among his things. He must have. He thought of everything. Bring them to me. Your service is not through until the dweomers are restored once more and my love is safe. Do you understand? You are not spent until Glass Town is secure. There is no release. You will live on to serve until I see fit to allow you to pass."

The Comedians bowed their head in acknowledgment.

When Crake looked up again there were tears in his eyes.

Hardly sympathetic, Clamp cuffed his partner across the back of the head with the only hand that was actually his, and rolled his eyes exasperatedly.

"This was his," Seth said, taking the bow tie out of the final envelope. He rose from his chair and met the uncanny conjuration in the center of the room. He lifted the bow tie to Marty Crake's mouth, clamping his free hand around the comedian's jaw and forced it open so that he could feed Crake the bow tie. "Taste him on it. Taste him on the cloth. Go on." He forced it all the way down with his fingers and closed Crake's mouth, causing him to swallow over and over until he could be sure the conjuration wouldn't regurgitate it. The Comedians might look human, despite the bluish light at their core, but they were anything but. When people talked about selling their soul to Hollywood, this was what they were buying. Immortality. Though not the kind of immortality they ever dreamed of. Sometimes it was better to be forgotten. To slip away. But the camera never forgot. That was the point of it; its sole reason for being, to remember. No matter how old an image was, how discolored or faded it might be, how blurred or granulated its composition or how badly it had deteriorated, it abided. A frozen moment. An eternity. And as long as it abided there was always going to be someone there to remember it.

Damiola understood that.

The magic was in sustaining the image, preserving the memory, and through his carousel he had found a way of bringing it back to life. It was good old Hollywood magic.

"It is all I have of him. But it is rich with his flavor. His sweat, drawn out by the stage lights night after night, soaked into that material. That is *him*. His essence. He is inside you. The man was unique. There wasn't another like him in this entire shithole of a place. Given that, it shouldn't be hard to find him amid all the filth of London. So go. Go forth. Hunt. Do not return here until you have found his secrets. He was a magician. He must have recorded the workings of every trick he ever did. Glass Town was his masterpiece. There must be instructions somewhere. Find them. I will save his greatest creation, even if I have to tear down half of London to do it. And you will not fail me. Do you understand?"

Crake chewed on the black tie.

The fat man looked at his other half and nodded. A star of the silent age, he had no words to say. There was nothing that needed to be said. Seth knew how this particular conjuration worked. There was nowhere Isaiah's get could hide that the Comedians couldn't find him.

15

SLEEPLESS

Julius Gennaro couldn't sleep.

That in itself wasn't unusual. He wasn't the deepest sleeper at the best of times, and living in the middle of what became the last bastion for whores and junkies every weekend night there was more than enough going on to wake him whenever he threatened to find refuge in it. He had been planning on moving out for the best part of a year, but without getting a roommate the ridiculous property prices in the city meant it was a choice of a desirable cupboard in a decent area or this.

This won for now, but it wouldn't win forever.

Something had to give.

There was an air of decrepitude about the entire area that could only be found in the old red-brick terraces of London. It wasn't so much that they'd crumbled as they'd been beaten down year after year through living done hard, skilled laborers being written off by the country they'd broken their backs for, their children and children's children left to grow up with a bitterness that went back generations.

A wag had painted a big red *NO* on the Hope Street sign under his window. That just about summed it up.

Tonight's insomnia wasn't just down to the usual backstreet symphony of the loved and unlovely, though. There were other reasons for it; chemically, no doubt, the caffeine had a large part to play in his mind refusing to settle. He'd never been a coffee drinker, but Taff insisted on doing the rounds of designer cafés and the greasy spoons, putting merciless pressure on his bladder and gulping down enough caffeine to keep a herd of wildebeests going on one hell of a rampage. But beyond the chemical there was something else: the suspicious little part of his mind that made him a half-decent copper refused to shut off. He had no idea what other officers were like, but with Julie, once his mind got hold of something it wouldn't rest until it had worked it out. He'd worry at it. Pull and push and prod until something gave. It was why he couldn't read books and made a lousy companion in the cinema—he was obsessed with *knowing*. And right now, lying in bed staring up at the shadows conjured by the chip shop's lights reflected over the galaxy of plaster spirals stippling his ceiling, he was obsessing about one thing: Taff Carter had never once ducked out of clocking off.

It was a stupid thing to be keeping him awake, but he couldn't let it go.

The thing was he knew his partner.

Taff was a stickler for rules and regulations. He was a by-the-book kind of man. That was just who he was. Some of the younger beat cops called him Jobby Carter—short for Jobsworth—behind his back, because where they were tempted to give an inch and take a yard, Taff was a stick in the mud, or up the arse, or any other variant of inflexible that came to mind involving sticks not bending.

Julie had always figured his partner was just a bit fixated when it came to routines.

Until tonight.

And that bothered him.

So he lay there trying to work out what was different about today. And what really got under his skin was the fact that there was nothing different about it. It had been pretty much business as usual, apart from the woman in white, the same as every other day they had spent together. So why had Taff bailed on him rather than head back to the station for the change of shifts? What was so urgent he couldn't do it ten minutes later?

Julie worked backward through everything he could remember, watching the shadows change as the owner of the takeaway closed for another night, the 2 a.m. shift done. As the sign went out, it left the moon to light his cramped little room.

Julie could smell the fat and grease in the air. It wasn't conducive to deep thought, but no matter how he looked at it, nothing out of the ordinary had happened, even if the shift had ended with a bit of excitement over at the Rothery. That was a common enough occurrence.

So why break the habit tonight?

It could only be the woman.

Taff had been single for as long as Julie could remember, not that they talked much about sex and women, or the lack of both in their lives. Taff was more of a rugby and real ale kind of conversationalist, though he had a surprising love of jazz, which didn't quite fit with the man's rough edges; whereas Julie was your metrosexual modern man happy to talk about art exhibitions, world news, politics, religion, changing gender roles, gay marriage, underground music, or anything else he'd found within the pages of *The Guardian*. Chalk and cheese. It made the shifts interesting.

But as far as he could figure, the woman was the only thing that made sense. And even then it was stretching the definition of sense to a point far off in the distance. Closing time wasn't exactly the ideal dating hour, unless you were paying by the hour and didn't want to worry about the niceties of social convention.

He sighed.

Was he overthinking things?

Was it just a case of Taff needing to be somewhere, all quite innocent, and trusting a friend to help him out no questions asked?

Maybe. Probably. But the problem was the no-questions-asked part.

As he pondered that, Julius couldn't help but wonder if there was any significance to *where* Taff had dropped him off? The Hunter's Horns was right on the boundary of the Rothery, by the green and the lightning-struck tree. They used to joke that beyond that corner lay nothing, like on the old maps that said *Here Be Dragons*. The only reason to drop him off there, so close to the station, was if Taff's business would take him *back* into the estate, wasn't it? Otherwise it would have been quicker to drive on. So was he meeting a woman in the Rothery?

Julie gave up on sleep for a while, and went through to the kitchen area—it wasn't an actual kitchen, just a workbench and a sink—to grab a glass of milk from the fridge and sit on the windowsill in the lounge and stare out into London.

By three in the morning he was so convinced his partner was in trouble he sent Taff a text asking him to call, just to let him know everything was okay, but of course there was no call. Why would there be? It was 3 a.m. and Taff would be off in the land of nod dreaming, no doubt, of big-breasted women to a soundtrack of soft jazz.

That didn't help Julius Gennaro sleep.

Just after three he jumped in the shower. The old pipes took an age to warm up, so he suffered five excruciating minutes of ice-cold water streaming down his body through gritted teeth, and toweled himself off colder than before he went in. He went back through to the kitchen area and brewed a cup of coffee, putting an extra spoonful of instant powder into the cup, and then tried Taff again.

Still no answer.

But again, why would there be? It was barely 3:15. And they weren't due back on duty until midafternoon. He was asleep, just like Julie ought to be.

He pulled on a T-shirt with a faded barbed-wire fist emblazoned on the chest and a pair of jeans already worn threadbare on the right thigh. Both were relatively new, designer secondhand chic, or in other words it cost a lot of money to look this scruffy. Julie stuffed his feet into a battered pair of Adidas, grabbed a leather jacket from a hook by the door, and headed out.

It was a night for firsts—the first time Taff had cried off from clocking out, and the first time Julie had visited his partner's house.

He saw a black cab on the corner, and ran down the middle of the road to catch it, waving his arms above his head to make sure the cabbie saw him and didn't drive off. Clambering in the back he gave the driver the address and settled back in for the ride.

Ten minutes later the black cab pulled up outside Taff's house.

Eleven minutes after he'd left the flat Julie stood in the street looking at the dark windows of Taff Carter's bedroom. All he needed was the boom box to hold over his head. He smiled at that.

He couldn't tell if there was a woman in there.

Part of him really hoped there was, and that his partner was getting lucky. It would be good to be worrying about nothing. But another part of him was convinced the dark windows meant something was wrong, which, given it was the middle of the night and every other window in the street was dark, was completely irrational. There was just something about the place that felt *off*.

Julie had two choices, ring the bell or turn around and head back to his own bed. The smart money was on option two, not that he would have been able to fall asleep, but he was never going to do that.

He rang the bell and waited.

When there was no answer he rattled the letterbox.

Then he rang the doorbell some more.

No answer.

No signs of a light coming on up upstairs.

No complaints or groans from behind the door.

He went down on his knees and shouted, "Taff!" through the letterbox, rattling it loudly enough one of the neighbor's lights came on and a hoarse voice shouted, "Shut the fuck up will you! We're trying to sleep! Don't make me call the police!"

"I *am* the police," Julie shouted back, shutting them up. He hammered on the door with his clenched fist, yelling Taff's name at the top of his voice until a light finally came on inside.

A few seconds later his partner opened the door.

Taff was dressed in a pair of piss-stained boxer shorts and a terry toweling dressing gown that hung open to the waist. He had a look of utter contentment and a pair of sunglasses on his face. He didn't say anything. He stood on the welcome mat and smiled, but there was no real welcome or warmth there. He kept the door between them and didn't move to let Julie inside. There was a faint bluish light on the landing behind him; a nightlight maybe. Was his partner afraid of the dark?

"Jesus, Taff," Julie said, relief flooding his system at the sight of the

Welshman. He hadn't realized how much of a state he'd managed to work himself up into until he saw Taff standing there in one piece, larger than life, a stupid grin on his face, obviously without a care in the world. "Why didn't you answer your bloody phone, you prick? Or the door? Or just . . . fuck it, mate, this isn't how you treat your partner. We're in this shit together. I was starting to get really worried about you."

"Worried? Why?"

Julie had to shrug ruefully at that. Why indeed? Because he hadn't clocked out? So much for doing a mate a favor. "You know me, letting my imagination run away with itself. Are you okay?"

"I'm fine. I won't be in tomorrow, though. I'm taking a personal day. I think I deserve it. Now go away, Julie. I want to be alone." Taff said. There was something in his voice, not anguish, not euphoria but something in between that had no business being there. Taff slammed the door in Julie's face before he could ask him about it, or why he was wearing sunglasses in the middle of the night.

16

ANOTHER FINE MESS

"So, what have you got for me today?" Julie Gennaro asked the desk sergeant an hour later.

"You should be asleep, kiddo. You look like hell."

"I should be," he agreed. "But as you can see, I'm not. And I hate sitting around, so I figured I'd roll in early."

"Ah, the dedication of youth."

"If that's what you want to call it."

"We've got a couple of drunks sleeping it off in the cells, Melissa's in with a woman who came in to report a sexual assault, got the doc waiting to do a rape kit. Other than that, pretty quiet, all things considered. They're having more fun over at Euston by the sounds of it."

"Yeah?"

The desk sergeant rifled through a sheaf of papers, looking for a printout. He put it on the counter between them.

"A CCTV shot from a robbery in progress on Stephenson Way about two hours ago. Take a look."

Stephenson Way was a few minutes walk from Kings Cross. A fairly unremarkable street, all things considered. There were dozens just like it in a five-minute radius of the train station. And on that unremarkable street there was an equally unremarkable brownstone building. The street and the brownstone might have been unremarkable, but once through the door everything inside was about as remarkable as you got, even in a city like London. This one particular building contained a hidden theater, a miraculous floating staircase, and the largest collection of magical memorabilia in the country. It was the home of The Magic Circle.

That alone was enough for it to have caught the desk sergeant's attention, but coupled with the image captured by the CCTV it was irresistible.

Why so? Because of the criminals.

Julie studied the photo of Marty Crake and Al Clamp, two of the most iconic faces from the black-and-white days of cinema, captured in the middle of breaking into The Magic Circle. They weren't wearing their trademark bowler hats and didn't have their familiar goofy expressions on their faces, but it was unmistakably them, even if they'd been dead for the best part of fifty years. There was nothing slapstick—or undead—about either of them. He assumed the burglars were wearing some sort of latex masks to hide their real faces. It wasn't uncommon to see Margaret Thatcher holding up a convenience store these days, with Neil Kinnock as her sidekick. Ronnie Reagan was ever popular, as were Elvis, Donald Trump, and Ronald McDonald, clowns one and all. Clamp's mask was perfect, right down to the detailing on the pencil moustache on the fat man's top lip.

Part of the image seemed overexposed, as though a bright light had damaged the film. Looking more closely at the pair, they appeared to be joined. It was obviously a trick of the angle, but the effect was unnerving.

"Okay, you got me. What did they steal?" Julie asked the desk sergeant, handing the photograph back.

"That's just it, imagine all the stuff they've got in that place, right? It's full of old tricks, props, posters, programs, toys, photographs; that sort of stuff. It's all valuable, sure, and to the right sort of collector probably priceless, but it's not like it's easily movable. I mean some barrow boy's hardly going to be selling it down the Portobello Road, put it that way. It's all specialist stuff. They've got a cylinder there that's a recording of Houdini's voice. A lot of old stage magicians bequeathed their tricks to the society."

"So, Crake and Clamp broke in The Magic Circle and stole some dead magician's trick? Why can we never get fun stuff like this?"

"Actually, according to the boys over in Euston they took a book, not a trick, but yes, it sure beats another knifing on the Rothery, doesn't it?"

"A book?"

"According to the museum's curator the only thing missing as far as he can tell is some old magician's journal. The thieves shattered the glass case it was in, along with a bunch of exhibits he'd donated, but left everything else behind."

"You've got to ask yourself what's in that book?"

"That place is like the Bank of England. You can't just walk in and walk out. They've got some seriously high-end security there to protect their secrets. And these guys didn't set off *any* of it. That means they are *good*. Pros. Even so, it doesn't make much sense: this guy has been dead for ninety-odd years. Every secret he had back then, no matter how revolutionary it might have been at the time, has to be pretty passé now, doesn't it? Penn and Teller have given every game away. Now it's all David Blaine and Criss Angel. Street magic, not old stage-show stuff like Paul Daniels."

"Doesn't mean the right someone wouldn't kill to get their hands on it."

"True, Julie. Sadly."

"So we've got a robbery, a dead magician's journal stolen to order. Some collector will be locking it away in his safe and it'll never see the light of day again. If it's valuable enough for them to go to these lengths to get their hands on it, they're hardly going to leave it lying around on the kitchen table."

"Again, very true. You're on fire today, detective. Casting pearls before swine. And speaking of swine, will your partner in crime be joining us this fine morning? Or does he have the good sense to stay in bed?"

"I just talked to him. He's taking a personal day."

"Taff having a day off? Fuck me. Seriously? First time for everything, I suppose," the desk sergeant said. "Why don't you go up to the dayroom, grab a coffee, put your feet up, and I'll give you a shout when something comes in."

He did as he was told.

Ten minutes later WPC Melissa Banks came into the dayroom to claim one of those horrible vending machine coffees before going back into the room with her rape victim. She was giving the doctor time to take his swabs and photographs and give the girl some peace. "Some nights I wonder what the hell I must have done to piss off the universe in a past life," she said, sinking down onto the couch beside him. "I've got a woman in there, battered bloody, half of her face bruises. It's pretty obvious she's been through hell, but she can't tell me a single thing about her attacker beyond the fact he looked like a movie star. That's it. A movie star. I ask you, Julie, what am I supposed to do with that?"

"Must be the night for it," Julie said. "Marty Crake and Al Clamp just robbed The Magic Circle."

She looked at him like he'd lost his mind, and shook her head. "What the fuck's the world coming to, mate? I miss the old days when things were simple. The bad guys wore striped shirts and carried sacks that said *swag* on them."

"It was never like that," Julie said, but he knew what she meant. It had felt cleaner when he was starting out. Now every fourth call was domestic violence, battery, or sexual assault. The villains didn't wear striped shirts and Zorro masks over their eyes. They dressed just like everyone else. There was no way to look at someone and see the monster inside without looking at everyone and seeing a monster inside—and that way lay madness.

17

THE BOOK OF THE DEAD

Seth Lockwood opened the door on the bitterly cold morning.

The sun was up, but frost was king. It owned every surface.

There was a thin gray mist in the air, but even that couldn't hide the curious deformity of his early morning visitors. Or more accurately, *visitor*. Marty Crake and Al Clamp looked up at him from the doorstep. There was something a little bit pathetic about them, he thought. Anyone who happened to see the exchange would have been forgiven for assuming the two went inside holding hands. The conjoined Comedians were fused at hand and hip, not holding hands. Their creation was flawed, but that didn't appear to have hindered their efforts to find Damiola's journal.

He hadn't expected them to return so soon; that they had could only be good news.

Seth could barely contain his eagerness as he led the pair back through to his upstairs office where the light still burned in the projector. Seth closed the door behind them, making sure they were alone, and gave the reel on the projector's arm a push as he passed it to take up his seat behind the desk.

The creature wasn't empty-handed. It clutched a leather-bound book in its two functional hands.

"Is that it?"

Clamp shrugged eloquently as Seth took it from them, the Comedians' silence not hindering their communication, rather it spoke volumes. Seth cradled it in his hands like it was the most precious thing he had ever touched, which, given what was at stake, it just might have been—if it had the answers he was looking for. The leather was soft and buttery despite its age.

Seth placed it on the desktop.

He ran his fingers across the cover, feeling every grain and indentation in the leather before he cracked open the spine and turned to the first page.

Being the Journal of Cadmus Damiola
And Containing the Fundamental Secrets of His Art

Seth inhaled sharply.

This was it.

Damiola's diary.

His secrets.

He could barely contain his excitement as he turned to the next page.

It was blank.

He turned the next.

Blank.

And the next.

Blank.

Every single page in the damned book was empty. There were no secrets here. Even in death the illusionist defied him. Excitement turned to rage as Seth drove himself up out of the seat and hurled the book at the far wall. The pages splayed open as it landed, taunting him with their emptiness. "Is this some kind of fucking *joke*?" He fumed, shoving his chair back. "Do you think it's funny?" The Comedians said nothing. They didn't move. "It's empty! I gave you one simple task and you *failed* me! Damiola, you sniveling little cocksucker, are you in there?" He stared at the Comedians as though they were somehow sentient, not merely projections brought to life by some ancient trickery. "Can you hear me?

I should shove my hand up your fucking arse and rip your bowels out, you prick."

The Comedians stared implacably at Lockwood.

"Can you hear me?"

He had no idea if the dead man could—if anything of him resided inside his creations, if they were still linked in any way, or if they were something else entirely: demons, angels, ghosts, echoes? It didn't matter; he wouldn't be defied. Not by them. Not when the cost of failure was so high. He was a man of violence. Born of violence. Raised in violence. At home with violence. At peace with it. They might not be flesh and blood, but that didn't mean he didn't have a few tricks of his own up his sleeves that would hurt them just the same.

He heard movement downstairs, probably that idiot son of his banging about in his wheelchair. Well, fuck him and fuck the wheels he rode in on. Seth clenched his fist. It would have been easy to lash out, to ride the wave of rage and unleash it in an explosive burst, driving his fists into the fuckers until they bled whatever it was creatures like them bled, but he knew from grim experience it was far more chilling to master his anger; to exist in a state of violent equilibrium.

Seth pressed his fist to his own temple, pushing so hard that it hurt the plates in his skull.

When he took his fist away he was calm.

"I do not accept failure."

Marty Crake blubbered, fidgeting as silent tears streamed down his face. Al Clamp remained calm, awaiting further instruction.

"One simple task, that was all you had. One task."

Clamp inclined his head slightly, then shrugged. It was a frustrating gesture only using half of the comedian's body. Crake looked down at the floor, but not Clamp. He met Seth's challenge head-on. He put a finger to his lips as though to silence Seth. But the gesture meant something else, didn't it? Quiet. Hush. A whisper. Secrets. What was he trying to tell Seth? That he'd somehow fulfilled his half of their pact?

"You failed me," he insisted. "I am your *master*. I brought you forth. I own you."

Clamp shook his head.

"Get out of my sight."

The Comedians held out their hands, as though chained and cuffed, asking for release.

"No," Seth shook his head. "Bring me what I need to repair the dweomers."

The Comedians turned and walked slowly across to the other side of the room, where they stooped awkwardly to retrieve the book from where Seth had thrown it. They brought it back to him.

They held out their hands again, miming release.

"You are done when I *say* you are done. I want that bastard's secrets." Crake pointed at the book.

"This? This thing is *worthless*! There's nothing in it! There are no answers in here!" He yelled impotently, tearing a page clean out of the journal, "Look at it. Where is the wisdom?" He crumpled the page up in his fist and walked toward the Comedians. "Can you read a blank page?" He held it up before Crake and Clamp's eyes. "Can you decipher its secrets?" He waited for an answer from the silent duo. "What does it say? How do I save Glass Town from ninety years of decay and dissolution? How?" He demanded. But of course they had no answers for him. Seth shoved the crumpled page down Clamp's throat forcing him to swallow the paper just as he had forced Crake to swallow Damiola's bow tie. "You don't have a fucking clue!"

Clamp spat out the paper, miming disappointment as he rubbed a curled-up index finger beneath his eye as though wiping away imaginary tears.

Seth drew his hand back, but checked himself a heartbeat before he lashed out and sent the projector spinning across the room. That kind of damage would have been irreparable. It might have been satisfying for a split second, but in the long run it would have weakened him, and that would have been the action of a fool. Seth clenched his fist again; so fiercely this time his nails drew blood from his palm, slowly mastering his temper. He didn't move or say a word for the longest time, until his breathing was calm and steady instead of the shallow ragged pant it had momentarily become, and he had stopped trembling. Every muscle was taut with barely suppressed rage.

"Give me a reason," he said, his voice surprisingly calm given the rage inside him. "Tell me why I should snuff your flame out. One good reason and it is done. You have my word."

The Comedians gestured toward the empty book, as though it not only had all the answers, it *was* their answer.

Unfortunately for them, it wasn't one Seth liked.

Crake's tears stained his cheeks while Al Clamp fumbled desperately with his tie, both parodies of their iconic selves.

"I gave you a chance," Seth said, sounding oh-so-reasonable. "You did not take it. Now given that you cannot find what I need, and have not won your release, there must be something else you can do for me. I know," he said, a slow smile spreading across his face. "You can stop Boone's brat from finding the weakness caused by the damaged lens. You can stop him stumbling into Glass Town and ruining everything. Can you do that? Are you capable of getting something right?"

Clamp nodded eagerly.

Crake mimed walking with his fingers in the air between them.

"No," Seth shook his head. "On second thoughts, that's not good enough. Kill the boy. Bring me his heart. Bring me his tongue. Bring me his hands. His cock. Bring him to me in enough pieces that all the king's horses and all the king's men can't put poor Josh together again. You can do that, can't you?"

Crake ran a finger across his throat, pretending to slit it from ear to ear.

"I want you to remember what I'm about to tell you, can you hear me in there, magician? If you can, then let this be written on your soul. Fail me again and you'd wish you could die."

18

AFTERNOONS AND COFFEE SPOONS

Josh left the flat in Rotherhithe armed with a map to a place that didn't exist and a head full of questions he couldn't answer. It was going to be a different kind of day, no matter what happened to him.

Daylight hadn't made things any clearer, but, and perhaps this was a small mercy, it hadn't brought any fresh revelations, either.

And no more movie stars had turned up at his door. That was no small thing, given the way yesterday had played out.

As he crossed back over the Thames, Josh knew one thing for sure, and only one: life wasn't about to get any *less* complicated. Now it was just a case of living with it.

He'd woken aching everywhere from one of the worst night's sleep he could remember. Guilt at not going home, or even checking in with his sister and warning her he wasn't coming back for the night, meaning they were going to worry about him and walk in on the wreckage of the burglary, mixed with a mind alive with the improbabilities plastered across the walls around him made sure of that. Names that until yesterday had meant nothing to him consumed his every waking minute: Damiola, Ruben Glass, Seth Lockwood, Eleanor Raines, even Hitchcock and Glass Town, the Opticron, and, of course, *Number 13*. They were all alive inside his head. They were more than just names. He felt like he knew them, even the famous ones. They had faces. They belonged to a secret geography of the city that he was beginning to believe only a chosen few knew or even suspected existed.

Suddenly he was one of that number.

He wasn't sure how that made him feel. Special wasn't the right word for it. Endangered might have been a better fit, all things considered.

And then there was the scene from *Number 13* itself, that moment where Seth Lockwood looked out of the film at him, wearing his new-found cousin's face . . . and there was the letter in his pocket that claimed Isaiah had seen Eleanor decades after she'd disappeared, only the woman hadn't aged a day, which, combined with the way Gideon's grandson had behaved behind the Scala, left him unable to trust anyone or anything. His head was spinning.

It was all in there, churning about. Refusing to settle.

Josh had copied the thirteen scorch marks from the floor map onto the one on the wall, along with the words *one for one,* before pocketing it, noting that while they corresponded with landmarks around Spital-fields, Aldgate, and Shadwell, they weren't in a straight line, Bermuda Triangle–like, or any other easily chartable geometric pattern that might have hidden an entire borough between the folds of the paper. Looking at the marks after he'd meticulously transferred them across offered up no clues, either. There seemed to be no rhyme or reason to any of them.

But they had to mean *something*, didn't they?

He felt the first fat heavy drops of rain as he made his way up Mansell Street, past the shiny arch of the Tower Gateway DLR station and the insurance offices and windows into a telesales world they offered, reminding him that tomorrow he had to return to the real world, his day spent chained to a desk chasing cold leads. He continued walking toward Aldgate, and eventually to the first landmark he'd drawn on the map, which turned out to be a stuffy little antiquarian bookstore wedged in between a thoroughly modern coffee shop with its mass-produced identical goodies and a pawnbrokers with one of its tarnished brass balls missing.

The words *Aldgate Librum* were written in an arc of flaking gold across the window, and beneath them *purveyors of fine escapes since 1929.*

Meaning five years before, when Eleanor Raines disappeared, it had been something else. Unfortunately there was no way of knowing what.

He stepped back into the road and looked up, checking out the façade. He couldn't see anything remarkable about the building itself. Like something out of Goldilocks it wasn't too big, wasn't too small, and was probably just right.

Shading his eyes, Josh peered in through the rain-streaked glass.

He couldn't see anyone moving about inside, but the paper card hanging from the window promised that the place was open. He tried the door. It creaked open, the old hinges desperately needing oil. Josh was hit immediately by the smell of old books as he stepped inside—one of the most unique, and to some romantic, fragrances in the world. To Josh it was just overwhelmingly musty, like there was no nourishment in the air to breathe.

The interior of the librum was crammed full of books of every variety imaginable, every age and condition, with weathered boards and cracked spines. Some of them had been loved like old friends, while others, still pristine had been cherished like assets waiting to be cashed in. A well-dressed old man—in cravat and morning suit no less—looked up from a ledger he was laboring over to smile at Josh as he shook the rain out of his hair.

"Welcome to my humble library, my new friend," the old man said, warmly. "I like to think we have the finest selection of out-of-print and antiquarian texts in the city, but I'd probably be lying if I said that." He winked conspiratorially, which made Josh smile despite himself.

"Thanks. I'm just happy it's dry in here," Josh said.

"Might I inquire if you are looking for anything in particular? We have a good selection of philosophy and psychology, religion is always a favorite, as of course are language and literature, while the classics are a mainstay of any shop like ours. We do have a rather fascinating local history section, if I do say so myself." He must have noticed the way Josh's interest perked up at the mention of local history, because he came out from behind his counter and swept a wide all-encompassing arm out to invite him to try his luck. *Pick a book, any book . . .* the gesture seemed to say. "We are rather at the mercy of what our customers bring in, or more often than not bequeath, as we help move a lot of collections for families of the departed, so there's no guarantee we have a particular book, but that's part of the fun. You never know what you might find. Rather like a lucky dip. You are more than welcome to browse what we have, make yourself at home, and feel free to ask questions. If I can possibly help you with your search, I will. I've spent so long in here among the stacks I'm pretty sure I know every book inside out." It was one of the more peculiar sales pitches Josh had ever heard, but like the shop itself, it had a certain charm.

Josh wandered over to the local history section and started to scan the spines, not really looking for anything in particular, but hoping something would catch his eye. "I don't suppose," he ventured after a few minutes, "you've got anything about an area called Glass Town, have you?"

"Glass Town? I don't believe so. Are you sure it is local?"

"Honestly, I'm not even sure it exists," Josh said with a shrug. What did he have to go on other than the obsession of a dead man and the gingerbread trail he'd laid down?

The old man joined him at the shelves and started seemingly pulling books down at random, thumbing through the pages to get the indices, musing thoughtfully to himself then placing it back on the shelf as one after the other let him down. Another came down and went back up. Finally, after maybe five minutes of theater, the bookseller turned to Josh and said, "Can you perhaps tell me a little more about this place? Perhaps some landmarks or characters, something else I can try and cross-reference?"

What names did he have? There had been so many in the articles, including of course his own family, but one seemed so logically linked to the whole thing and yet he knew absolutely nothing about the man beyond the fact that he shared his surname with Glass Town and Isaiah had described him as the worst of the lot in his letter, whatever that meant. He said, "Ruben Glass? I don't know much if anything about him, save that he would have been around in the twenties, maybe the thirties, and was somehow tied to a stage magician who went by the name of Damiola. Does that help?"

The bookseller shrugged. "We shall have to see, but that name *does* ring a bell," he lifted down a compendium of old *Strand* magazines from the day, scanning the adverts as well as the articles, until he found what he was looking for.

It was a small advert beside similar ones for gentleman's clothing, but where they promised an array of top hats and tails, this one featured a line drawing of a man, Ruben Glass, who cordially invited people to the opening of The Glass Film House on Latimer Road where he would be premiering the role that would make Myrna Shepherd one of the most talked about actresses of the time, raising her up to the pantheon of silent stars that included the stunning beauty of Louise Brooks and Greta Garbo: *The Flower Girl of Belgravia.*

Any link between Glass and the actress, even one as intangible as this, was enough to prove he was on to something, wasn't it? Could The Glass Film House be the same old cinema that lay in ruins behind the Scala? The derelict building was on Latimer Road.

"'Between Notting Hill and Wormwood Scrubs lies a vast desert of human dwellings . . .'"

"Sorry?"

"That was how Horace Newt once described Latimer Road," the bookseller said. "'A vast desert of human dwellings.' Paints a vivid picture of early twentieth-century working-class life in the city, don't you think?"

Josh had no idea who Horace Newt was, but he couldn't argue; his few carefully chosen words painted a particular vivid description of the squalor that must have been the city back then.

The bookseller took down another book; this one called simply *The London That Never Was: The Crime of the Century* and thumbed through the pages until he found what he was looking for. "Here we are," he said, "'Mister Glass was new money. He had a dream of creating a Hollywood in London a decade before J. Arthur Rank laid the first bricks of Pinewood.'" He broke away from reading to opine, "He was murdered, you know? Quite the scandal."

Now the man had Josh's attention.

"I didn't know."

"Yes, here we are," he stopped turning the pages. "There were a few books about it back in the day. This one only offers a brief summary, but has, I believe, all of the salient facts. There was talk of Hitchcock adapting one of the more famous accounts, given the salacious nature of the scandal, but obviously that never came to pass. Now I come to think of it, Glass Town *might* have been the name he'd suggested for his movie studio, a rough play on Holly Wood, but I wouldn't like to stake my life on it. There was a global economic crash, which halted the development of the entire film industry. You must remember it was just a fledgling industry at the time, and massive risk was involved, even if people were flocking to gaze adoringly at Valentino and Garbo up on the silver screen. Glass lost a not-so-small fortune trying to build his studio, money he had raised by drawing loans and favors from one of the oldest criminal families of the East End. I'm trying to recall . . . yes, here we are, Lockwood. That was the family. Thoroughly nasty souls. Of course nothing could ever be proven. When Glass was burned alive there was talk that the killing was a falling out among thieves. They found traces of silver nitrate residue on his corpse, believed to be a mocking reference to his failed endeavor, silver nitrate being an essential part of the filmmaking process back then."

"So Glass Town got him killed?" Josh said, his mind racing.

"I suppose you could say that," the bookseller nodded. "Fascinating case, all things considered. One of the first real gangland stories of our city. Of course, it's all but forgotten now in the shadow of the Krays."

"How about the stage magician, Damiola?"

"Other than you just mentioning it, I can't say the name rings any bells, but then I've never been a great follower of celebrity, but if he's of note, then perhaps there'll be something in here." He pulled down another book, this one seemingly a history of London theater and easily as old as the bookseller himself, and began leafing through it.

"Ah, here we are, Cadmus Damiola, I do believe we've found the fellow. Who needs the internet, eh? So, let's see what history has got to say about him, shall we?" The bookseller thumbed back through the pages to those referenced in the index, and started to read. " 'After delighting the crowds of the capital for eighteen months with his wondrous *Opticron,* a curious contraption that ostensibly allowed viewers to spy other worlds through its many lenses, the magician confounded fans and critics alike by walking away from the spotlight. Fêted by none other than Harry Houdini himself, Damiola gave his final performance on the evening of Saturday, 12 January 1924, in the Adelphi Theatre on the Strand, never to be seen again. The show had been booked to run for three more weeks, but all subsequent performances were canceled. Rumors abounded at the time that he had fallen foul of key figures in the East End underworld and that his disappearance may not have been entirely voluntary. A body, believed to be his, was found some five years later, and interred at Ravenshill Cemetery, in East London. All of his tricks, mechanisms, journals, and paraphernalia of his act, bar the *Opticron* that made his name, were donated to The Magic Circle by his heirs.'" The bookseller tutted and closed the book. "Well, well, well, quite the character, wouldn't you say? It does make you wonder if they may not be the same hoodlums who gave Glass such a hard time, doesn't it?"

Josh wasn't about to say what he thought, but it would seem to be linked, at least on the surface. Damiola's final curtain call was the night before Eleanor Raines disappeared. Glass was in Lockwood's debt, the magician in his pocket. At every turn he kept coming up against the specter of Seth Lockwood and his hateful family. It had gone far beyond the realms of coincidence.

They tried some of the other names, including Seth and Isaiah, but had no joy.

As an afterthought he asked the man, "Does the word 'Annwyn' mean anything to you?"

"Why, yes, it most certainly does. It is one of the many names they used to give to the druidic underworld during the age of the Celts."

"Underworld? Like Hell?"

"And Hades, and the others, indeed one and the same. It was ruled by Arawn, the Horned God, who himself is the root of the once and future king legend we associate with the mythical Arthur."

Josh had no idea why Boone had noted the name, Annwyn, not once, but twice, or how it related to the disappearance of Eleanor Raines, but the old man must have written it down for a reason, along with all of those mythological references on the third wall. He'd just have to keep chasing until he could make sense of it all. Boone had had a lifetime with this stuff, after all. He couldn't expect to unravel it all in a night.

He asked about the cemetery, as it wasn't one he was familiar with.

"Gone," the bookseller explained. "Lost in The Blitz. I'm not entirely sure what's left beyond a marker stone and a broken gateway, maybe a few of the old stones. It's not far from here, in the shadow of the Tower," he hooked a thumb back over his shoulder indicating the city's most famous landmark. "Which is of course where it drew its name, right on the old wall where the city proper ends and the East End begins."

The bookseller invited Josh to share a snifter in the hopes that he would tell him more about his interest in Damiola, Ruben Glass, his cinematic studio Glass Town, and the gangsters in Josh's family tree, but Josh wanted to visit some of the other places on his map before dark.

Not that he expected to find Glass Town—which if he was being brutally honest with himself, he doubted existed outside of a dead man's increasingly desperate obsession and another dead man's foolish dream—but it was a mystery and there weren't enough mysteries in the world anymore.

That, and it was his legacy.

Boone had wanted him to have Isaiah's letter, which surely meant that Boone had wanted him to carry on looking for Eleanor. He loved his grandfather, so how could he deny him his final wish? He couldn't, obviously. But there was a huge difference between taking a few days and dedicating the rest of his life to something. He wasn't Isaiah. This wasn't his story. Isaiah had never stopped looking for the woman he loved. He'd become so fixated on her disappearance he'd broken away from his own family, turned his back on his own brother, married her sister, and taken her name as he disappeared down the rabbit hole of his obsession. And then he'd passed it on through the family like some kind of perverse inheritance until it had found its way to his great-grandson. Josh wasn't going to let it claim his life. He'd give it another day, walk around the remaining sites on the map, chalk them off one by one, and if he didn't miraculously stumble upon the secrets of Glass Town and Damiola's trickery, then at least he'd tried, right? Couldn't say fairer than that.

He spent five hours wandering the streets around Aldgate, Spital-fields, and Shadwell, pushing through suits rushing to and from meet-ings, looking at the cracks in the pavement and the clothes the pedestrians wore, trying to see if he could pick out anything that looked obviously out of time. It was next to impossible, because London was a city en-tirely built around eclecticism and the aesthetics of dozens of cultures and time periods with fashion ranging from the baroque and steam-punkish to the plain old punk by way of burqas and band T-shirts and everything else imaginable. Kids wandered by in furry costumes with animal ears. No one walked around with a sign that said *I just stepped out of 1924* and no matter how intently he stared at the cracks in the pavement or peered around the corners of buildings he didn't once catch a glimpse of another world.

One by one he chalked off the sites with no more joy than the last, and none of them seemed to have anything in common with any of the others. A bar; a bookies; an abandoned church on a street corner, its steeple missing a dozen slates; an old movie theater that had died when the multiplexes came; a supermarket; a trendy clothes store; a second-hand record shop with its shutters rolled down; a café called Paper Cups; a block of maisonettes; the gates of a Jewish cemetery; the courtyard of a disused hospital that was in the process of being converted to luxury little pieds-à-terre; and a payday loan place, the modern ver-sion of the pawnbrokers, the stylized checkbook of its logo hanging out over the pavement. Some of them were abandoned, some quite obviously repurposed from whatever they might have been in another life, while a couple were untouched from the '20s, but there was no rhyme or reason to why Boone had marked them out.

He looked on the walls for a sign, a small tag of graffiti or something that would imply a link between the sites, but whilst there was plenty of creative street art on display at some of the sites the others were pain-fully bland. He looked for scratches or markings in the flagstones of the floor, remembering what his mum had always said about stepping on the cracks breaking your mum's back. He looked for anything vaguely cinematic, thinking that maybe that was the link. Nothing. Or rather plenty of things. He was in a city full of them. But none of them offered some readily apparent red thread running through them like the room back at Boone's secret place.

As the day wore on it grew more and more frustrating, feeling like he'd taken one step forward at the bookstore and two steps back since leaving it.

Josh browsed through the racks in the trendy clothes shop feeling very much out of place in his slept-in funeral suit. He walked through the Jewish cemetery, marveling at how the gravestones were packed in one upon another like a crazy game of dead-man Tetris to fill every available space, and listened to a tour guide explain how they'd buried the dead vertically instead of horizontally to make the most of the expensive real estate. It was practical if nothing else. He stopped for an overpriced latte in the café and posed as a potential buyer to walk around the hospital grounds.

Nothing.

Even though it wasn't on his map, Josh went to Spitalfields Market and walked the perimeter, looking down every alleyway and each narrow street around Brick Lane and thereabouts purely because Isaiah had thought he'd seen Eleanor there.

He saw more of London that afternoon and early evening than he would normally see of it in a month, but not once did he notice anything to suggest that Glass Town was anything more than an old man's obsession whatever it might have been once.

After a while it began to feel like he was going slightly mad. At one point he thought he caught a glimpse of a couple dressed as Crake and Clamp, probably on their way to a costume party. They certainly looked the part. But other than that, London presented him with its most mundane face. The most excitement he got was when a couple of spiky-haired girls ran past singing Duran Duran's "Union of the Snake" before disappearing hand in hand into a sex store on the fringe of Soho.

It was dusk. The offices turned out for the night. He didn't want to be seen by anyone he knew from work. Josh finally admitted defeat. He wasn't going to miraculously stumble into the lost world of Ruben Glass's cinematic ambition.

Hungry, he ducked into a not-so greasy spoon and ordered himself

an all-day breakfast, which really was stretching the limits of the definition of "all day," taking it into the night. He perched on one of the
high window stools to wait for it, and stared out into space. The rain,
which had been on and off all afternoon turned into a proper downpour.
Water rushed down the gutter, filling the drains faster than they could
carry it away. A couple of people rushed by, heads down, while a woman
walked more sedately through the rain, an umbrella obscuring her face.
She wore heels and stockings with a seam so straight it must have been
drawn in. It was only because he was staring at her legs that he saw the
newspaper headline on the side of the kiosk. ANOTHER FINE MESS AS
COMEDIANS ROB MAGIC CIRCLE. He couldn't help but grin and would
have gone to grab a paper, but the vendor was long gone. He craned his
neck trying to see the woman with the straight seams, but her brisk
stride had carried her out of sight.

With nothing to do but wait, Josh thought about calling home to
check in with Lexy, but as he fished his phone out of his pocket he saw
that it was dead, so that killed that idea.

A few minutes later the waitress brought over a chipped white cup
and poured a strong black coffee into it. He thanked her and continued
to gaze into the middle distance, watching the world go by.

He was out of ideas.

So much for solving a mystery that had haunted his family for generations with one day's legwork hoofing it around London like some half-
arsed Indiana Jones. He smiled wryly at the arrogance of youth.

Eventually the food came, swimming in tomato sauce. Two fried eggs
over greasy Cumberland sausage, rashers of bacon, button mushrooms,
and hash browns to soak it all up. It tasted exactly how a fry-up was meant
to taste, and starving, Josh wolfed it down like a death-row prisoner
knowing there'd be no last-minute reprieve.

So intent was he upon the feast he didn't realize the woman had returned and was watching him from the street corner.

19

ELEANOR

Eleanor Raines stood on the street corner as long as she dared, looking like the tragic central focus in a melancholic painting of the city in the rain.

He looked so much like Isaiah sitting there, framed by the window and the streaks of rain running down its glass.

So very, very much like him.

It was uncanny.

For a moment she caught herself thinking it might actually *be* him, that somehow he'd found a way to cling on to time without the need of the illusionist's prison, but the longer she watched him the more she became sure he wasn't the man she'd loved and lost for all that he looked so very like him. They could so easily have come from the same soul split in two.

He was different; the way he brushed the lock of hair out of his eyes so he could see the food, that he was left-handed when he ate, not right, that he touched his temple when he was thinking, massaging it counter-clockwise. He was narrower across the shoulder and broader across the smile as he thanked the waitress for the refill, but more than anything, he seemed content inside his own skin, happy enough to eat alone without needing to engage with the world around him. She liked that about him. Was that how Isaiah would have been if he'd been allowed to grow up normally?

She leaned back against the wall, angling the umbrella to better see the man in the café window.

He cradled his cup, gazing out into the middle kingdoms.

How could he be anything other than Isaiah's kin? Just look at him . . .

Of course, it wasn't the first time she'd seen him. Eleanor had watched him outside of the church yesterday as they buried Isaiah's boy. That was hard, not walking up to him before he walked inside and just holding him and pretending he was someone he wasn't, sharing his grief. But she'd had no business being there so she turned to go without saying a word only to see Seth leading his own son through the wooden lych-gate into the graveyard. Without thinking, she ran. She ran hard and fast, stumbling on her heels and having to grab a stranger to stop from falling in her panic. As he tried to help her she pushed away from him and ran on, knowing she was drawing attention to herself even as she did it.

She couldn't risk Seth seeing her.

He didn't know she was here, back in London.

He didn't know she'd found a way to slip between the cracks and escape her prison—if only for a few hours at a time. That snatched freedom was the most precious thing in her life. He could never know about it. *Never.*

But the boy had come looking for her, hadn't he? Even though he hadn't seen her, and she didn't know his name, he was trying to find her. Like father, like son, and now like great-grandson.

Maybe he'd be the one?

That was the only explanation for his tour today. He'd taken in all of the anchors, even if he didn't know what he was looking for, or how close he had been to stumbling up it. One, even two, might have been chance, but not all thirteen of them.

He was following Damiola's pathway, even if he didn't know it.

Which meant he knew about Glass Town.

And that, in turn, meant he knew about her.

So there was hope, wasn't there? Hope that he would be the one who finally freed her for more than an hour or two from that Hell of Damiola's making. Hope that one day it would finally be over. The bitter truth was that hope was a bastard that wouldn't leave her alone to die. She would have been better off without it.

She looked at her distant reflection, knowing even as she did that it was aging faster than anything around her, time desperately trying to catch up with her flesh. She couldn't stay out here much longer. Even a few minutes more out here breathing the air of the twenty-first century, drinking in the life that had outpaced her, surrounded by all of these things she barely understood and had no place being among, and there'd be no arresting its merciless assault on her flesh. And no hiding it from Seth. He wasn't a fool. He'd know what fresh wrinkles meant.

And would that be such a bad thing, to simply wither away and finally die? Eleanor wondered.

There was a limit to how long she could stay in the city before time and life caught up with her. She could feel it now, tightening her skin, drying it out and stretching it across her old bones. One day, maybe even one day soon, she'd stay out here and let it take her. It was tempting, the idea that it would all finally be over. But not today, no matter how much she hated her life, no matter how much of a prisoner she was to it, to Damiola, and Lockwood and that bastard Glass, it was still her life and she couldn't surrender it while there was still hope it might be saved.

Even if that hope had tomato sauce on his chin.

Using her lipstick she wrote a message for him on the wall, and hoped he would find it.

20

LOST GIRL

Josh cleaned his plate and set the knife and fork down at a slight angle on it. It always made him smile, but there was no getting around the little habits that were ingrained in him thanks to years growing up with Boone. There were proper ways to do things, like setting your knife and fork down together at five twenty-five on the clock face of the plate.

The weather had worsened over the last thirty minutes.

London looked particularly sodden, but then the city was getting used to flooding—well, vacillating between flood and drought, to be more factually accurate—and had been for the last few years. The weather reports were filled with freak floods, freak snows, freak hailstorms with hailstones the size of golf balls, and stock footage of people sandbagging their doors and canoeing down the middle of what had been the road. The rain never seemed to drain away, meaning every year the water table rose a little higher, meaning every year the streets flooded a little faster than the last as though Mother London was trying to wash away her sins. Even the Thames Barrier, the last great defense against the elements, built to save the city from flooding, was next to useless as the water table had essentially risen above its protection in the few short years since its completion.

A kid hunched over the curb, making a paper boat out of a nightclub flier to set sail down the gutter as a black cab aquaplaned around the corner soaking her. Unperturbed, the kid scrambled forward on her hands and knees and launched her paper boat in the taxi's wake. The little boat was stubborn.

Josh looked up from the girl and saw red writing on the wall that he knew hadn't been there ten minutes ago. He couldn't read it from where he was, and the rain was already making it run.

He pushed himself out of his seat and hurried out of the door and across the street, nearly getting himself run over in the process. The driver yelled something at him out of his window. He wasn't listening. He stared at the wall, and then grabbed the kid, who wriggled like a lizard in a tin trying to break free of his grasp. "Did you see who wrote this?"

"Get your hands off me, you fuckin' perv!" Only it sounded like *fackin* when she said it. "You want Yewtree chasing you?"

"Did you see who wrote this?" Josh asked again, ignoring her protests and twisting her around so that she could see the two red words dripping like blood down the wall: *Find Me.*

"I didn't see nuffin," the girl grumbled, but he refused to let her squirm away. "'n I'm serious about Yewtree so get your hands off me, mister."

"So you saw something?" Josh said, turning the double negative around.

"What? I just said, I didn't see nuffin. You stupid?"

"Forget it," he said, letting go of her collar. She went sprawling across the pavement, and then looked up at him like he'd completely betrayed her by actually letting her go like she'd asked him to.

"She went that way," the girl nodded down the street, toward the huge market hall filled with designer foods packaged up at designer prices.

"What did she look like? What was she wearing?"

The girl shook her head. "Dunno. Pretty. Long coat. I couldn't see her face because of the umbrella."

"Think. Please. Anything you can remember that might help?"

The girl sat there on the wet paving slabs looking up at him as she made a show of thinking. "Long yellow coat. Red umbrella."

He'd seen her, he realized. Not only had he seen her, he'd sat there admiring her legs, or rather the impossibly straight black seams of her stockings. It *had* to be her. "Thank you."

Josh started to run in the direction the girl had indicated, the soles of his shoes slapping on the wet paving slabs. The pavement was slick and slippery. He twisted and dodged around a couple of pedestrians shuffling along like the walking dead, and reached the corner, looking left and right.

The downpour intensified, the rain spiking up six inches off the road around him. He couldn't hear for the drumming and the whistle of the wind as it howled through the high buildings, rattling windowpanes and loose tiles. It was like staring out into a gale, but there she was, a couple of hundred yards away, about to disappear around another corner. It had to be her. And if he let her walk around that corner he knew he'd be letting her walk out of his life just like that. So the rain could pour and the wind could howl, he wasn't slowing down or stopping.

He ran faster, gritting his teeth and calling, "Wait!" after her, but his words were drowned out by the rain.

She didn't slow down.

She didn't look back.

She walked into the heart of the storm even as it whipped up into a righteous fury. The ferocity of it, and the speed it came on, was frightening. It was as if the elements were trying to keep them apart, the universe conspiring to keep its secrets.

Josh kept his head down and fought his way across the road, following her onto a narrower street. The tarmac changed into cobblestones halfway down the street. He looked up, trying to see her. The rain streamed down his face. He wiped it away, but it didn't matter how much he rubbed at his face it kept getting in his eyes, stinging and blurring his vision and making it impossible to focus as it tried to drive his head down.

There were no shops on this street.

Gone were the lunch restaurants and designer delis. Gone were the secondhand stores and the florists and the offices.

He stumbled into what quite literally felt like another world—a

Victorian slice of London that must surely have been unchanged since the time of the good Queen herself, and more aptly, since the days of *Number 13*. The cobbles were worn smooth and there was no white line down the middle of the road. If he'd reached out, he could have touched the buildings on either side of him as he ran down the middle of the street, it was that claustrophobic. There were fewer people here, but the street felt twice as crowded because it was so narrow. The second storey of the nearest buildings loomed in over him, casting deep shadows across the street as it narrowed yet again, until it felt no wider than his shoulders.

"Wait! Please!" Josh called.

She heard him this time, and visibly hesitated before she threw a backward glance over her shoulder. Despite the misstep she didn't slow down for more than a fraction of a second. She didn't need to, because Josh stopped dead in his tracks.

They were less than one hundred yards apart.

He recognized her.

Even with the rain in his eyes and the wind making it difficult to focus for more than a moment at a time. How could he not? She was the reason he was out here in the first place. She was the reason his great-grandfather had lost his mind and the reason Boone had lived a secret life all those years.

She was the woman who hadn't aged a day in ninety years.

She was Eleanor Raines.

And she really was beautiful. Not what they called beautiful in those glossy adverts and magazines he sold; beautiful in a truer, purer sense of the word. Not all sharp angles and shadows and heroin chic. None of the pictures plastered on the bedroom wall did her justice, he realized, and knew he was standing there gaping like a fool. The reality of Eleanor Raines made every photograph seem flat, dull, and lifeless.

In that moment he could see why Isaiah had refused to just let her go.

"Eleanor," he called, taking a step forward, knowing his voice wouldn't carry. He didn't want to shout for fear of breaking the moment. "Wait."

She turned away, breaking it for him, and carried on down the alleyway. The sound of her high heels clicking on the cobblestones was lost beneath the rain. She ducked down an even narrower passage, this one more like a shadowy crack between two buildings than a footpath. "Wait!" He called again, chasing her to the mouth of the empty alleyway. "Please."

He could hear something . . . children laughing? No. Not that. Birds. Starlings. He looked up and saw a vast flock of them banking on the fringes of the storm, the flock spiraling overhead tighter and tighter until their wing tips touched and they looked like a vortex in the sky, their black bodies the eye of the storm itself, casting a shadow over the streets below.

When he looked back down there was no sign of Eleanor Raines and nowhere she could have gone. No doors into the buildings that started the alleyway; no gates in the high wooden fences that continued it.

He was alone.

It was as though she'd slipped between the cracks and simply disappeared right before his eyes.

21

RAVENSHILL

He turned over every stone in the alley, physical and metaphorical, but she simply wasn't there and there was nowhere she could have gone.

Part of Josh began to doubt she'd ever been there, that he'd caught whatever sickness had driven the rest of the men in his family—all save for his dad, Barclay Raines, who'd died well before his time and in that case probably before the obsession could take hold—mad.

With no real idea what else to do, Josh followed the only clue he had left and embarked upon a pilgrimage of the dead. It was that or give up and go home for the night, and going home meant facing Lexy and his mum, and work in the morning, which felt too much like the real world for today. Today was the kind of day meant for creating his own Josh Stories his friends could trade with smiles at his memorial. He knew roughly where the old Ravenshill burial grounds were supposed to be, if not where they actually were thanks to the ever-shifting landscape of the city. One thing he'd already learned was that a lot could change in ninety years. Not least the contents of a cemetery in London, which wasn't something he would have ever imagined before the bookseller's explanation, and then of course it had made absolute sense. The Blitz had rewritten the landscape, and it stood to reason that the bombs wouldn't discriminate between the living and the dead.

He had no idea what, if anything, he'd find waiting for him at the end of his pilgrimage.

Graffiti on the walls offered the wisdom of a generation's worth of prophets. They didn't have very much to say, or maybe it was just a case of being too old to understand what they were saying? Wasn't that how it worked? Each generation had its own idols and martyrs, and where once it had been Timothy Leary now it was the Steve Jobs of the world— or whichever faceless suit had replaced his vision after cancer had claimed him—the youth bowed down to as they offered every sort of iGenius for download by the kilobyte if you had the right data package.

The city moved to the drumbeat of his heart, an insistent percussion that had Josh looking back over his shoulder on every street corner, not just looking left and right before crossing the road. She had been there, almost close enough to reach out and touch. He thought about Isaiah's confession to Boone, that he'd seen her, unchanged, in 1994, and realized that as crazy as it was, it was true. That was a game changer. It was one thing to keep it all at a distance and think of it almost academically, but it was quite another when it was the evidence of your own eyes. Eleanor Raines might have disappeared ninety years ago, but she had been here less than an hour ago as though she'd stepped out of one timeline and into another.

Josh sank down onto a bench seat, head in hands, ignoring the rain, and tried to think it through but there was nothing about it that made sense. The whole impossible scenario defied logical explanation. But there was no getting away from the fact that he'd seen what he'd seen.

She'd been running. From him? From Lockwood's goons? There were so many places someone could lurk unseen. The streets were nothing more than an elaborate rattrap. Unwelcome Boomtown Rats lyrics ran through Josh's mind as he doubled back on himself determined not to be caught. He glimpsed his reflection in a shop window: he looked harried, tired, and stretched thin. He couldn't be sure that was entirely an illusion of the glass. He checked the street signs against the basic map of the city he'd used to mark out the strange scorch marks on the wooden floor of Boones's secret flat, following its landmarks to be sure he was walking the right way.

Up ahead, he saw the gates of the burial ground as the bookseller had promised, and for a moment thought the pitted iron was all that remained of the cemetery because behind them rose gleaming towers of concrete and steel reflecting dozens of incarnations of London back through their blind windows.

He saw a little old man huddled up on a bench oblivious to the rain. The man, with the wisps of his white hair plastered flat to his scalp, looked up at him as he approached the wrought-iron gates. The iron formed the black wings of a raven, reinforcing the dilapidated cemetery's name. One side of the gates hung lopsided, only held in place by the rust. As he got closer he realized that the old man was actually a tramp, swaddled in layer upon layer of dirty old coats and torn trousers. He wore a pair of hobnail boots that had been resoled so many times you could tell the age of them by looking at the rings around the bottom of them. The smell was the worst of it; weeks-old piss fused into his coats was being released by the rain.

The old man nodded as he passed. He had the red vines of alcohol abuse across his cheeks and the tell-tale open bottle peaking out of one of his pockets as he leaned forward, watching Josh every step of the way.

The guy was creepy, but said nothing and made no move to stop Josh or beg for spare change to waste on the demon drink.

Josh ignored his audience and walked through the gates, passing into a lost part of London.

It wasn't miraculous.

Crossing the threshold didn't suddenly transport him to Oz or Narnia.

It didn't block out the sounds of the traffic or life on the other side, but it might as well have because Ravenshill was a different country. Josh let his feet take him down the overgrown path between the headstones, looking for Damiola's name on one of them. A tree to his left was ringed by crooked stones. There must have been two hundred headstones crammed together with only inches between them. None of their engravings were visible; the names of the dead lost. Moss and lichen clung to the weathered stone. There were no bodies beneath the stones—they had been destroyed during the bombings. The stone circle was all that remained of two hundred lost souls.

Time was the cemetery's worst enemy. It encroached everywhere. Its fingers wormed their way into every nook and cranny, filling them with natural signs of decay. The old stones could stand against anything apart from time.

Josh walked through the lines of graves.

There were no mourners here, and no signs of fresh flowers on any of the plots to suggest that any might come. It was hardly surprising, given the fact that the last interment had happened some sixty years ago. Other than the tramp guarding the gates, there was no one left to mourn these dead. Beneath the weeping willows, he saw an ancient mausoleum fenced off by iron railings. It was overlooked by two stone angels. The skeletal limbs of overhanging trees and the hungry roots of vegetation gone to seed reclaimed the structures on either side of the mausoleum. It wouldn't be too many years before they claimed it for their own. They were already creeping through the black railings. Crooked gravestones marked more of the nameless dead, their memorials weathered away. The place gave Josh the creeps.

He was just about to give up any hope of finding Damiola's resting place amid the ranks of anonymous stones, fearing the worst—that it was somewhere amid those ringing the tree—when he saw the mausoleum's gates properly for the first time, realizing that the filigreed metal looked like a magician's gloves caught in the moment of transformation from cloth to blackbird ready to fly.

He'd found Cadmus Damiola's tomb.

A deep crack ran through the wall where clematis vines had clawed it open.

The gate was locked, but judging by the state of the rust-eaten hinges, it wasn't going to provide any sort of obstacle. Josh looked around to be sure that he wasn't being watched—the tramp had left his bench and wandered off—and then boosted himself up, scrambling over the railings with their blunted spear-tip points.

He dropped down on the other side and stayed in the crouch, looking around again for prying eyes. He couldn't have looked more suspicious if he'd been carrying a hand-painted placard that declared he was a tomb robber. Satisfied he was alone, Josh crossed the short distance to the iron-studded crypt door, which like the gate, was locked. He hadn't thought this far ahead. The lock itself was more decorative than practical, the keyhole as big as his fist. He could see part of the mechanism through the keyhole, but without something to trip it, he wasn't getting inside. It was ironic, of course, after all the years Boone had worked so hard to keep him from becoming one of the Rothery kids, and here he was contemplating breaking into somewhere far more sacred than any two-up two-down because of the old man's obsession. It was contagious. His great-grandfather's madness had been handed down to him like some twisted heirloom. Seeing Eleanor had just cemented it for him. He couldn't *not* open the door after that. He owed it to her, to Isaiah, and ultimately to Boone.

He needed something thin enough and strong enough to work into the hole and turn the heavy tumbler without breaking and blocking the mechanism—assuming the tumbler wasn't jammed up with the rust of age. None of his keys were long enough to do the job. The answer was entwined in the elaborate iron gloves of the rusted gate. It took him a few minutes to worry free one of the thinner pieces of filigreed iron from the design, the rust flaking off in his hands and staining them a dull red as he did so. But he had what he needed: a makeshift lock pick.

A few seconds later Josh heard the satisfying clunk of the tumbler falling into place.

He took a deep breath, then pushed the door open.

The other side was absolutely dark, broken only by the shaft of faint light that encroached around him. Josh stepped inside. He hadn't thought to bring a torch, and with his phone dead the only light source he had was Boone's old petrol lighter. He took the battered tin from his coat's deep pocket, and rescued the lighter from inside.

He slipped the tin back into his pocket and wrapped his hand around the lighter.

A short flight of nine stairs led down to a second set of double doors. Even in the Stygian gloom he could just make out the accoutrements of the stage magician's craft carved into them. The doors were exquisite. A work of art that like the tomb itself spoke of surprising wealth, which jarred against the expectation of a man who had spent his life treading the boards of British theaters offering penny entertainments for the masses. How could he have accumulated the kind of fortune such an afterlife demanded?

There was only one answer to that, of course: Lockwood.

It was the logical leap as far as joining the dots of what had started out as a very cold missing person's case and was beginning to look like a grand criminal conspiracy that went back a century. Damiola had been in Lockwood's pocket, either through greed or fear, both great motivators on their own, but together surely irresistible?

Josh approached the door, resting the flat of his hand against the shape of a huge leafless tree and the curious Celtic knotwork carved into the door.

He opened the door.

22

THE MYSTERIES OF DAMIOLA

"There are no answers in there," a voice said behind him, scaring a month of his allotted years out of Josh with those six softly spoken words. "At least not the ones you are looking for."

Josh's heart was in his throat as he turned to see the old tramp silhouetted against the entrance. He was taller than he'd realized, close to six foot, and despite the thick layers of coats padding his bulk up, he was skeletally thin and showing obvious signs of malnutrition. His breath stank almost as badly as his damp coats. But even so, there was something about the man, a *presence*.

"I always knew someone would come looking eventually. I'm surprised it took you so long. Which one are you? You look like Isaiah, but you're not him. His boy?" Josh shook his head. The tramp had a slight accent, the lingering trace of something he couldn't place. "Poor bastard didn't deserve what was done to him. If I could do anything, I'd change that."

"Who are you?"

"No one anymore. I used to be him," he pointed over Josh's shoulder toward the doors and the tomb beyond them. "But now he's just bones and I'm a ghost, I guess. Or as good as. Funny what time does to you, but

I should know that better than anyone. But I'm more interested in who you are, boy, and how you fit in to this sorry story? Tell me that."

Josh started to say he wasn't involved, not really, but he'd been actively searching out the truth of Glass Town ever since he'd heard its name. Instead, he said, "Did you know my great-grandfather?"

"Ah," the tramp said, inclining his head slightly, piecing together the genetic puzzle but coming to a conclusion a couple of generations short. "That explains you wearing his face. Time moves on, always ticking on, *tick-tick-tick*. No matter how much we might want to grab a hold of its hands and slow it down to a more manageable pace, on it goes *tick-tick-tick*. Cruel bastard. So, the hunt has passed from one generation to another? You won't find it here, you know. There's no hidden door. Or, to put it another way, you're barking up the wrong burial place if you think coming here will help you get in, or get her out. I'll tell you what I told him that night; she's gone. Forget her. I'm good at what I do. Or at least I was. *He* was." He looked pointedly toward the doors behind Josh. "Go on, open the door. Disturb my old bones. There's nothing in there that will help you."

"How can you be in there and out here? You keep talking about the body in there as if it's you, like you're some ghostly guardian—" Josh wanted to say *but the moonlight isn't streaming through you, you're not some phantom.* "But he is you, isn't he? Somehow?"

"Somehow," the old tramp nodded. "Cadmus Damiola the Less Than Magnificent, at your service," the old man said, forgoing any bow or scrape because his old bones wouldn't allow it.

Josh studied him in the flickering petrol light, trying to peel away the layers of grime and time to get to the face the tramp had once owned. Despite the trickery of the shadows, he was sure he'd seen it before—or a version of it—on the poster announcing Damiola's grand tour on the wall in Boone's Rotherhithe flat, which meant the old tramp was telling the truth. Or at least a version of it, because that would have made him 120 years old, give or take a few rotations around the sun, and he was looking pretty damn spritely for someone who'd lived the best part of two lifetimes.

"Go on, open the door if you don't believe me. Perhaps I'm lying and enlightenment waits within?"

"How long have you been standing guard out there?"

"Longer than I thought," he said.

Josh didn't say anything, struggling to come to terms with the idea that the stage magician spent his days at the gates of the destroyed cemetery, guarding his own tomb. Why would anyone do that?

The lighter burned hot in his hand. There was only so long he'd be able to hold onto it before he had to flip the lid closed and plunge himself back into the pitch black darkness of the tomb.

He made a decision, then, turning his back on the tramp and stepped up to the door. As he reached out for the huge brass-ring handle he half-expected Cadmus Damiola to say that only the worthy shall cross the threshold and he had been deemed unworthy.

He didn't; instead, the old tramp said, "It is good that you don't trust what you've been told. Words are so often the basis for any misdirection; look at my hands, see, nothing up the sleeve, nothing hidden in them, but what's *this*? Is that your card? It is? I don't believe it," he smiled wryly, his tone mimicking the wide-eyed amazement of the spectator seeing the magic for the first time. "Don't you think if it was that easy to uncover the secrets of my greatest illusion of my life any of the many who have come looking before you would have found my secrets long ago? I mean, ask yourself this, how hard was it for you to find this place, truly?"

Josh flipped the lid closed on the lighter, giving the metal case a chance to cool down. He twisted the brass ring and pushed, but the door didn't budge an inch.

"Oh, well would you look at that," the old tramp muttered. "Maybe the hinges have rusted? You might want to give it a really good shove? Maybe that'll do the trick. Really put your shoulder into it."

Josh knew he was being played with, even so, he twisted the brass ring again, feeling the tooth of the hidden mechanism retract, and pushed hard but the doors didn't give.

"Curious. Perhaps something is blocking the way? Let me try for you."

Josh moved aside as the old man shuffled forward, placing the flat of his hand on the black wood. As he did so, the sigils carved into the wood flared as if aflame for a second, the fire chasing through the crevices carved into the door to bring the patterns to brief fiery life. For the silence between two heartbeats the dark passage was lit an angry red, and then plunged back into darkness as Cadmus Damiola opened the door. The sudden intensity of the light stung his eyes. "No, everything seems to be fine. After you, but don't say I didn't warn you. I promise you, it is quite the anticlimax. And I should know, given I've been the sole occupant since 1929. At some point I really should go back and die, I suppose. Come to think of it, you might want some light, save you from burning your fingers on that old Zippo of yours." The old tramp clicked his fingers and in response a stub of candle in the brass holder on the sarcophagus in the center of the room came alive, lighting up the crypt with a sizzle of sulphate.

It was a single flame, but more than enough to light the entire tomb.

"I knew you'd come. You or someone like you. Ever since I felt the first of the dweomers failing I knew it was only a matter of time until someone turned up at my grave. I thought it would be Seth, ordering me to restore the magic, to make it whole again, banish that place back to Hell, or Isaiah begging me to rip apart the veil once and forever. So much time has passed, so many years. I don't know how it could ever come to this, but it must be inevitable because here you are, and here I am, and I know what you are about to ask me—but first let me ask you why should I help you?"

He didn't have an answer for that.

"How do I know you aren't one of them?"

"Two days ago I knew nothing about anything. My biggest concern was that I'd screw up my grandfather's eulogy," Josh said. "And then I find a house filled with my family's obsession, articles, photographs, film reels, all of them about Eleanor Raines."

At that, the old man stiffened. "Did you release the Reels? Was that you I heard?"

"Did I what? I have no idea what that means. No. I don't think so.

I watched a few minutes of an uncut Hitchcock movie filmed in Rotherhithe. Is that what you mean?"

"No," the old man said. "But if it wasn't you, you have an enemy here."

"Seth," Josh said. "The question is, do I have a friend here?"

The old man craned his head as though listening to voices in the
wind only he could hear. "Yes, for now. As long as you stand against
Seth."

Josh entered the cramped tomb, the tramp a couple of steps behind
him. The old man was right and wrong at the same time. Everything
beyond the threshold was disappointing and extraordinary at the same
time. The light flickered, guttering in the breeze as it chased into the
small space, but didn't go out. The candlelight pushed the shadows away
from the sarcophagus. Josh didn't realize what was happening at first,
barely noticing the way the shadows on the far wall had begun to take
on some sort of shape, but as the flame settled down so, too, did the
shadows and their nature became clear: they were a map of sorts.

"My original designs for Glass Town," the old man said. "My greatest trick, and yet the only one I have never been in a position to take
a bow for. It will be nice for someone to appreciate the brilliance of it,
even if only for a short while. Sadly for you there is no way Lockwood
will let you live now that you have got this close, you do know that,
don't you?"

Thirteen stones on the walls were deep red in color, almost as though
stained with blood. Josh didn't need to check his own map to know that
they coincided with the thirteen points scorched into the floor of the
Rotherhithe flat and copied down there.

Josh looked from him to the sarcophagus and back again. Beyond
the shadows and the stone tomb there was nothing else in the crypt.
"How can you be in there and out here? It doesn't make sense. Not that
any of this makes sense."

"It's a long story, including more than a little alcohol, desperation,
a pretty girl, and a necromancer, but then aren't they all?"

"The best usually are," Josh agreed, as though there was nothing
remotely extraordinary about the fact the old tramp's nonexplanation
included the word necromancer. "I'd still like to hear it."

"I'm sure you would, boy, but it's my story to tell, not yours to ask for. So, look around you, are you satisfied? You've found the magician's tomb and but for a little light trick, it's empty."

Josh looked at the shadow map again. The lines blurred, merging and separating in the slight breeze, creating a second layout that looked quite different from the first. Those were the lines he tried to focus on, because they offered a map quite unlike the one he carried in his pocket. Was it a trick of the wind, or his first proper glimpse of Glass Town?

"How do I find it?" he said, pointing at the shadow map.

"Who says it's there to be found?"

"You wouldn't be guarding this place if it wasn't."

"Very true."

Josh had a dozen follow-up questions, everything from where is the door—if there was a door—and how did he open it, to why Damiola had made Glass Town in the first place and why he was still protecting it after all these years, what the scorch marks on his map represented, but he didn't have the chance to ask any of them; the old man tilted his head, seeming to sniff the air, then turned to look back out toward the cemetery. "He knows you're here. This isn't good. Come here." He placed a grubby hand on the center of Josh's chest. "Can you *feel* it? The disturbance in the night air? Not good. You've frightened him. That's not a good thing. A man like Seth Lockwood doesn't react well to being scared. He's like a cornered beast; he reveals his claws." Josh heard the movement then, a scraping of feet dragging through the gravel chips that made up the pathways between the graves outside. "There's something out there." Not someone, something. The old tramp had chosen his words with care. "We can't stay here. This isn't where we make a last stand, and that's what's going to happen if we don't go now." Cadmus Damiola snuffed out the flame that burned atop his sarcophagus, taking with it the shadow map, and hurried back toward the door, ushering Josh ahead of him.

He stepped out into the night and saw the weird light immediately.

Something. Like the apparition of Myrna Shepherd that had torn Boone's house apart looking for something.

"This way, hurry," the old man said, pulling at his sleeve.

Josh turned his back on the ghostly glow and followed Damiola out through the iron gates. Damiola drew them closed behind him, dragging the left side back on a broken hinge that left it hanging preciously, then uttered a short declarative Josh didn't catch—the words refused to settle in his mind, squirming around like the metal itself did as Damiola passed a hand across the filigree.

As with the door of the tomb itself, the rusted iron answered his touch with a ripple of flame; this one so hot it seemed to buckle and bow the metal to its whim. Josh saw the shapes of the birds wrought within the fretwork twist slowly as the birds began to tear free.

Damiola leaned in, exhaling a single sharp breath into the iron beaks of the miraculous birds, and then stepped back, giving the summoning room to complete itself.

It wasn't quiet; the shrieks of twisting metal sheering free of its welds drew an answering cry from the direction of the light. It was the sound of magic calling to magic, and it was as old as nature itself.

Slowly at first, but with evermore determination, the raven's rusted wings pulled away from the frame. It twisted its head to peer at its master with beady rust-pitted eyes, the rhythmic *whump-whump* beat of its wings almost masking the sheering snaps of the final welds that pinned it to the gate, and then the metal raven took to the air, circling once, twice, three times overhead, impossible and magnificent as it trailed the rocket's red glow of sparks in its wake.

The old man leveled a finger in the direction of the eerie light and whispered another impossible-to-concentrate-on command, his words lost in the squeal of rusted metal as the raven swooped low, skimming the tops of the weathered stones before chasing away toward the light reaching the edge of the cemetery just as two men shuffle-walked into the garden of the dead. The light couldn't separate the pair. Josh didn't recognize them, except there was something vaguely familiar about them. He didn't have time to dwell on it. The squeals of metal transformed into shrieks as the raven fell upon the men, who in turn threw up their hands to defend themselves.

"That should buy us some time."

"How?"

"Not enough to stand here explaining that or arguing about what we do next," the old tramp said, breathing hard. Beads of sweat peppered his forehead and ran down the red vines in his cheeks to tangle in the mass of his scruffy beard. He started to run, barking short staccato sentences in front of him as he did. "You want into Glass Town? You need to pierce the veil between worlds, to find a place of weakness, an oblique."

"A what?"

"A weakness in the veil between worlds, where one brushes up against the other. You want to find a way into limbo, into Hell, whatever you want to call it; you need to find a weakness. It is out of time. There is no secret door . . . I'm sorry . . ."

"You're wrong," Josh shouted at his back. "You must be. There has to be a door. I saw her. Eleanor. She was out here."

That stopped Damiola cold. "What are you saying?"

"I saw her."

"No. That's impossible."

"Like everything else you're talking about? Like flying metal birds and you being a hundred and twenty years old? Yeah, it's impossible," Josh said, bluntly.

"Glass Town doesn't work like that. What we did . . . you can't just slip into and out of the otherworld, it's out of phase with our own. Time is different there. You can't walk from one to the other and back again. So whatever you think you saw, you couldn't have. And you need to pray for all of our sakes that you didn't," he added, making the sign of the cross over his chest. "Even a crack in one of the lenses would be enough to doom it and everyone inside it. Once time slips in through the cracks it all comes undone. It's entropy. It cannot hold."

Behind them they heard the desperate howl—it could not have been further from a *caw,* it was an utterly broken sound—as the bird was ripped from beak to bowels; its shattered wings discarded by the duo as they lunged between the broken stones, on the hunt.

"What do I do?"

"Easy. You run. And you hope those things don't get through me, because I'm all that's standing between you and them." He reached into the folds of his coat for something stuffed deep in the pockets, and pulled out a small brass compact. "Sometimes the only way you can see through smoke and mirrors is with more smoke and better mirrors. Maybe it's time the whole thing came undone. Every trick runs its course. Look for my workshop on Cobb Street, over in Spitalfields. Everything you need is there. But know this, the closer you get, the more certain it is that Lockwood *will* kill you, not just try." He pressed the compact into Josh's hands, and closed his own hands around them. "Don't slow down, don't look back, just run and keep on running, boy. Unless you want to die, then by all means stick around here and let Lockwood's gets do it for you."

Josh saw the pair push their way awkwardly between gravestones, seeming to flicker in and out of focus as they came. He recognized them now: Al Clamp and Marty Crake, the comedy duo, and realized he'd seen them earlier that day. He'd been wrong; they weren't fancy dress partygoers wearing rubber masks, and they weren't tied together for some bizarre three-legged charity collection. There was no bucket full of coins between them. They were conjoined. Fused together.

"What do I do?" Josh repeated, unable to tear his eyes away from the grotesque comedians as they lumbered toward him.

"I've already told you," Damiola barked, and shoved Josh away.

Josh didn't need telling a third time.

He ran.

23

MIRROR KINGDOM

And he didn't stop running until the shock wave of the explosion hit him—so hard it flung him from his feet with all the force of a punishing fist to the solar plexus. Josh scrambled back to his feet, looking back over his shoulder at the plume of black smoke and licks of flame coming from the heart of the old cemetery. A few lights came on around him with faces appearing at the windows a moment later. From where they were it must have looked like a gas explosion. Not that many years ago the default fear would have been an IRA bomb, but times had changed. London wasn't the city it had been. Of course now there were other terrors, but that first reaction to an explosion and fire wasn't a bomb these days, even after the July 7 attacks There was always another reason.

He saw them coming out of the smoke: the Comedians.

There was no sign of the tramp, which could only mean one thing: They'd found a way past him.

Josh felt the sting of gravel on his hands as he dusted them off on his jeans. For a full ten seconds he stood stock-still staring at the deformed duo as they shuffle-walked toward him, the smoke billowing all around them. Then he remembered what they were: Lockwood's henchmen; just like the actress. He turned his back on them and ran.

Instinct took him through the East End streets, those narrow warrens where once upon a time Jack the Ripper and Spring-heeled Jack might have stalked, toward the bright new towers of the business district, and Cobb Street.

They were gaining ground fast.

He didn't know this part of the city half as well as he would have needed to if he wanted to plan any sort of escape route; instead he had to rely upon speed and luck and hope he didn't run himself down a blind alley.

Josh drove himself on, not letting himself think.

It was easier to run when you were terrified: the adrenaline flooded his system and cheated his mind into thinking he could run forever. Rain and sweat plastered his hair flat to his scalp. There were plenty of narrow little side streets and back alleys in this part of London. Josh gritted his teeth and took a left then ducked right down a narrow lane that cut a channel between an old haberdashery shop and a newsagent's.

He could hear the Comedians coming, their static howls and slapping palms mocking him every step of the way.

Josh doubled back on himself, realizing that he couldn't simply shake their pursuit. He needed to be smart—assuming they were somehow locked on to his scent, he needed to search out places that would mask his fragrance, or at least hide it among crowds of others. He remembered an old line about dogs losing the scent in water, and for one crazy second thought about hurling himself into the Thames and making a swim for it. The urge didn't last long, given the fact that he couldn't actually swim.

He saw the lights of a pub a couple of hundred yards away, and ran for it. He didn't stop running as he pushed through the doors into the snug. A couple of old heads turned to see what all the commotion was, but he kept on running straight toward the back of the room and the gold-painted hand pointing toward the gents. There were perhaps twenty people in the room. Not enough to hide away in, but the place stank of stale beer and cigarettes despite the smoking ban, and the all-pervading smell of old sweat. It reeked. But would it be strong enough to buy him the time to put some real distance between himself and the relentless Comedians?

Probably not, he thought fatalistically.

Not for the first time in the last twenty-four hours, he wished he had learned how to steal a car. It was pretty much a remedial skill for a kid raised on the Rothery, and if he lived long enough, it was a gap in his education he intended to plug.

Someone laughed, seeing his panicked left-right-left look before his gaze fixed on the painted hand, assuming he was about to shit himself, which wasn't entirely wrong.

Josh dodged around a man balancing three pints in stretched fingers, and pushed straight through the door, praying that he wasn't running himself into a literal dead end.

On the other side he was confronted by three possible escape routes, and used the threadbare carpet to make his choice, taking the least walked alternative, gambling it would take him to the fire exit. He guessed right. At the end of the passageway he hit the safety bar on the door, triggering the alarm, and ran out into the yard behind the pub.

The rain had eased off a little over the last few minutes, the worst of the storm having past. The yard was filled with beer barrels. The rain played them like a Jamaican steel band. Six concrete steps led down into the yard. Graffiti on the wall promised that God lived at the bottom of a pint of beer, and suggested the trick to finding him was as simple as drinking enough.

Josh ran straight at the gate. It was bolted. Rather than open it, he clambered up onto one of the barrels, teetering awkwardly as it threatened to roll away from under him, and launched himself at the fence. He kicked, scrambling up over the top—it wasn't graceful, but it was effective—and dropped down into the alleyway on the other side.

He hit the ground hard and kept on running.

The alleyway was lined with green plastic wheelie bins and black sacks waiting for the dustbin men to collect them. A stray dog curled up against the brick wall behind a restaurant, obviously familiar enough with the routines to know when the spoils were cast out. It saw him, but didn't stir itself.

Josh paused twice to get his bearings as he reached an alternative junction or alley end, and was forced between taking a right or left, or running straight on, not knowing where either eventually led.

Hearing the suddenly shrill chorus of starlings again, he looked up at the sky. The birds banked and swirled, and once more he seemed to be beneath the epicenter of their mad flight. Unintentionally, his random twists and turns brought him back to the alley Eleanor Raines had disappeared down. He saw the sign on the wall: *Cobb Street.*

He stopped running and looked back over his shoulder.

The street was empty, but he could hear them: the manic *slap-slap-slap* of their hands on the brick houses and the constant chatter of sharp teeth chomping mercilessly at his heels. They were coming for him.

There was something completely *off* about the street.

It felt like it belonged in another time.

Which it did, but he wasn't to know that.

Cobb Street was long gone from any modern map of London, replaced by the concrete and steel office blocks and the great sprawl of the indoor market. He rushed down the street with the Comedians on his heels.

Now that he was on their turf Clamp and Crake didn't rush to catch him; they didn't need to. Rather, they kept their measured pace, *shuffle-shuffle-drag, shuffle-shuffle-drag,* knowing that he would inevitably tire, and when he did they would fall upon him, bringing him down when he was at his weakest from what felt like hours of running.

Smoke and mirrors. The words stuck in his head as he ran down Cobb Street. The entire thing was an illusion. A grand trick. Cadmus Damiola was a stage magician, after all, so wasn't whatever he'd done to Glass Town just some magnification of his magician's art? *Like the iron raven?* Josh thought, casting another backward glance, but this time looking over the Comedians' heads. There was no sign of the magical construction in the sky. But if he was right, if it was just a trick, then what trick had Eleanor pulled on him to mask her disappearance? He'd turned over every stone in the alleyway, so how could she simply disappear into thin air?

There was nothing that looked even remotely like a workshop on the street. There were flats with bricked-up windows, others with curtains drawn for the night. Some were so narrow it seemed impossible to imagine people called them home.

Smoke and mirrors.

Sometimes the only way you can see through smoke and mirrors is with more smoke and better mirrors.

That's what he had now, didn't he, a better mirror? Josh fished the compact from his pocket and fumbled with the clasp, well aware that the Comedians watched him from the other end of the alleyway.

Facing away from them, Josh held up the compact and looked in the mirror, not sure what he expected to happen—if the magician's mirror would suddenly give him new eyes, or at least some new sharper perception, or if he would simply see some backward landscape in which the Comedians lumbered toward him in miniature. There was a blue moon behind them, or a blue-tinged streetlight, that cast their end of the alleyway in its peculiar ghost light, just as there had been with the actress in Boone's house. But beyond that there was an almost ethereal quality about them, as though the light somehow passed *through* them rather than around them. It was only a slight difference, but it changed everything. Smoke and better mirrors.

But that wasn't the only thing that caught his eye as being wrong about the reflection—but he couldn't know for sure without turning around to face the Comedians.

He was right; there, amid the rundown backs of the Victorian terrace, was a door—a split-stable door with the words *GOODS ENTRANCE* engraved in an arc across the lintel. There was a symbol beneath it, a Celtic knot around a leafless tree, branded into the door. It had to be the entrance to Damiola's workshop, because there *wasn't* a door there unless he looked for it in the mirror's glass.

Face front, the walls and windows seamlessly joined, hiding its existence.

Was this a first glimpse of how the magician had hidden away Glass Town? A prototype for the trick on a much smaller scale? There was no denying the fact the door wasn't there, and then it was when he looked at the street through the looking glass, only for it to disappear again when the mirror was removed from the equation. The magician's workshop was hidden in plain sight. If anyone would know the workings of that kind of trick it would be the man whose signature illusion, the Opticron, involved the manipulation of light and sight through lenses, wouldn't it?

Josh took four steps back toward the mouth of Cobb Street and the Comedians, then reached out with his free hand to fumble with the door. It was difficult doing everything in reverse, but after a couple of seconds of groping around he opened the door.

As the door swung outward, the Comedians entered Cobb Street. Close up, there was nothing funny about them. The fat man inclined his head slightly, seeming to sniff the air. *Just like a dog,* Josh thought, amending that quickly to, *a rabid one.*

There was no streetlight or shop sign or any other possible source for the weird blue-tinged light now. It emanated from within the fat man, Al Clamp. Only of course it wasn't the comedian, dead ringer for him or not. That thing in the alleyway was something else entirely, like the woman last night. They were a pair; both of them burned with the same weird light as if they were being projected into the streets by some god-like cine camera. The comedians shuffled a step toward him. Just the one. They didn't move comfortably.

Marty Crake's mouth twitched.

What frightened Josh more than anything was that somehow he was close enough to see that involuntary muscle spasm.

The *caws* of the starlings were the only sound in the otherwise silent alleyway. Al Clamp's gaze seemed to drift upward, drawn to the rau-cous birds. There was no iron raven up there to save Josh this time. The reed-thin Marty Crake came toward him—moving with an uncanny serpentine grace. Josh saw the way his hand was fused together with his companion's, the pair conjoined at hand and hip.

Josh couldn't seem to force his body to turn. Though his mind screamed *run,* his legs stubbornly refused to obey him. That one step over the threshold into the workshop was beyond him.

And then Marty Crake's mouth opened wider than ought to have been possible, and wider still as his jawbone dislocated with a shocking *snap.* The comedian's lips stretched back on row after row of razor-sharp teeth as his smile transformed into a death's head rictus.

Beside him Al Clamp loosed a shrill static shriek. Windows overhead cracked, then as the shriek escalated, shattered, showering biting-sharp shards of glass down on Cobb Street.

Josh clamped his hands over his ears, the paralysis that had gripped him broken finally, and nearly fell through the doorway as his soles lost their purchase on the slick cobbles. He reached out with his right hand, planting it flat on the side of the frame, and plunged into the darkness of Damiola's workshop.

They came after him, no hint of shambling or shuffling movement as they surged down the middle of the narrow street, their outstretched hands slapping against the brick walls and wooden fences on either side, playing them like the leather skins of battle drums as they ran.

If the wild drumming was meant to intimidate him, it worked, but not half as effectively as Clamp's unearthly static howl. That was so much worse. It was like a jolt of electricity pulsing through his blood. Every muscle tensed as it surged through him.

That noise removed any and all doubt that the Comedians were fashioned from the same stuff as Myrna Shepherd and that their sole purpose was to tear his soul apart.

He slammed the door behind him, praying it would keep them out.

Damiola's workshop was an incredibly narrow building, claustrophobic and cobwebbed, with only two rooms on the ground floor. The bare boards of a staircase rose at the far end of the uncarpeted hallway. With very little light, he mistook the mirrors at the end of the hallway for windows out into the street beyond. If he'd have looked more closely, or thought about the fact there was no light source in the workshop, he might have seen that the light was emanating from within the mirrors, and the landscapes he saw there bore no relation to what he should have been seeing through the window of an East End hovel, but rather looked to be perfect reflection of a greener, pleasanter land. Albion. The ancient England was surrounded by mirrors filled with mist. But fear stopped him from seeing any of that.

The first of the two ground-floor rooms must have been the magician's workroom once upon a time. It was filled with the dusty accoutrements of his art; sword cabinets stood empty, housing dust and spiders in place of a crisscross of deadly blades; elaborate water torture chambers, long-since drained dry; chains and handcuffs dangled from the ceiling, suspended on hooks where Damiola must have practiced his escapologist's act; the mirrors of a crude Pepper's Ghost trick lined up to cast his mirror image halfway across the room, all half-hidden in shadow; trapdoor mechanisms, hidden compartment triggers, all manner of curious contraptions and installations that simulated levitation and other illusions; linking rings lay on a worktop; a death-saw cabinet lay folded in two, no beautiful assistant's feet wiggling out of it; and so much more he couldn't describe much less imagine how they might function on stage. It was all here. Every part of the magician's craft. But it was all broken, unmade, or at least part-made. These weren't the finished articles; these were tricks in various stages of the design process.

He moved through them quickly, looking for something, but with no idea what that something might be.

The second room was given over to the three glassblower's ovens—the furnace, the glory hole, and the annealer—and the blowpipes, plaster, wooden molds, crucibles, and rails that had been set up for the pipes to ride so the magician could shape the glass while it was still red hot. There were hand-drawn designs on the scarred and pitted workbench. Josh looked at them as he moved through the room, assuming they were the blueprints for the Opticron or some variation of the light-manipulation illusion he'd been working on before he made his deal with the devil that was Seth Lockwood.

A large marble slab dominated the rest of the room, which was where the magician did his work.

The floorboards were stained with burns and scorch marks. Around the room were other glass objects, a vast array of lenses and the like surrounded the blueprints on the bench, component parts of the Opticron, no doubt, spare parts or misfires, it was impossible to say which.

Josh stepped over a pair of jacks that lay discarded on the floor.

It had obviously been decades since the furnaces were last fired up.

A thick layer of dust and grime had settled over everything. It all smelled so stale, like the air hadn't moved in the workshop for years.

The front door rattled against its frame, dragging him back to the here and now abruptly.

There was no back door.

That was his first thought. There were windows in the hall, and here in the workrooms, and plenty of things to break them with.

Josh had to fight down the urge to panic.

He needed to think.

Be calm.

But he felt sick.

Through the window in the magician's workshop—virtually opaque from the buildup of soot and muck clinging to it—he could see the rusty metal rungs of a fire escape descending from the roof, meaning there had to be a way out from the floor above that didn't involve trying to clamber out through wire-reinforced windows with the Comedians snapping at his heels.

The only way is up, he thought grimly, running for the stairs.

Even as he reached them, he threw a glance toward the array of mirrors, finally grasping the fact that they weren't reflecting the workshop, but not understanding their true nature as he climbed the stairs to the next landing. The slam of fists against the outside door chased him, pounding over and over until the wood splintered beneath the impact.

Josh had seconds at best to get out of there—at worst it was already too late—and two doors to choose from: eeny and meeny, with neither looking more like salvation than the other. He followed the geography of the house in his mind's eye and grabbed the knob of the second, yanking open the door directly above the glass room.

He stepped into room as the Comedians burst into the workshop, and was confronted by what appeared to be an enormous Heath Robinson contraption—some crazy juxtaposition of junk. There was a brass steam boiler heated by tiny kettles that vented steam that hit a brass plate above and condensed, only to pool in the pan and be dripped back into the kettles to boil again and again, thus creating the machine's own tiny ecosystem that turned the gears and complex pulley arrangements that were threaded by lengths of knotted string, manipulating a huge lens in the center of the room. There were mirrors, too: a bank of them with gilt-edged frames and foil-speckled glass where the silvering had worn away. Two contained absolutely no reflections at all, the thin light passing into them but reflecting nothing back out. Two others offered a glimpse of deserted streets and what looked like the false fronts of a film set.

Josh realized he was seeing Glass Town for the first time, but didn't have the luxury of time to appreciate just how incredible that was.

He looked around for something he could use to defend himself. Anything. Anything at all.

There was an old Imperial typewriter, which appeared to have a page from a manuscript still in the carriage. Beside it there was an old cine camera on a wooden platform.

None of the component parts of the contraption appeared to bear any relation to any of the others. None had any obviously apparent use. It was like the whole thing had been cobbled together to confound the eye, like an elaborate game of Mouse Trap. So many of the pieces appeared to be held together by duct tape and a prayer, but it *worked*. The reels whirred, and Josh saw that a film was threaded into the projector so that it spooled from one reel to another, and then onto a third—which fed it back to the first reel, insuring the film never played out. The camera's light was aimed right at the heart of the huge lens in the middle of the mechanism, and shone out through the room's only window as if projecting a new reality out there.

Josh didn't have time to wonder what trick he'd stumbled onto. He heard the Comedians' static shrieks taunting him as they dragged their twisted body up the stairs.

It came again, like broken laughter.

It was hideous.

Josh worked his way around the side of the room, having to squeeze between prongs that jutted out of the contraption and the wall, making his way over to the window. He could see the iron fire escape on the other side of the glass, but when he tried to open the window it refused to budge.

The sash had been nailed shut.

The Comedians appeared in the doorway, Marty Crake's red-raw gums peeled back on row upon row of teeth. There was no room on his face for anything else. Teeth. Teeth. Teeth. Teeth slick with spittle. Teeth clogged with gristle. Teeth filed to points, fashioned to rend and tear flesh.

White noise burst from his hideous mouth.

Josh tugged desperately at the window, but it wasn't opening.

Damiola had told him what he needed to do, he realized then, and it wasn't run.

24

THE SOULLESS CITY

He clawed at one of the nails, desperately trying to pry it free, but it wasn't moving. Splinters dug into his fingertips. He could see Clamp and Crake's reflections weirdly distorted in the hand-blown glass, and yet the reflections were somehow *less* horrific than the reality they offered as they came into the room.

The pulley, cog, and camera contraption occupied so much of the floor space they couldn't easily get to him. Josh made sure to keep it that way for as long as he could, realizing quickly that the Comedians seemed reticent to so much as touch the machine. He edged away from the window, keeping as much of the contraption between him and them as they worked their way around the room.

Another ghost shriek of static crackled out of the fat one's mouth. It seemed almost as though there were words trapped in there trying desperately to be heard.

Crake's rows of teeth chattered.

The white noise kept coming, along with it more and more snatches of something else, something so close to words, but not quite, that they sounded all the more sinister for the almost familiarity.

Josh backed away from the pair, taking one shuffling step for every one of theirs. He could almost imagine them going around and around in circles, the Heath Robinson machine between them, forever. Only that couldn't happen; they might not tire, but he most certainly would. And when he did, well, looking at those teeth, what happened after that was the last thing he wanted to imagine. He felt the sweat beginning to gather clammily against his skin.

"What do you want from me?" Josh asked.

Al Clamp answered that with a grin, his fat face looking anything but threatening as he followed his hungry companion around the side of the machine in that eerie not-silence that shrouded them. Every time his foot came down on one of the bare floorboards instead of being greeted by a creek or groan it was met by a burst of static and a surge of white noise that lanced through him, the filings in his teeth resonating sympathetically so they functioned as a receiver inside his head, amplifying the noise through the bones of his skull.

It was hell.

Josh caught one of the armatures dangling over the side of the contraption with his hip. It swung inward. A dozen other pieces of the peculiar device rattled and clanged, adding to the tinnitus wailing inside his head. The projection light veered upward as the platform supporting the cine camera tilted alarmingly and, the effects being felt along the many joints and joists of the contraption, the lens began to oscillate.

A weird humming emanated from the glass, barely audible above the sheer hateful sound of the white noise.

Even a crack in one of the lenses would be enough to doom it and everyone inside it.

Damiola had told him how to win this fight, even if he hadn't intended to.

Shhhhhhh, one of the Comedians' two heads seemed to say, while the lizardlike tongue of the other's flicked along the ridges of his teeth making a show of just how hungry he was. Spittle clung to the yellowed points. The fat man tried to wriggle his girth through a tight gap, reaching out for Josh. After that first question Josh hadn't said a word, so the Comedian had to be shushing the contraption, which made it all the creepier.

Josh edged another step back toward the door and the landing.

The fat man seemed to realize what Josh was doing.

He shook his head and stopped trying to push his way through a gap that wasn't there and moved back toward the door.

Crake's face full of teeth gnashed, rows grinding against each other as he chewed through another static howl.

This time the sound was enough to drive Josh to his knees as the plates of his skull threatened to tear apart. He clutched at his head, then, as his head went down, began to beat at his temples with the heels of his hands, trying to drive the torments out.

When he finally looked up the Comedians were barely an arm's length away.

Josh struggled to rise, placing one of his hands on the brass boiler. He recoiled, wincing as the metal burned his palm, but instead of fighting it, forced himself to put both hands flat on the searing plates and pushed with all of his might.

The rickety contraption concertinaed in on itself like a collapsing house of cards, though for one alarming second the lens seemed to stay suspended in midair before it finally fell.

The kettles spilled steaming water across the bare floorboards.

The duct-taped armatures pulled apart, buckling as one end tore free of the other and the entire thing came tumbling down.

The lens hit the floor.

One of the small kettles hit the lens, cracking it right through its convex heart.

The light from the cine camera stuttered and failed. As it went out the static howls of the Comedians reached a crescendo, shattering every piece of glass in the room. The cold wind howled in, bringing with it driving rain.

Josh didn't dare look away from Crake and Clamp.

The fat half of the duo moved forward, feet crunching through the debris. Those huge jaws opened again impossibly wide as the comedian's jawbone dislocated with a crack and continued to open to the point where it could have swallowed Josh's head whole. There was no answering howl, only silence this time. Profound, horrifying silence. It was so much worse than the static. His partner in crime grabbed hold of one wooden spur and yanked it free. He ripped the old Imperial typewriter free from the twisted wreckage and hurled it at Josh.

He barely managed to get out of the way as the huge lump of metal sailed out through the shattered window behind him.

Josh felt the sudden surge of fresh air against his scalp and didn't hesitate; he turned and hurled himself out through the shattered window right after the typewriter, hitting the iron floor of the fire escape on his hands and knees. His momentum carried him into the safety railings. Shards of broken glass cut into his hands as he pushed himself up to his feet.

He risked a look back into the room and wished he hadn't.

The deformed Comedians were slowed by the debris, but not stopped by it.

Coming out of the stuffy old narrow house, the air felt painfully fresh in his lungs as he gulped it down. The rain hit his face. He didn't know which way to turn. He looked up at the sky. The birds were gone. The sky was gray and full of soot and coal dust that hung over the rooftops in a cloud of man-made fog. Through the clouds Josh saw the lights of the stars. The constellations shifted, trailing light like an entire heaven filled with shooting stars. For a moment it looked as though every single star was raining down from the sky, somehow holding their alignments and patterns until they settled in a different part of the sky. Josh stood there for the longest time, gazing up at a different sky, until the crashes as the Comedians hurled pieces of the contraption aside to get to the window spurred him into motion.

The metal stairs were rain-slick and treacherous. Josh grabbed the iron handrail and clanged down the steps toward the ground as fast as he dared, setting foot in Glass Town without even realizing he'd stumbled upon it.

The woman with the red umbrella—Eleanor—waited at the foot of the fire escape, looking up at him, a look of absolute horror on her beautiful face.

25

GLASS TOWN

"*That* can't be here," she said, even before he'd reached the ground.

She wasn't talking about him.

She was looking up over his shoulder at the broken window of Damiola's workshop where the Comedians were framed by rotten timber and jags of broken glass. She didn't seem the least bit disturbed by the thing's appearance, taking the endless teeth and wide, wide mouth in her stride like it was something she saw every day in this place. "It can't be here. It just *can't* . . . There's no crack . . . It can't just walk into this place . . ." and then the horror as realization hit her. "Unless . . . Please God, tell me you didn't break the anchor?" She grabbed Josh by the arm and all but dragged him the last two stairs down to the ground.

He didn't know what to say.

He'd expected her to be thrilled to see him. Hadn't she just begged him in lipstick on the wall to find her? Hadn't his family been searching for her for the best part of ninety years, never giving up in all that time, and he'd *found* her? He'd imagined her throwing herself into his arms and, well, if not exactly showering him with kisses at least treating him like a conquering hero.

"Listen to me. Please. You have to get out of here. *Now*. Go. Before it tears the whole place apart!"

Which was easy to say, but there was no way he was going back up that fire escape when that thing was waiting for him at the top.

"Eleanor? It is you, isn't it?" Josh said.

"Yes. Yes. It's me. You found me. Clever boy. But if you're going to stand there wanting a pat on the back, I wish you hadn't. Not with that thing hunting you. You have no idea what you've done, breaking the anchor, leading that thing in here. Now please, no arguments, you have to *go.*" She dragged him away from the fire escape toward the end of the alleyway.

He could see the green metal dome of what looked like an old theater, the copper completely tarnished. There was a small railed-off garden in the square and a stone fountain in the center. The trees were trapped in perpetual autumn, the leaves forever browned and curled, but not yet fallen from the bough. That almost stopped Josh there and then. He'd climbed out of a wet winter window into an autumnal street? He felt his grip on the simple things—like where he was—slip along with those stars in the sky above them. "Oh, God, Seth's going to know you've been in here . . . you need to fix the anchor . . . get that thing as far away from here as you can and fix Damiola's infernal machine before the broken glass scars the place beyond all recognition."

The yard behind the magician's workshop was clean, unlike any of the others he'd run down in his flight from the Comedians. No wheelie bins, no black plastic sacks, or cardboard boxes or anything like that. No litter on the cobbles at all. Not even a page of yesterday's news blowing down the street. It was an absolutely sterile environment, like the film set it had been once upon a time.

Josh shook his head, stupidly. "Anchor? Scars? I don't *understand.*"

"Look," she told him, pointing up at the window where the Comedians were making an ungainly effort to climb out onto the fire escape. Crake's first foot clattered on the iron platform. The sound seemed to ripple down to them through the fire escape into the ground. "Look at its hand. Look at what it's done to the wooden frame." He did, though he didn't really understand what he was seeing. The window frame around the Comedians' hand appeared to be blistering. Curls of smoke peeled away from the timber. It was as if he were watching a piece of film burn under the heat of the camera's light, the frame around it shriveling back to pure white light. When the Comedians' first foot came through the window and set down on the iron fire escape the contact burned up another precious few inches, scarring the world. It was only one tiny part of Glass Town, but it had only been on this side of the illusion for a few seconds and in that time the first blister had popped revealing nothing beneath it. A negative. An empty space.

"What's happening?"

"That thing is one of my keepers . . . Seth calls them Reels. It's a joke. He's got other pets: Dailies, Rushes, Negatives. They're all part of the film world he stole me from. It's not human. I don't know *what* it is; a demon maybe, if you believe in them, a creature of the mists, a devil. Any of them work. I don't know how Seth controls it, what kind of pact he made with Damiola to take possession of the damned things, or if he just killed the magician and took them for his own. But he owns that thing and all of the others like it, body and lack of soul." She crossed herself as she said this. Josh couldn't help but think that whatever was going on it was well outside the help of any god, no matter how strong her faith. "And you being here, you are a threat to this place. It won't stop until you are dead and the threat is gone."

"I'm no threat—"

"You're *here*. You're Isaiah Raines's blood. You're the first person to set foot inside the confines of this damned prison of mine. That makes you more of a threat to him than any of your family has ever been. There's a weakness . . . a crack . . . He doesn't think I know about it. I'll take you there. Come on." She grabbed his hand and dragged Josh toward the gate in the garden rails, and through it, urging him to hurry as they rounded the fountain. It was only as he passed it, he noticed that the nymph in the centerpiece had Eleanor's face. It was disconcerting to say the least: a glimpse as to the depths of Seth Lockwood's obsession with the actress. Josh didn't get to dwell on the realization. Eleanor kept on running until they were out the other side of the small garden and standing in the middle of an empty street.

She looked at him then, seeming to see him properly for the first time. "Are you Boone's son?"

"Grandson."

"Already? So much time has gone. You look so very like him . . ."

"Boone?"

"Isaiah. You could be his body double. It's uncanny. I feel like I am face-to-face with his ghost. I just . . ." She reached out to touch his face, but stopped short and shook her head. "We don't have time for this. As much as I want to talk . . . to tell you things . . . Seth set that thing after you. It's a hunter. You've got to go. Please. Get as far away from here as you can. It's the only way you'll stand a chance."

He knew she was right—he had brought this thing here, but in his defense he didn't know where here was, or what it was he'd brought with him. Damiola hadn't told him any of it beyond setting him down in the right direction. The only thing he's said—really—was that even a crack in the glass would be enough to ruin the delicate balance his creation held in place, manipulating the veil between worlds. He hadn't told him to break that glass back there. He hadn't said tear down the fabric of the illusion or begged him to set the truth free. He hadn't even meant to tell him what the anchors were, but he had a map, the location of each one seared onto it, and he had a mirror to see through the smoke hiding them. "I only just found you." The objection sounded lame the moment it left his mouth, but he carried on, sounding like a child. "You wanted me to find you. You wrote that on the wall, didn't you? *Find Me.* That was you, wasn't it?"

"Yes. It was me. You know it was. But I didn't know you were a marked man. I had no idea he'd set the Reels on you. Believe me, if I had, I never would have dragged you into this. I'd have stayed hidden. I'm very good at it. I've been doing it for a long time. And, Jesus, just to be blunt for a moment, you weren't supposed to just *walk* in here. No one has been able to do that since Damiola's dweomers sealed the film studio set away. Do you have *any* idea what you've done? If he finds you here, he'll know the anchors are coming loose." She shook her head. "There's no telling what he'll do then. He's not like normal people. He doesn't like losing. He'd rather destroy the board than lose the game." That was a telling glimpse into Seth Lockwood's psychology.

Eleanor pulled on his arm again, forcing Josh to match her speed as she started to run through empty streets of Glass Town toward the crack that would lead him back through to the streets of London on the other side of the illusion.

He used every second he spent in the place to soak it in: every building, every window, every streetlight—gaslight, he realized—every car—none of them immediately recognizable, their badges naming them ABCs and Crossley's and other bygone models.

It really was like walking through a fully dressed, completely deserted film set masquerading as 1920s London.

It didn't feel real.

All the details were there, but it was like there was nothing behind their painted fronts: there was a factory, he saw, but no smoke rising from any of its chimneys, and a public house, but no welcoming light burning inside its taproom.

He looked back over his shoulder several times to see the Comedians following them, and behind the grotesque Crake and Clamp, a trail of silver footprints that smoldered and blistered a path all the way back to the magician's workshop. Josh had no idea how she could possibly hope to hide them from Seth or anyone else. Black curls of smoke rose from them, crying out: *Here, look at us, see us, we are* wrong, *we shouldn't be here* . . . then, through the smoke he noticed something else—a shadow-shape, a blur of movement. He tried to focus on it, but there was something decidedly wrong about the way it moved. He heard its claws on the street, scrabbling as the shape raced toward him.

Josh couldn't bring it into focus.

Eleanor grabbed his arm and dragged him down another empty street and then another, constantly looking back over her shoulder as the animal surged toward them; its powerful gait eating the distance between them too quickly for comfort. Glass Town was a vast empty townscape, but that meant there was no one to stop them as Eleanor dragged him into a house and slammed the door behind them, and kept on running out the other side, through another house and another. Contrary to his first impression, every interior was immaculate, frozen in time. He saw frames of everyday people and their everyday lives locked in place, everything just so, from the china on the table to the cutlery and even the coats hanging over the banisters. He didn't stop to think what the presence of all this stuff meant, he just followed Eleanor.

Finally, she stopped running, having led them into a dead end. They faced the brick wall. Josh looked back over his shoulder to see the Comedians approaching, the hound at their heels.

While it moved like a dog, snapping and snarling rabidly, but soundlessly at the air, it possessed a haunting X-ray-like quality of a photographic negative. The dark patches of fur were painfully bright, its eyes two bright white spheres that blazed demonically.

"There," Eleanor said, pointing at nothing.

"What is that thing?" Josh said, unable to tear his eyes off the animal stalking toward him.

"Seth calls it a Negative. There are three of them. I call them Hell-hounds. Black dogs. They keep me in this place . . . it's grotesque . . . like so much else that Seth Lockwood lays his hand to. Now go, before you *can't*. Through there." Josh saw a shadow that ran like a crack at the juncture of the red-brick wall and the house it butted onto. "It's a weakness in the veil. You can slip through, back into your own London. Go. Close your eyes if it helps."

Josh looked back over his shoulder one last time. The Comedians were no more than two hundred feet away, but the dog was so much closer, eighty feet and closing fast, less than five seconds from pouncing on him.

They weren't going to have the luxury of some long farewell.

"Come with me."

"I can't. It doesn't work like that."

"Of course it does, just take my hand. I've seen you out there."

"I can't leave this place—not for more than a few minutes. You'll see why when you leave. Now go."

"What about the—?" he didn't get to finish asking how she'd deal with the smoldering tracks of the Comedians or the rabid Negative. She didn't even ask him what his name was. Eleanor shoved Josh toward the shadow, and he found himself falling into it.

There was a moment—a singular moment that existed within the silence between his heartbeats—when there was *nothing*. It was the most frightening thing Josh had experienced in his life, despite lasting for less than a second. In that moment his senses failed him. There was no sight, no sound; he could taste the saliva in his mouth, rusty with blood, but there was nothing to feel, not above or below or around him, and no lingering odors, not even his own sweat. Nothing. It all simply ceased to be. Was this what death was like, an absence of everything?

And then he heard her say, "Save me," as he staggered out into the middle of a busy road, into the blaring of horns and the biting cold of the rain, the night and the stars gone, the sun high in the morning sky.

His senses came *alive* as he stepped straight into the path of a police car.

26

ETERNAL FLAME

Josh froze.

That hesitation saved his life.

Had he tried to run, the reflexes of the driver would have left him lying dead in the middle of the road. As it was, the man behind the wheel instinctively executed an evasive maneuver, slamming his foot down hard and yanking on the wheel, that had the police car slewing sideways across the road, tires shrieking as they burned rubber.

It spun past Josh as the Comedians emerged from the shadows.

They weren't so lucky.

The sounds of the impact were sickening as the radiator buckled around their tangled legs, Clamp thrown high into the air even as Marty Crake's head came down, his face cannoning off the bonnet to a chorus of shattering teeth before the pair were casually tossed aside by the momentum of the spinning car. The bodies cartwheeled across the white line, still seeming to hold hands to the horror of the witnesses, only to be caught by the front of a number 23 bus hurrying toward Aldwych. That second impact battered them beyond all recognition as they hit the tarmac and were mangled beneath the relentless forward motion of the bus. It didn't matter how hard the driver stamped on the brakes, the bus was moving too fast, and the stopping distance too far to save the Comedians from going under its speeding wheels.

Someone screamed, thinking they were watching two men in fancy dress die.

Josh still didn't move.

He was staring at the shadow, waiting for the Negative dog to emerge. When it didn't, he finally turned to look at the horror unfolding in the street. He watched as one of the Comedians' arms flapped weakly. Cars stopped all around him, people running to help, others crying or dead silent in shock, him an island of absolute stillness inside the chaos of it all.

People came out of the shops. Passengers poured out of the bus. Drivers opened car doors, all of them walking into the middle of the road, bringing the traffic to a stop. Every single one of them driven by morbid curiosity to see something they really didn't want to see.

And still Josh didn't move.

He heard someone yelling, barking orders at the others. He watched the bus driver stumble out of his seat, shaking his head, saying over and over, "I didn't see them. I didn't see them. I couldn't stop. They came out of nowhere."

Someone else shouted, "Don't try and move them. Don't. Just leave them."

"We should do something."

Voices. Voices. Everywhere.

"We have to help them!"

"Has someone called an ambulance?"

"Are they dead?"

"Do you think they're dead?"

"Oh, God . . . they're dead aren't they. Jesus. Fuck. Jesus."

And still Josh didn't move.

He didn't move when the young policeman came across to him and tried to guide him out of the road. "Are you all right, sir? Sir? Are you okay? Can you hear me? Are you hurt?"

Nothing.

Josh stared at a man sitting in the window of a café across the street.

The light above him was dim, so he couldn't see his face properly, but he could see more than enough. It wasn't some mysterious newfound cousin; it was Seth Lockwood. The same youthful Seth he'd seen in *Number 13*. Just like Eleanor, he hadn't aged a day in ninety years.

On the table in front of Seth there was what looked like some kind of glass orb, a lens of sorts, crusted in parts with dried blood. Until an hour ago, Josh wouldn't have thought there could be anything sinister about a glass ball. Now he knew better. Josh could see the small flame burning in the heart of the orb as Seth picked it up and balanced the glass on his palm. He rolled it out to the edge of his fingertips, then brought his hand around quickly so the orb seemed almost to stick to the back of his hand as it rolled, threatening to fall and shatter into a thousand pieces before he brought it back under control again.

All the while, Seth stared at Josh, never breaking eye contact.

"Oh, my God, he's still alive under there!"

"Help me get to him. Jesus. Jesus *fucking* Christ. What a *mess*."

"For the love of all things holy . . ."

"Look at his head."

"Fucking hell . . . how is he still breathing?"

"Oh, God. Oh, God. Look at him . . ."

There was a commotion behind Josh. He didn't turn. He didn't want to see what was happening. Hearing it was enough. The reflections in the café window were more than enough. Together they were too much. The ambulance sirens neared, but there was no way they were going to be able to negotiate the narrow street and its jammed traffic fast enough.

"Hang in there. Don't worry. It's going to be okay. The ambulance is on the way. Look at me. Look at my face. Don't close your eyes."

"Roll him over. We should roll him over."

"No."

"What if he chokes on his blood or drowns on it or something? We should put him in the recovery position, poor bastard."

"Leave him where he is. He's not going to choke; he's facedown."

Movement. The dragging of a dead weight across the tarmac as they pulled the Comedians out from beneath the bus. And still Josh didn't turn.

"I said—holy *fuck* . . ."

"What's wrong with his face?"

Josh watched as Seth leaned forward, and with a careless tilt of the wrist let the glass orb roll back to his fingertips, teeter on the edge, and then fall. The glass hit the linoleum floor by his feet. The impact shattered it and snuffed out the last flickering life from the flame at its heart.

Behind Josh, one of the Good Samaritans said, "It's too late. He's gone." And Josh knew that somehow Seth had relinquished his hold on the thing, letting it go into whatever passed for its endless night. That was the only reason it was dead, not the bus, not the crushing damage it had caused to the Comedians. They had served their purpose. By shattering the glass he'd extinguished more than just the light, he'd snuffed out whatever magic that had kept that thing alive.

Never taking his eyes off Josh, Seth pushed himself up out of his seat.

The fact that he was here, waiting for Josh to emerge from the shadow meant that he *knew*, didn't it? Meant that he knew it all. He knew that Boone had left his grandson more than just a lighter in his will. He knew all about Isaiah's legacy. He knew that Josh had found Eleanor Raines in her lost London prison. Which in turn meant he knew all about the weakness in Glass Town's invisible walls.

And he knew all of that because Josh had just stepped out of the place in front of his eyes.

Seth Lockwood was every bit the devil Isaiah had painted him to be.

27

LOST WEEK

Julie Gennaro left the car door open as he walked over to the dead men.

He hadn't seen them coming. They had quite literally stepped out of *nowhere,* right in front of him. He was shaking; not just because he'd hit two pedestrians, but because of what he'd seen as they'd gone up over his bonnet: that face. Those teeth. The impossibly wide, predatory smile as the mouth opened wider and wider, then spiraling shut like the metal jaws of a garbage truck as the guy's head came down, cannoning off the bonnet, before impact dragged the body away. It was like something dreamed up by a fever, a nightmare given flesh and set down in the middle of an East London street, and all Julie could do was stare at the bus driver's face as he tried so desperately to stop. The true horror of it being that he knew he couldn't.

It all happened so incredibly slowly, like some sort of jerky stop-motion film playing out, only it was real. Life-and-death real.

"Look at the mess. Poor bastard."

"Christ, he's *lucky* he didn't make it," another speaker, her voice almost reverential. "I mean . . ."

"Who would *want* to live looking like that?" One of the first responders finally said what they were all thinking. His voice—and callous disregard for human life—carried across the street, but no one was arguing with him. Death, in this case, was a small mercy.

"What about the other one? Can someone get him out from under there?"

Then, "Christ . . . he looks like . . . God . . . who? That old comedian?"

"Holy shit, they killed Crake and Clamp," a kid said, and laughed. *Laughed*.

Julie didn't need to see another corpse. He was more interested in the man who had been running away from the deceased. He had a story to tell.

He stood in the middle of the road, one foot on either side of the white line, staring across the street at something.

Julie went across to him. "You okay, sir?"

He didn't say anything.

Julie put a hand on his shoulder and asked again, "Are you all right?"

The man shook his head as though to say no, no he wasn't all right, how could he be all right, he'd just stepped out of thin air, chased by a monster that lay dead beneath a double-decker bus, why the ridiculous question?

"Sir? Are you all right, sir? Sir? Are you okay? Can you hear me? Are you hurt?"

"I need to get out of here."

"I don't think so, sir. What's your name?"

"Josh."

"Okay, Josh, you're a *very* lucky man, do you know that?" He shook his head again, denying any relationship with that particularly capricious lady. Julie didn't think arguing the point would help, so instead he asked, "Do you want to tell me what just happened?"

"I don't . . ." Julie couldn't tell if he was saying he didn't want to, or if he'd simply run out of words in the middle of saying he didn't understand himself, which given the face Julie had seen—all of those teeth, the eyes pushed back and away into the temples, swiveling like some apex predator's—was pretty fucking understandable, to be blunt.

"Stay with me, Josh. What happened? Why were they chasing you? Where were you all coming from? One minute the road was empty, the next I was trying not to kill you. Talk to me, Josh. I'm your friend here."

"I don't have any friends," Josh said, still staring toward the café across the street.

Julie saw a good-looking guy in the doorway who was staring right back at them.

"You know that guy?"

As he asked, the man in the doorway drew his finger across his neck in one smooth motion, as though slitting his throat. Julie recognized him then. He'd seen him a lot over the last month or so with Gideon Lockwood in the Rothery. Wherever Gideon was, there he was, on his shoulder, in the thick of it. That made the threat all the more visceral. The Lockwoods didn't piss about with words when actions would get the message across much more emphatically.

Josh nodded. "Seth," he said.

"Let's get you out of here, shall we? Then you can tell me what you've done to upset old man Lockwood. Come on," Julie wrapped an arm around Josh's shoulder and steered him toward the side of the road. The ambulance turned onto the street as they reached the pavement. The paramedics were out of it and moving spectators away before the engine had stopped ticking over. "Nothing to see here, folks," one of them called, shooing people back, making some breathing space for the crew to get in and work. "How about you let us do our jobs. Come on, thanks, yeah, back, back."

Seeing Julie's uniform, another one of the paramedics came over to him. "Everything okay here?"

Julie nodded. "I've got this guy. He's fine. Shock. He's a lucky lad. Could have been a lot worse for him."

"Hard to argue. I've seen the others," the paramedic said, nodding toward the bus. "Want me to give him a once-over anyway?"

"Nah, it's fine. You've got enough to deal with. I'm going to take him back to the station, ask him a few questions, see if I can work out what the fuck just happened here. Just waiting for backup to arrive."

The paramedic nodded, and was already halfway back to the worst of the accident before Julie whispered into Josh's ear, "I don't know what the fuck's going on, but I saw that *thing*. And either I'm losing my fucking mind, or some shit's happening here I don't understand. So we're going to talk. You are going to tell me everything you know. Understand? And before you think about lying to me, I know that guy—I know what kind of bastard he is, and that you're in trouble. Okay?" He didn't wait for Josh to answer him. Thinking about it, he knew the victims, too. Or at least of them. He'd heard a kid say they'd killed Crake and Clamp and laugh. That was the second time he'd heard those names recently, Crake and Clamp. They'd been behind The Magic Circle robbery and now they were dead. There was no such thing as a coincidence in his line of work, meaningful or otherwise. The world just didn't work that way. "Now, we're going to go over there and get into my car, we're going to close the door and drive away, and you're going to start explaining. Don't leave anything out. Don't try and hide anything. I'll know if you're lying. This is what I do and I'm good at it. Do we understand each other, Josh?"

Josh didn't say anything as Julie led him to the car, but he didn't resist, either, and compliance was as good as acceptance as far as the policeman was concerned. Julie put his hand on his head and eased him down into the back seat, slamming the door on him before going around to the driver's side. The child locks kept his passenger in place. He hadn't taken the keys out of the ignition when he'd abandoned the car. Before Julie could get behind the wheel he heard someone ask, "What the fuck?" only to be answered by an equally perturbed, "He's *melting*?"

"Fading."

"Where the hell did he *go*?"

"Jesus, I'm losing my fucking mind. There was a corpse here two seconds ago."

He didn't wait to find out what they were talking about. He clambered into the driver's seat, and with the sounds of fresh sirens rolling into the busy street, gunned the engine, putting the car into reverse.

He was two hundred yards from the scene before he said a word. When he did, it was only the one. "Spill."

His passenger looked back at him through the rearview mirror.

There was something about him that Julie recognized. Some nagging familiarity. He'd seen him before somewhere. But where?

Julie looked him in the eye, waiting for him to say something, but he didn't. And then it hit him; he hadn't actually seen the man before, not in the flesh, but he'd been looking—or rather not looking—at his face on and off for the last week on lampposts all across the Rothery. "You're him, aren't you? That guy who went missing from the funeral last week?"

"I don't think so," Josh said.

"Oh, no, it is you." He was sure of himself now. "I was out at your place twice. Once with my partner, responding to a burglary call in the middle of the night, the place had been tossed. A woman met us at the door. I thought she was the owner. She wasn't. I realized that the second time I was there, when I sat with your mother and your sister and they told me how you'd called to say you wouldn't be home that night, but then hadn't come home at all and they were frightened you'd gone after the burglars yourself. Oh, believe me, I *know* you. I've been turning the estate over brick by brick looking for you and dreading telling your mother if I'd actually found you under one of them." He shook his head. "Where the fuck have you been for the last week?"

Josh had no answer for that.

"Okay, well I guess I'm taking you home and you can explain it to your family," Julie said, indicating right at the end of the street, and merging with the main flow of traffic that would eventually lead them back to the Rothery. "What the hell kind of trouble are you in, mate?"

28

PRODIGAL SON

Josh didn't say a word all the way back to the house.

He didn't know what he *could* say.

A week?

It couldn't be a week since the funeral.

It was impossible.

But as they turned into the estate he saw the first of the posters his mother had glued up on one of the telephone poles. It was his face. The word *MISSING* was right there in block capitals above it and their phone number beneath it. He didn't know what he was supposed to think. He'd been at the funeral two days ago. He'd spent the night at the flat in Rotherhithe and then the rest of the day chasing clues left by Boone. He'd stood face-to-face with Damiola last night. He'd seen incredible things, yes, but they'd only happened to him yesterday. He'd seen an iron raven do battle with dead comedians with mouths like sharks. He'd met a woman who hadn't aged a day in ninety years, and set foot in a part of London that hadn't existed for just as long. He was surrounded by impossible things. What was one more?

He was about to ask the obvious question, but took his phone from his pocket to check the date and time on it instead, forgetting that the battery was dead. It didn't matter; he was already beginning to believe crossing the length of Glass Town had taken days not minutes.

I can't leave this place—not for more than a few minutes. You'll see why when you leave.

Now he was seeing why: minutes there were days here.

The policeman looked at him through the mirror again.

Josh turned away from his scrutiny, looking out through the window instead of making eye contact.

It was the first time he'd stopped running since the break-in, and with the adrenaline draining from his system he was left feeling utterly and completely exhausted. And lost. There was no fight left in him, just acceptance. If this was the way the world was, then this is the way the world had to be. It really was as simple as that. If a man could weave magic and make people and places fold away in space and time somehow, then men could weave magic and make people and places fold away in space and time. QED. Denying that, pretending it wasn't happening, that the wonderful wasn't possible, forcing himself to believe that the amazing wasn't actually part of the human condition, all of that, was counterproductive. It was. It had to be, because he'd experienced it. He'd run through streets in minutes only to emerge from them a week later. He'd been chased by monsters and talked to a woman who was 109 years old and looked bloody good for it. Who was to say what was and wasn't possible anymore? Not him, that was for sure.

The streets became more and more familiar until they finally pulled up outside of Boone's house. Only of course it wasn't Boone's house anymore, it was their house and only their house. That would take some getting used to.

The policeman clambered out of the car and came around to open his door.

Josh didn't want to get out.

But then he saw the front door open and he saw his mother, Rosie Raines, standing there, the look of desperate fear on her face. He knew what she was thinking in that moment: a police car at the door, the driver had to be the bearer of bad news. Then, even as grief tore at her, there was no mistaking the sudden overwhelming flood of relief as she saw Josh emerge from the back seat.

Rosie stood there for the longest time staring at her son, then came running up the drive toward the car, arms out blindly.

She swept him up in a fierce embrace before he could straighten up, only to push him away and start beating at his chest with the full force of her fists, weeping and gulping down air and trying not to choke and say something all at once. It took Josh a second to realize what she was saying: "I thought you were dead! I thought you were dead!" The same words over and over until they lost all sense and meaning. "I thought you were dead!"

Josh pulled her close, crushing his mother's fists between their chests and held her tight until she stopped fighting him. Rosie shuddered against him, struggling to breath, but he refused to let her go. "It's okay. I'm here," he said. "I'm home."

She leaned back, arching her spine to pull away from him so that she could look at his face, like she couldn't believe it was really him, that it had to be some horrible prank being played on her by the universe.

And then she hit him again.

Just once.

Hard.

Before she broke down into uncontrollable sobs, snot and spittle dribbling out of her nose and mouth as she tried to say thank you to the policeman who had brought the prodigal son home.

Then behind her, Josh heard his baby sister yell, "You bastard! You thoughtless fucking *bastard*!"

Alexandra Raines came running out of the house.

"Not the sort of homecoming you were expecting, eh?" the policeman said, wryly. "That's what happens when you disappear for seven days without so much as a peep."

"Where the hell have you been, Josh?"

He shook his head. It was no easier to explain now than it had been ten minutes ago and it would be no easier in ten minutes, ten days, or even ten years' time for that matter. There were no words that wouldn't sound like lies. "I don't know," he said.

Lexy was chalk to his cheese, salt to his pepper, yin to yang, tortoise to hare, and every other diametric and polar opposite. They couldn't have looked more physically different if geneticists had taken random eggs and sperm from donors and fused them in a petri dish. Growing up he'd tormented her mercilessly, claiming that she was variously the window cleaner's daughter, the postman's, the milkman's—while they still had a milkman—and in return she came home from art class one day to present him with a homemade birth certificate that named him heir of some Nigerian prince's millions. Family stuff. Normal. She was a nurse down at St. Thomas's by the river. She'd been on the long-term care ward for five months. She spent most of her nights looking after an old woman who never woke up. He knew everything about her; she knew every-thing about him. But the way she looked at him now it was like she'd never seen him before in her life. That scared him more than anything that had happened since the funeral. This was his baby sister, she *knew* him better than he knew himself.

"We should take this inside," the policeman said, gently easing them in the direction of the door. "Especially if you intend on killing him now he's home safe and sound." He nodded toward twitching curtains across the street. "Fewer witnesses."

Rosie nodded, allowing herself to be led inside. She didn't seem to realize it was a joke.

They'd cleaned up the mess since he was last here. The memory of the woman upstairs going through Boone's things was visceral; it gripped him, clenched his gut and twisted. He winced, looking in-stinctively toward the stairs like he still expected to see her waiting at the top.

The landing was empty.

There was no Myrna Shepherd looking down at him. Still, he shiv-ered at the thought of it.

"I'll make a cup of tea," Rosie said, as though she'd hit up on the last great secret of the universe in a perfect eureka moment. "You like tea, Officer Gennaro?"

"That'd be great," the policeman said. There was a look that passed between the policeman and his sister. It was there and then it was gone, but it had definitely been there. They weren't strangers. "We'll go sit down in the front room while you put a brew on."

She came back through a few minutes later balancing a tray loaded with the finest china and a pot of tea stewing. She took a seat opposite them. No one really seemed to know what to say now they were all face-to-face with no pretend errands to run. There was one question they obviously wanted to ask.

Lexy broke the silence, "Where have you been?" She leaned forward, her fringe falling over her face.

Josh looked at her, and for just a moment wished they shared some sort of telepathic bond so she could see it, so that he could make her understand. But he knew she'd never believe him, so he said, "I don't know," and offered a shrug.

"What do you mean you don't *know*?" Lexy pressed. His sister never had been one for letting go of a bone once she'd got her teeth into it. "Are you seriously going to pretend you've got amnesia? That you just woke up now and everything that happened since Granddad's funeral is just a bloody blur?"

"No. Not that." Josh said, helplessly.

"Then what? Why the hell didn't you just *ring*? Do you know what we've been going through here? We thought you were dead, Josh. We thought you were *dead*. So the least you can do is tell us where the fuck you *were*."

But he couldn't.

No matter what he owed them, no matter what they'd been through, he couldn't tell them where he'd been because it was one thing to think something, to come around to accepting it, no matter how impossible, even embrace it, but it quite another to *share* it with someone you loved when you knew they'd think you were mad for believing it.

He reached across and took his mum's hand, ignoring Lexy for a moment. The room reduced to two people. "I'm sorry, Mum," Josh said, and meant it. He'd never meant anything more in his life. She looked up at him with so much sadness in her eyes he thought his heart might just break beneath the burden of it. He squeezed her hand. He knew it wasn't just about him; it was about Boone and about his father and her own father. All of the men in her life, the ones she gave her heart to, always left her. He was her last man, and she'd thought she'd lost him just like she'd lost his dad when he'd gone out to buy that packet of cigarettes.

Life had a cruel sense of humor sometimes.

He didn't know what to say to make that better.

"They fired you, you know? Mike Nicholson called from the office. He was very polite about it, but said they couldn't keep your job open indefinitely. The second time he called he was less polite, concerned, I think, that you might never come home, but he said they had to fill your post. Still, you're home now, that's all that counts."

"Why don't you talk us through it, Josh," Julie Gennaro said, intruding gently on the moment. "Everything you can remember from the funeral onward. This is a safe place; no one is going to judge you. You never know, it might help saying stuff aloud."

"I doubt it," Josh said, letting go of his mum's hand to reach for one of the cups. He didn't drink from it. He cradled it in both hands. He couldn't look his mum in the eye as he explained what had happened after Boone's funeral, how he'd slipped out the back and met his "cousin" in the yard behind the Scala, how Lockwood had asked if Boone had left him anything in his will, and how he'd returned home to find some woman in the process of robbing the place. He didn't say she looked like a long-dead Hollywood icon. Or that she glowed blue. There were some things that didn't need sharing.

"And you think Gideon Lockwood was behind the break-in?" the policeman asked, pushing him toward the truth. "You think that he sent the woman to find whatever he suspected your grandfather left you?"

"Seth," Josh corrected him without thinking. "And, yes, that's exactly what I think."

"So, do you mind if I ask what your grandfather left you?"

"Nothing," Josh said, a little too quickly.

Julie Gennaro's lip twitched—maybe it was his bullshit detector pinging? Josh figured cops had fairly finely tuned BS detectors. People lied to them all the time, maybe not big fat lies; just little ones to make them look better or make sure they took themselves out of the frame. "That's a lot of trouble to go to for nothing, if you don't mind me saying, Josh."

"We haven't had the will reading yet," Rosie said, supporting her son. "We were supposed to do it on Monday, but with Josh gone . . ." She didn't finish the thought.

"Ah, so Lockwood might not actually be wrong then? There could be something? Any idea what it might be that Lockwood thinks it might be?"

"I wouldn't know," Josh said, finding it a little easier to lie now that his mother had given him a way to wriggle around the truth.

"Okay," Gennaro seemed to accept his denial at face value. "So what happened next?"

"You went after him, didn't you?" Lexy blurted the words out. "Oh, you fucking *idiot*. You promised me you weren't going to do anything stupid . . . but you went after Lockwood, didn't you?" Lexy pushed herself up out of her chair. She didn't know what to do with herself. She couldn't storm out, but she couldn't sit still, either, so she stood there, fists clenching and unclenching impotently. "What did you do?" What she really meant was what kind of trouble are you really in?

He could see the cogs clicking into place and 2 and 2 making about 6,027 as she leaped to all sorts of worst-case conclusions. He could guess what they were: He'd gone after Lockwood; lost, badly; and they'd taken him prisoner. That was the only way she could rationalize him not calling, not letting them know he was alive—because he couldn't.

That changed the way she looked at him.

She stared at Josh, looking for signs of it on his body; there had to be bruises, cuts, something, some marks to prove he wasn't just a fucking selfish bastard for making them suffer.

Josh held out his hands for her to see. "I'm all right," he promised, knowing she didn't believe him. "Really."

"Did they hurt you?" That was his mother's next question.

"No. I'm fine."

"Do you know where they held you?" That was the policeman.

"They—" he started to say didn't, but knowing that by denying that he'd been held captive he'd have to find another excuse for his disappearance, stopped himself. "Isn't it enough that I'm back? I'm not hurt. I'm safe."

"Obviously that's between you guys," Julie said. "If you tell me there's no crime here, there's really not a lot I can do apart from enjoy this touching family moment, but I'd advise you strongly to tell the truth." Josh shrugged. "Okay, well, do me a favor, walk me back to the car, will you? If that's okay with you, Mrs. Raines?"

Rosie nodded.

They left the house together. Outside Julie said, "Okay, mate, you're not a bad liar, I'll give you that, but you're far from a good one. What is Lockwood after and don't think about lying to me again. There's just me and you here. You don't have to worry about protecting your mother from the truth. I don't care what you're involved in, but I want to know what happened to you? What's going on here? You know a lot more than you're letting on."

"I really don't know if I can explain it."

"Try."

"You won't believe me."

"Again, try me. I've seen some shit over the last couple of hours. You never know, I might wind up being the friend you need."

Josh shrugged. "Okay, but it's better that I show you."

"Then maybe you want to let your mum know we're taking a little trip. Wouldn't want her thinking you'd disappeared again, would we?"

29

A PROBLEM SHARED OR TWO

LIVES RUINED

Josh took Julie to the flat in Rotherhithe.

"You wanted to know what Boone left me. This is it in all of its glory."

"This place?" the policemen asked, looking up at the dark windows. "Nice. Must be good to have rich relatives."

"You say that now, but you might not think so in a minute," Josh opened the door. "Welcome to the obsessive world of the Raines family, Constable Gennaro." Josh led him upstairs. "You might want to brace yourself; you're about to enter a whole lot of crazy."

Julie nodded, it all beginning to come clear. "So this is where you got to for a week? Some sort of love nest you didn't want to tell your mother about? No telephone I take it?"

"Ah, well . . . not quite . . . I think it's best if I just open the door and let you see for yourself," and so saying, Josh opened the lounge door and stepped aside to let the policeman enter the room.

There was a momentary silence followed by a slow whistle, which in turn was followed by, "Holy shit . . . you weren't kidding. What *is* this place?"

"My inheritance," Josh said. "This little lot is what Boone left me."

Julie turned and turned about, trying to take it all in, just as Josh had the first time he'd walked into the room. The sheer amount of articles and photographs Boone and Isaiah had gathered about Eleanor's disappearance and events surrounding it was overwhelming. But that was nothing compared to the web of threads linking them all. Crazy was the only rational word for it. The policeman walked across to the nearest wall, ducking under the colored yarns, to read some of the vast wealth of information plastered up there. "You think this is what Lockwood wants? Some old newspaper articles?"

"It's not what they are," Josh said, "it's what they're about. Read them." Josh waited for Julie to skim a few and get the gist of the crime the room was dedicated to before taking him next door. He was putting his trust in the policeman, with no real reason to think he was worthy of it, or that he'd keep it save for the fact he'd obviously seen the Comedians, even if he didn't understand what it was he'd seen.

"An actress disappeared nearly a hundred years ago? Seriously? This is the big mystery that kept you away for a week?" He shook his head like he couldn't quite believe the answer was something so *understandable* after all of the intimations he'd have to see it to believe it.

"There's stuff in here he'd rather no one knew," Josh said, looking toward the wall obsessed with Damiola's antics.

"Look, even if his grandfather was complicit in the kidnapping, it's water under the bridge now. We're talking about a century. Crimes don't last that long, no matter how shocking they are at the time. Unless we're talking something like Jack the Ripper, no one's interested, and even then it's purely academic. You need to face it, Josh, they got away with it. And believe me, that family have gotten away with a lot worse over the last twenty years."

"They haven't gotten away with it."

Julie looked at him, then he seemed to realize why Josh hadn't gone home and that it had nothing to do with love nests or lost weekends with lovers hiding away from the world. "You disappeared down a rabbit hole chasing this lot, didn't you? Jesus, mate, that's insane. Let it go."

"There's something I need to show you if you're going to understand, but you might not want to see it."

"There you go again, all vague and mysterious. Look, you need to know this: I'm a cop in London. The Rothery's part of my beat. I see the worst humanity has to offer every single day, without fail. And let's not forget what happened today. I might not have killed two men, but I hit them trying to get out of *your* way. I'm pretty sure there's very little you could say that will shock me."

"No matter what had happened out there, you wouldn't have killed two *men*," Josh said, but didn't elaborate. "And honestly, no matter what you think, you haven't seen it all. We can remedy that, though. Come with me."

They went through to the projection room, where Josh fed the film back into the reel while Julie worked his way around the walls, looking at Eleanor and Eleanor and Eleanor. "She was really something," he said after a while.

"That she is."

Josh powered up the projector and set the lost Hitchcock playing once more. If the policeman noticed the switch in tense from past to present he didn't say anything. "This was going to be her breakthrough. If she hadn't disappeared, she'd have been our Louise Brooks, our Garbo," and naming film stars he was immediately reminded of the woman riffling through Boone's room, Myrna Shepherd. The film flickered, the first few seconds blurry before it settled down. Josh added his own narration. "Hitchcock began shooting on his first flim, *Number 13*, in the early 1920s. It's a lost film. No one's seen it in years. The common belief is that the film itself was melted down for its chemical content; that being more valuable than what was on it. What you're watching is a little piece of cinematic history."

"Must be worth a pretty penny," Julie said, as though he'd just found Lockwood's motivation in all of this.

"I can't even begin to imagine what it's worth," Josh agreed. "A lot. It's Hitchcock, but not just that—it's the first-ever Hitchcock, abandoned because he ran out of money."

"So the way you're explaining this, maybe this whole mess isn't as mysterious as you think? Most things come down to money in the end, even with a nasty piece of work like Lockwood."

"This isn't about money. It never was. It's all about the girl. Eleanor Raines."

"Ah, the other classic motive. Sex and money; I'd be out of a job without those twin vices."

"I don't want to tell you anything about the film itself," Josh said. "I don't want to influence you in any way. I just want you to watch. No preconceptions. No prejudices."

"I can do that."

For the best part of half an hour the pair of them stood spellbound as the young director worked his magic, the actors and actresses telling their silent story of homelessness and murder.

Julie recognized the pub across the street, and realized the flat was in the middle of the set. He remarked as much. Josh nodded.

It wasn't much, but he was glad the detective had caught the geographic significance of Boone's secret place. Maybe he'd see the rest without prodding.

When they came to those thirty seconds near the end when Seth Lockwood drifted across the background of the shot, then turned to stare at the camera, out of the screen and straight at them Julie Gennaro pointed. "That's him . . . isn't it? The guy from the café?" He shook his head, doubting himself. "That's Lockwood."

"That's Seth Lockwood," Josh agreed. "I'm sure of it."

"This is what you wanted me to see?"

Josh nodded. "This is part of what I wanted you to see. Seth Lockwood in flesh, side by side with Eleanor Raines days before she disappeared."

"Well, there's no doubt it offers a compelling narrative in terms of means, motive, and opportunity, but I hate to break it to you, it's impossible. It can't be the same guy that was threatening you earlier, not if the film was shot almost one hundred years ago." Josh could see him struggling to make it fit. It didn't; that was the problem. The pieces didn't fit into any rational, mundane picture. "It's been tampered with, hasn't it? Edited. He's been added to the shot somehow. It's good. Clever. You almost had me. But he can't be there and here at the same time, not looking the *same*. It's not possible."

"And yet he's right there, believe me."

"Did you do it? Is this your handiwork?" And then, as the images flickered on unsteadily Julie saw a second familiar face projected against the wall and did a wild double take, shaking his head. "You? Okay, what the fuck's going on here? This whole thing stinks. You're playing me for a fool. All this you-won't-believe-your-eyes shit. Okay, well played. You almost had me, but I'm out of here."

"That's not me," Josh said. "That's my great-grandfather, Isaiah."

Julie thought about it for a moment. "Fine. Then applying the same logic, that's not Lockwood. If it can happen once, it can happen twice. That's *his* great-grandfather and your great-grandfather and by some freak of genetics you both look just like dead men. That I *can* believe. Just about. At least it's more believable than the alternative."

"It would be easier if that was true, but . . . " Josh shrugged.

"But. But, but *fucking* but . . ."

That was a big word.

But.

"I need to tell you something."

"That sounds eerily like a confession's coming?" Julie said.

"No. But if you don't believe what you've seen so far, there's no way you're going to believe the rest of what I've got to say."

"Frankly, you're right, I don't believe you. There's a scam here, I just don't know what it is, and I don't appreciate you taking the piss like this. I've got better things to do with my life than waste it being dicked by a bunch of petty criminals."

"There's no scam. But I don't know how to convince you other than to *show* you."

"Fine. Show me."

He spread his arms wide. He'd hoped the projection room would sell it, but he had other alternatives now, thanks to Damiola. Thirteen of them burned on the floor in the other room: the locations of the anchors. With Damiola's glass he would be able to peel back the layers of illusion hiding them and show the policeman. That would change the way he looked at the world. "Okay, come with me." He led Julie back through to the other room and knelt down, placing his hand on one of the scorch marks burned into the floorboard. It was where he'd found

Damiola's workshop and bludgeoned his way through into Glass Town. "These marks aren't random. They're important. It's a map."

"I can see that. London. But it's not right."

"It is. I'll show you. But you need to understand what's at risk. He can't know we're sniffing around. If he finds out . . . I don't want to think about what he'll do to Eleanor."

"By him you mean Lockwood?"

Josh nodded. "She made me promise. If he knows there's a way in, he'll kill her. Or us. Or both. Seth is a monster. I don't doubt that for a second. I've already seen some of what he's capable of. That thing you hit—"

"The men?"

"They weren't men," Josh said. "Not like you and me."

"Look, Josh, you seem like a decent guy, but I'll be honest with you, I don't believe a word that's coming out of your mouth. Did Taff put you up to this?"

30

THE TALE OF ONE BENT BASTARD

Taff Carter was in paradise.

Myrna Shepherd knelt between his legs, taking him into her mouth again.

There was more pleasure than he'd ever imagined in dying; that was the lesson she was teaching him. She was the most exquisite creature he'd ever encountered, which made it a lesson he was happy to learn, welcoming the fact that he grew weaker by the ejaculation, diminished, so that she might be sustained.

She looked up at him.

Her eyes were *alive*. That was his gift to her.

"Perhaps it's better if I live in your heart, where the world can't see me. If I'm dead, there will be no stain on our love."

This isn't love, he thought in some disconnected part of his mind, but didn't fight her. In a week he had gone from being an overweight slob of a man to the wretched wreck of skin and bone, stripped of fat, muscle degenerated to the point of emaciation, slouched on the couch in his dark lounge, and still she fed on him, even though there was nothing left to give. There was an unquenchable emptiness to the woman between his legs. That hollowness was in part what made her so compelling. That and her face; her beautiful, beautiful face.

This succubus was so much more than perfection; she was a distillation of beauty, a reduction of the divine. He couldn't imagine his life without her now, even if it meant sacrificing what little remained of it to feed her and keep her with him. *That,* he thought, *is a death worth dying.*

A song played on the stereo. He used to know what it was called. It had been one of his favorites before she came into his life. Saxophone. That was the instrument. Such a sad sound. Like so much else in the last week, the name of it had slipped away from him.

Myrna Shepherd's hand still cupped him. She worked him, even as it began to go flaccid. Each gesture was harsher than it was tender.

"I can't," he said, meaning he was spent, exhausted no matter that his body was trying to rise to the occasion, meaning he needed to rest, gather himself, but she was *hungry.* His traitorous body couldn't help but respond as she refused to let him shrivel.

Holding eye contact, staring deep into him, she took him all the way in to the back of her throat. Taff buried his fingers in the terry cloth of his dressing gown as she used her tongue to draw a hitching breath from his lips and with the glint of mischief in her eyes, she milked him until he stiffened beyond anything comfortable or pleasurable.

"Please." He said. "No." He said. "Please." He said. "Shit." He gasped. "Fuck." He screamed. And every muscle in his body tensed.

"My beautiful boy," she sighed. "We only live this life once, and if we are honest, once is enough."

He couldn't argue with her. He couldn't think beyond the need for this to be *over.*

Once, with her in his life, was more than enough for him even if it wasn't for her.

His orgasm when it came was furious. There was blood in the seed as it seeped out of him.

Myrna Shepherd wiped her mouth and stood, sated.

For now.

She still wore the white dress she'd arrived at his door in. During all their time together, each time they'd fucked, he'd not once seen her naked. It was almost as though she and the white dress were one, the fabric fused inextricably onto her torso while its folds billowed around her legs. But she was happy enough to raise her skirts for him.

Shepherd swirled her skirts as she walked away, kicking up her heel; after what had just passed between them it was a curiously innocent gesture, playful, but then it was impossible to separate what was genuine and what was an act with the woman. Or maybe it was all theater? That didn't mean he didn't appreciate her playing the ingenue, it was just hard to reconcile the two images of her, Madonna and Whore. Gideon Lockwood and his new boy had sent her to him, a "gift" to buy his loyalty for a few more years to come. It had felt like a bargain at the time, but what had Lockwood said, "Remember, you asked for it." Or something like that. Men like Taff Carter didn't get to fuck women like her. That was one of the fundamental laws of nature. No matter how much he wanted to deny it, pretend he was doing something noble or that he had no choice in the matter, the truth was he was a bent bastard, just like Lockwood had mocked.

Taff didn't care anymore. He was too exhausted to move. He just sat on the settee, dressing gown open beneath him, and stared down the bones of his rib cage to his cock where it stuck uselessly against his thigh. The blood scared him.

He didn't even move to cover himself when the doorbell rang, or a few seconds later when the door opened. He just reached down to cup his balls and cover his modesty.

Seth Lockwood strolled into the room all unpleasant smiles.

"Well if it isn't my little pet pig. *Oink-oink.* I would ask how you're enjoying my little gift, but I can see the answer to that a little too clearly for my liking. Do you think you could stop playing with yourself for a minute?" Taff didn't move. Seth waited. Taff looked up at him, eyes all but useless after the damage they'd taken from the succubus's thumbs, his brain running slow. "That means take your fucking hand away from your miserable little cock while I'm talking to you, you perverted little bell sniff."

Taff did as he was told.

"And cover yourself up. I really don't want to see the shit stains on your dressing gown, thank you very much."

He pulled the trailing edge of the terry cloth up over his groin, but didn't belt it.

"I'm very disappointed in you, Huw," the gangster said. "I thought we had a deal. Didn't we have a deal? I give you your lovely fuck toy, and in return you give me what I want? Wasn't that the deal?"

Taff nodded.

"So where's my glass? I don't see it. Unless you've got it shoved up your rectal passage? Have you got it shoved up there?"

Taff shook his head.

"I didn't think so. So, like I said, I'm very disappointed in you. Do you know what I do to people who disappoint me?"

"Hurt them," the Welshman said.

"Very good, Huw. I hurt them. So do you know what I'm going to do to you?"

"Hurt me."

"You're on fire. You're on fucking *fire*. Or you will be, at any rate," and so saying, Seth took a silver hip flask from his back pocket, unscrewed the cap, and splashed the contents all over the man and the couch in front of him as though he was dousing them in holy water. Only it wasn't holy water and it wasn't whiskey, either. The reek of petrol filled the cramped room.

Seth took a cigarette packet and lighter from his pocket.

"But you know what? There's been enough dying today already. I'm feeling forgiving. I can understand why you've been distracted. She really is something, a gift from the gods, and a miserable shit like you doesn't come into the orbit of such a heavenly creature often, I get it." He put a cigarette between his lips, lit it and inhaled, drawing the smoke into his lungs. He exhaled, letting the curls of smoke raft up in front of his face. "I do. Honestly. But there's a difference between my understanding it and my thinking it's okay." Seth tapped the ash off the cigarette tip. "From where I'm standing, you still owe me, Huw, and it's spoiling my good mood."

"What do you want?"

"Ah, good question. I've always liked a man who gets straight to the point rather than dicking about. Honestly, I want to watch you burn, but I can wait to have my fun. In the meantime I can use you. Your partner is getting in to be a real pain in the arse. You'd know what that's like," Seth said, lips curling into a sneer. "He cost me one of my people today. That's bad enough, but he walked out of there with the Raines kid, which is the last thing I need. I need him taken care of. Call it preemptive problem solving."

"Julie? You want me to kill him?"

"I said nothing of the sort. Jesus," Seth shook his head. "I want to meet him face-to-face. I want to *talk* to him, see if he's as flexible with his morals as you are. After all, once you go up in flames I'm going to need another pet pig to play with, and one thing I've learned is every piggy has his price. Bring him to me, Huw, let's see if we can do some business. If I were you, I'd hope that he's a chip off the little bent bastard block. Otherwise I *will* hurt you. Do we understand each other?"

Taff nodded. "Where should I bring him?"

"You know the old Latimer Road cinema in the Rothery? Bring him along in time for a midnight performance."

"There hasn't been a show there in years."

"Let me worry about that. You just bring the audience along like a good little piggy. The curtain goes up at twelve sharp."

31

DEAD ENDS

Julie was having none of it.

He drove with the window down and the stereo's volume cranked up. It was summer music, vibrant and far too perky for the cool night, just the way he liked it. You could trust music in a way that you couldn't trust people. Certain tunes made you feel good while others brought you down. They were attached to memories, of course, but that didn't change the fact that you knew what you were getting with a song in a way that you didn't with people. It was all about masks with people. They might appear perky and vibrant on the outside, but on the inside be tortured and twisted up.

He trusted Josh Raines about as far as he could throw him.

There was something *off* about the guy. It wasn't just that his story didn't add up. Julie considered himself a pretty decent judge of character; it went with the territory. But it was hard to get a read on Raines. He came across as a good guy and seemed genuinely distraught about the hell he'd put his mother through over the last week, but not enough to actually come clean about what had happened. Sure, there was enough weirdness in that flat of his to last a week if you decided to disappear down that particular rabbit hole, but a century-old crime? An obsession with some long-dead actress? Okay, he could accept it was a bit freaky that Lockwood and Raines *looked* like their counterparts in that long played-out story, but looking like someone wasn't the same as . . . as what? Living a hundred years without aging?

Julie shook his head.

Yeah that was some weird shit.

But that was pretty much par for the course these days.

He was worried about his partner, and with good reason. Taff had been acting way out of character ever since he'd failed to clock off a week ago. Julie had been around to his place a couple of times to check in on him. Taff was never out of his damned dressing gown and insisted on wearing those stupid sunglasses inside like he was some kind of rock star on a weeklong coke binge. He looked bad, and smelled so much worse.

Julie decided to pay him another visit after he'd finished with this wild-goose chase.

Beside him, Josh had a badly drawn map open on his lap and was giving him directions a couple of turns at a time.

The only reason Julie was humoring him was because of the Comedians. What were the odds of two thieves matching the description of Clamp and Crake both robbing The Magic Circle and then being involved in a fatality that signaled the end of Josh's disappearance? Sometimes when something stinks it really is shit and Josh was in it up to his neck.

He'd almost managed to forget about those teeth, but then he'd spent the last hour working pretty hard to convince himself that what he'd witnessed was actually the distortion of impact as his car had plowed into the screaming man, and everything else he'd thought he'd seen had been nothing more than a trick of that weird slow-motion momentum as adrenaline kicked in, everything moving so fast but seeming to go so slowly.

And he almost believed it.

"You'll want the next left," Josh said. "Followed by a sharp right about twenty feet after that, then we should start looking for somewhere to pull up. We'll need to go the rest of the way on foot."

Julie flicked the indicator on, signaling his intent, and edged the squad car over to ride along the white line for a hundred feet, waiting for a break in traffic before he swung across the other lane. Cars lined both sides of the road, constricting it so completely that Julie had to keep glancing toward the wing mirror to be sure it wasn't grating its way down the street one unlucky parked car at a time.

There was no obvious break in the snake of vehicles parked along the curb.

Up ahead he saw a woman emerge from one of those overpriced boutiques balancing what looked like a big cake box on one hand while trying to fumble her keys out of her too-tight jeans pocket. Behind her a couple of guys from a building crew hung off the scaffolding, paying her backside far more attention than the job at hand right up until the moment where half of the roof came roaring down the plastic bins and emptied out into the skip in the street below. They gave each other a rueful smile as if to say the shock was worth it, and judging by the woman's curves Julie was inclined to agree. He couldn't remember the last time he'd seen a woman naked without the filter of a computer screen between them. Weeks had slipped into months and into that weird territory beyond that where it was only natural to worry that sex wasn't actually like riding a bike. "Be a gent," Julie told his passenger. "Hop out and help the lady with her things." He saw Josh's confusion and smiled. "Don't worry, she'll think you're one of the good guys. Goes with the wheels."

Josh did as he was told.

A minute later the woman was pulling out into traffic in a car that must have cost eight times his annual salary and leaving a space for Julie to pull into. He locked the car and joined Josh on the pavement. " 'Onwards, Macduff.' "

Beside him Josh looked left and right, then back over his shoulder, on edge.

"No one's following us," Julie assured him.

"How can you know that?"

"Because this isn't Gotham and the bad guys don't have superpowers. Take me to this irrefutable proof. I want to believe you're not a complete twat, Josh. I want to believe that you wouldn't just fuck with your mum like that and disappear for a week, but I'll be honest, right now I'm finding it hard."

"I'm telling you the truth."

"We'll see."

Julie followed him around another corner, stepping into what seemed at first glance to be a back alley behind the row of designer boutiques, but the street was cobbled. There weren't many cobbled streets left in the city. He could think of a few around Neal's Yard and Covent Garden, pandering to the tourists and that whole Ye Olde World thing they wanted to see, but not around here. That wasn't the only thing that was noticeably different about the street. He looked up at the darkening sky. There was nothing remarkable up there, but the air tasted *thick,* like it was laced with smog or coal dust or Christ alone knew what other pollutant the factories farther along the river were pumping out. The difference in the quality of air between where they'd parked the car and where they stood now was so stark it felt like he'd suddenly developed asthma. "Okay, we're here, what are we looking for?"

"I'll know it when I see it," Josh Raines said, taking a small gold compact from his pocket.

"Trust me, you look beautiful," Julie said.

Josh didn't take the bait. He opened the compact, holding it slightly to one side of his face so that he could see over his own shoulder, then began to slowly turn in a full circle, obviously looking for something and equally obviously not seeing it. Julie watched him turn in five circles, each successive one a little more frantic than the last as he failed to see whatever it was he was looking for.

"Let me guess, it's not there now?"

"I don't understand," Josh Raines said. He'd stopped spinning around, and was walking down the alleyway, using the mirror to guide him instead of just looking where he was going.

"I think I do," Julie said.

"No. It should be here."

"Of course it should."

"Something's wrong." He opened and closed the compact, shaking his head. "It should be here."

"What? What should be here? Where Lockwood held you hostage? Is that what we are talking about?"

"It should be here," Josh said again.

"You've got to help me, Josh. I need to know what you're looking for. Are we looking for a door? Is that it? Maybe you're wrong. Maybe it's the wrong alleyway? These places all look the same. Let me have a look at the map."

"It's pointless," Josh said, handing the paper over.

"Then what am I doing here?" Even so, he looked down at the map, seeing the street where they'd parked the car, and tracing the route they'd taken from there to the mark drawn on the map. They were standing right in the middle of it, whatever it was supposed to be. "What am I looking for?"

Josh held out the compact, offering it to him. "Look in the glass, can you see anything different? Anything wrong. Look at the street."

And just for a moment Julie thought about humoring him.

He raised the compact up to his face, but instead of looking into the glass snapped the lid closed.

"This is ridiculous," Julie said, handing the mirror back. "I don't know what you're trying to prove here, Josh, but I'm done. If you get serious about wanting help against Lockwood, you know where to find me, but until then you're on your own."

He started to walk away.

"Wait!"

Julie looked back over his shoulder. The guy seemed to have shrunk by a foot in the few seconds since he'd turned his back on him. He looked broken. "What for? So you can come up with a better lie? Here's the thing; I'm not interested. Whatever mess you got yourself into with Lockwood, you're on your own. I don't envy you. That family . . ." he shook his head. "They are nasty little fuckers."

"You've got to help me," Josh said.

"No, actually, I don't."

"He'll kill me."

"That may be the first true thing you've said to me all day," Julie Gennaro said, and walked away.

32

HOT LEADS AND LOOK-ALIKES

A few hours later a scattering of pebbles against the glass brought Julie Gennaro to his window.

He hadn't been able to sleep.

He hadn't tried. He'd been thinking about Josh Raines. He'd got under his skin—or at least his predicament had.

He couldn't understand why the guy had been so insistent on showing him stuff if he'd known there was nothing to show. That didn't make sense. He'd obviously expected to find something there, some conclusive proof that would sway Julie to his side, and because of that part of him was inclined to cut the guy some slack. It wasn't hard to see he'd been dragged all the way to hell and back and was still deep in the stress of shock, but he wasn't helping himself. That alleyway had been a dead end. The problem was crazy seldom made sense. And that flat over in Rotherhithe was a whole hoarder's paradise full of crazy.

Even so, Julie couldn't shake the feeling that he'd be reading about Josh propping up some motorway flyover if not tomorrow, then the next day, or the one after that. Like it or not, he felt responsible.

He'd walked away.

He was a cop.

He was supposed to put himself in the line of fire, not deliberately turn his back and walk away from it.

"Protect and Serve," the Americans said. It was the same job over here, even if it didn't have a fancy motto.

He should have forced Josh to tell him the truth. None of this follow-me-you-need-to-see-it-with-your-own-eyes bollocks he'd let the guy babble on about. He'd let himself get carried away in Josh's story and forget the one simple truth: Joshua Raines was in trouble. He should have just sat the guy down somewhere safe and leaned on him until he broke. It wasn't as if he would be a tough nut to crack. He was pretty much begging for help. He wasn't the first person to get in trouble with a bunch of bastards like the Lockwoods and he wouldn't be the last.

Julie couldn't sleep because he knew he'd fucked up, plain and simple. He'd let himself get worked up because he couldn't shake the feeling that he was being screwed with, and everything Josh Raines said and did from that point on just made it worse. Looking at the street through a mirror? That was hardly normal behavior.

Instead of sleeping, he'd written everything he knew about the case on a piece of paper.

Assuming he could find the guy in the morning, Julie decided he'd take him somewhere safe, a non-hostile environment, somewhere out of Lockwood's reach. Then it would be down to Josh to talk. He couldn't force him to tell the truth. Unless, of course, Josh had had a change of heart and was out on the street right now, ready to bare his soul?

As another scattershot of grit hit the glass Julie pushed himself out of bed and went over to the window.

Even through the streaks and smears it was obvious it wasn't Josh Raines down there.

Taff stood in the street grinning up at him like some bedraggled Romeo. His usually unruly hair was matted flat to his scalp and his clothes hung on him, two sizes too big for his bones, like rags on a skeleton. He was still wearing those bloody sunglasses.

Julie wrestled with the latch on the sash window. There was a trick to opening it. The window latch had been painted shut once upon a time, though most of the gloss had been picked away over the intervening years. The wood around it was a honeycomb of woodworm that threatened to crumble as soon as any weight was applied to it. He worked the window up inch by inch, then leaned out to shout down, becoming Juliet to Taff's rain-soaked Romeo. "Why didn't you ring the bell?" *Hardly, hark, what light from yonder window breaks?* he thought.

"Chop-chop, Julie, places to go, people to be," his partner called up.

The change in him over the last week was harrowing. Taff was dying. That was the only logical conclusion he could make looking down at his partner. Erratic behavior, rapid and inexplicable weight loss, his hair unkempt and thinning, deep dark bags under his eyes—he was a shadow of the man he used to be. But that it had all happened to him in a week, that his body had been so utterly ravaged in such a short time that was something else. That was shocking. Even cancer didn't devastate a man so absolutely, so rapidly.

"What are you going on about?"

"Got a meeting. Need you to be on your best behavior, so, in the immortal words of *The Price is Right*, Julie Gennaro, '*Come on down,*' pretty boy. More haste less speed and all that. Don't want to be late."

Julie crumpled the piece of paper he had in his hand and tossed it at the bin in the corner. There was one word written on it. It was all he'd managed in an hour of thinking:

Lockwood.

He kept coming up against the name; here a Lockwood, there a Lockwood, everywhere a fucking Lockwood. That family was haunting Julie. Their influence on the Rothery was pernicious, and the more he dug into the goings-on of the criminal underworld, the more he began to grasp just how much of a cancer they had always been in the body of London. There was an entire wall in Joshua Raines's flat given over to the crimes of the Lockwoods dating back a hundred years. They were shockingly varied in scope and brutality. It wasn't a stretch to see how Joshua Raines had demonized them, reframing Gideon and Seth Lockwood as bogeymen, but in reality all they were was a pair of old-time Bad Boys cut from the same slab of unpleasantness as the Krays and their fellow hoodlums.

But Josh's outlandish claims that the old patriarch, Seth, who had kidnapped some silent movie star over ninety years ago, was the same new Lockwood kid that had turned up in the Rothery recently? Well that wasn't helping his case, that's for sure. Yes, there was a more-than-passing similarity between the man in the old movie and the new kid on the block—assuming the footage hadn't been doctored—but that was genetics, wasn't it? There were only so many variations of the same DNA-rendered face that were possible before the family tree started to repeat itself.

Everything comes back to the Lockwoods, he thought as he grabbed the battered leather jacket off the back of the chair and headed down to the street.

It wasn't a comforting thought.

They were the kind of people you just didn't want to get mixed up with, not if you valued the simple things like two testicles and them both being attached, not doing a bloody yo-yo impression.

He slammed the door behind him and half-ran down the narrow stairs. "What's up?"

"Long story, Julie," Taff held the car door open. "You're driving. Get in and I'll tell you all about it on the way."

There was someone sitting in the back, a woman. She had her head down and a scarf wrapped around the lower part of her face so all he could see were her eyes.

He thought about not getting in, but Taff put a bony hand on his shoulder and eased him down, just as he would shoehorn a suspect into the back seat of the squad car. Taff closed the door and came around to his side. He moved awkwardly, running his hand across the rooftop as he went around to the passenger seat.

Julie turned in his seat to introduce himself. "Hi."

She didn't answer him.

He shrugged and turned back to face-front, but kept on watching her through the driver's mirror. She met his gaze with amazing eyes, the pair of them sharing a moment of disturbing intimacy through the backward land of the glass. In that moment all he could think of was doing unspeakable things to the woman—or more accurately having her do them to him. He shivered, the chill running down every bone in the ladder of his spine. There was something very familiar about the small part of her face he could see. She seemed to be saying: *This is me, all of me, I see you.* And all he could think, lost in her eyes, was that he wanted her to consume him. She was such a beautiful woman, but there was so much sadness in her eyes.

"Fire her up, buddy boy," Taff said, slapping his thigh and breaking the moment.

Turning the ignition, the radio crackled with some long-lost minute of the '80s, though it was only half-tuned into the station.

Julie didn't indicate as he pulled out into traffic.

"Okay what's the big secret?"

"It's a surprise."

"Where are we going?"

"Work. Hot lead. Big case. Gonna crack it wide open. You'll see. They'll pin a medal on us for this one, *mon ami.*"

"Pretty hard for me to drive somewhere when I don't know where we're going."

"You can find your way, I believe in you, but you only have so long," the woman said from the back seat. There was a weird distorted quality about her voice, like it was crackling over a distant sound system rather than coming out of her mouth. He wasn't sure how he was supposed to respond to that. *"Before your life disappears in this ugly country."* There was something familiar about that. It was such an odd thing to say, but he was sure it wasn't the first time he was hearing it.

"In other words: 'Onwards, Macduff,'" Taff offered a translation, and Julie realized where he'd picked up that particular mangling of the Bard.

They drew level with a silver Volvo at the first set of lights.

"Does this have something to do with where you've been all week?" Julie asked.

Taff seemed to think about it for a moment, inclining his head slightly to the left, then the right before he offered his partner a wry grin, "It's got *everything* to do with where I've been, boyo," which was no help at all. "Faster. Time's a-wasting."

His hand fluttered up toward his glasses.

The woman in the back seat hissed and his fingers fell away.

Julie peeled away from the junction, leaving the silver Volvo standing at the lights. After a few minutes Taff reached out and grabbed the wheel, pulling down hard on it and taking the car off the road. The front wheels hit the curb, mounting the pavement as the back end slewed and the car slid sideways; they nearly hit an elderly homeless woman struggling with a shopping trolley filled to overflowing with bulging grocery bags filled with her pathetic life as she shuffled along the road. She wore slippers on her feet and her stay-ups were around her ankles.

She stared daggers at them as they raced away, shaking her fist uselessly at their back window.

"Jesus, Taff, what the *fuck* do you think you're doing? Are you trying to get us all killed?"

Taff just chuckled and shrugged. "Missed the turn."

"Just let me drive the damn car. Where are we going?"

"Take us over the water."

Shop façades blurred into one, as though the stores themselves were offering cheap clothes, vegetables, curries, and new homes all under one roof.

Five minutes later he knew where they were going; there was only one place they *could* be going: the Rothery.

The woman in the back seat didn't speak again the rest of the journey, but she did reach out at one point to rest a hand on Taff's shoulder, although through the mirror it seemed as though her hand rested an inch *inside* it, burrowing down into the muscle and bone, not on it.

Julie noticed that weird blue luminescence again.

He'd assumed it was down to late-night streetlights washing back into the car, but it wasn't, it came from the woman. He didn't know how she did it; makeup maybe? Some sort of pigment in the powder? And in that moment, he knew exactly where he'd seen her before; Joshua Raines's house, the night they were called out to respond to the break-in. He didn't like it. He didn't like it one little bit. He looked at Taff. What had his partner got himself mixed up in?

Once they were inside the labyrinth of the estate itself it was a little more difficult to guess what their final destination would be, but Taff talked him through it turn by turn until they pulled up outside the boarded-up front of the old Latimer Road cinema. There was another car parked across the street, by the back of the Scala, but otherwise the street was deserted.

It was like stepping back in time.

The billboard still advertised the last matinee performance, a triple bill, *The Punishing Kiss, The Devil's Flesh,* and *Wallflower Girl.* There was nothing particularly remarkable about that, apart from the fact that it had survived years of exposure to the elements and aerosol cans of the Rothery unscathed, but right there next to the devil, right there delivering the killer kiss, right there with her anything-but-platonic eyes, was the woman in the back seat. The eyes were unmistakable, as now he saw it in its natural habitat up on the billboard, was her face.

Myrna Shepherd.

He turned to look at her, and then looked back at the poster, then back at her again. It was her. Somehow. And she'd been at Josh Raines's place the night he disappeared. Forget Taff; what the fuck was *he* getting involved in here? Dead movie stars in the back seats of police cars? Old-school criminals from those brutal, postwar days back and giving it large around their old stomping grounds? Josh Raines's obsession with the coldest case in town was beginning to make sense, and that was maybe the most unnerving part in all of this. That lost Hitchcock film and the madness of Raines's flat in Rotherhithe didn't seem so outrageous. He felt like he was teetering on the edge of a deep dark hole. It was ridiculous; all of it. Ridiculous. She had to be some sort of lookalike, one of those paid Kissogram girls or something, someone who made her money off her looks. She *couldn't* be the same woman from the posters in front of him. Forget Occam's razor, she just couldn't be.

Julie took a step back toward the street—away from the car, away from the cinema, away most importantly from the woman and his partner.

Taff leaned on the woman in white as he clambered out of the car. Julie refused to think of her as Myrna Shepherd. She was just the woman. She didn't have a name. His partner moved uncertainly despite the easy smile on his hollow face. "Inside we go, don't want to keep him waiting." The woman helped Taff up the five steps to the old cinema's glass doors. The concrete was cracked, the doors blacked out.

Taff reached out and pushed against the door, and against all the odds it opened.

There was no light inside. Julie followed him inside. As he ventured into the old foyer, he tasted the must of fifteen airless years in the back of his throat.

With every step farther into the old cinema, Taff seemed a little weaker than the last, the simple act of walking exhausting him.

"What's wrong with you, mate?"

"Nothing. Life is good, Julie. You worry too much."

"Maybe. Maybe not. What are we doing here?"

"God, you're full of fucking questions today, aren't you? It's a bust, Julie. I told you. A deal going down. We're about to do our job. We're the good guys, Julie. We're on the side of the angels. I've been watching this gang for a while. Got a tip it was happening today, and didn't want to leave you out of the glory, partner. We're a team. One for all and all for one."

Julie Gennaro wasn't buying it. He didn't need a sixth sense to know this didn't feel right. "We should call for backup."

Taff pushed the sunglasses back onto the bridge of his nose.

He pointed toward a door marked *SCREEN ONE*. The sign above it was lit, whereas the sign above the door to *SCREEN TWO* wasn't. "We're gonna make the front pages with this one, boyo."

Julie remained unconvinced, but what could he do?

He followed Taff and the woman into the dark theater.

33

THE LAST PICTURE SHOW

The inside of the old Latimer Road cinema stank of stale air and forgotten dreams. It wasn't difficult to imagine what the place used to be: while the concession stands were gone, the glass cases were preserved like museum exhibits, thick with a patina of dust, still displaying their stickers offering popcorn and Pepsi at what now looked like bargain prices. There were posters for films Julie could barely remember promising they were coming soon. Great swathes of the old red carpet were sodden underfoot from cracks in the glass skylights. Looking up, Julie saw several birds nesting inside the rafters.

He heard a ruffle of sound off in the distance. Bird wings.

"I don't like this, Taff."

"*Shhhhh.* We don't want to show our hand too early, boyo. Let's get a bit closer to the action before we announce ourselves, shall we?" But for all the reasonableness of his words, Taff made no effort to keep his voice down. His words echoed through the foyer of the old cinema. "Screen One. That's where the magic's happening," he said, allowing the silent Myrna Shepherd look-alike to lead him by the arm. Julie was struck yet again by his reliance upon the woman and just how awkwardly he actually moved, but he followed his friend.

Where the red carpet wasn't wet it was worn threadbare by the scuffing of feet and ground-in popcorn.

The woman seemed to be coming animated—*alive*—the closer they got to the double doors at the end of the corridor. A cardboard cutout of a B-movie action hero waited where the usher would have stood once upon a time collecting tickets.

He heard noises coming from behind the doors.

Voices.

But they were far too loud for it to be normal people talking, unless their conversation was being broadcast across the loudspeaker system.

A chink of bluish light seeped through the crack between the double doors cutting a vertical slash through the darkness ahead of them. Taff pushed his way through, the Shepherd look-alike one step behind him, steering him forward with her hand on his shoulder.

Julie followed them, the big doors swinging closed behind the three of them as they stepped into the theater.

He could just about make out the tiers of old red-velvet chairs curving around the room. There were twenty rows and more down to the big screen where a black-and-white film was playing.

He recognized the scene from outside The Peabody building where Eleanor Raines and Claire Greet shared the screen for a few seconds. Magnified a dozen times to fill the huge screen Eleanor's beauty was even more obvious than it had been in all of those publicity stills back at the flat.

Number 13.

It was proving to be remarkably popular considering it was supposed to be lost.

Huge crystal chandeliers dominated the ceiling, their lights dimmed for the feature presentation.

Gideon Lockwood sat in a wheelchair on the dais before the screen, and behind him, Seth, stood with both hands on the old man's shoulders. The constantly moving light of the film played with their features like putty, remolding them over and over again. The light lent his skin a peculiar oleaginous texture.

"Ah, Huw, so glad you could join us," Seth called, his voice carrying up to them easily. "And good of you to bring Mr. Gennaro with you. Julius," he said amiably, "I've been looking forward to meeting you."

"I can't say the same," Julie said, trying to work out what—beyond the fact that Taff appeared to have delivered him to the gangster—was happening.

"Such hostility. I was rather hoping we could be friends."

"I've got enough friends," Julie said.

"One can never have enough friends in this life, Mr. Gennaro."

"Are you making me an offer I can't refuse?" he turned to leave, but found the woman blocking the door. She lit the entire auditorium far more effectively than the backlight of the scene on the screen. There was no getting away from the fact that the luminescence came from *within* her. It wasn't makeup or pigment or anything applied to her skin. There was a shoal of light swimming around behind her eyes.

"Please, do me the courtesy of listening. And if you still feel the way you do, you're free to go. You have my word."

"Listen to him, Julie. It's not what you think. It's worth hearing him out. He's special."

"He's not fucking *special,* he's a crook, Taff. Remember what they are? They're the people we're supposed to protect everyone from."

"Please?" Seth said again, still smiling amiably. "I'm not like Gideon here. I'm not trying to take over the city and have no interest in setting your feet in concrete and dropping you off the Embankment."

"The times they are a-changing, is that the lie you're peddling?"

Seth nodded. "Well, the only way you'll find out is to listen to me." He motioned toward the front row of velvet seats directly under the big screen. Julie was sorely tempted to just push past the woman and go, but for the fact that Seth was screening that supposedly lost Hitchcock movie and Eleanor Raines was up on the screen again, surely proved at least *some* of Josh's less fabulous claims as far as the criminal went. Besides, he told himself, listening wasn't the same as selling his soul.

He looked at Taff for reassurance, but none was forthcoming.

"Fine," Julie said, walking down the stairs to the front. The old man,

Gideon Lockwood, hadn't said a word. There was obviously a shift in power happening, Gideon handing his corrupt little empire over to the latest bastard spawn of his loins. "Okay, I'm all ears," he said, taking a chair.

"When you have a meeting like this I think it's important to know what you want out of it before you say a word, that way, when tempers fray you've just got to think: 'What's my motivation here? What do I want? What do I stand to gain? What could I lose?' Of course, that's difficult from your side, as you had no idea this was going to happen, but from my side, well, I'll admit I've got a very clear endgame in mind. We have a situation developing, Julie—can I call you Julie?" Julie didn't answer him, so Seth took his silence as tacit acceptance and carried on, "Huw speaks *very* highly of you, Julie, and as you can see, Huw and I have a rather special relationship—"

"You mean you bought him."

"I appreciate a man who speaks his mind. Yes, my family have paid good hard cash for young Huw's loyalty over the years. It was a smart investment for people in our line of work. With someone like Huw, you're buying a bit of insurance. But as you say, things are changing. For one, I don't intend to run the family the way old Gideon here has," he dug his fingers deep into the old man's shoulders. That was when Julie noticed his hands; they weren't the smooth powerfully masculine hands of a young man in his prime. They were liver-spotted and deeply lined. They were the hands of an old man who had spent his entire life grafting with them.

He looked up at Seth's face, trying to decide if it really was the face of the man in the film, or just some familial similarity. He didn't really grasp the complexities of genetics, but it didn't seem unreasonable that men born a century apart could bear more than just passing similarity if they came from the same stock.

Seth put up with his obvious scrutiny with no obvious objection, but Julie noticed the way his fingers dug deeper into Gideon's shoulders. The old man didn't so much as flinch beneath his touch.

"I need someone I can trust," Seth said. "An honest man. Not a bent bastard like Huw here."

"And you want to buy me to be your 'good man'? Seems to be counterintuitive to me."

"Not a good man, Julie, an *honest* one. There's a difference. I've got no interest in whether you're good or not, that's between you and your maker. But to answer your question, it's all about love."

"I'm sorry, despite the nickname, I don't swing that way," Julie said.

"Ha! A wise guy. Excellent. Look," his fingernails dug deeper into Gideon's shoulder. "I know you saw my cousin. I saw your little accident. I have no idea what stories he has filled your head with, but he's not to be trusted that one."

"And you are?"

"I'll never lie to you, Julie, which is more than can be said for a lot of people. Honesty is very important to me. There's a history between our families, the Lockwoods and the Raineses. It goes back to Gideon here's father, and Josh's great-grandfather, Isaiah. See, his real name was Isaiah *Lockwood*. He was Gideon's uncle."

"Okay, so assuming that's not a lie, why should I get involved in a domestic dispute, especially one that goes back a long time?"

"I could say something melodramatic, like lives are at stake."

"You could, but that would make you a liar after all, considering one of the first things out of your mouth after we walked through the door was that you don't intend to run the family business the same way as your grandfather. I have to take you at your word that you're cleaning up your act."

Seth smiled. As smiles went it was about as warm and friendly as a forest fire. "I think I like you, Julie."

"Great," Julie said with little enthusiasm.

"So, to business, besides your honesty, I want your help."

"Of course you do."

"Nothing sinister. Nothing illegal. I want you to watch out for young Josh. He's meddling in things that are going to get him hurt. I don't want that, he's family after all."

"And who's going to hurt him?"

"Who? Why *me*, of course. Just because I don't intend to run the family like Gideon here doesn't mean I'm not capable of some very nasty things. I think you need a little demonstration, it's important that you understand who I am. Huw, take off your glasses, let's get a look at that ugly mug of yours," Seth told the Welshman.

Taff did as he was told, leaving Julie to stare at the mess of scars where his eyes had been.

Julie pushed himself up out of his chair, backing away. "What the *fuck?*" He was shaking. "Taff? *What have they done to you?*"

"I can see," Taff said, his smile utterly beatific. He reached out for Shepherd's hand. "For the first time I can *really* see."

"They've taken your *eyes.*"

"No, she's *opened* them, Julie. That's different." Taff argued.

"Fuck me. Fuck. Oh, fucking no. Just no. Jesus fuck." Julie couldn't seem to wrap his tongue around any other words. He was caught looking from Taff to Seth to the hideously radiant Myrna Shepherd and back again. "So . . . if I don't do what you want, you'll do this to me?"

"I wouldn't dream of it," Seth said reasonably. "Huw *asked* for this. It was his choice. Huw's *happy*—aren't you, Huw?" Seth asked. "He's the hero of his own life. He got the girl. And what a girl she is. Look at her, Julie. Take a *good* look. Wouldn't you say she was worth any price?"

Julie shook his head. He had no words.

Seth smiled that damned smile of his. "Good. I'm glad you're not like your partner. You see, Huw here is a bitter disappointment to me. I gave him everything he asked for. More. And in return I asked for so little. Now I'm out of patience. Myrna, dearest," he turned to the woman who was tenderly stroking the stubble of Taff's gaunt cheek. "You have my permission to *feed.*"

Without a word, the woman in white leaned in to kiss her beau, and as her bluish lips touched his, reached up around the back of his head and tangled her fingers in his hair. It might have been the most tender of kisses, but for the fact that her face bled into his, losing all semblance of individuality as the two became one. Lost in the ecstasy of it, Taff reached up for her hair, trying to reciprocate even as she sucked the life out of him.

34

LOVE BITES

It began with a twitch. The twitch grew into a tremor. The tremor in turn became a shiver, the shiver intensified into a convulsion as their lips touched. There was nothing intimate about the contact. Electric, yes, but not *intimate*. Her fingers moved up around the side of his face to cup it in her hands. They left a glossy trail that puckered his skin as it quickly dried. The track glittered silver in the old cinema's low light.

A soft sigh escaped Taff's lips and for just a second, the flicker between frames, Julie could almost believe it was bliss.

It really did look like he was enjoying it.

He mirrored her movements, reaching up to cup her face in his hands, trying to pull her so close it was impossible to tell where she ended and he began. He met her kiss with desperate lips. Julie could hear his partner's breath coming in ragged gasps as he was forced to choose between breaking contact and breathing.

The woman was the embodiment of the old Hollywood hedonism, right out of the Garden of Allah and its legendary sewing circles along the dirt track that was still to become the real Sunset Boulevard. Tallulah Bankhead, Greta Garbo, Marlene Dietrich, Barbara Stanwyck, Joan Crawford, Marilyn Monroe, Ava Gardner, Lauren Bacall, Jayne Mansfield, all names to conjure with, all linked to the excesses of that famous villa in its heyday. And Myrna Shepherd stood side by side with every one of them, a classical beauty so far out of the league of mortal men as to be up among the pantheon of the immortals and here she was, on the verge of devouring Taff Carter in front of his eyes. Even in the grim ruin of the old movie theater, the light—what little there was of it—loved her, but then, like all true beauty she carried it within her.

Taff was exactly where he wanted to be, a willing victim.

His hand moved up the curve of her spine, fingers pushing against fabric that didn't move. It was the second hint at her impossible nature.

"I suppose there are worse ways to die," Seth remarked, happily providing his own soundtrack to the murder playing out before them.

"I don't know what sick game you are playing here, but I don't want any part of it," Julie said.

"You can't walk out, you're the guest of honor. This whole piece of theater is just for *you*. Ever heard that phrase damned if you do, damned if you don't?"

Julie turned his back on the stage and managed three steps back toward the aisle before Taff cried out. There was a world of hurt in the sound.

Against the backdrop of Hitchcock's lost film, his partner and the movie siren worked their bodies against each other, each movement frantic, hungry, desperate, as the pleasure quickly faded, born again as pain.

She moved sinuously against him, never breaking contact with his temples even as his bliss was transformed into whimpers and his whimpers became moans.

There was no mistaking the agony in the sounds gurgling deep in his throat now.

Behind Taff the images on the big screen flickered by disjointedly, remembering a London long since lost. The film provided a curious backdrop to his torture.

The woman's teeth drew Taff's tongue tip slowly out of his mouth, into hers. It wasn't erotic in any way. It was like watching a black widow's sexual cannibalism.

She bit down on it, tearing into his gums with her teeth with shocking ferocity. Now there was blood; a single track of it down the stubble of Taff's chin and more of it frothing around his teeth. She bit him again, harder this time, pulling and pulling as if his face might peel away beneath her teeth to expose the bones beneath. She tangled her fingers in his hair and yanked his head back. Taff gasped and opened his mouth wider. The blood spilled down his neck. Drawn to it, she leaned in, tasting his stale sweat on her tongue, and then she bit down again, around his Adam's apple.

"Please," Taff begged, the muscles of his neck corded against the pain. For a moment Julie actually thought he was so far gone he was begging for more. But the second "Please," banished any misconceptions. He saw the panic in his partner's face as the woman tore free another mouthful of meat and gristle.

Seth placed a comforting hand on Julie's shoulder. "It really is a tragedy. Well, actually no it isn't. He deserves everything that's coming to him. He was willing to give you up to save his own skin. That's our Huw. Like I said, in a meeting like this you need a clear idea of what you hope to achieve. I know what I want out of this."

"What?" Julie said.

Seth had something in his hand.

A Browning Hi Power, 9mm with thumb safety. It was the weapon of choice for the armed response units of police marksmen. Julie knew it well. It was the only gun he'd ever fired. The Browning had a thirteen-shot clip.

"You. My honest man."

Seth offered him the gun.

"There's one bullet in the chamber," Seth said. "You've got a choice. You can put it in my head, then the delightful Myrna here will turn on you and we'll all end up pushing up daisies, side by side for all eternity, or you can put it in your partner's head and end his suffering. Mercy or murder? That's why we're here, to see if you are the kind of man I think you are."

Julie didn't even think about it, he raised the gun, leveling it so the black eye aimed squarely at the bridge of Seth Lockwood's nose. "I think I'll take option three, this ends here, *Seth* Lockwood. You're under arrest."

Lockwood just laughed. "You see that, Gideon? I was right, the boy has got some brass balls on him." The old man didn't say a word. "I like a fearless man, don't I, son?" Still the old man kept his silence. "So, Julie, cards on the table, no lies or pretty promises, I could use a guy like you now that Huw's on the outs. I'm a good friend to have, believe me, but I make a lousy enemy."

"I get the picture," Julie said, not lowering the gun.

"Do you? You're still thinking of me as the villain of the peace. I'm really not. I might not be the victim, but I'm far from the villain."

"Are you trying to tell me you're the hero here?"

"Aren't we all the heroes of our own lives, Julie? The only thing you need to remember is that Huw brought this on himself. I *liked* having my own pet pig. I didn't ask much of him, one thing in fact, and in return I gave him exactly what his heart desired. I even warned him before I gave him the monster, but he was adamant that she was all he had ever dreamed of, so we sealed the deal. What am I supposed to do? It's out of my hands, Julie. I didn't make the rules. Here's the only thing you need to know: I don't want to be here any more than you do. So, let's just get this over with, either kill me or kill him, but for fuck's sake kill one of us. All you've got to do is pull the trigger. You can do that, can't you?"

Taff echoed Seth's "Please."

It was the last coherent thing he ever said.

The woman's thumbs pulled his mouth open wider and wider until the skin was stretched taut, and then she pulled it open farther still; Taff's pleas became gurgles as his tongue bloated. It took Julius a moment to realize what she was doing—folding Taff's tongue back on itself so it filled his throat, and she then kept pressing it back as he gagged on it, but she wouldn't let him choke. She was tender with her torture.

She lingered a moment to marvel at her handiwork, tracing a finger from his lips to his belt before she reached down, unzipping him as Taff stood helplessly by. There was nothing erotic in the move, and yet Taff ground his hips against her as she slipped her hand inside his pants.

Her grip tightened.

A desperate moan escaped Taff's lips.

"You might want to do something," Seth said, quite matter-of-factly. "It's all about the *nasty* from here on in. He's a dead man. It's just how much he suffers before the end, and that's in *your* hands."

"I can't—" Julie said, shaking his head. His hand was shaking, too. The gun felt impossibly heavy in it, as if the entire weight of his partner's life had been conferred onto the cold metal.

He thought seriously about pulling the trigger—the gun aimed squarely at the woman. He thought about putting the bullet in *her* head, but doubted it would stop her. Whatever she was, she wasn't flesh and blood. Was he going to need a silver bullet to put her down? How did you stop a silver screen siren from devouring your partner? The world had stopped making sense. Suddenly he was in a city of movie stars and monsters where the movie stars *were* the monsters and all he could think, staring at Myrna Shepherd as she drained the life out of his partner was: *If he was right about something as insane as this, what else was Josh Raines right about?*

Stage magicians, gangland thugs, kidnapped actresses, all of it?

As his eyes were drawn once more to the image outside The Peabody and the look that passed across that black-and-white Seth Lockwood's face he actually started to believe it *could* be.

Saliva and blood dribbled from Taff's chin as he started to come undone.

"She's going to feed on him now. It won't be pretty," Seth said. "To all intents and purposes, she's a succubus, a sexual demon," Seth was quite matter-of-fact about it, as if sexual demons were commonplace in his world. "It's how she sustains herself. You're doing your friend no favors by prolonging his demise."

It was a miracle Taff was still standing.

"It'll be a long time before she lets him go, Julie. A lot of suffering can be packed into very few seconds when you know what you are doing. Pull the trigger. We've got stuff we need to talk about."

"No," Julie said. "I'm not going to do anything you want me to."

"That's a shame. I was hoping we could work together like grown-ups. Maybe you'll change your mind after a few more minutes watching poor old Huw suffer?"

"I won't," Julie said. This was his line in the sand, the point he couldn't cross. Not by choice. Not willingly.

The woman reached out, pawing at the bloody mess around Taff's crotch as his legs finally buckled. Still she wouldn't let him fall. His breath came fast, hitching in his throat as he struggled to suck air in around his bloated tongue. The tears she'd ripped into his gums and cheeks were the only reason he wasn't suffocating on his own blood and bile.

The stink was overpowering. Raw. Wet. Meaty.

There was so much blood.

But that wasn't the worst of it; it was the sound: the suckling.

It was all over Myrna Shepherd's face as she pressed her mouth to his wounds, sucking at his cock and balls with all the tenderness of a piranha.

"Hel," Taff begged, as much of the words *help me* as he could manage, his empty eye sockets staring blinding at Julie. "*Puh eez.*"

And there ended Julie's resistance, in the face of his partner's agony. Julie pulled the trigger.

He hadn't even realized he'd been pointing the gun at Taff until the blood-red rose flowered in the center of his face and the meat punched out through the back. It was a bloody mess.

Taff collapsed in a whorish sprawl, more blood than a single shot could ever have caused pooling around his corpse as the woman crawled her way up his belly, blood-slick hands up to her mouth as she scooped up his innards hungrily.

"We'll just hang on to this for safe keeping, I think," Seth said, prying the Browning from his fingers.

Julie was shaking.

This wasn't happening.

It couldn't be.

He hadn't just killed his partner.

This was some alternate reality where everything he held dear had gone with that bullet. In this place he wasn't his own man anymore. He was Lockwood's bitch, body if not soul.

He surrendered the gun, knowing it was the worst thing he could possibly do. Seth took the murder weapon from him.

"What about his body? You can't let her just . . . eat him . . ."

"Don't worry about that, now that he's no longer with us she'll lose interest in poor old Huw pretty quickly," he turned to the ethereal actress who was crouched over Taff's corpse. She turned her head to look at Seth, obviously responding to her master's voice. Lockwood offered her an indulgent smile. "Won't you, my dear?"

Her mouth opened and static crackled out of it followed by a line Julie had heard a thousand times. It was one of those iconic movie moments everyone thought they could imitate, like Bogart's beginning of a beautiful friendship or Mae West's invitation to come up and see her. *"I'm frightened . . . but when you strip away all of the things I'm afraid of the only thing that remains is love . . . I'm just a fool in love . . ."* Though far from sounding seductive or enticing, the line sounded positively repugnant, like the promise of a serial killer to his next intended victim.

"We'll put Taff somewhere no one will find him, trust me. It'll be like he never existed. Now, I think it's time we talked about what you can do for me, Julie. For starters, my cousin Josh. He's becoming an inconvenience."

"I'm not going to kill him for you," Julie said, unaware just how similar his words were to his partner's when Lockwood had asked him to deliver Julie to the old cinema. If he had been, perhaps he would have been more afraid that a similar outcome awaited him should he fail his new paymaster.

"What is it with you policemen and death? Always assuming everything has to be so absolute? Convince him to let this go. That's all I'm asking. I don't care how you do it, just find a way."

"And if I can't?"

"I'll have to convince him."

35

DOWN AMONG THE DEAD MEN

It was a familiar feeling. He'd put himself out there, taken a risk, told the other person the secrets of his heart, and they'd walked out on him. It wasn't love this time, but he could so easily have been describing his love life. It wasn't as though he lived in a Joy Division lyric, but in matters of the heart Josh had never been all that successful. It was the same when it came to understanding people. He'd thought it would be different with Julie, that the young policeman would understand because he'd seen the Comedians with his own eyes and experienced the dread their presence conjured, but it wasn't.

He looked at the gold compact for the umpteenth time, turning it over and over again in his hands. It was curiously lacking in ornamentation or embellishment. There were no engravings, not even a crown hallmarking or any indication of its carat. The hasp was well worn as were the hinges, and when he opened it he saw the vines that cracked the mirror's face where the silvering had begun to wear away from the back of the glass. There was a dent the size of his thumb in the top of the case. He closed it and slipped it into his pocket.

Josh lay on his bed, still dressed.

He could hear his mum snoring softly in the next room. It was a re-markably normal sound, the only thing remotely normal about the last day—or was it a week? It was hard to believe that something as simple as the passage of seconds, minutes, and hours could be so totally undermined.

The compact was his only link to Eleanor. Unfortunately, he couldn't trust it. He'd learned that the hard way. But he'd promised he'd save her so what was he supposed to do now?

It was a rash promise. A stupid, unkeepable one. The kind of thing lovers said all too glibly, knowing that reality could never come back to haunt them, but they weren't lovers. They weren't even friends. She was a face on the wall, a few seconds on film, nothing more. She wasn't his obsession.

Or she hadn't been until now.

Obsession, desire, to want something so badly it hurts, to be willing to trade everything you had for the one thing you didn't . . . Here he was, wide awake when he should have been dreaming, seriously contemplating that kind of deal with the devil.

Nothing was going to be resolved by lying on his back looking up at the ceiling. He needed to get back out there. So what if he didn't have Julie Gennaro on his side? He'd done fine without him so far. Better than fine. He'd found the flat down in Rotherhithe; he'd found the map marking out the anchors of Glass Town; he'd found the magician who'd conjured the illusion up; he'd even found a way inside. And he'd done it all by himself. He didn't *need* Julie Gennaro.

His thinking was wrongheaded. The compact wasn't his only link back to Glass Town; the magician was, too, he realized. Cadmus Damiola. It began with him, and assuming he'd survived the Comedians, the end of Glass Town rested with him. He was the one man who knew *all* of its secrets.

Josh pushed himself up off the bed and padded silently across to the window. He looked out across the street at the row of identical windows, at the neatly trimmed hedges, and the lines of garbage bins on the curbside, and was struck by just how *normal* it all was. Through the double glazing, he heard the distant full-throttle roar of a motorbike powering toward one of the bridges that would take him across the river.

It was hard to believe that beneath the veneer of banal bricks and mundane mortar there lay anything approaching a secret life of London when other miracles passed by unremarked every day. But he'd seen it with his own eyes, set foot in it—however briefly—and now hungered to return there. That was what happened when you let the idea of the impossible, of hidden cities and men trapped forever in the prime of their lives, into your life; it wasn't much of a stretch to start to see all of the little miracles that otherwise went unnoticed every day. The inner city became a red-brick miracle, the suburbs a wisteria-covered wonderland fit for any Alice who tried to find it.

So even if Damiola was dead maybe his part wasn't over in all of this?

It was somewhere to start again, but this time he wasn't about to run out into the middle of the night. He went downstairs and wrote a note for his mother, telling her not to worry, which of course guaranteed she would, and called a cab to take him across London.

Twenty minutes later Josh stood outside the rundown old cemetery feeling woefully underdressed for the cold. The magician had given up his vigil at the gates. Josh stepped between the lopsided raven's wings. The cemetery at night was a very different animal to the cemetery by day; the shadows of the dead clung to the dark places, lending the old stones the feel of perdition. Walking down the gravel path it was easy to imagine the lost souls trapped within the cemetery's crumbling walls, unrepentant even as their eternal torment began in earnest, their cries being drawn out of their dead lips even as the gravel crunched beneath his feet.

But perhaps that was just the wind?

He resisted the urge to call out. If the magician were here, he wouldn't take kindly to being summoned in that manner. Instead he walked among the gravestones, his breath becoming louder in his ears with each step until it drowned out the crunch of gravel underfoot. The specter of the mausoleum rose out of the shadows ahead of him. The moonlight transformed what had been a modest structure into an imposing house of the dead. The gates still hung open though they lacked the ornamentation they once had thanks to Damiola's defensive magic. The bird he'd conjured forth from them was reduced to a tangled heap of wrought iron on the grass. Behind it the door to the tomb itself was still open a crack, the ancient oak embossed onto the door casting deeper shadows around the lock.

There was nothing to suggest that the magician had survived the showdown with Seth's Comedians, but plenty to intimate that he hadn't.

He was sure he could smell blood on the air as he pushed the door open wide.

So many things begin with something as simple as opening a door. It wasn't just a clumsy metaphor for life's choices. It was more than that. There was the fear of what lurked on the other side of a closed door, of what made those sounds in the night; there was the hope that went with the idea that stepping through could lead to something different, somewhere new; there was the belief that somehow the door protected you from the outside world and the knowledge that it didn't.

Josh went inside.

The passageway leading down to the chamber beyond was dark. There was a vague flickering light at the far end. No doubt that was another metaphor for the path he was on, Josh thought as he descended the few steps into the tomb proper.

He heard labored breathing in the darkness up ahead.

He walked cautiously toward the light, not sure what he expected to find waiting for him there.

This time he did call out, just the one word, "Hello?"

The call went unanswered.

He walked slowly toward the light, entering the tomb.

For a moment he thought it was empty. The single source of light, a guttering candle stub that didn't seem to burn down—despite the fact the wick was buried in less than a fingernail of wax—reflected in the steel toe cap of a worn-out boot that stuck out from beneath a pile of rags.

Cadmus Damiola was a broken man.

Beaten, battered, and cast aside by the Comedians before they came after Josh, he lay now beneath layers upon layers of grimy and filth-ridden coats that shrouded his ruined body.

The magician looked up.

He didn't seem surprised by the intrusion as he said, "You again?"

"You're not dead," Josh said.

"I am. I told you, 1929. It says so on the door. It's just taken a while to catch up with me." He held out a hand. Josh could see dark lines that at first he mistook for fine hairs across the back of it until he saw them for what they really were: cracks. "I'm coming apart," Damiola explained, no fear in his voice, only resignation. "It can't be helped. Death is catching up with me after all of these years. I'm done. Now it's only a matter of how long before I unravel. Leave me be. I'm too tired for all of this. I've told you what needs doing. It's your fight now. Seth has bested me for the last time. There are only so many times you can get knocked down and get back up again. I don't have the indignation to go down fighting. I'm done. I'm out. Just leave me alone."

"I've been there," Josh said, not exactly a protest, not exactly begging the old man for help, but hoping those three words would catch his interest. That had been the point, after all, hadn't it? By giving him the compact and telling him where to go, Damiola had been guiding him to the hidden city within the city. He wanted him to tear the illusion down, to find a way to save the girl. "I've been into Glass Town," Josh held out the gold compact. "That's what you wanted me to do, wasn't it? Find your workshop, find the way through to the other side." His lips were suddenly dry. He crouched down beside the magician. "When I went back to try and find another way in . . . it didn't work. The mirror didn't show me the way. I didn't know what else to do apart from come here to find you."

Damiola shook his head. "Impossible."

Josh didn't know if he meant it was impossible that he'd set foot in the hidden city, or that it was impossible that the mirror hadn't revealed a second way in to him. "I know how it works," Josh pressed on. "I know that it messes with time."

"You don't understand what you are talking about, do you? It's all just words to you."

"I might not know *how* it does it, but I was in there for a few minutes, inside Glass Town, and when I came out the other side a week had passed. I know how it works, how you hid them from Isaiah."

That stopped the magician's denials.

He didn't say anything for the longest time, and when he did finally make to speak, a vicious bout of coughing rattled his old bones. He wiped the spittle from his lips with grubby fingers. It was a full ten seconds before he said, "I thought the anchors dilated time, like an optical, spatial, and temporal illusion, city within a city, hidden behind glass, an hour within a month, a year within a hundred, all coming together to slow the passage of time, but I was wrong, it was so much more than that. They keep the way through the veil into the otherworld closed on this side, but open on the other."

"The Annwyn?" Josh said, as though he understood. It was a convincing lie.

"Perhaps you aren't as clueless as you look, dear boy. Yes, the Annwyn, the druidic otherworld, the underworld, Mictlan, Naraka, Diyu, Duzakh, the lake of fire, the outer darkness, what we now call Hell was so much more in the understanding of our ancestors. I didn't know. Not at first. I was naïve enough to think it was my masterpiece; that I was in control. That I had fashioned a miracle; not tapped into a nightmare. But in reality it was just a prison." The magician hawked and spat in disgust. "It was such an amazing feat . . . the sum of my life's work, bringing two phases of existence together. And for what? So that bastard could escape from his crimes and live happily ever after? What a travesty."

"Then help me. Help me stop him."

"You can't beat the devil, boy."

"He's not the devil, he's a lunatic."

"Oh, no, no; he's so much more than that. He doesn't need horns, he has the heart of Lucifer inside him."

"If you've already given up, why did you give me the compact? Why did you send me to your workshop?"

"Honest answer? To keep the glass out of Lockwood's hands," Damiola explained, shuffling his back up against the wall. The cracks in his neck and cheek were deeper and more pronounced than they had been a few seconds ago. "It was only ever about getting the glass away from me while his playthings were so close. All these years he'd left me alone. I'm sure he thought I was dead. Now he knows I'm not. Those freaks of his will have spilled their guts as soon as they reported back to him."

"They never made it back. There was an accident. They got hit by a bus."

"That wouldn't have stopped them," the magician said.

"It did."

"No," the magician shook his head. "The only thing that could have stopped them would be Lockwood snuffing their light out. As long as that flame keeps on burning, they live."

"They're gone."

"Then he made a mistake."

"That's good, isn't it? Proves he's not unbeatable."

"It just proves he's impatient," the magician said.

"And that's something we can use against him," Josh said. "Just help me. Tell me how to fight him."

"I already did. I told you his weakness. He's obsessed with the woman. It's beyond desire. He needs to possess her. The problem is what it means for her, that woman he took, Eleanor. To beat him, you damn her. Is that a consequence you are willing to face? If it is, you know what to do."

"There must be another way."

"If you've been there, you understand. You know what I am saying. Beyond the glass one year passes as one hundred. You were gone barely fifteen minutes if you lost a week. Eleanor Raines is almost a year older than when he took her. She's still the same vibrant young woman he ripped out of time."

"But that's good, isn't it?"

"It means she can never leave the other place."

"She can," Josh protested. "She was at my grandfather's funeral. I saw her again not far from here."

"I'm not making myself clear. She can't leave what you call Glass Town without the universe making moves to protect itself. It's bigger than her now. The world as we know it is a delicate ecosystem. Eleanor Raines doesn't belong here. She is intrinsically linked to the London of the 1920s. That is her place in space and time. Take her out of it and you create an absence. An Eleanor Raines–shaped hole in the universe.

If you then put her here, now, in the London of today, that creates a fault line between then and now," he lifted his hand again, "like these, but instead of being limited to one man's frail body they are all around you. Cracks in the here and now as time looks to reassert itself. Her being here creates paradoxes by the minute. Think of reality as a sheet of glass, and all of those paradoxes are little hairline fissures in it. It doesn't take a lot to shatter it. Her being here is like taking a hammer to that glass. It is as simple as that." The magician shuffled up against the wall, using it to help himself stand. He was weak despite the absence of any obvious wounds beyond the cracks in his skin. He leaned on Josh for support. "Existing outside the Annwyn, even for a few minutes, is enough for the whole thing to start unravelling. She can't come back. The consequences are too much to bear."

The magician snuffed out the stub of candle, but the tomb didn't go dark. There was a second source of light, Josh realized, as Damiola brought forth a ghost with the slightest turn of his right hand and index finger.

It looked like Eleanor. Exactly like her save for the fact that her red dress had a vaporous hue, no solidity or substance to it. The conjuration was absolutely still. Josh could see straight through her to the wall behind her. The red light cast an ashen glow across the magician's face. Damiola coughed, phlegm rasping at the back of his throat wetly. Josh didn't know how the old man was doing it—some sort of optical illusion. That was how he did everything wasn't it? Mirrors, with or without smoke.

The woman slowly turned in place to face Josh and as she did she began to crumble. It began as a single black crack through her cheek, then another and a third, as her complexion was ruined. The cracks became a web of black lines.

"Time forces itself to catch up with her," Damiola explained, as the ghost aged rapidly, her youthful beauty replaced by a hard-worn middle age, which crumbled into those twilight years in a matter of seconds. "The reality is that Eleanor Raines is over one hundred years old. She can't be here and not be over one hundred years old. It doesn't work like that. And people don't live to that kind of age. Seventy? Eighty? Ninety, maybe, but there's a limit; no one lives forever, not even me, and what happens then? The natural order reasserts itself. There's no other way this ends for her."

"There must be."

"Why? Because you want one? Because it's unfair?"

"Because of Seth. He is out here now, in our London, coming and going as he pleases. He hasn't turned to dust. He's not aging like that. He's just . . . him."

"Then he's never left the safety of the illusion."

"He has. I've seen him. He was at the funeral. He threatened me afterward. He was there when I stepped out of Glass Town a week after I set foot in it, waiting. He's spending a lot of time outside of the safety of the illusion."

"Maybe he cut his heart out and keeps it buried in a lead-lined box, beating away?" Damiola said. Josh couldn't tell if he was entirely joking.

"Would that work?"

"I don't know. I don't know everything, lad. I'm not ineffable. I didn't create that world, I only opened the door."

"What if I kill him?"

"Hard to do if his heart's in a box," Damiola said, offering a wry smile. "But, assuming it isn't, it won't change a thing. And to be honest it could do more harm than good. You don't know what the effect of spilling blood in there will do. Blood is strange, it carries the essence of life in it, and the essence of life is time."

"You say that like it's a bad thing,"

"I know it can't be a good thing, that is enough. Everything is connected. I don't know how quickly it will happen, hours, days, maybe, but it will happen. So to beat Seth you shatter the anchors, allowing the door into that other place to close once and forever, bringing about an end to Glass Town, and you win. The years will race in to fill the void, catching up with themselves. Look at her face. Look at what's happening to her."

This time as the ghost of Eleanor flickered, the cracks widened to finger-thick fissures now, its light went out like a pinched flame, casting them in darkness.

The silence in the tomb was absolute.

"There *must* be another way," Josh said finally.

"You either break them all and shatter the illusion forever, no going back, let time take both of them, or you repair the broken anchor by using the glass from the compact—it's the same stuff that I used to push Glass Town into the underworld in the first place, and the only piece of glass that remains—and in doing so trap her in that place for another hundred years, or however long it takes for the anchors to finally fail. The world will have forgotten all about both of them, and us. So at least you won't have to watch it happen, but it is going to happen. So, what is it to be?"

36

FRIENDS LIKE THESE

Julie Gennaro was in over his head, and thanks to the Lockwoods learning a very important life lesson: You didn't need water to drown; you could do that just fine on dry land.

He looked up at the windows of Joshua Raines's Rotherhithe flat.

There was no obvious way in apart from the front door, which suited him just fine. He'd taken something from the evidence room at the station: a bump key.

The science behind it was pretty simple, all he had to do was slip the key into the lock, bump it hard, once, maybe twice, and fool the tumblers into thinking they'd been tripped and that was that. It was an essential bit of every thieves' kit. The skill was in fashioning the key, not using it. The principle was simple enough, by not sliding the key all the way in there was one pin at the end that wasn't tripped, and when the key was bumped it forced it deeper into the keyway. The specially designed teeth worked to fool the pins, and the lock thought it had been opened. It only took a second, and done right barely left a trace on the barrel.

As he walked up to the door Julie couldn't help but glance back over his shoulder, just the once, to see if anyone was watching. It wasn't exactly the behavior of an invited guest, but he'd done it before he could stop himself. It was still a couple of insomniac hours before the dawn chorus so he was banking on the fact that there was no one around but the birds to see him acting like an idiot.

He shuffled up to the door and did the trick with the bump key, praying it would work.

It did.

He opened the door quickly and closed it behind him without looking back.

The hallway smelled musty. He hadn't noticed it the first time. He'd been too busy trying to take in the craziness of the Raines family obsession, struck by the sadness of generations of men never getting over the kidnap of the woman they were named after. He stepped through the sea of unopened mail, newspapers, and gaudy fliers and restaurant menus, then climbed the stairs two and three at a time to the top. He wanted to be in and out quickly, less chance of being caught, as he reached the top of the stairs he was struck by how little thought he'd given the crime.

Lockwood wanted him to convince Josh to let it go, but how was he supposed to do that? This thing, the story of Eleanor Raines, had clearly obsessed his family for generations. It wasn't as if he could just lean on the guy and say it'd be bad for his health like some dodgy scene in a gangster movie. He needed to be cleverer than that.

And that was hard, because right now his brain wasn't working properly.

The key to stopping Lockwood *had* to be in one of these rooms. He was banking his life on it. That was what Josh Raines had been trying to tell him, when he'd brought him here and again when he'd dragged him out to that empty street at the other end of the city wasn't it? Julie needed him to be right. But facing the sheer mass of information gathered in the flat, it quickly became obvious that the problem was identifying that single piece of information amid all of the madness.

He needed to think smart, use the time here alone to really get a grasp of everything on those walls.

The first time he'd skimmed stuff, his mind already made up even before he'd ducked under the first red thread to read about some long-forgotten stage act, a bunch of long-dead East End villains and weird ancient mythology. Between then and now he'd come face-to-face with celluloid sex demons and murdered his own partner.

Everything was different now.

He needed to absorb it all, let it wash over him, lose himself in it in the same way that Josh had obviously done in that week he'd disappeared.

But he didn't have a week.

He wasn't even sure he had until sunrise.

Where to start?

He looked around for something, an image, a headline, something that would serve as a cipher to unlock the whole puzzle, and chose a photograph of Eleanor Raines. He crossed the bare floorboards with their scorched-in map of London, ducking under the cat's cradle of red threads linking the articles and images, and spent a full minute just staring at the woman. He stood on the scorched words, *one for one*. They didn't mean anything to him so he ignored them. There were enough things he didn't understand without worrying about three little words.

There was no getting away from the fact that she was beautiful. Not modern beautiful, not heroin chic or Hollywood plastic, properly beautiful, timelessly beautiful. It wasn't hard to imagine two men becoming so utterly obsessed with her they went to war. Men had gone to war over less.

He followed the red thread from her portrait to an article mentioning the entrepreneur Ruben Glass and his failed attempt to get a movie town established in the East End, which was where a young director by the name of Hitchcock was looking to shoot many of the scenes of his first movie, *Number 13*. Glass, it seemed, was heavily invested in the success of the young director's first movie. Until today—yesterday now—Julie had never even heard of it. The article was dated more than a decade after the disappearance of Eleanor Raines, but that wasn't what caught his eye, it was a reference to a coup the young director had tried to pull off, a cameo from none other than the Hollywood goddess

Myrna Shepherd. According to the reporter there was no proof that she'd ever been on set, and with the film itself lost, no way of ever knowing as Hitch refused to talk about *Number 13* save to say that it wasn't very good.

Did a sex demon with Shepherd's face feasting on his partner count as a link?

Once that image had crept back into his thinking there was no getting away from it. He'd tried telling himself it was mercy, but that was easy to say, harder to believe. He'd pulled the trigger, even if there'd been no choice. He had his partner's death on his hands. That was the sort of thing that changed a man. Forever. For good and bad. Whatever sort of man Julie Gennaro had thought he was, he wasn't; he was something else now. Like it or not, as long as Seth had the murder weapon he was Lockwood's man. And that meant facing the very real possibility that there would be more blood on his hands before this was over.

He followed the red threads to another article, this one about a rumored falling out among thieves, with a new Lockwood rising to fill the power vacuum left by the disappearance of Seth. Gideon Lockwood. Seth's son. At seventeen, the article claimed, young Gideon had committed more atrocities than any of the generations before him, hiding the worst of his brutality in the ruins of The Blitz. Julie tried to picture it; a new breed of gangster emerging during the horrors of the Second World War to run the streets of London, getting away with murder under the camouflage of the Luftwaffe's nightly bombing raids. All of those images of Londoners coming together at the time of the city's greatest need vanished in rock dust and rubble and opportunity. There was always someone who would look to profit from the pain of others. It was a case of entering the family business, with all the ruthless aplomb of the bastard who went before him. It made fascinating reading, but it didn't solve anything.

Julie crossed the scorched floorboards again, following another thread.

There were thirteen scars on the wooden floor. Josh had tried to explain what those marks meant, or at least give him a practical demonstration with that mirror of his, but there had been nothing to see, no matter how insistent Josh had been that he was about to offer up miracles. Julie stood on the same scorch mark that represented the street where he'd last seen Josh turning in desperate circles, looking for something in the glass that wasn't there.

Julie Gennaro was drowning and there was no easy way to save himself. Lockwood had him by the short and curlies. Whatever came next, whatever person emerged, it wouldn't be Julie Gennaro even if it walked like him, talked like him, shared his past and his face; it wouldn't *be* him. That Julie Gennaro was dead and had been from the moment he pulled the trigger to save Taff.

This thread took him to an entire wall dedicated to Seth Lockwood's gangland empire, and from that another mosaic of newspaper cuttings obsessed with the missing actress.

These things, no matter how exotic they seemed from afar, only ever came down to one of two things, sex or money.

He needed to keep it simple.

Follow the money. Find the lady—or in this case the lady's bones and hope some sort of evidence had survived that could be used to bring down the Lockwoods. Good old-fashioned police work. That was what this entire room was all about, even if it got lost in Crazy Town. There were key players in this and Lockwood was only one of them. There was Isaiah Raines, the stage magician Damiola, the moneyman, Ruben Glass.

Follow the money. Find the lady.

Lockwood had been so eager for him to believe he didn't want to be here, but if not here, where?

He was standing on top of the answer, he realized.

Glass Town, where else? That was where every single thread tangled together in one angry red knot after all.

But before he could find a way out of this Hell of Lockwood's making, Julie heard the telltale sound of the key in the door downstairs followed by panicked surprise at the revelation that it had been forced open.

Julie counted to five as Josh came running up the stairs, fearing the worst as he raced into the room pumped up on adrenaline.

He didn't move.

He stood in the midst of the red threads, his feet on two of the anchors, and faced Josh. He had no idea what he was supposed to say. There was a moment, the silence between heartbeats, when Josh clearly couldn't place him, and then he seemed to collapse inwardly as the fear gave way to recognition.

"You? What the *fuck* are you doing in here?" The subtext being: *I thought you were him. I thought you were Seth. I thought he was going to kill me in my own house.*

How did he answer that?

Carefully.

"Looking for you."

"And you just thought you'd break in? Why did you come here? Why not come to the house?"

"I could lie to you, but I won't. I thought about going to the Rothery to find you, but I didn't think you'd be there. I didn't want to turn up on your mum's doorstep and bring more worries for her. But that was only part of it. Lockwood owns the Rothery. If I turned up on your door, he'd know." He met Josh's doubtful stare and decided to push his luck. "You don't beat a man like Seth Lockwood if he knows you are coming."

"Now you want to help me?"

"No. I want to understand. You tried to show me something back there . . ."

"And you didn't want to see it," Josh said. "So what's changed?"

I gunned down my partner because he was being gorged on by a ravenous sex demon, because he'd sold himself to the Lockwoods, because he was corrupt, and now Seth Lockwood has me by the balls and he wants you out of the picture, Julie thought, but he didn't say any of that. Instead he said, "We both know there's something going on here, I may not understand it, but just because I don't understand, it doesn't mean it isn't happening. That accident, where I picked you up, the two guys in those masks—"

"The Comedians, no masks; that's what they were, who they were. They were fused together at the hand and hip," Josh corrected him.

"Whatever. It was no coincidence Seth Lockwood was in that café, was it? He was waiting for you. He wants to hurt you. And this," Julie spread his arms to encompass the contents of the room. "All of it, from the floor to the ceiling, this is why, isn't it?"

"I showed you the film. You saw it for yourself. He's not Gideon Lockwood's grandson, despite all appearances, no matter how impossible it sounds, Seth Lockwood isn't just named after Gideon's father; he *is* his father."

"You showed me the film," Julie said.

"But you still don't believe me, do you?" It wasn't so much an accusation as a statement of disappointed fact.

Julie didn't know if he could sell the next part. It's hard to peddle something you didn't believe in. "I don't *not* believe you," he said, shrugging. "Put yourself in my shoes for a minute, it's hard to take it all in. You're talking about a world I'm not familiar with. The kind of stuff you are telling me, long-dead actresses breaking and entering, conjoined comedians hunting you?" He looked down at his feet, seeing for the first time the distortion of the map and the streets he'd never seen in his London, and put two and two together, "And this," he jabbed his foot toward one of the anchors, letting Josh assume he knew what it meant. "It's a lot. It's *more* than a lot. You want me to believe Seth Lockwood is, what, the devil?"

"Not the devil," Josh said. "The devil doesn't exist, Seth does. That makes him so much worse." Julie couldn't help but smile at that. Sound logic.

"Then prove it to me. Make me understand, Josh. Because right now all I see are the shadows you're jumping at," he deliberately turned slightly, his gaze going to Eleanor Raines's beautiful face where it was taped up on the wall, "And a hundred-year-old obsession that's anything but healthy."

Josh looked at him. Julie wished he knew what was going through his mind. "Why have you come here? What's changed? You didn't want anything to do with what I had to say. You basically left me to die back there."

He didn't say anything else for a moment, then said, "Bit of an exaggeration, but I take your point."

"So what happened?"

"I saw the woman who broke into your house . . ." he swallowed, biting back on the memory of Myrna Shepherd crouching over Taff's corpse, his blood smeared across her lips and chin. "There was nothing natural about her."

"Because she isn't. But that's not it. It can't be. You're lying to me—or at least not telling me the truth." He was shaking his head over and over.

"You're right," Julie said, wishing that Josh Raines wasn't half as perceptive or good at reading people as he obviously was. That made it so much tougher to sell him a lie. So he kept it as close to the truth as he could. "He killed my partner right in front of my eyes."

"Seth?"

Julie nodded. "You can't fight him, Josh. He's untouchable. He owns the Rothery and plenty of other places besides. Just think about it for a second. He killed a police officer before my eyes, acting with impunity, knowing I couldn't touch him. That's a special kind of monster. So, ask yourself this, is it really worth it, all of this, this family feud or whatever it is? Is it really worth dying for, because he *will* kill you."

"What do you suggest I do?"

"Walk away."

"Is that your advice as an officer of the law?"

"No. That's my advice as a human being. You didn't see what he did to Taff. It doesn't matter whether he's thirty or one hundred and thirty; this is his town, mate. He might pretend he's not Gideon, and that might be true, but that doesn't mean he isn't a different kind of monster. You can't beat him. None of us can."

"I can't walk away," Josh said.

"How are you going to fight him?"

Josh looked down at his feet and for a moment Julie thought it was the cowed gesture of a broken man. It wasn't. Without looking up, Josh Raines said, "I know how it works now. All of it. The grand trick. The great illusion. I know how he did it. How he spirited away Eleanor, all of it. And I'm going to bring the whole thing crashing down. I'm going to burn it to the ground if I have to. Let him come for me, I don't care. I'm not going to fight fair. I know his weakness."

"Okay . . . then I guess you're going to need some help," Julie said. "Wind me up and point me in the right direction. I'm in. I owe it to Taff."

37

THE UNSEEN REALM

JANUARY 13, 1924

Damiola had doubts.

He had walked a full circuit around the perimeter of the veil—where this London and the mists of the Annwyn brushed up against each other with their barriers at their thinnest. The implications of what Lockwood wanted him to do were dire and he couldn't pretend otherwise. He barely grasped the full weight of the magic he'd tapped into, though best he could tell the anchors he had developed would force the veil between here and there to be held open on that side while closed at the same time on this. In itself that wouldn't have changed the city, but with his manipulations to push Ruben Glass's failed studio through the veil and act as a bridgehead into the underworld, those anchors would effectively banish the place into limbo forever. Limbo. Purgatory. Hell. The Otherwhere. The Otherworld. The Underworld. There were so many names for what lay on the other side of the veil. He thought of it as a shadow world, or half world, even called it Mist World for that was all he ever saw of it; rolling endless mists. It was Damiola's belief that those mists had last impacted upon this world in the days of myth and were responsible for the dragons and demons of all of those impossible stories, but he had no way of proving that. The veil itself ran along intersecting ley lines, which themselves tapped into the elemental power of the land itself, the raw earth magic that was being mercilessly consumed by the revolution of mankind—marking out the anchor points where the lenses would be placed. The planning was meticulous. It had to be. Even a fraction of an inch, an eighth, or sixteenth variation and the light paths would be off and the weave would fail. It was that precise. And he couldn't afford to be wrong. Lockwood would kill him if he was.

Again.

Kill him again.

It wouldn't be the first time.

Lockwood had come to him three months ago with a proposition: He had money behind him, and wanted to use it to make Damiola the most famous performer in the country. He should have been suspicious. All of those clever words and dangled promises, temptation that played on his vanity, the idea that everyone would know him for the innovator he was, putting him up there with the likes of Thurston; Houdini; Robert-Houdin, the man Houdini took his name from; the Great Lafayette; even Thurston's prodigy, that damned Dane, Harry August Jansen, who wasn't half the magician he was. Cadmus Damiola would have—in a very real way—immortality. Offer the world, you want something major in return. It's simple economics. What Lockwood wanted, no more, no less, was the girl.

To think this all started with something as pure as love.

They were barely kids, the pair of them, Isaiah and Eleanor, but it had been doomed the moment Isaiah's older brother Seth had decided he needed to take the one thing that made his brother happy and make it—her—his own. He didn't care about the cost, figurative or literal. It had started with pretty trinkets and flattering words, turning her head with promises of fancy restaurants and West End dance clubs, then diamonds and pearls, and then the ultimate play, once he'd learned the secret yearning of her heart, stardom.

She had dreams of the silver screen that eclipsed walk-on parts in low-budget movies and wanted to stand side by side with Valentino, Flynn, Garbo, and Myrna Shepherd, who she'd met on the set of *Number 13,* the one day Shepherd was there. They'd barely exchanged a word, but Eleanor Raines had fallen in love with the star every bit as obsessively as Seth had fallen for Eleanor. That was when Seth had thrown his lot in with Ruben Glass and used his connections to help the entrepreneur crystallize his dreams of Glass Town, a huge theatrical studio in the heart of London, and grease the right palms to make it happen. The city was corrupt, everyone understood that, that there were levels of power that couldn't be reached without a certain amount of ruthlessness, where cash was king and violence its bagman. Seth controlled the streets in the ways that councilmen and cops could only dream, and he offered his influence to Glass in return for one thing, the promise that Eleanor Raines would have the bright lights and leading roles. Glass wanted his dream so badly he'd agreed, and Seth had taken the promises to his brother's girl. Of course she had been tempted.

He'd given her everything she had ever dreamed of, surpassing any promises his younger brother could ever make good on.

But Seth hadn't banked on love.

She'd refused him.

There was one thing she wanted more than fame, more than the bright lights and the promises of stardom: Isaiah.

That should have been an end to it, but men like Seth Lockwood didn't take no for an answer. That was how they had got to where they were in this life.

That first night when he'd turned up at the stage door, Damiola had thought he was a fan looking for an autograph, or perhaps to discover the secret of magic, so he'd greeted him with an indulgent smile.

He'd listened, but unlike the girl, he'd fallen for the promises and pretty lies, and believed in the illusion Seth wanted him to create. He should have known getting into bed with men like Lockwood and Glass his life could never be the same again. He had, to an extent. He wasn't naïve. What he hadn't grasped was the fact that his death wouldn't be, either.

Damiola couldn't think properly.

He had a show to put on tonight, his swan song.

He'd never intended it to end this way, but there was no way he could stay in London after tonight. He needed to get away; anywhere, it didn't matter, just far away from this place. Far away from Glass Town.

From the outside looking in, Cadmus Damiola had it all. He was on top of the world. The write-ups in *The Evening Standard* and the *London Post* had been incredible. The good people of London had fallen for the wonders he had to show them. They gasped in awe at the new worlds the Opticron offered up, not understanding that they were truly seeing other worlds through the lenses that pierced the veil and offered glimpses of paradises and purgatories. They queued around the block for hours for tickets to the matinee performances, hoping for a glimpse of the miraculous.

The evening's show, three weeks before the final curtain call of the tour, had been sold out for months.

Life didn't get better than this.

Life didn't get worse than this.

Satisfied with the sigils and the alignment of the lenses, there wasn't much left for him to do except prepare for the greatest vanishing act of his life—and he wasn't talking about making part of the city disappear. He headed back to the workshop to run through the tricks one final time, before going to the theater. He walked quickly through the rain-swept streets toward the Adelphi Theatre down on the Strand, the steel tips hammered into his heels clicking on cobbled stones as he did.

The playbill beside the theater's glass doors promised the Lord of Illusions would confound the mind and delight the heart. The illustrations, meant to hint at the tricks to come included self-decapitation, levitation, ghostly spirit faces of fallen soldiers, and at the center of them all, the Opticron. The poster boldly proclaimed: *Witness the Wondrous Opticron! Watch As It Opens Windows into Fabulous New Worlds! Marvel at the Miraculous Sights It Has to Show You! You Cannot Believe Your Eyes!*

If only they knew, he thought to himself, going inside.

The stage manager nodded to him, offering a polite, "Evening, Mr. Damiola," as the magician swept through the foyer toward the main theater.

The lights were low, the stage clear.

Hands worked quietly in the background, securing the traps, checking the acoustics and the rigging and every other eventuality that needed to be in place before the curtain went up. He might be the star of the show, but there were more than a dozen stagehands behind the scenes making sure the tricks went off without a hitch.

The main attraction hung suspended from the ceiling on steel cables: the Opticron.

He caught a stagehand's eye and told him to lower it so that he could give the machine one final check. It took three men and twice as long to lower the huge contraption down onto the main stage as it took to raise it. It looked like a huge water boiler with a dozen peculiar appendages and apertures like a metallic octopus. There were levers and dials, and valves to vent steam when the levers were pumped. It was all smoke and mirrors. None of it was necessary. It was all about putting on a show for the audience, giving them what they expected, which was a huge and powerful machine to look into the future or the past or wherever wonderful he chose to direct their attention. The truth was he didn't *need* tricks. He was what made the machine work. And he could only do that because of what Lockwood had done to him that night down by the Thames Embankment, pushing him down beneath the ice, chained up, mocking him to the point of death and beyond, only to have his goons bring him back, coughing and spluttering into the world he'd left behind. The natural laws of the universe didn't apply to the unnatural— which was precisely what he had become, a living dead man.

Lockwood had never understood his role in creating the Damiola that stood center stage now. Something had happened in that icy water. It wasn't simply a case of drowning, though that was what had happened. It was the coming back that had changed him. He'd been there, in the darkness, in the mists, newly dead, taking his first steps toward what came after, when he'd been pulled back to this life, the river pumped out of his lungs. And as he'd choked on that first reborn breath he'd become a different man. He had seen the face of creation, what some called God, but which was so much more than that, had been touched by the threads of life and death that run through all things, the spark that is the magic of existence, the ancient energies that hold the world together, and he had grasped his own insignificance in the scheme of things; his place in the mosaic of eternity. He understood now what God was; it was everything, all of us, every life lived, every magical spark, every soul, that at the end came together in the raw energy of the universe and simply was, the beginning, the end, and everything in between. He had taken up his place in the pattern only to be ripped out of it and dragged back down to earth, forced to live on.

How could he not be changed by that?

It was late at night, the same night that he had died and returned, and Damiola had been in his workshop when the white gloves he wore on stage for close-up magic had begun to twitch on the tabletop and move of their own accord. He'd been thinking about an elaborate re-working of the classic rabbit in a hat trick, this one with white doves, and the gloves had responded to his imaginings: the thumbs tangled and knotted, forming a crude head with fingers for wings. The satin bird tentatively took flight, struggling to lift itself at first, as though his doubts held it back, but gradually grew more confident and circled the workshop, with each circuit becoming more and more dovelike in appearance until finally he threw open the small window upstairs that overlooked Glass's film set, and the impossible bird disappeared through it, banking in the dark sky before it flew off over the make-believe rooftops of that fake city.

That was the first time something in his mind came to pass, but it was by no means the last. It was all the little things at first, vague thoughts in his mind that seemed to cause the world around him to suffer until it danced to his tune. The police-issue handcuffs that were the stock-in-trade of his escapology act simply fell away from his wrists; the padlocks securing the buckles of the asylum-stamped straitjacket sprung open, the leather straps melting away from the metal buckles. Nothing could contain him. Not even a locked coffin. He began to test the limits of enchantment, working through his repertoire of illusions and grand tricks one by one until he drove swords through his own body and lived, and locked himself in the water torture cabinet with no hope of escape—and didn't need to because the water couldn't kill him twice. That was when he knew for sure that the stage magician Damiola, Lord of Illusions, was no more. He had died forever in the river. And at the same time Damiola the magician was born.

But it wasn't until he grasped the fundamentals of where that magic was being drawn from that he truly understood the extent of his gift.

He was tapping into the mosaic.

He was drawing from the divine spark.

He was leeching off the raw elemental magic of creation.

Damiola possessed a keen scientific mind. He was rigorous in his planning when it came to his act, and methodical in its execution. He needed to understand the mechanicals. That was the way his brain worked. So, he approached his new gifts with the same scientific grounding, seeking understanding. In the days after his rebirth, he approached Alkeran, a fakir touring the country with a show that promised to unravel the mysteries of the subcontinent. His own act might have been little more than smoke and mirrors in the early days, but Alkeran offered him his first glimpse of what could only be called true magic, the greatest of which allowed him the grace to leave his body and soul and walk a short way. He studied for two months with the fakir, who himself had died and returned in a ritual of rebirth practiced by his people. That was how he knew the secrets of the mosaic, though he had a different name for the Annwyn, naming it Alam Ghaib, the Unseen Realm. Alkeran taught him that there were certain places in the world where the veil between the Unseen Realm and their own world was perilously thin, and other places where the sacred geometries intersected in nodes of power. These sacred geometries as he understood them followed what the British called ley lines and were more potent in the open air with grass or dirt underfoot, not the concrete and steel of the new world. The ancient fakir's wisdom humbled Damiola. He learned everything he could and still felt like he was barely scratching the surface of the old man's knowledge when it came to the old earth magic, but even so he couldn't truly believe until his first opiate-induced soul walk where his consciousness left his body and rose higher and higher into the heavens and beneath him saw all of the shimmering energies of the land rippling out in the vibrant colors suffusing the landscape.

Then he truly understood the magic of creation and just how insignificant he was.

Even so he wasn't brave enough to stand against Lockwood.

The man was a brutal idiot. He couldn't tell the difference between sleight of hand and proper, genuine, laws-of-physics-defying magic. How was he expected to grasp the idea that by taking Damiola to the Otherside then dragging him back again, his thuggery had opened doors that couldn't be closed again?

Damiola checked each of the optics in turn, moving around the Opticron slowly, content that the world they offered was no farther away than a few streets beyond the theater's walls. Each of the thirteen street corners that formed the perimeter of Glass Town and the anchors for his grand enchantment were reflected in the lenses.

Everything was in place.

All that remained was to wait for the final curtain.

Damiola stood in the center of the stage, looking back toward the doors. Banks of red-velvet seats tiered up away from him toward the gods. Gilt statues peered on from the sidelines, their golden faces imperious. The place smelled of magic. It was the one place in the world he truly felt alive. Damiola smiled to himself, offering a few practiced flourishes toward the bank of seats, going through the motions. It was hard to imagine that after tonight he would never set foot on a stage again.

But, in the immortal words of the Sufi poet, Rumi, "It is what it is."

God help him.

There was still time to stop Seth, to back out. Her fate wasn't sealed yet. It was still in his power to influence the outcome of the evening. If he didn't play his part, Lockwood would fail. But what price his betrayal? He wouldn't be any more likely to return to the stage and enjoy the adulation of the crowds. He would never rise to the ranks of the true greats as his gift so richly deserved. He would become a footnote on the criminal history of the city; a performer fitted for cement shoes and left to feed the fish in the polluted river. Any victory could only ever be pyrrhic. But was that better than absolute failure and being party to Lockwood's vile enterprise?

Yes. Undoubtedly. But did he have the balls to go up against the gangster? That was a different question. He'd only know the answer when it came time to act, but had no faith in his own resolve.

He was a weak man.

He saw the silhouette of a man waiting in the wings. It took him a moment to make out the familiar features. Seth Lockwood. Damiola breathed deeply—once, twice, three times—steadying himself before he left the stage.

As he descended, Damiola cast one last lingering glance up toward the Royal box where more of his backstage team were finishing resetting the props for the evening's penultimate trick in which a flaming bird—a phoenix—would fly across the stage and disappear as he clapped his hands, bursting into a shower of burning confetti. It was all about timing. There was no magic to it, only artifice, but it was pleasantly visual and grand.

"What are you doing here?" Damiola asked, not waiting for his visitor to announce himself.

"I didn't trust you to go through with things on your end, so I decided to make sure you didn't have a change of heart." There was no mistaking the menace behind the words.

"Everything is in place," he assured Lockwood. "I've paced out the perimeter, I've checked the sigils, I've calibrated the lenses and run the calculations to the nth degree, backward and forward. The numbers are right. The alignment is set. Come midnight there will be a window of time, an hour, no more, when Glass Town exists in our time stream and out of it, but then as the hour passes the anchors will weigh it down one by one and time will begin to slow within its boundaries. Once that happens, you won't be able to cross in or out of it. You'll be forced to live out your days within the streets of Glass's movie world."

"I know all this," the gangster said impatiently.

"I'm sure you do, but it bears repeating. Are you sure this is what you want?"

"I know my own mind, magician."

"You are consigning yourself to Hell, do you understand that?"

"Where I shall be the Devil, not one of his pitiful penitents. Believe me, I am aware of your superstitions. I shall be king there just as I am king here, wherever *there* may be." And that was the end of the argument.

"I have prepared certain defenses, I shall have one of my men deliver them to you before the curtain goes up. Their use is self-explanatory.

They are powerful magics, Seth, and once set in motion they can't be recalled, remember that. Time will try and fix itself, I'm absolutely sure of that. The longer Glass Town is removed from our today, the harder entropy will work to ensure that time finds its way in through any cracks or weaknesses in the lenses to where it is hidden. The glass must be maintained at all times. Should one anchor fail the entire feat will come undone, and when it does, the years will catch up with you, Seth. You can't escape them, we are all beholden to time, even if it only feels like you've lived for a few weeks or months. If the lenses fail, you will experience the toil of every single lost year. You will age years in moments. And, if enough time has passed, you will die."

"Then they better not fail," was all the gangster said to that.

"Is owning her really worth all that?"

"And more," Lockwood assured him. "I love her, magician. One day you might be lucky enough to understand what that means. I'd move heaven and earth to have her. It is that simple. That absolute. I have made my peace with this, magician. I know what I am doing, what it means. But the simple truth is I cannot bear to be even a day out of her orbit. She is the earth to my moon." For all the poetry, all Damiola could see was madness in Lockwood's eyes. There was no love here. "She will be mine, with or without your help."

"And your brother?"

"Fuck him."

"I will do what I have to do," Damiola said, and knew he would. He hated himself for it, but he was weak. The last and greatest trick of his career. It would have to last him a lifetime.

He never made it as far as the stage that night. The crowd formed a long line around the theater waiting for the doors to open, without realizing that Damiola was out there among them. He walked down the line, smiling to the few people who did a double take, almost recognizing him before he moved on to the next until he found Eleanor Raines deep in conversation with one of the women from that doomed film they were working on. No one seemed to understand that Ruben Glass was destitute, that the half-built Glass Town was the folly that ended him as a power player in the city, and that the movie he'd invested his fortune in—like the studio city he dreamed of—would never be finished. Hell, come sunrise, there would be no sign of him or his doomed empire anywhere in the city, including the streets it was built upon.

Eleanor recognized him.

Smiling, she introduced him to her companion, "Cadmus, this is Claire. She's the star of our picture. Claire, this handsome devil is Cadmus Damiola, the star of the show we're all queuing up here so diligently to watch."

"Charmed," the magician said, taking her outstretched hand and raising it to his lips.

"Likewise," Claire Greet said, offering a slight curtsy. In most company, she would have been the most attractive woman present, but even her rare beauty paled beside Eleanor's. "I trust you are going to put on quite the show for us, Mr. Damiola."

He inclined his head slightly, a wry smile spreading across his lips. "I hope you will find it unforgettable," he said. "If you would excuse me, dear lady, I need to talk to Eleanor."

"Of course, of course. Don't worry, I'll keep our place in the line." He ushered them away. Eleanor followed him to the street corner. He breathed deeply, knowing what was going to happen. It had all been carefully orchestrated like some grim dance.

He rested a hand on her shoulder.

She looked at him.

She knew something was wrong.

He didn't waste his breath trying to reassure her.

"What is it? What's wrong, Cadmus? What's happening?"

"It's your man," he said, not saying which corner of the love triangle he meant. Considering his profession, he was a lousy liar. The trick was to keep things as close to the truth as he could. "He's in trouble."

She looked nervously toward her friend, who was completely oblivious to their conversation, tapping her toe to some barely audible tune being pumped through tiny speakers in the awning, then back to Damiola. She trusted him. If he said Isaiah was in trouble, then Isaiah was in trouble. So many things communicated wordlessly between them.

They all came back to the only word she said aloud—the one word that by chance meant he wasn't lying to her. "Seth . . ."

He nodded.

"He's going to hurt him," he said, delivering the line in such as way as she couldn't possibly misinterpret the amount of pain involved.

"You can't let him. Please, Cadmus, you have to do something."

He nodded again, hating himself. "I'll take you to him, then the pair of you, you're going to have to run. Seth won't stop until both of you are dead. You do know that, don't you? He's obsessed. There's no happy ending here."

"I know," she said, sadly, like she'd always known, but had been blind to it for the longest time, attracted to the flame of fame he promised and knowing deep down she was going to get burned. "Where is he?"

"I'll take you to him," Damiola said. She didn't know him as well as she thought she did. If she had, she'd have noticed the slight tick in his cheek that he got when he was lying.

"What about the show?"

"We'll be back in time, don't worry." He looked up and down the street, seemingly checking for a taxicab. It had only been a few years since the city was awash with horse manure with over eight thousand hansom cabs working the streets, but they'd all but died out over the last couple of years. Now the fares went to Austin Low Loaders with eight thousand of those trawling the streets for passengers. There was a horse-drawn four-wheel growler outside Kelly's across the way, and beside it a couple of Rational motor cabs waiting for fares from The Savoy. Damiola had no intention of flagging down either. He raised a hand, catching the eye of Seth's man who was parked up two hundred yards down the street.

A minute later he was bundling Eleanor in the back of the car and giving the driver the address of one of the anchors. It was a relatively short drive. He had no urge to make small talk. The driver, though, was happy to fill the silences with a stream of barely comprehensible cockney babble. The streets rolled by to his commentary. Damiola checked his pocket watch. Time was running out. If he didn't time the incantation to perfection, there was no telling what would happen. The only thing he knew for sure was that Seth Lockwood wouldn't accept failure. That was why he was doing it, he realized. It wasn't about helping Seth spirit her away; it was about banishing Lockwood from the streets he terrorized.

When he thought of it that way his cowardice was almost noble.

They pulled up outside one of the many churches of London. This one was a little different as its gargoyles hid one of the magician's lenses, serving as an anchor point for his great conjuration. "We're here," he said.

There were three men waiting on the church steps, their faces obscured by the shadows cast by the steeple. Ruben Glass stood beside Isaiah Lockwood.

Isaiah came running down the steps toward them. Seth shoved him in the back, sending him sprawling down the stairs. He was on his hands and knees, battered and bloody from a proper beating, as they clambered out of the car.

"What have they done to you?" Eleanor wailed, dropping to her knees beside the love of her life. She cradled him in her arms. She didn't care about the puddles or what they would do to her dress.

Seth stayed up in the shadows.

Misdirection.

Showing the audience what they wanted to believe. The brothers were day and night to each other: one light, the other dark; one tall and thin; the other shorter, stockier. They should have been easy to tell apart, but she wasn't looking at what was in front of her, she was looking at what Damiola wanted her to see. That was the foundation for a lot of illusions. A wig to change the hair color, stoop a little to make yourself appear smaller, dress in your brother's clothes; the illusion will hold because it's not being scrutinized.

Thinking it was Isaiah, she helped Seth stand, allowing him to lean on her.

Seth didn't look up once. No eye contact. He lifted a dirty hand to his brow, and breathing hard, said, "It is time, Cadmus." Their voices were different, of course, and Seth made no effort to mask it. Eleanor wasn't listening for the subtle differences. She thought she was saving

Isaiah and nothing was going to change that until the denouement, and by that time the trick would have been played, the outcome assured. She would only see what the magician wanted her to see until it was too late to change anything.

He breathed deeply, calming himself. He was committed to this course of action. He had been ever since he'd taken the gangster's coin. You get involved with a man like Seth Lockwood, he's not content until he owns you body and soul. And he's always looking for ways to make it so.

Damiola began to intone the first few words of the invocation, feeling the faint tingle beginning in his fingertips spread quickly down the length of his arms, trammeling the bones of his rib cage to collide in a spark that ignited inside his heart, giving birth to the first true magic London had seen in generations.

The words when they came were laced with the raw elemental energy of that spark.

He raised a hand as though in farewell.

A ghostly blue glaze engulfed it.

Inside the glaze the light crackled and sparked with life as he drew on the alignment of the elements around him, the unique power of the place, and in turn its place within time, to fuel what would be his last illusion.

It still wasn't too late to back out, to turn around and walk away.

As though sensing his moment of hesitation, Seth rasped two words: "Do it."

Damiola reached up, whispering the final syllables of damnation.

The light sparked from his fingertips, hitting the lens in the center of the anchor and refracting to follow the precise lines he'd calculated that would take the light from lens to lens around the thirteen anchors completing the circuit of Glass Town.

It was a heart-stopping few seconds while they waited to see if his calculations were right, and then the sizzling line of blue-white light came racing from the lens of the last anchor streaking through the air to rejoin the first, completing the ring of blue fifteen feet above their heads.

The air stank of magic.

He couldn't remember what it had been like before when he couldn't smell the impossible. When you knew what you were looking for it was unmistakable. It was all around him, in the fresh-cut grass, in the cinnamon from the bakery on the corner, in the thick choking smog of the city and every other incredibly vivid aroma. It was the essence of magic that amplified the natural odors to the point that they were so much more powerful than any other smell in the vicinity. It wasn't some fragrance of its own. Standing there in the middle of the dirty East End street it was the reek of garbage, of rotten cabbage and urine, so much stronger now than they had been when they'd emerged from the car. There were other fragrances that refused to be overpowered by the garbage, most notably the turgid smell of the river and its murky water.

Seth grabbed Eleanor's hand and pulled her back behind the line of magic.

She fought him instinctively, recoiling from his touch.

She knew in that moment that he wasn't Isaiah, but it was too late for her.

The air between them rippled like a summer haze.

Seth turned her toward him, the wig on his head lopsided and almost comically covering half of his cruel face.

Eleanor pushed back against him, her hands on his chest. Seth reached up, gripping her by the wrists as she struggled against him. There was no mistaking who it was, or how she'd been tricked, and in that moment she seemed to move to hit him, the motion becoming a blur. Her face turned away from Seth to look hopelessly at the magician. The betrayal in her eyes burrowed into him.

Damiola watched as the magic trapped them.

There was nothing he could do now.

No place or time for regret.

He had damned her.

But it was hard to believe he couldn't just reach and pull her out of that place. Just for a second he even contemplated it, leaving Seth trapped alone on the other side, but before he could move they changed, becoming ghosts as they slipped out of time.

He hadn't noticed Ruben Glass come down the church steps to stand beside him. "That deserves a stiff drink, my man. By God does it. I can't believe that I get to wake up in a London without that bastard Lockwood tomorrow. You don't know what a great thing you've done, magician. What a great, great thing. You've saved us all."

Damiola shook his head, not so much in answer, as in denial. They were gone. "Not her. I didn't save her."

"Collateral damage," the businessman shrugged as if to say such is life. "The way I see it, it's better some woman I don't know gets hurt than me. And the way things were going, Seth had gone off the deep end. If you'd failed, we'd both be dead by dawn. Losing some real estate is a small price to pay. Lockwood's gone. We're free of his vicelike grip. That makes today a good day no matter who had to be hurt to make it happen."

"You're all heart," Damiola said.

"Better than that, I'm a free man, magician. Smell that? That fresh air? That's hard-earned, my friend. Every breath is a treasure. He's gone. Think about it for a moment. He's *gone*. I can't believe it. He's fucking well gone. Look around you; this is what London looks like without that bastard. And it's *beautiful*. Now try and tell me that's not cause for celebration?"

All Damiola could say in answer to him was, "What have we done?"

"Won," Glass said.

He wasn't so sure.

38

CLEAN SLATE

Seth closed the door behind him.

Rosie Raines led the way through to the sitting room, offering him a choice of tea or something stronger and a seat. Seth was all smiles as he took the cup from her. The room was nothing special. There were the obligatory family portraits on the mantelpiece. It was interesting to see his brother's face diluted across a few generations before it settled unerringly back in the same set of features with Josh.

"I'm sorry to turn up on your doorstep unannounced, especially at this ungodly hour, but I was hoping to catch Josh before he headed out to work."

"He's not been home all night," Rosie said. "I never know whether he's coming or going these days. Not that it makes much difference to him. He lost his job at the magazine when he did his disappearing act after the funeral."

"Some people find it difficult," Seth said, pretending empathy. "It really is a lovely house you've got here," Seth said, lying through his teeth. It was anything but lovely by any of the yardsticks he would have used for his own taste. It reeked of the old man who had lived out the last two dozen or so years of his life cooped up in it. There was little of the woman's personality on display. Indeed, since Boone's passing it had become something of a shrine to him.

"There's a lot of living been done here, that's for sure," she said, "but I don't think I'd call it lovely. Boone was never one for creature comforts, and even after he took us in, well, this was always his house."

"And now it's yours," Seth said.

"But I wish it wasn't," Rosie admitted with a resigned shrug. "I could quite happily have waited another twenty years to inherit a few bricks given the alternative."

"I'm sure. It must be a hard time for you. Like losing your husband all over again," Seth said, watching her reaction.

She looked down at her plain slippers, then up, offering a wan smile. "Thank you for coming to the funeral. It meant a lot."

"It was nothing, honestly. These family feuds can be a bit silly if you ask me. Best to keep the past where it belongs rather than keep stirring it up."

She smiled at that, and raised the bone china cup to her lips to take a sip of the steaming drink.

"I appreciated it, and what you said. You and Josh, you're family, you're the future. I won't be here forever. I worry about what will happen to him. He's a bit . . ." She seemed to struggle to find the right word, only to settle on, "lost."

"The sickness of us millennials, I'm afraid," Seth said. "I can't help but think it was easier before, now everything is at your fingertips and you're carrying around the collective knowledge of the world in your pocket. Meet a nice girl, the first thing she does is check out your digital footprint, where's the romance in that? It was so much easier when it was just that old, old story of boy meets girl."

"Quite," Rosie said. "And to be honest, sometimes I think he'll never meet anyone. He doesn't even seem all that interested most of the time. I wouldn't mind if he brought a nice young man home, either, if that's what he wanted. That's all a mother wants, you know, for her kids to find someone nice to settle down with and be happy. That's not so much to ask, is it?"

"Very enlightened of you, Rosie. I can't imagine old Gideon reacting the same way if I brought a charming young man home," Seth laughed at the thought of it. The woman was annoying him in a perfectly useless suburban housewife kind of way. Her entire world revolved around these four walls, the extent of her horizons the end of the cul-de-sac they lived on, or stretching it, the short line of shops around the corner. "It's what makes the world go around, Rosie. You don't mind if I call you Rosie, do you?"

"No, that's fine; we're family after all," she simpered. It made his skin crawl.

"Rosie," he smiled his most ingratiating smile, like a salesman offering the world. He shook his head. "It's so hard to grasp, after all this time, growing up alone, thinking there was just me, looking at the way my grandfather ruled this place with a rod of fear, me hidden away from the world," he enjoyed that line, that was clever, that was almost telling the truth, "you start to think that's all there is to life, that this small circle of people around you is everything."

"I can imagine," Rosie Raines said. Of course she could, he was describing her life.

"If I'm honest, it gets so lonely," he said, again that grain of truth as he thought about Glass Town, about the year he'd spent trying to convince Eleanor Raines to love him like he loved her, and how all of that time together just left him feeling lonelier than he ever had before. But she didn't love him. She didn't even like him. That made Glass Town his prison as much as it was hers. He'd thought about killing her not so long ago, and had come close to doing just that. If he couldn't have her, then no one would. But, when it came right down to it he couldn't bring himself to do it. That was when he'd left her to rot. He'd always known there was a weakness in Damiola's design—a crack where one of the lenses was flawed that allowed him to slip in and out of that place. It had happened twenty years after they had disappeared, a Luftwaffe bomb hit the street and tore away one side of the building. It was a miracle the glass had survived at all.

He could have killed her and walked away, into the twenty-first century and no one would have been any the wiser. It was a case of be careful what you wish for. Given his time again, he'd even come to think he'd swap places with Isaiah; let his brother have the girl after he'd used her up. There were always prettier girls. There were always more willing women. He had money, he had power; he could have anything he wanted in this place. It didn't have to be Eleanor Raines. So what had made him do it then? He thought, looking at the woman across from him. He could have her, if the whim took him. She wouldn't fight much, and the fighting only added to the thrill as far as he was concerned. So why Eleanor? The answer was simple: She was in love with his brother. His brother didn't get to win.

He breathed deeply, needing to bring his focus back to the here and now before the bitterness and anger slipped through. "And suddenly I find I've got a whole new family I'd never heard of? It's like getting a second chance at life, Rosie. Maybe that's a bit melodramatic, but I'm sure you know what I mean. Look at us sitting here having a nice chat, me and my new . . . aunt? I guess that's right. It's really something, isn't it?"

She smiled at that. "It is," she agreed.

"Did you know about me?" Seth asked, wondering if she would admit it even if she had.

She raised her cup to her lips again, taking another sip before answering. "Not really. You have to remember I married into the family. I'm not a Raines by birth; not like Josh or Barclay. I never knew Katherine; she was already dead before I met her son. There was only ever Boone, and he didn't talk much about the past. Barclay certainly didn't. I don't know what had happened between them, but he hated anything to do with the family."

Seth resisted the temptation to say that he'd been there the day her husband died, in that little tobacconists, or that he'd brought to life the kid, just like the Comedians, and made sure the knife was rammed home before he allowed the demon to fade. The old grudges ran deep. He'd thought he was ending Isaiah's line at the time. He'd made a mistake. He wouldn't make another one.

He leaned forward in his seat, hands cupped around the warmth of the bone china. "I want to know everything about you guys. Josh, his sister. I don't suppose you've got any old home movies or anything?"

"Oh, there's a few, on tape somewhere, I'll see if I can rustle something up for you to have a look at."

"That would be wonderful," Seth said.

"You can't have had it easy growing up," Rosie said.

He barked out a sharp, bitter laugh at that. "You could say that. It was certainly an experience. The kind of stuff happening around me as I grew up, the people and the way they were all so afraid of the old man, it colors how you see the world. You start to think you're untouchable. That violence and crime is a genuine answer. People look at you differently, too. They're frightened of you because of your name."

"I can only begin to imagine, but I liked what your grandfather said at the funeral, about the past being dead, wiping the slate clean, about you boys finding each other and starting again. Family's important."

"It's everything," Seth agreed. "What time did you say Josh was getting home?"

"I didn't. I never know whether he's coming or going these days. He's hardly here. After the funeral . . . I thought he'd done something stupid, he loved that old bugger like a dad, and finding him at the bottom of the stairs like that . . ." she shook her head.

Seth resisted the temptation to say he would have willingly swapped places or how much he would have enjoyed seeing the old man broken at the bottom of the stairs, one less of his brother's bastard line in the world. Instead he said, "I was really hoping I'd get to talk to him. I don't suppose you have his mobile number to hand? Maybe we could call him, let him know I'm here? I'm sure he'd come running if he knew I was."

"Oh, yes, of course, it's programmed into the phone. I never remember any numbers these days. Not like when I was younger and you knew maybe a dozen off by heart. Funny how times change, isn't it? We'd be lost without things like speed dial."

Seth smiled. "Would you mind?"

"Of course not. You boys should get to know each other. Would you like a top-up?"

"I'm good," Seth said. He hadn't taken a single sip from his cup. "But if you could find those old tapes while we're chatting, that would be great." Rosie offered no indication she'd caught the impatience in his tone, but he was going to have to be more careful if he wanted this to work. He offered that salesman's smile again as she picked up the old plastic phone's receiver and pressed the top button—speed dial 1, making the call to the most important person in her life. The little things you learned about someone just from being observant. Josh came before his sister, Alexandra. It didn't say Lexy. It was her full name. His wasn't. Good to know.

Rosie stood while she waited for the call to connect, whispering "Come on, come on," into the plastic mouthpiece, then smiled as Josh obviously picked up.

"Hello, love. Yes, no, everything's fine," she said. "Just wondering where you are? Ah, there's someone here who wants to talk to you, hold on love, I'll hand you over."

Seth reached out for the receiver. "Hello, Josh, Cousin Seth here. I've been really looking forward to talking to you."

"What the fucking fuck are you doing in my house?"

"I've just been having a pleasant chat with your mum, Cuz. She's truly delightful. I envy you."

"What do you want?"

"I was hoping you'd be here."

"If you hurt her, I'll—"

"Don't be silly, it's fine. It's hardly a wasted journey. I've seen where you grew up, seen a few family photos," he looked over at the mantel-piece where the three generations of Raines men stared back at him. "I've enjoyed myself, and I think Rosie has, too. We've bonded over stories of how hopeless our generation is when it comes to matters of the heart."

"What do you want, Seth?"

"I hope what you're doing isn't too important for you to take some time out. I think you and I should have a sit-down. Like I said at the wake, we really should get to know each other better."

"I don't need to know you better. I know exactly who you are, Seth. I know what you've done. How you betrayed your brother, how you kid-napped Eleanor. I know all about Glass Town."

"Do you now?"

"I found the magician, Seth. Think about that for a moment. He told me how to hurt you. I can end this."

"You don't want to do that," Seth said, choosing his words carefully. He kept that salesman's smile on his lips as he leaned back in the chair, projecting an image of easy conviviality. "That's too much, really. A simple get-together at the pub would suffice. You know the place, The Hunter's Horns, on the edge of the estate. I can be there in a few minutes if you want?"

"It's not happening, Seth. Not in a million years."

"I'll be there for a few hours. If you can make it, it would be really great to see you. After all, we're family. You've got to look after your own."

"I swear, you raise a finger to her, to either of them, and—"

"You kill me, Cuz. You're a funny, funny guy. I didn't expect that, but you need a sense of humor at a time like this. It's a good quality to have. I'm really looking forward to getting to know you better. I think we're going to be the best of friends."

"You don't frighten me, Seth."

"I should. It's good that your mum's so close. Just around the corner. I can pop by any time to say hi. She's promised to sort some old family movies out for me so we can have a good old reminisce together," he looked at her for confirmation that she was indeed going to sort the tapes out. She was already on her knees in front of the big old dresser rooting through the labels of dozens of VHS cassettes looking for the past.

"You're welcome anytime," she said over her shoulder, just loudly enough for her voice to carry down the line to Josh.

"Well, then, there we have it, a standing invite," Seth said, all smiles.

"Fuck you."

"All you have to do is stop what you are doing for a little while. That's not such a lot to ask, is it? We really should raise a glass to the old man; send him off in style. My treat, Cuz. What do you say? Clean slate? Come around to the family place. The way I see it, it's as much your inheritance as it is mine. The sins of the past don't belong to us. We've got a chance to be different. Blood. That's my sales pitch," he smiled at Rosie, who nodded encouragingly.

"She begged me to save her from you. That's how much she hates you, Seth. She wants out of the prison you made for her, and I'm going to get her out. I know what I have to do. I know how to stop you."

"There's something you really need to know about me, Josh, there's *nothing* I wouldn't do for my family and the people I love. Nothing. I really am looking forward to seeing you again. I think we understand each other."

39

POSITIVES AND NEGATIVES

"Jesus fucking fuck."

"What? What is it?"

"He's in my fucking *house*. Jesus fuck, Julie, he sat there beside my *mum,* taunting me. Fuck. Fuck. Just . . . fuck."

"Slow down," Julie said. "What did he say to you?"

"He told me I should be frightened of him . . ."

"You should be. I am. Anyone in his right mind would be."

"He's not going to win, Julie. He's not. We've got to stop him."

Julie looked at his watch. "Listen to me, Josh. You need to stay calm. Okay?" He put his hands on Josh's shoulders and forced him to look him in the eye. "What is this about?" He didn't let Josh answer. "Eleanor Raines. That hasn't changed. Nothing has actually changed, has it? No, that's not true, one thing *has* changed: you know how to beat him. Right?"

Josh nodded, but it was obvious he was fighting every instinct to head for the stairs and race all the way back to the Rothery, playing right into Seth's hands.

"You still know how to beat him, don't you?"

Josh nodded again.

"Right, so nothing has *really* changed. You still hold the same hand you did before you picked up the phone. He's trying to call your bluff."

"He's in my house," Josh repeated, as if he could make Julie understand the implications of what that meant by sheer force of will.

"I get it. I do. I know what you're dealing with better than anyone, remember? He killed my partner. I know exactly what he's capable of. But I've put my faith in you. I need you to come through. Otherwise, to be blunt, I'm fucked. So get a grip. What did he want?"

"To frighten me."

"Right, but what did he say? You asked him a couple of times, what did he say?"

"That he thought I'd be there. That we should take time out; sit down together. He wants me to go to his family's pub, The Hunter's Horns."

"You don't want to do that."

"No shit."

"No, I mean if you're going to meet him, it should be neutral ground, not walking into the belly of the beast. You don't stand a chance on their turf. You've got to be clever about this."

"I know exactly what I've got to do; I've got to destroy the anchors Damiola put in place. Shatter them and bring the curtain crashing down on Seth Lockwood once and for all."

"It sounds easy when you put it like that," Julie said. "Look, do me a favor, hold fire a couple of minutes, I'm desperate for a piss. Point me in the direction of the bathroom, then we'll head out and do some shattering."

"Through that way," Josh pointed.

Julie locked himself in the bathroom, then opened the window. He took his phone from his pocket and dialed the number Seth had put in his contact list. It was picked up on the first ring.

"Julie, Julie, Julie. I hope you're calling with good news?"

"I'm with him now," Julie whispered, leaning his head out of the window so the wind could blow away his words. It wasn't foolproof, but he needed to get a message to Lockwood without tipping Josh Raines off to the fact that he was playing both sides against the middle. "He's coming for you."

"Good. Let him come. I'm ready. I'll rip his fucking balls off and make yo-yos out of them."

"He reckons he knows how to beat you," Julie hesitated, not sure he really wanted to throw his lot in with Lockwood. The silence on the other end of the line was expectant. He seriously thought about hanging up, flushing the toilet, and heading out of the flat, out of the city, and then ultimately out of the country. It was a big world. It might all be connected, but you could still disappear if you were willing to forego certain creature comforts. "He said he's going to destroy the anchors. I don't know what that means, but he seems pretty sure it'll fuck you up."

"That can't happen, Julie. I'm putting my trust in you now. I need you to handle it. Look after me and I'll look after you; that's how this arrangement of ours works. And remember, I know where the bodies are buried. Well, the body, at any rate. Don't disappoint me. When you know which anchor he intends to target, send word. I'll do the rest." Seth killed the call.

Julie slipped his phone back into his pocket, and then closed the window.

He flushed the toilet and ran the taps before he unlocked the bathroom door.

Josh waited for him at the top of the staircase; no sign that he'd heard the hushed conversation.

"Okay, where are we going?"

"Two choices, an abandoned church, or an abandoned cinema; the others are too public."

"I'm not a particularly religious guy," Julie said.

"And the lens setup is probably easier to find in a cinema," Josh mused. "Given there's a whole projection room filled with the kind of equipment Damiola would have used."

"Makes sense. And it seems fitting, you know, looking for a lost actress in an abandoned cinema. There's something right about it. Where's the cinema?"

"It's the old one on Latimer Road."

"I know it," Julie said. Too well, Julie thought, remembering vividly what had happened the last time he'd set foot in the place. He had no intention of going back there. At the very least Taff's blood was still on the floorboards; at the very worst the woman was still there. "But, you know, there's a lot to be said for an abandoned church, including the whole having fallen out of favor with God thing. Think about it, if you were Lockwood, where would you expect you to go? The cinema, right? Everything about this revolves around movies: Hitchcock's lost film, an actress that disappeared right off the set, even the place, what did you call it, Glass Town? Used to be a film studio, our failed attempt at a Hollywood. So if I were him, I'd be *expecting* you to go to the old Latimer Road cinema. I vote for the church. Try and blindside him. Any advantage we can get, right?" He hoped he'd sold it hard enough without overselling it. He didn't want Josh thinking he was trying to steer him away from the cinema for any reason other than that it made sense to try and outthink Lockwood and exploit any slight advantage they could maneuver.

He willed Josh to say they were going to the church.

"Makes sense," his unsuspecting partner agreed.

"I'm driving," Julie said, heading for the door.

"You don't know where you're going," Josh called, heading down after him.

"That's why you're navigating."

He popped the lock so that Josh could clamber in, and in those few seconds took his phone out to text a single word to Seth: *church*. He couldn't be more specific than that, both because of the time it took to type out even a short message and because he didn't actually know which church was their destination. Seth would, though. He slipped the phone back into his pocket and got in.

"What were you doing out there?" Josh asked, as he got in beside the wheel.

"Just checking in to see there were no messages from the station. I'm supposed to be on duty in an hour, but that's not happening. Obviously."

They drove a while in silence, both men wrapped up in their own thoughts. Julie followed the occasional left, right instructions, resisting the temptation to point out it would be much easier if Josh just told him where they were going. He tried to picture the map scorched into the floorboards and work out where the church was based on their current route, but his mind didn't work that way. He envied the cabbies who, armed with The Knowledge, could plot the fastest path between any two points in the city unerringly, taking into account traffic flow and congestion. He could barely manage to find his way through some of the backstreets around the Rothery and he'd been driving them for the best part of a year.

He reached down to put the stereo on. He was fidgety and didn't want his passenger to realize just how nervous he was. The CD started playing. It was one of Taff's. It was the absolute last thing Julie wanted to hear. Keeping his eyes on the road, he leaned forward and fumbled with the buttons to switch it over to the radio, picking up the jarring fiddles of the Levellers on a slightly off-station Absolute Radio. "Better," he said even as the static crackled across the airwaves.

As the streets grew grubbier and darker, so, too, did the music. It didn't matter; Julie wasn't listening to it anymore. He was trying to figure a way out of the mess he was in.

It took another ten minutes and twice as many turns as they tacked a way across the capital before the church with its gaping hole where there should have been a spire and bats up in the belfry came into sight. It looked curiously lopsided, like a caricature of a haunted house up on a green and unpleasant hill—this one surrounded by ring after ring of cracked and broken tombstones. The roof had collapsed over the altar and several of the stained-glass windows were broken, letting the elements in.

They parked the car and stood at the old lych-gate. It looked like it belonged on a much grander structure than the dilapidated church. Julie looked around. There was no sign of Seth, but that didn't mean he didn't have eyes and ears in place. Weeds had reclaimed the path that wound its way through the gravestones to the imposing archway where there used to be huge double doors. The greenery turned the granite slabs into tiny cobbles. Immense tree roots rose out of the ground to reach up over some of the graves, while the patron saints set to look over them lay on their sides—chipped, weathered, and broken. Julie saw a headless statue atop one of the graves, hands still clasped in prayer. Beside it words had been hammered into the lead above a sunken mausoleum's door. The sign said: *The Flesh Also Shall Rest In Hope.* The wingless angel lying on her back amid the tall grasses didn't offer much hope, Julie thought bleakly. The old churchyard grounds were heavily forested off to the left; while on the right, red-brick factories crowded the skyline. None of the gravestones were regular or whole. Several of the granite skirts that had outlined the shapes of the graves were buckled and balanced precariously where the ground beneath them had slipped away forming undulating hills that rippled all the way to the tree line.

"What is this place?"

"An anchor," Josh said. "There's a lens somewhere here, one of Damiola's glasses."

"How do we find it?" Julie asked, but Josh already had the battered compact in his hand. He turned his back to the derelict church and raised the compact high enough so that it showed the building in the glass.

"Here, look," Josh said, urgently. "Can you see it this time? Tell me you can see it."

Julie didn't know what to expect when he looked in the glass, but it wasn't the sight of a halolike crackle of energy running around the rooftop or the sight of the spire fully restored, black slates glittering with early morning dew. A too-white line chased through the halo's core, sparking as it passed through the hands of a leering gargoyle perched on the corner of the rooftop. A glint of sunlight reflected off the glass in the gargoyle's grasp. "I see it," he said. "I don't understand it, but I see it; up there in the gargoyle's hands."

Josh Raines nodded. "Damiola's glass. There are thirteen of them ringing the perimeter of Glass Town. It never disappeared. It was never redeveloped after the film studio failed. The magician did something that moved it a step out of time, I think, or pushed it through to another place that exists a step out of time from us. On the other side of those lenses time slows down to the point that one year passes in a hundred on this side."

Julie shook his head. "How the fuck is that possible?"

He turned around, looking at the church without its spire. The gargoyle was still in place, though half of his face appeared to be weathered away to the point that it looked as though the poor creature had

had a stroke. The spire wasn't the only thing that was missing. He couldn't see the halo.

He looked in the glass again, reassuring himself both were there, then looked back at the reality of the church and its crumbling walls.

"I just don't . . ."

"I can't pretend that I understand the where's and why's either, beyond saying it's magic, but it is what it is. There's no point standing around arguing the physics of it. This is how we beat Seth. We shatter that lens, bringing down this corner of the illusion. Without it, the magic can't hold. Then we go after the next and the next until there's none left. Seth was born over a century ago, all we have to do is wait for time to catch up with him."

"You make it sound simple," Julie said, looking up at the deformed gargoyle.

"As easy as breaking glass."

"What can possibly go wrong?" Julie muttered to himself, looking around for any sign that the gangster had arrived. Behind them, nothing moved. Not even the leaves on the trees in the slight breeze. The silence was unnerving. "So, how? I mean, have you thought about how you're going to get up there?" Julie pointed up toward the gargoyle that was perched about twenty feet above their heads.

It was obvious that he hadn't.

He looked about for something to throw at it, crouching down to pick up a fist-sized rock. He threw it and missed by a good three feet, the rock powdering part of the old stone where it hit.

"This could take a while," Julie joked.

"Not helping."

"Wasn't trying to."

Julie glanced back toward the lych-gate again. There was no way Seth wasn't going to pull something. He wouldn't just stand by and let them destroy the glass given just how important it was to his survival. Lockwood had given him one task: convince Josh to let it go. He'd failed abjectly at that. Josh was more determined than ever, but that was Lockwood's fault; he'd gone blundering in in his size twelves threatening Josh's mother. He didn't have to do that. It wasn't big, it wasn't clever, and it made no sense. It wasn't a smart play. The problem, as Julie saw it, was that Lockwood *was* clever. He was deliberate, manipulative, and dangerous. That he'd pushed Josh into lashing out couldn't be some unforeseen side effect of him trying to be too clever for his own good. He wanted Josh to lash out. Somehow, someway, it benefited him. It had to. But if Josh was right and that by breaking the lens he'd doom Seth, how could that be winning?

"Who are you expecting to see back there," Josh said, a new stone in his hand.

"Just thinking," Julie said. "This is a mistake. We shouldn't be here."

"What?"

"It's a trap, it's got to be. Think about it, why did he make your mum call you?"

"It was a warning," Josh said.

Julie was unconvinced, and would have been even without knowing his own part in the setup. "Or it was meant to force you into action," he suggested. "This is a man who has lived his life scaring the living fuck out of people. If there's one thing he knows how to do it's put the frighteners on people. He knew you'd do this, go after the anchors. It's your only way to hurt him, you said so yourself, but look around you, he hasn't tried to stop you. If you accept he's not an idiot, and that he's been one step ahead of you—at least one—every step of the way, that means he *wants* you to do this. He's counting on it."

Josh shook his head. "No. No. That's not right. It can't be."

"It has to be," Julie said, realizing the extent of just how badly he'd been lied to. "He's going to kill you here. You said it yourself, right at the beginning; he's going to kill you. He doesn't want you to stop looking for Eleanor Raines; he wants you dead, like your dad, like your granddad. He wants his brother's line ended, and you're the last. It's all about family for him, and when Isaiah took her name he stopped being a Lockwood. He stopped being family. He became the enemy."

Josh continued to shake his head, but Julie could see the doubt creeping in. He looked around again, seeing this time all the places Lockwood could be lurking, all of the culverts and tumbledown stones and realizing just how vulnerable they were out there in front of the church.

"We should get out of here."

"Go if you want, I'm not going anywhere. I came here to destroy the anchor, that's what I'm going to do."

Julie backed up a couple of steps, his feet crunching on the gravel underfoot. "Don't do this. You're playing into his hands. I know you think this is your idea, but it's not. It can't be. He's too fucking shrewd for that. He's playing you, Josh. He wants you to break that thing," but Josh wasn't listening. He walked up to the side of the church and reached up, feeling out the crumbling stones for makeshift handholds.

A couple of seconds later he boosted himself up and started to scramble up the side of the church, the cornerstones between his legs. Halfway up, with the gargoyle still out of reach, he leaned back looking for more handholds. It was the kind of stupid maneuver that, had he been unluckier, would have ended with him breaking his neck, but whatever god, angel, or devil who looked after idiots was watching over him.

Julie saw Josh reach out for the glass sphere hidden in plain sight within the gargoyle's stone talons. Josh leaned out perilously, straining to tease the glass free with his fingertips. Julie could hear the sizzle of the current surging unseen through the lens as it chased around the cordon of Glass Town maintaining the century-old spell. Josh leaned a little farther, his weight very much being taken by the fingers of his left hand as he flapped upward with his right, trying unsuccessfully to dislodge the glass.

Julie heard a dog barking in the distance. The sound made him shiver, as though someone had walked over his grave. He didn't like this one little bit. It was all wrong. "He's going to kill you," he said again, even though Josh was too far away to hear. He was absolutely sure of it.

And then Josh cried triumphantly, pulling the magician's lens free of the gargoyle's clutches. He held it aloft like Liberty's torch, then with what felt like slow-motion horror to Julie, let it spill off the end of his fingertips and fall.

It shattered on the chips of stone twenty feet below.

The barking intensified: closer, louder, savage now.

Julie looked around for the source, expecting to see a pack clawing up the road, snapping and snarling.

Nothing.

He turned back to look at Josh, and through the open arch where the church doors should have been saw the shimmering haze of a dark street and up above he saw a stray moonbeam and around it, streaks of shooting stars as if all of those thousands of points of light were falling from the sky. When he looked down from that impossible sky he saw a dog—only it couldn't be a dog, it lacked any kind of tone or color, like a photograph in negative. The dark patches of fur were blisteringly bright; its eyes two blazing white spheres in the center of its skull. It tore up the street that was somehow—incredibly, impossibly—through the archway. Behind the Negative, deep in the heart of the abandoned church where the movie-set street opened up into a Victorian square, he saw a woman in a red dress. He knew her. Even across the distance—across the time—she was unmistakable.

Eleanor Raines's screams chased the dog as it barreled out through the archway.

Still, the rabid animal didn't make a sound, yet the barking all around him intensified in its savagery, the strays of this London raging against its unnatural presence. How many dogs were there out there, descending on the derelict church? Ten? Twenty? The pack's howls spiraled, becoming a dizzying cacophony.

Julie felt the warmth leech out of the air as the Negative prowled toward him, its nearness placing a chill deep in his heart that spread through every vein and artery, putting ice where there had been hope. He felt his vision blur, the dual city within a city before him swimming out of focus as he struggled to cling on to his sense of self. Julie felt himself diminishing, the world around him pitching beneath his feet as he clung to the nearest gravestone to stay upright. The dog closed the distance between them from thirty feet to ten.

Julie stumbled back trying to put precious distance back between them, but in doing so lost his grip on the headstone and with it, his footing.

He went down, unable to take his eyes off the Negative as it loomed over him, salivating, strings of black spittle stretched out between sharp teeth. The Negative pressed him down, claws on his chest. He could see the rapid rise and fall of its rib cage, the flare of its nostrils, those strings of spittle snapping as its white eyes burned, but it still didn't make a sound.

He clawed at the ground, trying to push himself up, but the weight on his chest kept him pinned to the dirt. Try as he might, there was no getting out from under the beast. Julie wriggled desperately beneath the Negative, but couldn't dislodge it. Its breath tasted strange on his face. It wasn't brimstone or anything Hellish. It was blandly chemical. He reached up to push the thing off, and where his hands came into contact with the Negative's flesh, they came away stained black. He couldn't feel anything. No tightness of skin. No burning.

Those too white eyes stared through him.

Those eyes were *fierce*.

The Negative lowered its mouth to feed, teeth opening as it sought out the heat of his pulse in his throat. When he thought all was done, the Negative's black teeth inches from sinking into his meat, he willed himself gone, out of his head, somewhere it couldn't hurt.

The pain never came.

The grotesque monstrosity stopped and tilted its head, nostrils flaring as it sniffed at the air—once, twice, three times—its head swiveling left and right, before it turned to stare up at the still-stranded Josh clinging on precariously to the wall.

It bounded away from Julie, leaving him gasping, shivering and dizzy from the shock that somehow he was living not dying. He could feel the warmth of blood on his chest, a very mortal reminder that things didn't have to stay that way.

He was on his feet a moment later, hand pressed to his chest, his blood dribbling out between his fingers where the Negative's claws had pierced his flesh, and yelling barely coherently, *"What the fuck is that thing?"*

He didn't expect an answer.

Certainly not the one he got.

"My pet," Seth said, emerging from the sanctity of the abandoned church. "Don't be afraid, Julie, she's not here for you. You've done well. I couldn't have done this without your help. Now," Lockwood turned to look up at Josh. "Do come down from there before you fall and hurt yourself. And you will; she has that effect on people. She really sucks all the fun out of life. Tell him, Julie. You know what I'm talking about. I can see it written all over your face, plain as day."

The Negative prowled around the ground beneath Josh, waiting for him to fall. Julie could still feel the dread its nearness had instilled in him, the sheer overwhelming urge to just give up, to curl up fetally, and surrender.

"I can't . . ."

"Don't be so modest, Julie. You've got quite a way with words. You must have, to have lied so convincingly that young Josh here swallowed your bullshit."

"It wasn't like that," he said, telling himself that, telling Josh that, telling Seth that. Not one of them believed him.

"What's happening to me?" Josh moaned. "I can't see. Oh, Christ . . . I CAN'T SEE!"

"Ah, that's not good," Seth said, quite matter-of-factly.

And then Josh lost his grip.

40

HANDS ACROSS LONDON

The world was turned on its head.

Josh twisted against the chains trussing him up. The place—wherever it was—was dark. The air against his skin was cold, making him think it was some sort of warehouse or meat locker. Somewhere Lockwood wouldn't be disturbed while he dispensed his tortures. Somewhere Josh really didn't want to be.

Time passed.

Too much of it.

The darkness was dislocating and disorientating. It threatened to consume him. He was alone with his thoughts, and that was the last place he wanted to be. Images of the Negative plagued him. Was it out there in the silence? He couldn't feel the ice where his bones ought to be, so surely that meant he was safe from it, at least for now?

The last thing he remembered was losing his sight; then falling.

So maybe it wasn't dark at all, maybe this was his life now?

A world of nothing.

He struggled to straighten up, reaching to clutch his legs and for a moment at least relieve the pressure of the blood pounding through his skull. Surely the bones couldn't take the relentless pounding. Something inside had to give eventually, a tiny blood vessel somewhere deep inside the labyrinth of his brain rupture in a fatal aneurysm and end him. Folded double, struggling to stay upright long enough to reach up with his right hand to fumble with the chains binding him at the ankles, Josh felt the weight of the thick padlock rattle against the chains as he wrestled hopelessly against his bonds. He was going nowhere. He fell back down, resigned to whatever the darkness had in store.

More time passed. It crawled, it raced; it lost all meaning.

Josh listened desperately for any sign that he wasn't alone, fearing that Seth was just going to leave him hanging until he slowly dehydrated and starved to death.

Finally he heard something. It wasn't a comforting sound.

Rats.

He heard them scuttling about in the darkness, getting braver, edging closer. Their claws scratched on the concrete floor.

He missed the silence.

How long would Seth leave him hanging?

A day? Two? Too long?

Out in the darkness he heard the roll and slam of steel shutter doors going up and down, followed by slow, measured footsteps.

"Who's there?" he called out. "Who is it?"

"No ghost," Seth said. "No demon, no devil, and definitely no salvation. Just me." He was nothing more than a voice in the darkness. "I hope that's enough?"

The chains rattled as Josh turned again, wriggling around frantically like a daddy longlegs under a magnifying glass on a bright summer day. The sound swelled to fill his head, overwhelming his senses.

Footsteps echoed as Seth slowly paced around him.

The first punch landed with shocking savagery, crunching into his solar plexus. The impact spun him around in another dizzying twist. The second, a sucker punch to the jaw, split his lip and left him dazed and gagging with nothing to focus on. Flashes of light—fireworks of white every bit as intense as the Negative's eyes—went off inside his skull. The seconds it took for them to stop were filled with burning pain.

He grunted, trying not to give Seth the satisfaction of knowing how badly the blows hurt.

"That's better," Seth said, sweetly. "Want to make sure you are focused on just how much trouble you're in, Cuz."

"It's over, Seth, I won," Josh said, tasting blood on his tongue.

"Hmm? Interesting idea," Seth said after a moment. "What makes you think that?"

"I broke the glass, the magic can't hold."

"Well, well, well. It seems that you're not an idiot after all. Wrong, but not an idiot."

"Take the piss all you want, Seth. You lose. Time is stealing into Glass Town. You're wasting what little of it you have left to hurt me? That's fine. If that's what you need to do, have at it. I don't care. It's over, *Cuz*. I beat you. *Bang-bang,* you're dead." His voice sounded hollow in the vast space beyond the dark.

He had no idea where he was; one of Lockwood's old warehouses down by the Thames, maybe? Somewhere his body could be conveniently dumped? *If this was how it was going to end,* he thought fatalistically, *at least it ends with a win. I've had worse days.*

"You really don't have any idea, do you? Jesus, you poor fucking fool, Josh. I really thought you were brighter than that. Listen to me; I'm not dying any time soon. Ever, if I have my way. There's so much living left to be done. Some days it feels like it hasn't even *started.* I own this city, both versions of it, back then and here and now. I *own* it. I'm the most frightening fucker you've ever met. The most dangerous fucking fucker of all the fuckers out there. I'm the King Fucker. And that means I don't lose to scrotes like you. All that blood's going to your head. You look like a big purple cockhead about to explode."

"Is that supposed to frighten me?" Josh said, the words braver than he felt. He was alone in the dark, trussed up like a piece of meat in a slaughterhouse waiting to go under the knife.

"It should, if for no other reason than I can back my words up." To drive the point home Seth delivered another punishing blow, this one into the soft stuff of his stomach. The pain took endless seconds to subside.

Seth stepped back. Josh tried to follow the sound of his footsteps as he circled him slowly, the echoes and silence between each one filled with menace.

"You ever hear the phrase 'putting the frighteners on someone'?"

"I know what it means."

"Good, now I understand you don't want to give the magician up. I respect that. No one likes a grass. But I'm going to take a moment to show you just how wrong you are about everything. I'm going to let your level of fuckedness sink in, and then I'm going to give you a choice."

Josh heard the flick of a metal lid going back followed by the rasp of a milled wheel on the flint as a small flame sprung to life before him. Behind the flame Seth looked like a man possessed, the dancing red light reflected in his wild eyes.

It hurt to focus, stinging tears from him, but he didn't care because it meant he wasn't blind.

Seth held out his free hand.

There was something in it.

Josh blinked against the tears filming his eyes, trying to make out what it was. It took him a moment. It was the battered gold compact Damiola had given him. Slowly, Seth manipulated the clasp to pop it open.

There was no reflection of the flame inside the compact.

There was no glass in it.

"Imagine my surprise when I walked over to where you'd fallen, expecting to find that you'd broken your neck in the process, but instead found *this* lying in the shards of broken glass? Talk about killing two birds with one stone. I'd been looking all over London for this, and you had it all the time. The magician's looking glass, the locus of the whole web of illusions, the secret to Glass Town, and it was in your fucking *pocket*? Priceless. I'd had the Comedians tearing apart the city looking for Damiola's damned glass. I fed that bent fucking copper to one of the Rushes because of this thing. Now I understand why he failed me. I thought he was just too busy fucking the life out of his movie star whore, but no, it wasn't there to be found because you had it all along."

He didn't say anything else for a while, seeming to savor the irony of the situation.

"You want to know *why* it's so wonderful that you turned up with this when you did? That piece of glass is exactly what I needed to repair the damage you'd done. In fact it was the only thing that would. How delicious is that?"

Josh wasn't looking at the glassless compact anymore, he was focused intently on the imperfections of the hand holding it. He'd never noticed it before, but then they'd hardly spent any time together. The fourth finger of Seth's left hand was cut short at the knuckle and had no fingernail. Maybe Damiola's half joke about Seth defying the ravages of time by cutting out his own heart and hiding it in a lead-lined box wasn't so far from the truth after all. The fingertip wasn't exactly vital, but if it meant he never truly left the confines of Glass Town, then the relative immortality its loss conferred was surely worth the sacrifice to a man like Seth?

Seth capped the lighter again, taking what little light there had been with it.

Josh welcomed the darkness. It meant that Seth couldn't see his face and there was no way he could betray himself.

"You interest me, Josh. I see a lot of my brother in you."

"That's not particularly reassuring, given what you did to him," Josh said.

"Funny, I like that. For a while back there, I loved him. He was my best friend. We were *brothers*. Proper brothers. He helped me do what needed to be done. We started out side by side and ruled this city together. You didn't know that, did you? The Isaiah you know is the broken man hunting for his lost love, but that's not who he was. Not when we were young. He was ruthless. He had it in him to be a fucking *warrior*, Josh. A warrior. I was nasty, but he was capable of so much worse than me, because he was so cold and calculating about it. If I was fire, he was ice. I swear; you met him, you wanted to be him. Everyone loved Isaiah. But you crossed him at your peril. Christ, he could hold a grudge. But then, look at the mess you're in, that's because he could never let anything go. It's been a hundred fucking years, he's as dead as a fucking dodo, and he's *still* got you lot doing his dirty work. That's some serious grudge holding."

"You ruined his life."

"He ruined it himself. I just wanted one of the pieces. One. I left him everything else. I left him our fucking *kingdom*. In return I only ever wanted to be left alone. He was the most powerful man in London and he threw it all away. For what?"

"Love," Josh said, as though it were the most obvious thing in the world.

"Don't make me laugh," Seth said. "Love? What is that? Honestly? Some fleeting obsession with a face? Your heart skips a beat because you like someone's bone structure? You suffer some insane impulse to be inside someone and can't think about anything else? What is it they say, 'One person is pretty much like any other lying down?' We're all wet; we're all hard. We're all basically the same meat. So what are we talking about? A chemical reaction? Some kind of hormonal thing we're helpless to resist? How the fuck does that make you feel, Cuz? A slave to the chemicals that make up your flesh? It'd depress the hell out of me, to be brutally honest."

"Says the man who made part of London disappear because of a woman."

"Yeah, well, therein lies the mystery of it, doesn't it? Love. Ask me today and the truth I'd have to tell you is very different from the one I would have had for you in 1924. So, here's my offer: let's put an end to this silliness, no more Lockwoods and Raineses, come back into the fold. Unify the family. Be my right hand, brothers in arms."

"Let's get the band back together?" He felt ludicrous saying it, hanging there by his feet, the blood pooling inside his head, Seth's prisoner.

"That or just agree to go our separate ways, East is East, and all that shit."

"What's in it for you?"

"Like it or not, we're family, Josh. My blood flows in your veins. That's got to count for something in this fucked-up world we live in, hasn't it? What are we without family?"

"I don't trust you."

"And you shouldn't, but you're alive aren't you? I could have let the Negative drain you until you were nothing but an empty husk; that's what it does, you know. Your magician friend created it to be a guardian on the threshold, to make sure nothing got into or out of his precious

Otherworld. I could have put my hand over your mouth and nose and watched you kick and scream pitifully until you ran out of air. You couldn't have stopped me. I could have killed you back in the street when you ran out of Glass Town straight in front of Officer Gennaro's car. It wouldn't have been difficult. It was chaos. Cars, buses, people. I could have made it look like an accident. But I didn't."

"Am I supposed to thank you?"

"Maybe you should. You owe me. Can I ask you a question, Josh?"

"Can I stop you?"

"What have you got?"

"What do you mean?"

"I mean you don't have the glass. That means you can't see the anchors anymore, they're lost to you. You can't find your way back into Glass Town. Your ally, the man who promised to fight at your side to bring me down? Julius Gennaro is my bitch. After he put a bullet in his partner's head he became mine. His prints are on the smoking gun and the body's hidden away where no one is going to find it unless I want it found. I own him. How do you think I found you? He told me where you were. So, I'll ask you again, what have you got?"

Seth waited for an answer.

Josh didn't have one for him.

"I can tell you if you like: You've got nothing. I'm offering you a way out of this nightmare, Josh. No recriminations. I'm not saying you and me forever, but we can finish what Isaiah and I started. Think about it. It's symmetry. It fits. It's right. Take your time, don't just be pigheaded and dismiss my offer."

"And if I say no? Then you kill me?"

Seth didn't answer that, not at first. He simply walked another circuit around him in the darkness.

"Is that your answer?" he asked finally. "Because honestly, I'll be pretty disappointed if it is."

Josh said nothing.

"Man, you're making this so fucking *hard*. It doesn't have to be. Just let it go, Cuz. Please. Not for me, for the people around you that you love. Do it for Rosie. Do it for that lovely sister of yours; what's her name again? Alexandra? Pretty little thing. Do it for them. Forget you ever heard about Glass Town and Eleanor Raines. It'll be better that way. Because as much as I might want to, I won't kill you. I promise you that. What I *will* do is strip you of everything you have ever loved. Everything that's ever meant anything to you. I'll take everything you've ever cared about, everyone you've ever cared about, and I'll put a torch to them. I'll burn them until there's nothing left but bones and ash. It's who I am. So think about it, and remember that whatever happens now, it's on you. You did this. I gave you a way out. All you had to do was take it, not try and be clever and piss on my outstretched hand."

Seth didn't say anything else.

He didn't need to.

He walked away, leaving Josh hanging by the feet in the darkness to regret what he hadn't said.

The death rattle of the shutters rolling up and slamming back down into place filled the darkness, stealing hope far more cruelly than the Negative had. He squirmed against the chains, thrashing about in an attempt to pull himself up for more than a couple of seconds. Josh snatched hold of the chains around his feet, rubbing the skin of his ankles raw and bloody as he tried to work them loose.

There was no way he was getting out of here.

He fell back, tears of frustration burning his cheeks.

He hated Seth Lockwood with all of his soul. He hated Julie Gennaro for betraying him. But most of all he hated himself for losing. He'd had the glass, he'd known what he had to do, but he'd broken his promise. He hadn't saved Eleanor. He hadn't even come close. She'd put her faith in him, and he'd let her down by playing right into Seth's hands. The taste of disappointment was as bitter as the blood in his mouth. Who was going to save her now?

Seth was right; he had nothing.

He saw a light—the beam from a torch spearing through the darkness up ahead, roving all over the place, to reveal the contours of his dark world. He was inside some sort of warehouse. Chains and hooks for freight hung from steel crossbeams. Crates lined one corrugated iron wall. They were stamped with the crest of some company that had gone out of business long before he'd been born.

"Take me to him," a brittle voice said from behind the light. A few seconds later the light was bright in his face, and there were hands on his body.

"Don't try and move. Hold on."

It was Julie. He wrestled with the padlock securing his chains. He didn't have a key. He had a pair of bolt cutters.

"Get away from me," Josh hawked and spat a wad of bloody phlegm into the middle of the light. As defiances went it was petty and pointless. He wasn't getting out of here without help, and like it or not, his betrayer had just become the cavalry.

Beside Julie a man in a wheelchair looked on. Gideon Lockwood, the king of East London in his wheelchair chariot. Josh had been wrong when he'd seen him at the funeral, he wasn't a shrunken soul; he had been hiding his strength behind the ravages of age.

The old man rose slowly from his chair, coming to stand in front of Josh. "Before we free you," he said, "I want you to promise me one thing. Promise me that you will kill my father."

It hung in the air between them, demanding a truth he was more than happy to give.

"I'll try."

"Cut him down," Gideon told Julie.

"With pleasure."

41

THESE DREAMS

Seth drew the film out of the old cassette. He'd watched it on fast-forward until he'd found what he was looking for: Barclay Raines caught full frame looking toward the camera; love in his eyes, the sun in his face, his son disappearing off camera. It was the perfect shot. He wasn't entirely sure what he had in mind would work, but if it did, well, it would be sheer poetry. He clipped the individual frames out and fitted them into the barrel on Damiola's Carousel, then carried the old praxinoscope out to the car. He didn't bother locking the door. No one would be foolish enough to rob him.

It was only a few streets back through the Rothery to the house on Albion Close where Rosie Raines would have all of her Christmases rolled into one. He smiled at the thought of his own generosity.

He clambered out of the car and crouched down on the grass outside of her house, the carousel in the dirt beside him. There were lights on in other houses around the cul-de-sac, but no one was playing nosy neighbor. He scratched out a pattern in the dirt, each stroke rendered with precision. Satisfied with his artwork, he took a knife from his pocket, flicked open the blade, and drew a shallow gash the length of his palm to drip blood onto each of the symbols carved into the ground before he took a match from the box in his pocket, and lit the candle in the center of the zoetrope with it. He let more blood drip into the wax puddling around the base of the carousel. His blood sizzled, crusting around the candle, the smell of burning rich in the air as he conjured forth one of the Rushes.

He turned the small handle through seven revolutions until the drum spun under its own momentum, before he opened the carousel's hood.

The flickering candlelight was projected into the middle of the small garden in front of him.

Slowly, with each rattling revolution of the carousel, a man's stuttering silhouette began to take shape within the light.

Two more turns of the handle and the flickering frames settled on the shape of a man, his face still indistinct as the drum rattled around another revolution. It didn't become any clearer as he whipped the small handle around another couple of turns, setting the drum to clattering against the central rod it spun around. The man before him became ever more substantial. In just a few seconds it looked as though he had never died at all. Barclay Raines stood in the middle of the grass. The amber glow from the streetlight betrayed the solidity of the illusion.

The match burned out as the carousel came to a stuttering stop.

Barclay Raines turned to face Seth. His smile was just as it had been in the home movie. Unlike Myrna Shepherd, who had been conjured from a much cruder image, Barclay Raines's face was beautifully rendered. He wore the same casual white cotton shirt and jeans he'd worn on that day, the lick of unruly hair that refused to follow the line of his parting seemed to ripple in the wind, so perfect was the illusion. Unlike Myrna Shepherd, he was also rendered in vivid color.

Seth stood slowly and walked up to the man he'd had killed—at least tangentially—once already in this lifetime, and stood face-to-face with his invocation.

He walked around the apparition, looking at it from all angles. It was perfect in every detail. It was Barclay Raines. Right up until the moment it opened its mouth and a burst of static crackled out of it, but beggars couldn't be choosers. Besides, Rosie Raines wouldn't see that far into the illusion. It didn't need to be a smooth talker or woo her with promises of love. The heart wants what the heart wants. And in this case the impossible yearning of grief left to fester slowly for nearly two decades would make sure there was nothing rational about the way she welcomed him.

"You'll do," Seth said, resting a hand on the apparition's shoulder. He leaned in close, whispering his instructions into Barclay Raines's ear, feeding it with the most basic orders. "Make her love you," he said, knowing it would. When he'd explained the nature of the Rushes to Julie Gennaro he'd called Myrna Shepherd a succubus, a female sex demon. Seth didn't believe in the Catholic version of Hell, the brimstone and fire landscape of Lucifer, his black wings spread out to cast a shadow across the infernal wasteland. But these things, the Rushes, were as close as the world came to demons, brought to life from the mists of that other place. Damiola had called it the Annwyn. He called it Purgatory; it was more appropriate than Glass Town. It was a crude but accurate description of the supernatural paramour. Night after night, day after day, the Rushes would lie with their victim, weakening them as they fed off their essence. "And don't let her stop until there is nothing left of her to give," Seth commanded, condemning Rosie Raines.

Once those words were inside the conjuration they became its imperative, its raison d'être. They couldn't be denied. It couldn't leave this realm before they were carried out and Rosie was spent.

The apparition turned away from him, toward the house where Rosie Raines was sleeping, and moved away hungry for the kill.

——

Rosie tossed and turned, the sheets clinging to her bare legs. The mattress was soaked with sweat. She looked up again at the dream, so perfectly realized, as the man she had loved and lost moved up between her legs. It felt so right to have him there, to feel him moving inside her again. There had been no one else. When he'd left her, she had broken; the fragments of her splintered heart beyond ever being glued back together. Eventually she'd stopped dreaming about him or thought that she had. She'd stopped yearning for his familiar kiss and started to forget every little thing that made him *him*; his taste on her tongue, his sweat, the way he breathed, the shallow-fast inhale-exhale in the darkness as he lay beside her exhausted, the way he chewed on his lip nervously, the way his hair tried to defy its parting, all of the little things she had lived with every day that went with him when he died.

She reached up to touch his face.

It was a dream.

It had to be a dream because of the way the light from certain angles seemed to pass straight through him.

But it was such a beautiful dream she didn't care.

She missed him. So much.

She'd learned to live with the absence of him, but never without him.

Which is why when she'd opened her eyes and seen his ghost standing at the end of the bed instead of being frightened she had reached out to him. His shirt was rumpled—it was always rumpled, he didn't like to waste time ironing when the day would just drop the creases out anyway—and open at the throat and falling away to expose the sweep of his collarbone for a tantalizingly brief second as he leaned forward like they were the most intimate inches of his body, there briefly, then snatched away. She remembered the first time she'd kissed him there, outside the old Latimer Road cinema after their first date almost thirty years ago. It had been one of the last films the old place had ever shown. She'd pressed him up against the wall and kissed the way down the vein at his throat to the bone and along it, little salty butterfly kisses. She'd forgotten about that. Somehow, in all of the living they'd done together and then apart, she'd forgotten one of the most basic and fundamental memories of her life.

He was cold. So cold.

She started to ask him if it was cold in heaven, but stopped herself, frightened that the sound of her voice talking in her sleep would be enough to wake her and take him away again. She drew him down, feeling his familiar weight on top of her, and kissed his lips that felt like ether, so soft were they against hers.

It felt so real.

But it had never been this heady, this desperate, her body answering to his touch of its own accord, pressing against him, pushing, trying to maintain the sweat-slick contact at all times even as the sheets gathered up around her body pulled away from the mattress by their sex. That wasn't a word she'd usually use, it had always been lovemaking, making love, but this was more urgent, more carnal than any coupling they'd had before, as though in death Barclay had become some sort of movie star lover, a Valentino or Gable, confident that he knew how to play his wife's body. She stopped thinking and just focused on savoring the dream. Her breathing quickened, her back arched up away from the damp sheets.

Rosie's body wasn't the tight curves and muscle of youth, it had rounded and softened, lined and sagged with age as she grew into and out of it, but it was still her, more her in fact that it ever had been because it had been her for so much longer, but her dream lover hadn't aged a day. He was still caught in that perfection of youth. The memory of him was frozen in that moment, with him looking that way, but then she'd never seen an old version of his face. It had never had the chance to crease and wrinkle as it won the lines of life lived hard on the Rothery.

The moonlight stained a jaundiced yellow by the streetlight swelled to fill the room. Each and every detail of her imagination was perfect and so powerfully precise. The single bead of sweat on his upper lip, the imperfections in his irises, the flecks where Barclay's beard grew through in patches, even the way he moved, the response of his body to her hands, all of it. She'd never been a particularly imaginative woman—or lover if she were honest—but this dream was so vivid. She was in control of it, too. She was moving in time with him, sharing his rhythms, but acting as well as reacting, reaching up to tangle her fingers in his hair and draw him down, reaching around to place her hand flat against the small of his back and feel his cold, cold skin as he leaned in to greedily suckle at her throat, not just simply tossing her head back and gasping. She let go of his hair, her fingers following the sweat down his spine.

It was physical, but being dreamlike so much more. It was as though he could see into the deepest most secret parts of her soul and work to satisfy needs and desires she'd forgotten ever having. He might never return, so this dreamtime was it, her chance to do everything she'd ever missed, to savor every moment she'd lost, to feel the way she had felt for one last time, to fall in love all over again, knowing that when she woke she would lose it all all over again.

"I love you," she whispered, so quietly she couldn't possibly wake herself.

He smiled down at her.

That look in his eyes, the sheer happiness of the moment, was heartbreaking all over again. How many times could she stand to lose him?

None.

Not another one.

"Don't ever leave me," she whispered, her hand resting against his cold cheek. "Not again."

She didn't hear what he said in reply. Being a dream his words were lost in a weird crackle of white noise. Maybe she'd fallen asleep with the television on?

It didn't matter.

For tonight she was complete.

For her, tomorrow would never come.

42

GOING HOME

The dawn chorus was breaking out all across the city.

Josh stumbled away from the car, angry with himself for ever being stupid enough to trust Julie, battered from Seth's beating, and more than anything, exhausted. But not broken. Despite everything, not that.

His body was driven by primal urges now: eat and sleep.

A wave of nausea swept over him as he walked way from the creosote-stained fence that ran around the perimeter of the pub's beer garden. Before he crossed the street and headed back into the Rothery he stopped, needing to lean on the nearest lamppost before he pitched over.

He looked left then right, out to freedom, into perdition.

The Rothery: an estate of constant perpetual damnation and ruin, a punishment for the unrepentant Londoners who once upon a better life had dared to think things might be different once they moved into the fancy houses the council were building down by the river. So much for hope; that existed to be crushed. They were offered up like sacrifices to Lockwood's clan, willingly, eagerly, all in the hopes that it would be different this time. It wasn't. The walls around them might be new and shiny, but the same feuds and fears ruled their lives. But Josh was tired of keeping his head down; of keeping away from the gangs of youths clustered on the street corners in their hoodies and tattoo sleeves; of avoiding the skinheads with their beer bellies and bovver boots; of skirting the worst streets where dealers doled out tinfoil squares in return for the addicts' dole money; of looking at the bonfire piles of bed frames, gutted settees, and foam-stuffed mattresses, planks of MDF and chipboard, shopping trolleys and plastic bags advertising discount grocery stores waiting to burn.

This was his home and he hated it.

He rubbed at his temple, closing his eyes rather than looking at the decay that gripped his little patch of England. These were the places in the heartland where the fear and hatred of the immigrant fueled the fracture of hearts and minds. They couldn't grasp the notion that these foreigners who could barely speak the language and had no qualifications to speak of weren't taking their jobs and their women, even when it was spelled out for them just how desperate they were, and the difference between the words immigrant and refugee and how rather than fear, these people needed kindness and help. It was too easy to point at the scary headlines and blame ISIS for all the woes of the world, and brand these desperate strangers with the same hate.

His headache wouldn't go away.

He couldn't remember if the last thing he had eaten was that all-day breakfast in the greasy spoon a couple of days ago, when he'd first seen Eleanor Raines, or not. That couldn't be right, could it? But that would explain why he felt so out of it. His side still ached where Seth had hit him with that sucker punch. He tentatively felt around the area where it hurt. Something was broken in there, he was sure of it.

He crossed the road, going home.

Josh saw an old woman out walking her Yorkshire terrier. He'd seen her a thousand times before and always nodded, a polite little ritual of recognition. She started to smile at him, then took in his discomfort and dishevelment and asked if he was all right. Josh nodded and assured her that he was fine, just tired and that it had been a rough night. He had no idea if she heard half of what he said because her little ball of hair barked incessantly at him until he limped away.

He saw a handful of people heading into the city to work: not the briefcase-wielding gents of the "City," but the sandwich makers and the street sweepers, the office cleaners and the shop assistants. Invisible people. A woman looked his way, but she was too wrapped up in her own world to wonder about what had happened to him for more than the briefest glance.

He reached the mouth of Albion Close.

He should have felt safe, back on familiar ground.

Home.

But the first thing he saw was the open door.

Sorrow had its limitations, but fear was boundless.

He ran the hundred yards to the door, every possibility of what was waiting for him on the other side bouncing around inside his mind. And then when he got there he couldn't bring himself to enter. He stood on the threshold, shaking, only the single possibility left in his mind. He knew what was waiting for him. Seth had promised to strip him of everything he loved.

Josh called out as he went inside.

There was no answer.

He checked downstairs first. Despite the fact that she was an early riser, there was no sign that Rosie had come down for breakfast. No dishes on the draining rack, no cups in the sink. No crumbs from the thick sourdough bread crust on the chopping board. Her tea bag—Darjeeling, she always had Darjeeling with a slice of lemon in the morning—was on the counter beside her favorite cup, left there last thing before she went to bed. There was an eerie silence about the place, he realized, where there should have been the voice of the early morning deejay. He breathed deeply, slowly, steeling himself before he headed upstairs.

"Mum?" he called again. "Lexy? Hello?"

No answer.

He reached the landing. Rosie's bedroom door was open.

He didn't want to go inside.

He really didn't want to go inside.

But he had to.

Josh stood on the threshold, half-in half-out of the room, struggling to make sense of what he saw.

Rosie was on top of the tangle of bedsheets, naked, her skin mottled like marble, her mouth open wide in a rictus of ecstasy, hands bunched into fists clawing up the cotton. Her legs were splayed wide, offering sights he could never unsee. But none of that mattered, because the one thing that wasn't there was life.

He didn't move from the doorway.

Unflattering light streamed in through the open curtains, accentuating the details of death: the skin around Rosie's lips was chapped and dry, there were dark patches, bruises or love bites, around the bay of her throat and more of them in a hungry line down to the bloated blue-lined breasts.

He couldn't look away.

He willed a single breath to hitch in her throat, for her body to buck and cough and come back to life, but there were no miracles to be found here.

"I'm sorry, Mum," he said, meaning it. This was on him. This was his fault. Seth had made that abundantly clear as he walked away and left him hanging. If Josh taken his offer, she'd still be alive.

Whatever happens now, it's on you. You did this. I gave you a way out. All you had to do was take it, not try and be clever and piss on my outstretched hand.

It really was that simple.

He could pretend it wasn't. Seth *was* a bastard and that even if Josh had said he'd stop, give it all up, forget about Eleanor and Glass Town, he would have done this to punish him down the line, maybe not today, maybe not tomorrow, but sometimes the old movie quotes were on the money. Pain was a tool for a man like Seth. Tools were to be used.

The horror of it hit him slowly. The realization that she wouldn't be down to boil the kettle or use that tea bag on the counter, that she wouldn't just quickly run the vacuum around or dust the mantel or rearrange the photos there by half an inch then move them back to exactly the same spot a few minutes later, all of those little things that she would never do again slammed into him with all the grace of a hammer to the side of the head.

Josh fell to his knees and howled, head in his hands. Over and over. Just howled and howled as he surrendered to the grief as it tore at him. It was the most human and inhuman sound.

The tears came between gasps.

They weren't so much stages of grief as harrowing cliffs he plunged off one after the other, battering his body to a pulp on the way down. There was denial, that he simply couldn't be seeing what he was seeing; there was bargaining as he begged whatever god was left to watch over this fucked-up world to bring her back, to trade their places; there was rage far beyond even the blackest of anger that Seth had come into his home and violated his life in such a brutal manner, leaving his mother like that, shamed, broken, discarded; and there was overwhelming sadness as the cloying grief tore at him and kept on tearing until there was a Rosie Raines–shaped hole in his life for every day to come. There was no acceptance. There would never be acceptance.

He curled up on the floor beside her bed.

What I will *do is strip you of everything you have ever loved. Everything that's ever meant anything to you. I'll take everything you've ever cared about, everyone you've ever cared about, and I'll put a torch to them. I'll burn them until there's nothing left but bones and ash.*

He didn't move for an hour.

He couldn't. It was as if the rigor mortis was settling into his body, not the one on the bed.

Finally, he crawled to the head of the bed, and reached up to draw the sheets up over his mother's body, affording her at least some dignity in death.

He stood at the base of the final harrowing cliff: vengeance.

That took all the strength he had.

His world slowly narrowed down from the streets outside in the Rothery, to the house, to the room, to the woman on the bed, and with every heartbeat refocusing on that look on her face. "You burn my life," he said, his first coherent words in what felt like hours. "And I burn yours."

They were easy words to say, but there was little to prevent them from being hollow. Anyone could stand in an empty room and act the big man. But outside these four walls how could he fight back? Everything Damiola had told him was useless without the compact. Without the glass, he couldn't see through the illusion to find the lenses, so no matter how desperately he wanted to walk out of his mother's bedroom, find the closest anchor and shatter it into a million tiny pieces, move on to the second and the third and keep going to make sure there was no coming back for that bastard Lockwood, he couldn't. And even if he could, it wasn't *enough*. The idea of time creeping in and slowly catching up with Seth wasn't enough *hurt*.

Josh looked at his mother.

No, death could never be enough payback for what Seth had done to her, not in a million years, however long that would take to pass in Glass Town.

Josh pulled the blanket up over her face and walked out of the room, out of the house, and out of the Rothery without looking back.

43

GRAVE INTENTIONS

He didn't know where he was going until he got there: the cemetery at Ravenshill. The gates hung open. He didn't venture inside. Instead, he sat down on the bench where he'd first mistaken the magician for a tramp. He put his head in his hands and prayed. What for, he had no idea: guidance? The twisted wreckage of the iron bird to fly again? The spirits of the ancient dead to rise up before him from the dirt with a few words of wisdom or a lost spell of damnation known only to those who have passed? There were no miracles to be had, ghostly or metallic.

When he looked up, he saw the faded letters that marked someone's passing. It was the first grave inside the cemetery wall. Looking at the stone, there was no hint of the life the dead man must have lived or the person he must have been, just a dash between the years when it began and ended. That was the important part, where the living was done.

Josh wrestled with the overwhelming sadness and the disbelief laid over it. In the course of a few days, he'd lost his grandfather and his mother. The only person he had left in the world was Lexy, his sister. Beyond that he had no family, no friends to speak of, and no job. He was one of the endangered generation, at risk of becoming lost to the great hopes shunted onto their shoulders by parents who'd grown up with mottos like *Loadsamoney*—with the eponymous character waving wads of cash at the screen with only one care in the world—as their guiding lights. That was the sum of his dash.

And now here he was, in the shark tank about to get feasted on by an old-school gangster who by rights should have been dead for fifty years. It was hard to get his head around just how insane it all was. Every time he thought he had a handle on it something happened to twist his sense of perspective. It had been that way from the moment he learned that the man trying to ruin his life was his own flesh and blood. That this was his family legacy. He looked down at the flagstones beneath his feet. The heel of his right foot was halfway across one of the black cracks. "Step on a crack, break your mother's back," he said, and then started to laugh hysterically, like there was nothing funnier in the world.

The laughter lasted a good thirty seconds before it choked in his throat.

It was Isaiah's fight.

It should be him going up against Seth.

"Indeed it should," a voice said. "And before you ask, no, I didn't read your mind, you were talking to yourself." The disheveled man sat down on the bench beside him. Cadmus Damiola.

"How did you know I was here?"

The old man smiled. "Magic," he said, offering a wry smile along with a slight shrug. "Well, that and I heard you laughing."

Josh nodded. "I was coming to find you."

He looked at their surroundings. "Did anyone ever tell you that you spend an unhealthy amount of time in cemeteries? Anyone would think you were trying to talk to them."

"Who?"

"Them, all around you, the dead."

"They don't have much to say."

"They seldom do, lad. They seldom do. And when they talk, none of it is good, so it's best that they keep what they've got to say to themselves if you ask me."

"I lost the glass," Josh admitted, offering up his empty hands. "Seth has it."

"Well, then, it is a good thing he doesn't know how to use it, isn't it?"

Josh looked at the old man, not sure he understood. "He repaired the lens I broke when I tried to fight him."

"He may well have, but that's not using the glass, and to be brutally honest, that wasn't fighting him, lad, that was playing into his hands. Fighting him means using your head."

Josh was quiet for a moment. When he spoke again it was to say, "I want to hurt him."

"I know you do."

"No. Really hurt him." Josh thought about it for a moment, looking for words to put into context the level of hatred he felt for Seth Lockwood. "I'd reach down his throat and punch my way out of his arsehole if I could," he said at last.

"And quite a pretty word picture that is."

"He killed my mother last night. I found her."

"I'm so sorry. Death is a bastard. There's no comfort in that, but it's the truth."

"She had nothing to do with this."

"There are always innocents caught in the cross fire. Especially when it comes to your family."

"He did it to punish me because I wouldn't join him. He had this idea we could somehow become one big happy family. Me and him, ruling this place side by side, like it had been with his brother, before . . ."

Damiola shook his head. "I find that very doubtful, lad, no matter what words he might have used. His only intention was to inflict pain. You have to know your enemy. I know him. I've known him for the worst part of ninety years. There's not a single sentimental bone in his body. Family has never meant anything to Seth Lockwood. If he offered you a hand, it was only to draw you close enough to twist your arm until it breaks. There was never an offer of friendship, only a way for him to win."

Josh couldn't argue with that. He'd had the same thought.

"Yesterday I wanted to kill him. I stupidly thought I could beat him. He killed her to punish me for smashing the anchor at the old church. I thought it would be enough, that it would let time catch up with him like you'd said. One hundred years lived in one hundred minutes or however long it would take to all come rushing back. I thought it would put an end to everything . . . I thought we'd be free."

"But you don't anymore?"

"No, now I know there's no escaping him."

"So do you still want him dead?"

Josh shook his head. "No. Not anymore. Dead is too clean. I want him to live," Josh said. "For a very, very long time. He can live forever for all I care, as long as he is in agony for every single second of his wretched life."

"That kind of anger is dark, lad. You might not feel that way in a week or a month."

"He killed my mother," Josh repeated. "The way I feel isn't going to change. There's no going back from that. There needs to be a reckoning. Balance."

"And you see some sort of balance in pain?"

"I want to hurt him. And I mean *really* hurt him. I'm not talking about punching him in the face or kicking him in the bollocks. I want to hurt him so badly he can't remember who he is for all the pain he's in."

"And how, pray tell, do you intend to do that?"

"Magic."

Damiola raised an eyebrow at that. "Do tell."

"There must be a spell. Something."

"Must there?"

"One last trick? You've got powers. I know you have. Look at you, you're into a second life in terms of years and look younger than my grandfather."

"And that's why you were looking for me?" Damiola said, pushing himself up from the bench. "You want me to do your dirty work? Sorry to say I'm finished, lad. Look at me. I don't have the strength. These old bones are done. I shouldn't be here. I should be rotting away in there," he hoisted a thumb over his shoulder in direction of the mausoleum. "This isn't my fight anymore. I'm not the hero, I'm a bit-part player, and my cue to exit stage left has long gone."

"You started this," Josh had been thinking it since he buried his hands in prayer. It might have been Seth's obsession and Isaiah's love that kept this family feud running for the best part of a century, but it was Cadmus Damiola's magic that made it possible. It was Damiola's grand illusion that stopped it from simply burning itself out. Without him the brotherly feud would have ended in the '20s. There would have been blood, but that would have been an end to it. Instead, because of Damiola's magic, they'd been kept apart. They'd been denied that resolution. Those hatreds had festered on both sides of the invisible wall between Glass Town and London. They took on a life of their own, becoming, in a sense, immortal.

"And you think it falls to me to finish it? Is that it?"

"No. This is on me. But I can't do it alone."

"I told you, lad, I don't have the strength," Damiola held up his hands, offering them as proof. All Josh could see were the thick veins of dirt crusting them. "I'm spent. Or all but. Death's standing at my shoulder, waiting to finally get his bony hands on me."

"Then make your death mean something. Help me."

"You're good with words, lad. Quick on your feet. Make my death mean something. Get revenge on Lockwood. Who wants their deaths to be meaningless? Who wants the bad guys to win in this life? No one, am I right?"

"You came looking for me," Josh said. "You didn't do that out of the kindness of your heart."

"Clever lad."

"You came here to die?"

"I died a long time ago. Nineteen twenty-nine was the last time. Nineteen twenty-three the first. I came here to see about making it stick this time."

"You're going to help me?"

"I've been helping you all along, if you didn't notice."

"Eleanor described Glass Town as her prison," Josh said. He'd been thinking about it for a while without realizing he was actually thinking about it.

"That's what Seth asked me for."

"But it's as much his prison as hers, wasn't it?"

"It was meant to be. A few streets lifted out of today and hidden away in the Otherworld, pushed through a weakness in the veil that ran along the ley lines here. My teacher used to call them obliques; I prefer ley lines. But he's been coming and going freely for years, as you pointed out, without time catching up with him, so maybe I'm wrong about everything, boy."

"I know how he does it," Josh said, remembering Seth's missing fingertip. "You were right, he has left a piece of him inside Glass Town. Not his heart in a lead-lined box, though. His fingertip. That means he never truly leaves, doesn't it?"

"Ah," Damiola said, nodding thoughtfully. "It does indeed. He always was a devious bastard. I should have known he'd find a way around the restrictions the enchantment imposed on him."

"But we can make it work for us," Josh said, no idea if that was true or not. "We have to. So, you can't make anything new, you're too weak, does that mean you can't work with something old? Old magic."

"I'm not sure I follow, lad. Old magic? All magic is old. All magic is rooted in the mosaic. The mosaic is life. God. Our old Celtic brethren understood that better than we do today, worshiping the land for her majesty and might. They understood earth nodes and ley lines and how those primeval forests gave back to the land whereas our modern buildings just drain from it."

Josh shook his head.

"I'd been focused on destroying the anchors, but that's only one way of doing this, and it's the one he's expecting. That's why he beat me at the church. He's got his pet defenses, that dog-thing that sucks the life out of you, and the Comedians and whatever else he can conjure, so he's prepared to defend Glass Town. He's expecting me to go after him head-on. And I was stupid; I told him I knew the secret to beating him. I told him I knew about the anchors. But maybe that wasn't such a bad thing?" Josh was thinking on his feet now, but it was beginning to make sense. The makings of an idea were taking shape. "What if we *don't* try and destroy it? Do the unexpected, right? What if we *use* it?"

"How would you intend to do that, exactly? He can come and go as he pleases, so as we've already decided, it's not much of a prison."

"Not at the moment it isn't," Josh said, standing up. He was getting excited now. His mind was buzzing with possibilities. "But we've got thirteen lenses. You've already done the hard stuff. You know where they are. You know how they function better than anyone. How they simultaneously keep one side of the veil closed and yet the other open, like a two-way mirror."

"I do indeed."

"You said Seth doesn't know how the glass works; you do, you made it. It's your magic."

"Yes."

"The lenses are physical things, too, aren't they? Not just some magical trace."

"Yes," the old magician said again.

"Objects can be moved. I held one of the lenses in my hand. I shattered it."

"And as you remarked, Seth repaired it with the glass."

"That's not what I'm thinking. If I'd moved it, the barrier between here and Glass Town would have moved with it, wouldn't it?"

"Theoretically," the magician conceded. "The thirteen points are anchors. The veil is tied to the anchors, not to the ground the anchors are set in. It's harder to bind magic to a place than to a thing, a residual effect from days magic still ran along the ley lines."

"Right, so they don't have to be *there*?" Josh stressed. "That's what I'm getting at. They don't have to be exactly where you placed them. We could move them."

"I honestly don't know if the spell would hold or rip apart. There's nothing to say the whole thing wouldn't just leak away."

"But if it did?"

"If it did," Damiola said, with a shrug. "You tell me?"

"It doesn't have to ward off the entire movie lot, does it? Glass Town. The illusion could be refocused around a single house. Or even a single room," and now it was slowly crystallizing. He liked it. It was simple. Elegant. Poetic even. It was the kind of thing a Lockwood would do. "Only one way in, one way out, no cracks he could exploit. He'd be forced to live out his entire life in that one room. No view, never seeing the sun again. Alone forever, to slowly go mad from it. A man living out the end of his days in a deep dark hole."

"He wouldn't last long without food and water," the magician noted.

"Then you drip water in, down the walls; just a trickle, enough that he wouldn't dehydrate. But so little of it he'd always be thirsty and forced to press his lips up against the stone to get any kind of refreshment. As to food, stack the place with tinned food, enough to last a very, very long time, assuming he was ever industrious enough to work out a way to break open the tins. No tin opener, no tool he could use to end his own misery. You give him a chance; it's just down to how desperate he is if he takes it. And if he can't work out a way to break into the tins, then maybe the nearness of food—right there in his hands, but with no way to get into the tin to eat it—would be the kind of mental anguish that would tip him over the edge?"

"You're describing torture."

Josh nodded, his expression cold. "That's exactly what I'm describing, a lifetime of torture, however long or short that life is."

"And that is the kind of pain you are hoping to inflict on Seth?"

"Not even close," Josh said, and meant it. "I want him to be so desperate he finds a way to feed himself, even if it means chewing his own arm off. I want him to be so desperate to see the light he claws his own eyes out in the end, just for those few moments where sparks and flashes ignite behind them before he's forever blind. I want him to live in the dirt, grubbing around on his hands and knees, clawing at the walls of his prison until his fingernails are shredded and bloody and the idea of feeling the sun on his face is some impossible dream, like coming face-to-face with God."

"I don't know that I *should* help you," Damiola said, looking back across the headstones in the direction of his mausoleum. "That kind of vengeance would change you. You wouldn't be you anymore. You'd be him. In defeating him, you'd become another generation of the bastard Lockwoods."

"Don't call me that. That's not my name."

"But it is your blood, boy, and that makes it your legacy. Listening to you now just proves that. All of that violence is in you, just like it is in Seth. You might look like Isaiah Raines, but your soul is pure Isaiah Lockwood."

Josh wasn't about to admit just how right he was, but there was no ignoring the second idea bubbling away in the darkest recesses of his mind. Seth came and went because he'd sacrificed a fingertip. Josh wasn't against making the same sacrifice if it meant a century to take his rage out on Seth. That wasn't something he was about to share with Damiola, but he couldn't stop himself from making a fist, then as he caught himself doing it, relaxing it. He deliberately flexed his little finger a couple of times in the process imagining it not being there.

Damiola gave no indication that he caught the small tick. Josh tried to deflect the old man's attention from it, because whatever else he might be becoming, he wasn't and would never be a particularly good liar.

"You've been guarding that tomb of yours for years, waiting to see who would come looking for you. That's why you sit here, isn't it? Guarding. Watching. Not knowing who would turn up or what they would want from you, but you knew they would come wanting something. And they did. Things were set in motion, secrets exposed and a chain of events begun that culminated in the death of my mother. That's the long and the short of it. Now either we go into this like victims, and try to save ourselves, and maybe we will or maybe we won't. The alternative is we take him on on our terms. That tomb of yours, apart from anything else, is designed to keep the dead in and the living out. Four walls, no windows. It's isolated. Look around you; no one comes or goes, there are no idle passersby. It's almost a lost part of the city. It would make the perfect prison. It's exactly what we'd need. The only other possibilities are my grandfather's old flat in Rotherhithe or the house back on the Rothery. We could hardly make either of those disappear."

"Theoretically no more challenging than making the old tomb vanish," the magician said. "But I take your point."

"What if instead of shattering the lenses we use them to move the barrier? Rebuild the illusion on a much smaller scale? Use it to isolate your mausoleum? Then all we'd have to do is lure Seth out to the graveyard, which shouldn't be that difficult. The only question is could you repurpose the illusion?"

"It could work," the old man said. "But are you sure this is what you want to do?"

"Yes," Josh assured him, making a fist again, flexing his little finger again.

"You're forgetting about the woman, aren't you? The actress. Eleanor Raines. She's still a part of this. What about her part in all of this? Glass Town is her prison, too. Do you intend to keep her in that dusty old tomb with Seth?"

"No."

"But you can't set her free, it doesn't work like that. Tear down the barrier surrounding Glass Town and you damn her. That hasn't changed. It's the natural order of things. She cannot survive now that she's been out of time for so long. I thought this was all about saving her?"

"I can't save her, you've made that abundantly clear."

"And that means you're not even going to try? Instead you're going to actively see to it she has no hope of ever being saved?"

The accusation hit him hard.

"You said she can't be saved."

"I've been wrong before, lad. I'm not ineffable. I'm just an old man who once upon a time made a bad decision."

"And that's why I'm offering you a chance of redemption," Josh said. "To put right what you did."

"You're not. You aren't proposing we make a time machine and somehow go back to that night and change the outcome. I can't put right the mistakes I made."

"Then think of it as a chance to make amends."

"And if I have no interest in that?"

"Then perhaps you'll find peace in the death you so obviously want." It sounded more like a threat than he intended it to be.

"This life is not such a bad place to be," the old man said, turning his back on Josh. He walked slowly through the cemetery gates, forcing Josh to follow him.

Despite having decades on the old man, Josh struggled to keep up and was breathing heavily by the time he reached the rusted iron gates of his tomb. "Can you do it?"

"Stop asking can and ask will," the old magician snapped, stepping into the darkness beyond the threshold.

"Will you?"

"God help me, and God help that poor woman, but I will do what you need me to do. Now leave me alone, lad, there are things to be done if this isn't going to end in the deaths of us all."

Josh lingered on the threshold for a minute or two, expecting the old man to emerge again, but he didn't. He thought about going in there after him, but to what purpose? He'd gained all he could hope to here. There were other pieces he needed to align if they were going to have a prayer of luring Seth into their trap, not least getting Seth to the abandoned cemetery.

But he had an idea how that might be done, but it would mean relying on someone who had betrayed him once already. Betrayed then rescued, Josh amended, hoping the second act outweighed the first in terms of where Julius Gennaro's loyalties lay.

He pulled his phone out of his pocket as he walked back toward the cemetery gates.

"If I'm going to keep my promise to Gideon, I'm going to need your help," Josh said even before Julie had managed his single word of greeting.

"Yes."

"I know how he got to you. I know about your partner." That was greeted by silence. "I know where the bodies are buried."

"What do you want me to do?"

"The right thing. Make sure the old man knows that Damiola is still alive."

"And that's important because?"

"He's the man who made Glass Town. All of this begins and ends with him."

"Okay, so I tell him the guy's still alive, then what?"

"Then you tell him where to find the magician. The old Ravenshill Cemetery. That's where he's buried."

"You said he was alive."

"He is."

"And that's all you need from me?"

"Bolt cutters."

"What?"

"Bring a pair of bolt cutters and a blowtorch along," Josh said.

44

THIS OLD MAN'S WAR

The one benefit of old age is knowing that you are dying a little more every day and not caring. It brought a kind of uncaring invulnerability with it. *What's the worst you can do to me,* it said, *kill me? What's the difference between dying today and dying tomorrow?* Brutal fatalism had its charms. There was no getting around the fact that his days were numbered, Gideon Lockwood had known that ever since his father walked back into his life. This town, as the old cliché went, wasn't big enough for the both of them.

There was no heroism or nobility in the old man's bones. He was and had always been a hard bastard. Frailty didn't change that. It didn't change his mind-set or just how far he'd go to win. The apple didn't fall far from the tree. The tree in this case might look younger and prettier, more vital and vibrant, but it was still rotten through to the core. He was old, not stupid. He was well read, not ignorant. Events as they were unfolding around him were tragic in the Shakespearean definition of *tragedy,* the protagonist brought down by his own flaws: Othello by his passions, Hamlet by his indecisiveness, Seth Lockwood by his obsessions. Empires fell for less: some raised up from sand and silk, others from bloody knuckles and sawn-off shotguns. People are always and have always been their own worst enemies, and his father was no exception.

Seth was driven by his obsessions. Once upon a time they'd been about a girl, before that they'd been about bringing the estates around the East End under control, before that they'd been about playground power. Gideon had never known his father. He'd disappeared into Glass Town when he was born. Isaiah was the legitimate heir to the brother's empire, but had no interest in it so others came along and claimed the spoils while Seth was gone, capitalizing on his absence, leaving Gideon to be raised by East End nuns.

He'd been gone so long he ceased to matter. As Gideon grew up, he grew tired of hearing what a man his old man was, a proper criminal's criminal, someone who commanded the respect of a room full of proper hard bastards without having to say a word. Always it was Seth this, back in Seth's day that, it never would have happened if Seth was still here, and on and on with a level of reverence that bordered on the pathological. Gideon got sick of hearing about it before he grew out of short trousers. But not sick enough to think about his old man as anything short of a god when it came to these streets. Seth Lockwood gave, and Seth Lockwood took away. With that in mind, he had slowly and systematically gone about taking back his father's empire one street corner at a time. By the time he was nineteen, he'd put his father's specter where it belonged, in the ground far, far behind him. When people said the Lockwood name now it was Gideon they were terrified of. He was their bogeyman. He was the one who made their lives a living nightmare. He surpassed any evil his old man had ever considered, but still the legend of Seth Lockwood lived on.

There was a delicate ecology in place around the estates, a balance between the criminal fraternity and those paid to keep it in check.

So when he'd come back after all these years, unchanged, acting like it was all still his by the divine right of bastards, Gideon watched that delicate balance come undone. Seth still acted like it was 1924; the lawmen ill-equipped, underpaid, and absolutely corrupt. He threw his weight about, making a lot of noise, putting the frighteners on local businesses and ordinary decent criminals alike. He didn't like the way Gideon ran things and made no attempt to hide his contempt. This was all his; that's what he'd said that first night back. This was all his, and he was taking it back for as long as he needed it. Not a word about why he needed it, or how he had resisted the ravages of age and those deep cuts of time's knife; just that he was taking it all back. No pleases, no thank you for all that he had done to keep the family business together after he'd disappeared down the rabbit hole. None of that.

Why couldn't he just stay *gone*?

Wishes and fishes, right there. He couldn't because he didn't. And now Gideon was going to have to deal with him, even if doing so killed him.

He didn't mind.

Everyone died.

So he waited for Seth in the taproom of The Hunter's Horns. Marcus, the bartender, had left a glass of Rastignac XO on the table for Gideon before he'd folded up his towel and left him alone in there.

There was no music. The only sounds were down to life passing by outside.

His conversation with Gennaro had been most enlightening.

He would play his part, and he would enjoy it.

Gideon savored a sip of the old brandy, rolling it around his tongue before swallowing. It was beautifully smooth going down. He put the glass back down and took a thick hand-rolled Cuban cigar from the tin in his inside pocket, snipped off the end, then lit it, puffing several times on the tightly packed leaf to get it smoking. To hell with smoking regulations, this was his pub. He remembered the man he'd bought the cigars from, a big Swede who hadn't quite grasped English, introducing himself as sixty-five and retarded. That put a smile on the old man's face. "Hello, I'm Sven Ingvar, I'm sixty-five and retarded." But not as brilliantly memorable as the next thing he'd said. "I lost my virginity to a hooker in Havana. I don't know if I have any children." Lucky man, that Sven Ingvar, Gideon thought, as he leaned back in his chair and closed his eyes, enjoying the smoke while he waited for his father. All families were fucked up in his experience.

It didn't take long for Seth to arrive.

He didn't appreciate having been summoned.

"What was so important that we couldn't do this over the phone?"

he said, without preamble. The door slammed behind him as he stalked into the snug and sat himself down across the table from his boy.

"Here we are, finally. Father and son," Gideon said.

"Spare me the whole we-should-do-this-more-often guilt trip. I know, I know; I'm a rotten father, never took you to a football match, wasn't there to teach you how to ride a bike, none of that bonding stuff. I get it. I doomed you to a lifetime of angst and self-loathing. The whole Oedipal thing and not being able to form functional relationships? Mea culpa. Mea maxima culpa and all that crap. We've already done this, I freely accept it's all my fault."

"You think you're so clever, don't you?"

" 'Don't you, Dad.' Or 'Father.' Or, if you prefer, 'sir.' "

"You walked out on us. On all of this."

"Ah, the empire. Yes, I admit it, I didn't want it anymore."

"No. You wanted her."

"The heart wants what the heart wants," Seth said, obviously growing bored with the whole touchy-feely moment he thought was happening here.

"Didn't you used to be someone? I mean a real man? That's the bit I don't get. How you could walk away from who you were—*and then come back*?"

"Who I am, son. Who I *am*. Remember, it's only last year for me, barely time to scratch my arse. You've grown old, my hometown's gone to the dogs, but me, I'm still the same old cunt I've always been. And I came back out of necessity. I don't want to be here any more than you want me here. This place reeks of mortality."

I'm not the only person dying here, Gideon thought, but kept his own counsel. He raised the brandy glass to his nose and breathed in the heady fumes. It was the simple pleasures he was going to miss most, he thought, like a good piece of battered fish and chips with a side of mushy peas. Even the thought that this might be the last conversation he'd ever have didn't bother him half as much as the thought that he might never smoke another one of these most excellent cigars again. He inhaled slowly, savoring the smoke, then let it corkscrew up in front of his face.

He tapped the ash off into the small silver ashtray beside the brandy glass. He refused to be rushed.

"I don't have time for this," Seth said, finally.

"Answer me one question, then you can go."

"Fine. Ask."

"What do you see when you look at me?"

Seth leaned back in his chair. He thought about lying, but shrugged and told the truth. "Nothing," he said. "I don't feel anything, either. No great regret. No sadness that I never saw you grow up. No remorse at abandoning you to the nuns. No dreams that it might have been different. There's no parental pride. I see a stranger."

"Look again," Gideon said. "I'm what you could have become if you fulfilled your promise. I'm you, perfected."

That put a smile on Seth's face. "I don't think so, son. You're just a shadow of the man I used to be."

Gideon shook his head. "The world's moved on since you were here. I don't know whether you've really had a chance to take it all in, you've been so obsessed with your demons, and trying to grasp what's become of the world you left behind. It's subtler for one thing; the racketeers and gangsters are all dead. Protection is a mug's game. When you left this place it was all about extortion and opportunity—"

"And no matter what year it is, that doesn't change."

"Maybe not, but the how of it does. Back then there was honor to it. Ordinary decent criminals they used to call us. There was honor among thieves. There was a code. You knew where you were with your own kind. Now it's all happening in the shadows. It's online. Hackers are a bigger threat than heavies. You want to frighten someone you go for their information, their client base, you isolate them, you breach their security, and blow their relationships. You do stuff that's frankly beyond me; I'm a dinosaur in this new landscape, but you? You're clueless. You have no idea what it's really like out there. Kids hold all the knowledge of the world in their pockets. They can talk to each other, and I don't just mean a telephone conversation, they can reach out to hundreds of thousands of people all at once. A picture can go around the world before you've walked down the street. It's so much harder to be what we were, Dad. You've actually got to be clever, not just mean. What you don't realize is you kick-started that change with your twisted need for possession beyond all normal reason."

"I hardly changed the fucking world, son, you're exaggerating my importance. That's just time. Time's change. It's the nature of the world."

"You didn't change the world. You changed *me*. I changed the world."

Seth smiled at that. "You think a lot of yourself, don't you?"

"Because I've lived the life you walked away from. You name it, I've done it, and worse than you could ever imagine. Everyone you knew, your entire world, they're all gone. Every last one of them. No one remembers you. Do you know how they'd treat you if they were here now? They'd spit in your face. You broke the code. Now you're an irrelevance. I'm not. People are frightened of me, Dad. Me. Not you. They respect me. Not you. The name Lockwood still means something around here. That's down to *me*. Not you."

"So you called me here so you could show off a bit before you shuffled off this mortal coil? Isn't that a bit, oh, I don't know, *needy*? What do you want me to say? Well done? I'm proud of you? Fucking hell, son, did no one ever tell you that you talk too much?"

Gideon leaned forward, planting both his hands on the table and started to rise. Slight tremors ran the length of his arm as it took his weight. He stared into his father's eyes.

"I fantasized about killing you," he said.

That brought a smile to Seth's face. "And then thought better of it, I assume? I'd snap you in two, son."

"Oh, I wouldn't do it myself. It's been decades since I've got my hands dirty. But I've got an army of people who'd happily do it for me."

"Ah, right, you're the Big Man. Sorry, I forgot for a moment."

"Do you want to know a secret?"

"What the fuck are you talking about now?"

"It's a secret that will damn you, Dad. I know it will. So, I'm asking you if you want to know it, not simply telling you it. Think of it as a courtesy."

"Have you lost your fucking mind? Is that it? You've gone gaga in your old age? Good to know senility runs in the genes. I'll do my best to stay away from old age."

"Is that a no?"

"I'm not interested in playing games with you."

"It's not a game. I don't play games. It's a fact. I think you want to know it, so I'll make the decision for you. Cadmus Damiola is still alive."

Seth didn't flinch. His lip curled. He shook his head. "You really have lost it, haven't you? He's dead and gone."

"I don't particularly care if you believe me or not. That doesn't change the fact he's alive."

"And what if he is?"

Gideon's smile was sly. "Then Glass Town can be saved, can't it? You said yourself, that's why you returned. All you need to do is find the magician. And I know where he is."

"Do you now?" Gideon nodded. "So what's it going to cost me? That's what this is all about, isn't it? Money, power, *something*? What do you want? You called me here to negotiate, so let's negotiate."

"You don't have anything I want."

"Oh, that can't be true. Use your imagination a bit. Be creative. How about the carousel so you can torment your enemies with the Rushes? Or the projector? The Reels are nastier, more fully formed, but they're both quite effective terrors. You haven't even seen the Negative in glorious action."

"You don't have anything I want," Gideon repeated.

"I don't believe you, boy."

"What I want is you out of my life. The magician's hiding out in the old Ravenshill Cemetery. Do with that information what you will."

"You've just made an old man very happy, son," Seth said, pushing himself up until he was face-to-face with his boy. "For that reason I won't kill you. Because, and now it's my turn to let you in on a secret, I've been thinking about doing just that for a long time now. You sicken me. You're a poor excuse of a man. But if you're wrong, if this is a lie or a trick, I'll come back here and I'll burn this place to the ground with you inside it."

The threat wasn't so far removed from what Gideon had in mind himself.

He said nothing.

He didn't sit down again until he was alone.

It was done. It was down to young Joshua now.

He breathed deeply, and then took another slow draw on the cigar.

He'd miss these simple pleasures.

He left the cigar smoldering in the silver ashtray, walking unsteadily upstairs. He needed the banister to stop himself from falling. In so many ways he wasn't half the man he used to be, but in others he was twice the man he'd ever been. He thought about calling Julius Gennaro, but he needed to do this alone.

The hallway reeked of stale cigarettes and beer soaked into the thread-bare carpet. There was a dark stain beside the wall that he remembered being blood. The unlucky bleeder had been on his knees when Gideon had grabbed a handful of his hair and slammed it into the William Morris wallpaper. It had made quite a mess. These walls contained so many memories, most of them brutal. He opened the door to the office. He'd run the family business from this room for the best part of sixty years. It had been his sanctuary. His one place where he could get away from the world.

It hadn't felt like his since Seth's return.

"Time to take back what's mine," he said, walking unsteadily across the room to his desk. The projector was in the center of it, Damiola's Carousel still spinning away eerily beside it, the little wick in the middle burning endlessly. He gathered the carousel up in his arms. It was heavier than he'd expected, but not so heavy that he couldn't heft it and hurl it at the wall behind his desk. The drum broke away beneath the impact, the card popping out of place and flapping against the metal prong that had held it inside the drum's curve. The wax dribbled down the metal as the wick burned out.

He picked it up again and slammed it into the wall over and over again, each impact sending fragments of the machine flying until the bare metal frame was all that was left, and even that was buckled beyond salvage.

Gideon took the envelope from the safe next and made a small bonfire out of the cutouts in his wastepaper bin. It took less than a minute
for the old cards to blacken and burn, thirty seconds more for them to
shrivel. He turned his back on them before they became ash. The projector was considerably heavier, so he started his vandalism by wrenching
the reels off the armature and unspooling the film. It gathered in stream-
ers around his feet, as he pulled more and more free.

Gideon tossed the reel aside.

He shattered the bulb and the glass lenses.

Then and only then did he pick up the projector and carry it out to
the stairs. Gritting his teeth, the old man lifted it over his head and threw
it down the stairs. It didn't make it all the way to the bottom, hitting
several steps on the way down. The impact from each bent and buckled
the arm until it hung uselessly away from the projector's body.

He wasn't done.

He went down to the yard out back where two plastic containers were
filled with petrol, and carried one of them back up to the office, the other
he left at the top of the stairs. He doused the entire office in petrol, splashing it about everywhere. The stench was overpowering. He stood in the
middle of the room, sloshing petrol over the rug, the desk, and chair,
all across the books in the bookcases, the wooden floorboards, and then
dribbled a trail down the hallway to the staircase. He discarded the petrol
can in favor of the second, splashing his way down the stairs. In the main
taproom he doused the curtains and bar in petrol, then set about smashing the bottles one by one until the entire place reeked of alcohol.

Satisfied, he sat back down at the table and took up the cigar again,
sucking in a last glorious lungful of smoke before he touched the
smoldering cigar tip to the petrol soaking slowly into the tabletop, but
when it was obvious it wasn't going to ignite, drew on it, bringing the hot-
tip flame back to life, before he tossed it carelessly toward the bar.

For a moment nothing happened. He thought he was going to have
to push himself up out of his chair again, not sure he had the courage
to go through with it twice, but a faint whisper-rush of noise as a line of
bluish flame caught and spread up and over the bar meant he could sit
back in his chair.

Gideon raised the brandy glass to his lips.

He was ready to go now.

None of Damiola's creations would survive the flames, not the Rushes, the Reels, or the Negatives, none of them. The Hunter's Horns would be scoured from the landscape. It was the end of an era. The last Lockwood was leaving London.

He'd played his part. Seth was going after the magician, headfirst into whatever tangled web Joshua Raines was spinning. There was nothing more to be done.

He felt the heat on his face, contracting the red vines across his nose and cheeks, and the bite of it scouring the back of his throat as he drew another deep puff on the cigar.

This was the heart of his empire.

This was his throne room.

This was his coffin.

The flames chased across the carpet to the wooden door dividing the snug from the taproom, burning blue as they engulfed the wooden surface. They streaked up the velvet curtains as fiery lines raced across the flock wallpaper where the petrol had splashed.

The heat was incredible.

He choked on the thick smoke as it stung tears from his eyes.

He reached out with a trembling hand for the brandy glass, then raised it to his lips.

Gideon drained the glass in a single swallow and then closed his eyes and waited for the flames to take him.

45

BREAKING GLASS

One thing Gideon Lockwood was right about was just how much the world had changed over the last generation. Years of specialist education could be replaced by a couple of minutes on Google, *The Anarchist Cookbook,* and a brief stop at the Minute Mart. Josh followed the instructions step-by-step, putting together some makeshift explosives out of everyday household cleaning items.

Since he'd lost the compact he had no way of knowing exactly where the anchors were, but thanks to the MacGyverish wonders of the internet he didn't need to. He put the plastic carrier bag on the ground between his feet and looked up at the gargoyle. He couldn't see the halo anymore. Josh crouched down on the floor, emptying out the contents of his shopping bag. Aluminum foil, an aerosol can of air freshener, and an old box of sparklers left over from Bonfire Night. He peeled off a sheet of foil, spreading it out across the gravel, then uncapped the air freshener and stood it in the middle of the foil. Moving quickly he took the sparklers out of the box and scraped them so the sparkler dust landed on the foil. He gathered the foil up, closing off the package. That was all he needed. He took one of the unused sparkler wires and poked it into the base of the foil, then using Boone's lighter, lit the sparkler and backed quickly away to hunker down behind the nearest row of graves.

It took less than a minute for the fuse to burn out.

For the longest second of his life nothing happened. Josh started to stand, thinking it was a dud. He'd been careful to make sure the sparkler dust was in the biggest possible pieces and that none of them had got under the can of air freshener, like the instructions said.

The sound of the explosion was eardrum shattering—far more violent that he'd imagined it could possibly be, as the canister was torn to shreds by the violence of the detonation. The shrapnel sprayed every which way in a lethal hail of aluminum. Josh ducked back down beneath the protection of the headstone, eyes firmly fixed on the ground beneath his feet. He heard a second detonation, this one quite unlike the first, deeper, more resonant, as the lens shattered in a coruscating shower of blue-tinged sparks far brighter than the makeshift bomb had been. He counted out eleven in his head, adding one for good luck, before he risked looking up from behind the safety of the headstone.

The devastation wasn't anywhere near as bad as the sound suggested. The gargoyle and the stained-glass window beside it had taken the worst of it. The shrapnel had shredded half of his face and blackened scorch marks ran down the church wall from his perch to the ground. The window was gone. He could see the glow of flames inside the church.

Josh pushed himself up from his crouch and hurried around the side of the abandoned church toward the archway that once again had become a doorway into another world.

Eleanor Raines waited on the other side.

He looked at her. He wanted to say something clever, some line about how he'd promised he'd save her, but she'd never been in more danger in all the years since Seth snatched her. She smiled tentatively toward him, but didn't move. She looked around for signs of danger, but was alone on the other side of the broken barrier. There was no way of knowing if, once she set foot on this side of the veil, she'd be able to go back. He didn't want her stepping out of Glass Town until he was sure there could be no going back for any of them, and that meant finding Seth's missing finger.

He walked into the church.

Seven steps took him out of today all the way to the threshold of the film studio that had been Ruben Glass's century-old folly. This time the streak of stars in the sky above him—visibly only through the holes in the church roof—was less jarring. It didn't feel as if his gut had been twisted by Time's invisible hand. He didn't look up or around. He didn't want to see any of it.

He focused on Eleanor's face.

There were flames between them where his homemade bomb had done some serious damage. A dozen pews, those closest to the shattered window, were ablaze. The effect as the flames burned across a century was disconcerting. They appeared to flicker in and out, caught between burning bright in the here and now and ceasing to be—or yet to be—where Eleanor waited all those years ago.

Josh walked down the center of the aisle, his hand slick with blood. He looked down and saw a shard of glass digging into his palm. He hadn't felt it hit. He closed his fist around it, concentrating on the pain as he made the final few steps into Glass Town ignoring the weird flickering of the flames, then pulled it out and cast it aside

"You came back," Eleanor said. "I didn't think you would. Not when I saw Seth take you a moment ago. Where is he?"

"Not here," Josh said. He didn't have time to think about her, about what being there with her meant. She looked at him wide-eyed. That Audrey Hepburn line about the beauty of a woman being seen in her eyes had never been truer. "We don't have long." He took Eleanor's hand. She trusted him. "This has to end here. We have to beat Seth once and for all, no going back, but I can't do it without you."

She nodded. "I'll do anything you need me to. Anything to be free of this hell."

"Does Seth have a secret place here? Somewhere he goes to be alone? Somewhere he might hide something?"

She nodded. "More than one," she said, then shook her head. "But there's only one place off-limits to me."

"Then that's where we want to be. Take me there."

Eleanor looked over his shoulder, back toward the real world. She hesitated.

"You can trust me," Josh told her.

"It's not that," she said. It was painfully obvious she longed to leave her prison, but she didn't question him. She took his hand and led Josh away from the archway back into the deserted streets of Glass Town. This time it didn't feel like a lost world, it felt like a false one. He could see the chips and flakes in the paint and the cracks in the fake façades that exposed the truth of the illusion they'd been cobbled together to hide. It was far less magical than Ruben Glass had intended when he'd hired the set builders to hammer it together. From this angle, Josh could see one of the thick two-by-fours that braced the false front of the church wall through the shattered window. That window and the plank of wood presented a disconnect. He knew that logically the view was a hundred years away, because he'd looked in from the other side to see the burning pews, but there had been no supporting beam out there, only the scorch marks where his homemade bomb had detonated. He shook his head, not wanting to dwell on it.

Coruscating sparks showered down from the ragged edge of the halo where the lens had been torn away to end the illusion. The halo writhed and crackled, lashing against what little of the optic remained to anchor it. It would all unravel given time. Mist crept in through the cracks, bringing the icy chill of that other place with it.

He had no intention of being inside the illusion when that happened.

He followed Eleanor to the end of the deserted street.

It was quiet. Eerily so. But then it was hidden away from the rest of the world and all of its noise. Josh was about to dismiss the creeping sense of unease as just that, when a crackle of white noise set a chill in his heart. The Negative prowled around the corner. The great dog tossed its head back and barked another static hiss, then lowered its head and charged toward them.

Josh couldn't move.

His feet wouldn't let him.

There wasn't a star in the sky above them. The Negative ran hard and low, keeping its body close to the ground. Its nostrils flared as it sniffed them out. Another burst of white noise escaped its jaws. It had his scent. It breathed Josh in, then howled up at the moonless sky. With ten feet between them the Negative stiffened, muscles taut, ready to pounce, but even as it rose to its full towering height Josh saw the blisters in its fur. The Negative's claws raked across the cobbles, leaving deep gouges in them. It was painfully easy to imagine what they would do to skin and bone.

Eleanor threw herself between Josh and the beast, her hands up in front of her face as she braced for the impact that never came. The blisters on the Negative's fur spread, popping and shrinking back like film burning under the camera's too-bright light. Through the quickly spreading wounds in its flesh Josh saw the street behind the Negative. The beast howled its static roar again, then fell silent as the lower part of its jaw was lost to the blisters. It raked a claw across Eleanor's red dress that should have opened her from breastbone to sternum, but passed right through her as if she wasn't there.

She looked down at her chest and then at the ruin of the creature before her.

This dissolution was fast, the blisters spreading all across the Negative's body, blackening as they spread, then bursting to leave behind nothing more than a smoldering hole in the beast that grew as more and more blisters spread. Wisps of blackened smoke curled away from the wounds, spreading out across the Negative's flesh until it was entirely consumed and the gouges in the cobbles were all that remained of the Negative. The smoke tangled with the encroaching mist.

The stench was sickening.

"I don't know how you did that," Josh said, his heart hammering, "but I'm not complaining. Come on."

"It wasn't me," she said.

"Then we've got a guardian angel. Let's not waste it."

He followed Eleanor through three more streets, working their way toward the center of the lot. Up ahead he saw the domed roof of what he mistook to be some sort of place of worship. It wasn't. It was a movie theater. Light speared out of the single aperture in the dome with searchlight intensity. It arced out toward the barrier. He was looking at the source of the halo. The root of the conjuration, which kept the Otherworld open on this side of the veil.

"In there," she pointed unnecessarily. He was already climbing the steps toward the doors. Chains were looped through the push bars, secured by a heavy padlock. It didn't matter. It wasn't like they were going to get arrested for breaking and entering. He pulled his jacket off and wrapped it around his fist, then without thinking about how much it might hurt, slammed his fist through the glass. Without unwrapping his fist, he punched out the jagged splinters of glass left behind in the frame, then clambered through into the dark of the cinema.

It was musty inside, with no light save for the little that filtered in through the windows and doors. Deeper in, he'd be moving in pitch black. Where would Seth hide his treasure? Not near the door, for sure. Up in the projection room? That was the most likely option, wasn't it? Not down in the theater itself, up out of the way, somewhere safe. The reality was that there were thousands of places in this building he could have stashed the tip of his finger. The chance of finding it was less than zero unless it was simply waiting to be found. He took Boone's lighter from his pocket, flicked the wheel, and shone the tiniest light on the darkness.

Unlike the buildings they'd passed on the way here, the cinema wasn't a shell behind the false front. It was a proper building, curling wallpaper on the walls, and the red carpet underfoot looked as if it had never been walked on. This would have been the heart of the movie lot, he realized. The place where Ruben Glass intended to hold his glorious premieres, welcoming the bold and the beautiful one and all to marvel at the opulence of the new theater. Gold statues of Egyptian gods and goddesses were set in recessed sconces along the walls. There was more gold along the carpet rails and the banisters set along the walls. In full daylight, it must have been a throwback to the opulence of the time. Huge spiderwebs clung to the chandelier above him and spread across the ceiling like the draped fabrics of sheik's tent. He really didn't want to encounter the arachnid responsible for spinning out that grand design as he ventured deeper into the place in search of the stairs. The lighter was hot in his hand by the time he found them.

He climbed two at a time, Eleanor a couple of steps behind him.

"What are we looking for?"

"You wouldn't believe me if I told you," Josh said.

Their voices echoed through the empty spaces.

"Try me, you might be surprised."

"A finger. Well, a fingertip."

"You're right, that's definitely not what I was expecting."

Josh explained how that fingertip allowed Seth to pass into and out of Glass Town freely without the risk of time catching up with him because as long as it remained here he never truly left. He couldn't tell if she was impressed, or angry she hadn't thought of it herself. At the top of the stairs he turned to see her holding one hand in the other. He pretended not to notice.

The one advantage of the absolute quiet was that he could hear the tick of the projector wheel coming from up above them. The second set of stairs was behind a door marked *Projection Room*. There was a warding carved into the wooden threshold, and within it a crude rendition of a woman. As Eleanor tried to follow him through, it stopped her midstep. A lingering piece of Cadmus Damiola's magic that kept Eleanor Raines out of the room. Try as she might, she couldn't cross the threshold.

"I'll be back," Josh said. "Keep an eye out. Yell if we have any unwelcome visitors." She nodded. He climbed up the old wooden risers one step at a time, each one groaning underfoot. The room beneath the dome was small—the ceiling barely high enough for him to stand upright in it. A weird projector stood on a table in the middle of the round room. It was unlike any film projector he'd ever seen. There were loads of windows all around it that were shuttered so no light shone out through them. The single source of light in the room speared out from the heart of the machine, aimed at a lens that amplified it as it arrowed it out through the glass window which acted as another lens, intensifying the flickering light as the projector wheels rattled on endlessly, with no film to project. The set-up wasn't unlike the weird Heath Robinson contraption with all of its kettles and brass plates and condensers he'd found above the glass shop the first time he'd stumbled into Glass Town. But this was different. This was the source. This was where the magic happened.

This was the Opticron, he realized. It had to be.

If he opened those shutters, he'd see other worlds. Wasn't that what was supposed to happen?

He wasn't even remotely tempted to find out.

What he was tempted to do was kill whatever was powering the damned device and bring down the barrier, but not until he'd found Seth's fingertip. He needed the light to see by.

It's got to be here somewhere, he thought to himself. There were glass cabinets, like museum display cases, around one side of the curved wall. On the other were racks of film canisters. What better place to hide something in a projection room, Josh realized, going over to the racks and lifting down the first can. It was labeled *Number 13 Daily Print.* There were twenty more, each with the same handwritten label, the only difference being the date stamped beneath it. He looked for the last date in the sequence, then twisted the lid off the can.

It was empty.

He cast it aside, and pulled the next one out.

Another empty can.

The third one contained a small loop of film, nothing else.

The fifth can he lifted down rattled in his hands.

There was no film inside. The can contained a bone. The distal phalange of Seth Lockwood's missing little fingertip.

Josh fished it out of the metal canister and pocketed it.

He knew exactly how he was going to dispose of the damned thing. He wasn't going to salt and burn it; Seth wasn't a ghost. As evil as he was, he wasn't some sort of demonic entity, either. No, he had other ideas.

But first, he intended to bring down the veil and pull Glass Town out of limbo for the first time in a century.

He looked around for a plug, but the Opticron seemed to be powering itself on thin air. Josh started trying to fumble around with it, looking for some sort of off switch, but he was clueless. Clueless and frustrated. Grasping the contraption from the base, he lifted it from the table and carried it toward the small window. He hefted it up onto his shoulder, then ran the final three steps to the wall, hurling the Opticron through the window.

The glass shattered as Damiola's machine spilled out of his fingers. It teetered on the edge of the window frame for a moment before it toppled. It was a long way down. He heard the twisted detonation of impact as it hit the street. No matter what magic powered the contraption, there was no chance it could have survived the fall.

The darkness all around him testified to that.

The barrier that had kept Glass Town hidden away from the world had fallen.

Using the lighter, Josh followed its tiny light carefully back down to where Eleanor waited.

"It's done," he promised her.

They left the cinema hand in hand like so many young lovers before them. What they stepped out into wasn't Wonderland. The Opticron lay in hundreds of pieces strewn across the road. Each one of them glowed with the same eerie pale blue ghost light he'd seen emanate from within Myrna Shepherd, but it was fading fast. Josh looked up at the sky where the stars were streaks of silver, every single one of them up there a shooting star. "It's all coming undone," he said, and it was. All around them the world that had been hidden away for so long was rolling out to take its place within the London of today much to the consternation of late-night revellers who suddenly found themselves facing walls that hadn't been there a few moments before, unsure of just how much they'd had to drink as they approached crossroads that they knew like the back of their hands only to realize there was an entirely new choice to be had that they'd never taken before. Those movie set streets forced their way into the city, staking a claim on some of the most expensive territory in the world.

It was a magic night.

People were going to wake up to a different London in the morning, but at least they'd be saved the hysteria of watching Glass Town unfold before their eyes. That would have been too much, even for the endless possibilities of the capital.

The night wasn't as dark as it should have been—that was because of the trailing stars. It was going to take a while to familiarize himself with this new geography of the city. They needed to get over to Ravens-hill before Seth found the old magician. That was five miles away.

The cut from the shard of glass in his palm made his fingers ache. Josh flexed them a couple of times, imagining what it would feel like to be without the smallest of them.

In the distance he could see the white faces of skyscrapers towering over the lowly buildings below. New money always rose to the top, while old money was content just to be, spreading out behind the marble façades below.

They walked together through the utter silence of this forsaken place. Up above the stars slowly shortened with each step they took until they were single points of light up there in the heavens. Surely that meant that Glass Town had finished unfurling around them to take up its rightful place in the heart of the city? And that being the case, then surely that in turn meant time had been restored, Damiola's grand illusion undone?

There was no going back.

In destroying the Opticron he'd effectively killed both Seth and Eleanor even if the years hadn't caught up with them yet. He could tell by the look in her eyes she knew it, but she was focused on being with him right to the end, making sure that Seth couldn't somehow find a way to cheat death and walk away from this again. Not that Josh would let him. This had stopped being about Eleanor and Isaiah and Boone for him. There was only one person this was about now: his mother. Seth had killed her, and for that he was going to pay the ultimate price.

He saw ragged silhouettes of people coming into focus as he approached them, and ignored their confusion as he passed.

"What the . . . ?"

"Did you see that?"

"Where the fuck did they come from?"

"What the hell is this place? Where's the fucking chippie? I'm dying for a kebab . . . Could have sworn it was here. Must have taken a wrong turn back there."

And on and on the blather went, meaningless words from meaningless people. Josh took Boone's tin from his pocket. His hands were shaking. He needed something to do with them. The adrenaline was flooding from his system, reality pouring in just as it had in the wake of the halo's undoing. He didn't want anything to do with it. He rolled a cigarette, then lit it. The cold air had him squinting into the near distance. He saw what he was after, the carapace of a beetlelike black cab idling on the corner.

"Come on," he said, grabbing Eleanor's hand again and running.

The chill became a cold breeze, the cold breeze an icy wind as they ran headlong into it. The night sky filled with starlings and pigeons and all manner of city birds, their migration battered by the unforgiving wind.

At the end of the street he noticed a dozen or more cats side by side with just as many dogs, all of them crowded around the ragged edge where the barrier had come down. The air was peculiar, rippling with bruised purple light that replaced the halo as Glass Town entered the twenty-first century. It was like seeing the Northern Lights on a London street: impossible, but absolutely beautiful just the same.

He could have sworn he heard voices in the wind, but he ignored them. That way lay madness.

They ran past the windows of uninhabited houses, eyes fixed on the cab on the street corner and its indicator, which wasn't signaling any intention to move out before they reached it.

Josh waved frantically toward it, hoping the driver would see him in the mirror before he pulled away.

"Ravenshill," Josh said, clambering inside.

"Sorry, guv, I'm done for the night. Got to get home to the missus or she'll have my guts for garters."

"Please," Josh said. "It's only a couple of miles. We can pay."

The driver caught sight of Eleanor Raines in the rearview mirror and changed his mind. "Come on then," he said, buckling up. "So, what the hell was all that fuss back there? Sounded like a bomb going off."

"They're filming something," Josh said, hoping the man would buy the lie. He'd read something somewhere about a movie or television show being shot every single day in the city, so it wasn't an outrageous stretch of the imagination to think the BBC's special effects crew might be blowing something up even if it was the middle of the night.

"Ah, you coming off the set, guv? Had a few celebs in my cab, you can always tell the real ones, like the lady here, they've got a certain something. A luminescence."

Eleanor smiled sweetly at him. "Something like that," she said. "Believe me, it's been a really long day."

"Amen to that, love. This shift feels like it's lasted a hundred years." There was no answer to that.

46

THE MAN IN THE MIRRORS

The taxicab dropped them at the crooked gates.

"Can't say's I've ever been out this way," the cabbie noted, taking the crumpled twenty from Josh. He made no move to break it. Instead he waited, the protracted silence becoming meaningful, though far from profound, until Josh said, "Keep the change."

"Good man. Much appreciated. You folks have a good night doing whatever it is you intend to do in there," he raised an eyebrow toward the old cemetery. He chuckled knowingly as he said, "I ain't gonna judge." Though clearly he was. That last line was delivered through a smirk.

Josh helped Eleanor out of the cab before slamming the door.

The cab was gone before they were through the raven gates.

Josh looked around, but there was no sign of Seth. He took Eleanor's hand again and led her through the graves to the magician's mausoleum.

The old man waited for them in the shade of the overgrown willow. He ignored Josh. He couldn't take his eyes off Eleanor.

"I trusted you," she said. "I thought you were my friend," she said.

"I know," he said. "I'm sorry," he said. "I was weak. I made a mistake. More than one. It was a long time ago—"

"For you."

"For me," he agreed. "I am not the coward I was, dear lady. You have to believe me."

"You will forgive me if I don't."

"I am trying to make amends."

"It's not enough," Eleanor said, and he didn't argue. Instead, he turned to Josh. "It is ready."

"Good."

"I'll ask you one last time, are you certain you want to do this?"

Josh nodded slowly.

"There can be no going back once it is done."

"How many times do I have to tell you: This is what I want."

Josh heard the high-pitched *squeak-squawk* of lovesick bats flitting back and forth behind the mausoleum. He realized it was the first sound other than voices that he'd heard in a long time.

The second sound—a car's engine—came a few seconds later.

Josh saw the flashing blue light as Julie Gennaro's squad car pulled up at the gates. "I'm going in. When he gets here, tell Julie to follow me into the tomb. Give us a few minutes' privacy."

"What are you planning?"

"Nothing," Josh lied. Damiola knew he was lying. Eleanor knew he was lying. Neither of them called him on it. "Just give us a couple of minutes."

"If there are a couple to give," the magician said.

He ducked past Damiola before the old man could protest, and walked into the darkness of the tomb, only it wasn't dark anymore. A candle burned in the main burial chamber. For a moment he thought it was a lot more. It was an optical illusion. A trick of the mirrors the magician had arrayed around the tomb. They were the same mirrors Josh had seen in Damiola's workshop, the ones offering different views in their reflections, though, now he saw a hundred thousand flickering candles, going deeper and deeper into an endless mist, and beside the flames, like an infinite array of ghosts, each wearing his face. Staring at it for long enough would be enough to drive a man out of his mind. He approved.

He heard footsteps behind him.

He didn't need to turn to see who it was. A hundred thousand Julie

Gennaros stepped into the tomb. He had a backpack slung over his shoulder.

"You took your time," Josh said to all of his reflections at once.

"You try laying your hands on bolt cutters and a blowtorch after midnight. It's not as if I could just wander down to the hardware store."

"But you got them?"

Julie nodded. "I did indeed."

"Good. I want you to do something for me, Julie, and I don't want you to argue. We don't have time to waste. Seth will be here any second, and this needs to be done."

"I'm not liking the sound of this."

"It'll hurt me more than it hurts you," Josh said. "I promise you that."

He knelt on the floor in front of Julie and held up his hand, fingers splayed. "I want you to cut the tip of my little finger off."

Julie shook his head. "Are you out of your mind?"

"It has to be done. Just get it over with before I change my mind."

"Christ," Julie said, but he did what he was told. He dropped his shoulder so the backpack swung around and landed on the small flagstones that tiled the ground at his feet; then unzipped it, reaching in for the bolt cutters.

"It's going to be messy, and I'm going to scream. You'll need to cauterize the wound with the blowtorch. Just ignore my pain and get it done. I'm relying on you, Julie. This is your one chance to make up for betraying me to that bastard. Do this and we're even."

"Are you sure?"

"People keep asking me that," Josh said, no trace of humor in his voice. "Do it."

He took a T-shirt from his bag, wadded it up, and gave it to Josh. "Something to bite down on."

Josh nodded and stuffed it into his mouth.

He looked like a sacrificial pig staring wide-eyed at its butcher.

"Keep your hand steady," Julie said, opening the bolt cutter's jaw and resting Josh's fingertip on its teeth. Josh closed his eyes. He didn't want to see the mutilation happen. "This is seriously fucked up, mate," Julie said, shaking his head as he clamped the handles together.

There was surprisingly little resistance as the bolt cutters sheered through the bone.

Josh screamed into the T-shirt, gagging on the cloth as a spray of blood fountained from the wound. He clutched at his ruined hand, but Julie dragged his good hand away so that he could get at the wound with the blowtorch before he lost too much blood.

Josh swayed on his knees, threatening to black out.

Julie back-handed him across the face, not sure what else to do. Josh's panicked eyes flared wide open. "It's only going to get worse," Julie said, encouragingly.

Josh nodded, eyes red with tears. His breathing was fast and shallow, his nostrils flaring as he drew in breath after ragged breath.

Moving quickly, and doing his best to ignore Josh's agony, Julie lit the blowtorch. He held it in his right hand as he grabbed Josh's wrist with his left and applied the blue-hot flame to the wound, turning the flesh to blackened charcoal.

It took less than a minute, but in those sixty never-ending seconds Josh was sure his heart was going to stop. The pain was *blinding*. All he could hear was the roar of the blowtorch. He stopped feeling anything. His entire hand might as well have been on fire.

And then there was a *pop*, then nothing.

Silence.

Josh toppled onto his side, clutching at his ruined hand.

It was too late for regrets.

"Come on, mate. Up." Julie helped him stand. His legs were like jelly. Josh leaned on Julie. It was all he could do not to pitch forward face-first into the dirt. With his good hand he fumbled in his pocket for Boone's cigarette tin.

"Where's the bone?" he asked.

"Fuck knows," Julie said.

"We need to find it," Josh sank to his knees and started feeling out across the stone floor, trying to find it. It took another minute. The fingertip already felt dead.

Seth would pay for what he'd done to his mother.

Damiola was explaining to Eleanor what he needed her to do as they walked out together into the night.

She nodded several times, eager finally to be playing a part in the grand deception. She promised she wouldn't fail him. He believed her. Lying was in her blood. It was why she would have been one of the greats, but for the fact Seth had stolen her future away from her.

Eleanor left to take up her position.

They didn't have to wait long for Seth Lockwood to arrive.

He strode through the twisted iron gates with their buckled ravens and walked straight toward them.

"Well, well, well; quite the family gathering," Seth said, spreading his arms wide, as though to embrace them all. "And all for me? I'm honored. At least I think I am. Cuz, you don't look good. Actually, you look fucking *awful*. I would ask what happened to you, but frankly I'm amazed you made it out of the warehouse without being eaten by the rats. So, it's good you dragged yourself out of your pit, even if you're too fucked up to hurt a fly, it'll be enjoyable to finally put an end to your side of the family tree." He turned to Julie. "Officer Gennaro, now *you* I didn't expect to see here. I thought we were done with you, to be brutally honest. Not a lot to offer anyone on either side. A bit part, but played well, especially the final betrayal. Always a winner that. But, you're done. You've served your purpose. You should go now." Julie looked at Josh, not sure who he was supposed to be taking orders from now. In the end he thought better of staying and walked off, leaving Josh to stand on his own two feet. As he did so, he noticed the old magician's eyes flicker down toward Josh's ruined hand. Maybe the mutilation made sense to him?

"And, Cadmus Damiola, as I live and breathe. I thought you were dead. Actually, I was sure you were dead. It seems I was wrong. Or maybe not. You don't smell good, old man. In fact you smell like you've been dead for sixty years."

"That's about right," the magician said, adjusting his grubby coats. He scratched at his beard.

"Well, that's the pleasantries dispensed with. Where is she?"

"Here," Eleanor said, stepping into view. There was something strange about the way the light seemed to suffuse her body. She stood before the door of the tomb. She'd moved into position silently while Seth grandstanded.

"Let's get this over with," the old-time criminal said, as if his being there was such a hardship. "I haven't got time for this shit." He turned to the old man. "You don't have to die here. All I want is for you to repair the damage. Give me another hundred years with the woman I love. Give me the time to make her love me. That's all I ask."

"She doesn't love you," Josh said.

"And who the fuck asked you, Cuz? Be quiet. The grown-ups are talking. Eleanor?" He reached out a hand for the actress. She shook her head slightly. "Well, now, that *is* disappointing. I guess I'll just have to kill everyone. It's not like I don't have the best hiding place for your bodies." Seth reached into his pocket and pulled out an old six-shot revolver, leveling it at the woman. "What is it they always say in the movies? If I can't have you, no one else will. That's it."

Eleanor didn't move.

Josh could see the steady rise and fall of her breasts. She was calmness personified. He wouldn't have been half as calm in her place.

And then, amazingly, she turned her back on him, offering a guilt-free shot, and took two steps toward the mausoleum's entrance.

"Don't you *dare* walk away from me! No one walks away from me, woman," Seth howled at her back as she disappeared inside. He waved the gun from the empty doorway to the magician, to Josh, and back to the empty doorway again, frozen helplessly to the spot. "Don't any one of you fuckers *move*," he barked, finally breaking the spell that bound him. He followed Eleanor, stopping on the threshold. His face was lit gold by the infinite candlelight burning off that single wick. He turned to look at Josh. "You try anything, I'll put a bullet in your face. Understood?"

Josh didn't say a word.

He didn't move.

He gave no hint he'd even understood the words coming out of Seth's mouth. The black agony pulsing from his ruined hand gave him something other than Seth to concentrate on. He clenched his fist, biting back on the sudden flare of pain that lanced up his arm in response. He couldn't imagine his hand would ever be the same again.

Seth disappeared inside.

Damiola reached out to rest his hand on the lintel above the doorway, touching the carving of the ancient oak tree. The stone flared bruise-purple in response to his touch, a fine curtain of northern lights shimmering across the entrance as the magician entered his tomb. Josh pushed through the barrier, following Damiola inside.

"What trickery is this?" Seth demanded. His endless reflections stared back at him. There was no sign of Eleanor Raines anywhere inside the tomb. The candlewick flickered beneath the breeze that chased them in, then suddenly stopped, leaving absolute stillness in its wake.

"This is how it has to be," the old man told the criminal. "Glass Town is gone."

"It's true," Josh said, coming into the tomb behind him. "I destroyed the Opticron. It's lying in the street outside Ruben Glass's movie house in hundreds of pieces. There's no magic left in it. There's nothing to keep it trapped in the Otherworld. It's free of limbo. It's back here, where it belongs. It's over. You're a walking dead man. Can't you feel all of those years rushing back into your body, clawing away beneath your skin?"

Seth exhaled slowly, a sly smile spreading across his feral features. "You're pathetic. Just like your father. Just like Boone and Isaiah. All of you, absolutely pathetic. I'm going to enjoy killing you, boy, and then your sister, claiming the full set."

"The full set?"

"You didn't know, did you? Let me explain: I'm the plague as far as your family is concerned. Mother. Father. Grandfather. A push down the stairs. It wasn't difficult. He was a frail old man. I almost regretted it. Almost. If he hadn't worked out that the anchors were failing, that the whole thing was coming apart, he might have lived a few more years, maybe even lived to see the next generation of Raines take their first faltering steps. And wouldn't that have been something? Fresh blood for the feud. Conjuring the kid, yes *that* kid, from the Chaplin movie, to stick his knife in dear old daddy; then using the Rushes to have your old man fuck his wife to death. Poetry."

"You bastard," Josh spat, the pain of grief eclipsing anything he felt from his hand. He clenched his fist, jamming the stub of his severed finger into his palm. The sunburst of pain was enough to drown out his other senses as Seth gloated over the havoc he'd wreaked in his life.

"Absolutely. You seem to forget, this is all business as usual for me. This is what I do. You're in my world. You think you're so clever, but you're not. I'm not an idiot. I was king of this city before you were born. I've taken precautions."

"You mean this?" Josh held his hand out. The fragment of bone that had been Seth Lockwood's fingertip a hundred years ago rested on his palm. "The king is dead," Josh said bitterly. "Long live the king."

Josh took three quick steps toward Seth, grabbing hold of his jaw and slamming him back against one of the many mirrors hard enough to have a spiderweb of cracks race across it like wings at his back. The candlelight didn't waver. The flame hadn't burned down a millimeter. It wouldn't. It would burn for a hundred years and a hundred more. On and on. Unlike the three men in the tomb it was eternal. With his good hand he pried Seth's mouth open, and before he realized what was happening, Josh rammed both bones—his own fingertip and Seth's that he'd found in Glass Town—down Seth's throat, pushing his fingers in, curling back the other man's tongue until he gagged and choked on the bones before swallowing them. Josh stepped back.

Seth fired two shots, both missing. Before he could fire a third, the gun tumbled from his fingers and clattered to the floor. It spun in place for a second, the barrel scraping on the stones, then shot across the floor, coming to rest at the magician's feet. "Don't look so frightened. I'm not about to let you die, *Cuz*." Josh turned to Damiola. "Do it. Banish this place."

The old man crouched down, placing his hand flat on the stones, and began to chant. The words were in no language Josh had ever heard. It was the oldest of English, bearing no resemblance to their modern tongue. The flagstones shimmered in response to his words. Filaments of bluish light chased along each and every crack, creating a latticework of raw energy that enclosed Seth Lockwood.

Mirrors behind the magician began to move, sliding across the doorway to seal the tomb.

Damiola lifted his hand from the stones, the energy dissipating in a chase of crackling electricity as it surged away through the cracks in search of the fastest route to the earth. The old mausoleum had been built on a confluence, a crossing of ancient power lines. It was potent ground, deliberately chosen. Some of the ancient magic still resided in the dirt, not yet choked to death by the concrete and steel of the city beyond. It was precious little, but it was enough.

The old man stood slowly, looking every one of his years.

He reached out for Josh's hand, and then pulled him back through the glass, leaving Seth screaming at the walls of his mirror prison.

Josh reached out with his ruined hand and rested it on the cold surface. There was no ripple or give in it, and it didn't matter how many times Seth beat his fists bloody on the other side, Damiola's last grand enchantment wouldn't let it break.

"I'll find a way out," Seth raged. Josh could only hear him when his hand was in contact with the glass. Somehow it conducted the words through from there to here, even as time began to slow around Seth and deny them any sense. He emptied the four remaining bullets into the glass. They had no noticeable effect, the mirror absorbing them as they fell somewhere out of time. "So help me God, I'll find a way out and I will end you!" Seth screamed.

"No, you won't," Josh said. "There are no anchors to fail this time. Before there was always a way back, because the anchors kept the veil open on one side. This time you are gone. Banished. You are in Hell. The old races used to call it the Annwyn. It is a place of ghosts. There's no fake movie set for you to pretend life goes on as normal around you, you will wander alone through a shapeless landscape, endlessly the same, wreathed it mist to hide whatever creatures lurk in the mists. That infinite solitude will strip you of your mind long before your body fails you."

Josh stayed there for an hour, watching Seth prowl around the infinite glass prison, confronted by an endless array of impotent doppelgängers reflected in the backward land of the glass. His pacing slowed and slowed until he appeared to be frozen in the mirror world. Josh wished that time flowed the other way, that Seth was being thrust into the future so that a century on the other side of the glass might pass in a single year on this side. That way he could have watched the man break, his spirit crumble.

He wasn't going to feel that satisfaction staring at Seth's twisted face trapped in time.

He felt hollow.

Winning hadn't solved anything.

The world wasn't a better place.

And there was still one more grief to face: Eleanor.

He hadn't saved her.

He was a hollow man who had won himself a hollow victory.

How was he going to face her? How was he going to tell her he'd failed to do the one thing she'd asked of him?

Josh turned his back on Seth and walked away, leaving him to slowly rot.

Damiola stopped him before they walked out into the light. "I know what you've done, lad. You're going to need to get that hand of yours seen to."

"I will, eventually."

"Before it festers."

Josh nodded.

"I won't let you damn yourself, lad. I know what you've got in mind. I knew the moment you said you'd worked out how Seth came and went as he pleased. I didn't think you'd go through with it. I guess I didn't realize how badly he'd hurt you. But, know this, I'm going nowhere. I've got nowhere to go. This is my tomb, after all. I'll sit vigil on that bench out there guarding this place just like I've done for the last hundred years. I won't let you back in. The gateway to the Annwyn is closed and has to stay that way . . . you may think you can just walk into Hell and kill him because part of you is in there with him, or live forever out here, but the cost of that, the price, is too much, boy. Let it end here."

"You won't live forever," Josh said.

"That's what you think," the old man smirked, putting his hand on Josh's shoulder. "Stranger things have happened."

47

THE FINAL CURTAIN

"Pepper's Ghost," Eleanor said, explaining why she'd not reacted to having the gun pointed at her. She could see that Josh rather enjoyed the irony of an illusion that was already half a century old when she'd disappeared so thoroughly fooling Seth.

They were talking about everything apart from the one thing that was truly important: What happens next. Because, for Eleanor Raines there was no *next*. This was it. They both knew it. There was no point trying to say everything was going to be all right. It wasn't. Not that way. There was no happily ever after for her. She couldn't live in this new world, and there was no way back into the prison that had been her life for the last year, not that she ever wanted to go back there. As far as the world was concerned she'd been dead for a hundred years. It was time for reality to catch up with the headlines.

"I want to see it all for one last time," she told Josh.

He really did look so much like Isaiah—so much so she could almost imagine she was walking through the streets of London toward Primrose Hill to watch the sun rise one last time with the man she loved.

There were worse ways to die.

She was frightened it was going to hurt. Of course she was. How would her body, still so young and soft, react to the ravages of time, all of those years finally staking their claim on her?

"I shouldn't have promised," he said, halfway up the hill. She could tell he was struggling with the fact that in real life it was hard to be a hero, and so much easier to fail.

"I never should have asked it of you. Not those two words. Not 'save me.' I should have said 'free me.' Because it was never about being saved. Not the way you think. Not in the damsel in distress being plucked from the tracks barely seconds before the train rolls over her, foiling the villain's dastardly plans." That was an end that was hackneyed even before she set foot on the set outside The Peabody and heard Alfred Hitchcock utter that magic word for the first time: "Action!"

No, what she had meant with those two words was more about putting her fate into her own hands finally, letting her die on her own terms.

Of course she'd dreamed about making a new life here in this London ever since she'd bumped into Isaiah in Spitalfields. But she was a woman out of time. She didn't belong here. She didn't belong anywhere anymore. Everyone she had ever known was gone. Even the stars overhead were different tonight.

"Sorry," he said.

"Don't say that," she told him. "You gave me my life back. You ended a nightmare that haunted your great-grandfather, your grandfather, and ultimately saw both of your parents murdered. You did what none of them could. You won."

"So why does it feel like I lost so badly?"

"Because it's all still raw. But in time you'll feel different about all of this. You glimpsed the miraculous. You made a difference. And in a very real way you did save me."

"I killed you," he said.

"That, too," she said, with a wan smile. "But there are different routes to salvation, sweet boy. I get to see my true murderer banished to a very literal hell. How many murder victims get to say that?" This time the smile was sweet, and for just a moment he smiled back and she saw the man she had loved written all over his face. Dying with him beside her wouldn't be so terrible. It was as close to a perfect end as she could have hoped. She was ready to die now. Maybe she would be reunited with Isaiah, maybe she wouldn't. It didn't really matter. All that did matter was that Seth wouldn't be there.

She could feel it happening already.

But that was fine.

She'd never wanted to be saved.

She was free, walking the real streets of London one last time, not those fake wooden ones of Glass Town with their empty insides, and that was all that mattered.

Sunrise was only a few hours away.

She walked toward it, looking forward to climbing the hill and seeing the city in all of its glory for one last time, knowing that there would be no tomorrow for her.

THE END

ACKNOWLEDGMENTS

A great magician never reveals his tricks. Luckily I'm not a great magician, so I can spill my guts to anyone who'll listen. At this point, that means you, because you're still here. A lot of people have helped make me look better than I am, so this one goes out to them.

To Peter Wolverton, as insightful an editor as a writer could ever ask for, for bringing out the very best of the story you've just read, and all the team at St. Martin's who worked so hard to make this happen. Most notably, to Jennifer Donovan for running interference.

To my agents, Judith Murray and Chris Wellbelove at Greene and Heaton, who put up with my mad ideas.

To Mike Nicholson, Thomas Alwin, Stephen Morris, Andy Coulthard, and Stefan Lindblad for the coffee and friendship that made the obsessive search for Glass Town so much easier than it might have been alone. To Pat Cattigan for years of fantasy football rivalries to match the best of them. To Marie, my long-suffering wife, who won't read this line and will never know. . . . I could say anything at this point. Anything. I could promise a shopping spree in London, all-expenses paid, and she'd be none the wiser. Don't blab. This can be our secret.

And for my next trick . . .